Praise for the novels of Sharon Sala

"Veteran romance writer Sala lives up to her
reputation with this well-crafted thriller."
—*Publishers Weekly* on *Remember Me*

"Chilling and relentless…"
—*RT Book Reviews* on *The Chosen*

"Wear a corset because your sides will hurt from
laughing! This is Sharon Sala at top form. You're
going to love this touching and memorable book."
—*New York Times* bestselling author
Debbie Macomber on *Whippoorwill*

"[A] rare ability to bring powerful and
emotionally wrenching stories to life."
—*RT Book Reviews*

"Perfect entertainment for those looking for a
suspense novel with emotional intensity."
—*Publishers Weekly* on *Out of the Dark*

"…knows just how to steep the fires of romance
to the gratification of her readers."
—*RT Book Reviews*

"Sharon Sala masterfully manages to get
deeply into her characters."
—*RT Book Reviews*

Also by SHARON SALA

THE CHOSEN
MISSING
WHIPPOORWILL
CAPSIZED
DARK WATER
OUT OF THE DARK
SNOWFALL
BUTTERFLY
REMEMBER ME
REUNION
SWEET BABY

SHARON SALA

Rider on Fire

and

When You Call My Name

Recycling programs
for this product may
not exist in your area.

ISBN-13: 978-0-373-60628-3

RIDER ON FIRE & WHEN YOU CALL MY NAME

Copyright © 2014 by Harlequin Books S.A.

The publisher acknowledges the copyright holder of the individual works as follows:

RIDER ON FIRE
Copyright © 2005 by Sharon Sala

WHEN YOU CALL MY NAME
Copyright © 1996 by Sharon Sala

Printed in U.S.A.

CONTENTS

RIDER ON FIRE   7

WHEN YOU CALL MY NAME   245

RIDER ON FIRE

The Oklahoma Outlaws, my state chapter of Romance Writers of America, has less than forty members, and a half dozen of those are breast cancer survivors. Devastating illnesses are never fair. They didn't get to pick and choose the trials and tribulations that came with living their lives, but by golly those girls know how to live it regardless.

Because I am so proud to be an Outlaw, and because I love and admire those women so much for showing us what's really important in life, I would like to dedicate this book to them.

Ladies, this is my "pink ribbon" for all of you.

To Peggy King, Jo Smith, Willie Ferguson, Julia Mozingo, Chris Rimmer and Donnell Epperson, and to all the women everywhere, including my editor, Leslie Wainger, who have been forged in the fire of cancer and lived to be inspirations for us all—
PINK FOREVER!!!

Chapter 1

The small squirrel was just ready to scold—its little mouth partially opened as it clutched the acorn close to its chest. In the right light, one could almost believe the tail had just twitched.

Franklin Blue Cat called it The Sassy One. It was one of his latest carvings and in three months would be featured, along with thirty other pieces of his work, in a prestigious art gallery in Santa Fe. He hoped he lived long enough to see it.

Franklin often thought how strange the turns his life had taken. Had anyone told him that one day he would become known the world over for his simple carvings, he would have called them crazy. He would also have called them crazy for telling him that, at the age of sixty, he would be alone and dying of cancer. He'd always imagined himself going into old age surrounded by children and grandchildren with a loving wife at his side.

He set aside the squirrel. As he did, the pain he'd been

living with for some months took a sharp upward spike, making Franklin reel where he stood. He waited until the worst of it passed, then stumbled to his bedroom and collapsed on his bed.

He considered giving Adam Two Eagles a call. Adam's father had been the clan healer. Everyone had assumed that Adam would follow in his father's footsteps. Only, Adam had rebelled. Instead, he had taken the white man's way and left the Kiamichi Mountains to go to college, graduated from Oklahoma State University with an MBA, and from there gone straight into the army to eventually become one of their elite—an army ranger.

Then, during the ensuing years, something had happened to Adam that caused him to quit the military, and brought him home. He'd come back to eastern Oklahoma, to his Kiowa roots, and stepped into his father's footsteps as if he'd never been away.

Adam never talked about what had changed him, but Franklin knew it had been bad. He saw the shadows in Adam's eyes when he thought no one was looking. However, Franklin knew something that Adam did not. Franklin knew it would pass. He'd lived long enough to know life was in a constant state of flux.

As Franklin drifted to sleep, he dreamed, all the way back to his younger days and the woman who'd stolen his heart.

Leila of the laughing eyes and long dark hair. He couldn't remember when he hadn't loved her. They'd made love every chance they could get—with passion, but without caution.

Sleep took him to the day he had learned that Leila's family was moving. She'd been twenty-two to his thirty—old enough to stay behind. He'd begged her to stay, but there had been a look on her face he'd never seen before, and instead of accepting his offer of marriage, she'd been unable to meet his gaze.

His heartbeat accelerated as he relived the panic. In his mind, he could see her face through the back window of the car as her father drove away.

She was crying—his Leila of the laughing eyes was sobbing as she waved goodbye. He could see her mouth moving.

Franklin shifted on the bed. This was new. He didn't remember her calling out. In real life, she'd done nothing but cry as they drove away. It was the way he'd remembered it for all these years. So why had the dream been different? What was it she was trying to say?

He swung his legs to the side of the bed and then stood, giving himself time to decide if he had the strength to move. Finally, he walked out of his bedroom, then through the kitchen to the back porch. The night air was sultry and still.

He stood for a few moments, absorbing the impact of the dream, waiting for understanding. At first, he felt nothing. His mind was blank, but he knew what to do. It was the same thing he always did as he began a new piece of work. All he had to do was look at the block of wood until he saw whatever it was that was waiting to come out. Only then did he begin carving.

Following his instincts, he closed his eyes, took a slow breath, then waited for the words Leila had been trying to say.

It was quiet on the mountain. Almost too quiet. Even the night birds were silent, and the coyotes seemed to have gone to ground. There was nothing to distract Franklin from watching his dream, letting it replay in his head. He stood motionless for so long that dew settled on his bare feet, while an owl, feeling no threat, passed silently behind him on its way out to hunt.

And then understanding came, and with it, shock. Frank-

lin turned abruptly and looked back at his house, almost expecting Leila to be on the porch, but there was no one there.

He turned again, this time looking to the trees beyond
his home. He'd been born on this land. His parents had
died in this house, and soon so would he. But there was
something he knew now that he had not known yesterday.

Leila had taken something of his when she'd left him.

His child.

Right in the middle of his revelation, exhaustion hit.

Damn this cancer.

His legs began to shake and his hands began to tremble. He walked back to the house, stumbling slightly as
he stepped up on the porch, then dragged himself into the
house.

What if he could find his Leila—even if she was no longer his? He wanted to see their child—no—he *needed* to
know that a part of him would live on, even after he was
gone. Tomorrow, he would call Adam Two Eagles. Adam
would know what to do.

Adam Two Eagles rarely had to stretch to reach anything. At three inches over six feet tall, he usually towered
over others. His features were Native American, but less
defined than his father's had been. His mother had been
Navajo and the mix of Kiowa and Navajo had blended well,
making Adam a very handsome man. His dark hair was
thick and long, falling far below his shoulders—a far cry
from the buzz cut he'd worn in the military. But that seemed
so long ago that it might as well have been from another life.

This morning, he was readying himself for a trip up the
Kiamichis. There were some plants he wanted for healing
that grew only in the higher elevation. It would mean at
least a half day's hike up and back—nothing he hadn't done
countless times before—only today, he felt unsettled. He
kept going from room to room, thinking there was some-

thing else he was supposed to do, but nothing occurred to him. Finally, he'd given up and prepared to leave.

If he hadn't forgotten the bag he liked to carry his herbs and plants in, he would have already been gone when the phone rang. But he was digging through a closet, and ignoring the ring would have been like a doctor ignoring a call for help.

"Hello."

"Adam! I was beginning to think you were gone."

Adam smiled as he recognized the voice.

"Good morning, Franklin. You just caught me. How have you been?"

"The same," Franklin said shortly, unwilling to dwell on his illness. "But that's not why I called."

Adam frowned. The seriousness in his old friend's voice was unfamiliar.

"So, what's up?" Adam asked.

"It's complicated," Franklin said. "Can you come over?"

"Yes, of course. When do you need me?" Adam asked.

There was a moment of hesitation, then Franklin sighed. "Now, I need you to come now."

"I'm on my way," Adam said, and hung up.

In less than fifteen minutes, Adam was pulling up to Franklin's house. He parked, then killed the engine. When he looked up, Franklin had come outside and was waiting for him on the porch. He smiled and then waved Adam up before moving back into the house. Adam bolted up the steps and followed him.

A few minutes were wasted on small talk and the pouring of coffee before Adam urged Franklin to sit down. Franklin did so without arguing. Adam took a seat opposite Franklin's chair and leaned back, waiting for the older man to begin.

"I had a dream," Franklin said.

Adam set his coffee aside and leaned forward, resting his elbows on the arms of his chair.

"Tell me."

Franklin relayed what he'd dreamed, and what he believed that it meant. When he was finished, he leaned back and crossed his arms across his chest.

"So, can you help me?" he asked.

"What do you want me to do?" Adam countered.

Franklin sighed. "I guess I want to know if I'm right, if Leila and I had a child. I want to know this before I die."

Adam stood, then paced to the window, absently staring at the way sunlight reflected from his windshield onto a wind chime hanging from the porch. He knew what Franklin was asking. He just wasn't convinced Franklin would get the answer he desired.

"So, will you make medicine for me?" Franklin asked.

Adam turned abruptly and asked, "Will you accept what comes, even if it's not what you wanted?"

"Yes."

Adam nodded shortly. "Then, yes, I'll help you."

Franklin sighed, then swiped a shaky hand across his face.

"What do you need from me?" he asked.

"Something that is remarkably yours alone."

Franklin hesitated a moment, then left the room. He returned shortly carrying a carving of an owl in flight.

"This was my first owl. Would this do?"

"Are you willing to sacrifice it?"

Franklin rubbed a hand over the owl one last time, as if imprinting the perfection of the shape and the feathers in his mind, then handed it over.

Adam took it. The wood felt warm where Franklin had been holding it, adding yet another layer of reality to the piece. Then he took out his knife.

"Are you still on blood thinner?" Adam asked.

Franklin nodded.

"Then hair will have to do."

Franklin sat down. Adam deftly separated a couple of strands of Franklin's hair from his head and cut them off, wrapped them in his handkerchief and put them in his pocket.

"Is that all you need?" Franklin asked.

Adam nodded. "I will make medicine for you."

Franklin's shoulders slumped with relief. "When will we know if it worked?"

"When someone comes."

"When? Not if, but when? How can you be so sure?"

"I know what I know," Adam said, and it was all he would say.

For Franklin, it wasn't enough, but it would have to do. "Then I will wait," he said.

Adam nodded, then picked up his coffee cup and leaned back in his chair and took a sip.

Franklin picked up his cup as well, but he didn't drink. He tightened his fingers around the mug, letting the warmth of the crockery settle within him as he watched his old friend's son.

Adam was looking out the window, his eyes narrowing sharply as he squinted against the light. Franklin thought that Adam looked a lot like his father. Same strong face — same far-seeing expression in his eyes, but he was taller and more muscular. And he'd been beyond the Kiamichis. He'd lived a warrior's life for the United States government.

Franklin set his coffee cup aside, folded his hands in his lap and closed his eyes.

It was good that Adam Two Eagles had come home.

Within an hour after arriving back at his home, Adam began the preparations. He drank some water before going out to ready the sweat lodge. On the way down the hillside, he got work gloves from the toolshed and a small hatchet from a shelf.

A sense of peace came over him as he worked, gathering wood and patching a small hole in the lodge. Tonight he would begin the ceremony. If Franklin and Leila had made a baby together, the Old Ones would find it.

He hurried back to the house, gathering everything he needed, then walked back to the small lodge above the creek bank.

He undressed with care, shedding his clothes a layer at a time. By the time he'd dropped his last garment, a slight breeze had come up, lifting his hair away from his face and cooling the sweat beading on his body. The first star of the evening was just visible when he looked up at the sky. He checked the fire. Ideally, there would be someone outside the lodge continuing to feed the fire, but not tonight. Tonight the fire that he'd already built would serve the purpose.

He lifted the flap and crawled in. Within seconds, he was covered in sweat. He sat down cross-legged, letting his arms and hands rest on his knees. With a slow, even rhythm he breathed in and breathed out. Then he closed his eyes and began to chant. The words were almost as old as the land on which he sat.

The hours passed and the moon that had been hanging high in the sky was more than halfway through its slow descent to the horizon. Morning was but an hour or so away.

Inside the sweat lodge, all the words had been said. All the prayers had been prayed.

Adam was ready.

He crawled out of the lodge. When he stood, the muscles in his legs tried to cramp, but he walked them out as he then moved behind the lodge and laid another stick of wood on the fire.

With the sweat drying swiftly on his skin and his mind

and body free from impurities, he reached into his pack and took out the carving, as well as the hairs he'd cut from Franklin's head.

Some might have called it a prayer, others might have said it was a chant, but the words Adam spoke were a call to the Old Ones. The rhythm of the syllables rolled off Adam's tongue like a song. The log he'd laid on the fire popped, sending a shower of sparks up into the air. Adam felt the prick of heat from one as it landed on his skin, but he didn't flinch.

Still wrapped in the cloak of darkness, he lifted his arms to the heavens and began to dance. Dust and ashes rose up from the ground, coating his feet and legs as he moved in and out of the shadows around the fire. He danced and he sang until his heartbeat matched the rhythm of his feet.

The wind rose, whistling through the trees in a thin, constant wail, sucking the hair from the back of his neck and then swirling it about his face.

They were coming.

He tossed the owl and the hairs into the fire, and then lifted his hands above his head. As he did, there was what he could only describe as an absence of air. He could still breathe, but he was unable to move.

The great warriors manifested themselves within the smoke, using it to coat the shapes of what they'd once been. They came mounted on spirit horses with eyes of fire. The horses stomped and reared, inhaling showers of sparks that had been following the column of smoke and exhaling what appeared to be stars.

One warrior wore a war bonnet so long that it dragged beneath the ghost horse's feet. Another was wrapped in the skin of a bear, with the mark of the claw painted on his chest. The third horse had a black handprint on its flank, while matching handprints of white were on the old warrior's cheeks. The last one rode naked on a horse of pure white. The wrinkles in his face were as many as the rivers of the earth. His gray hair so long that it appeared tangled in the horse's mane and tail, making it difficult to tell where man ended and horse began.

They spoke in unison, with the sounds getting lost in the whirlwind that brought them, and yet Adam knew what they'd said.

They would help.

As he watched, one by one, they reached into the fire and took a piece of Franklin's essence to help them with their search. Then, as suddenly as they'd appeared, they were gone.

Adam dropped to his knees, then passed out.

Chapter 2

DEA agent Sonora Jordan was running after a drug dealer when she fell into the twilight zone. One moment she was inches away from grabbing her perp, Enrique Garcia, and the next her gun went flying as she fell flat on her face. The shot that would have hit her square in the back went flying over her head. Instead of the heat and dust of Mexico, she was in the shade of a forest and hearing the sound of moving water from somewhere up ahead.

She lifted her head, and as she did, she saw a tall, older man standing on the porch of a single-story dwelling that was surrounded by trees. His skin was brown, and his hair was long and peppered with gray. There was a wind chime hanging by his head that looked like a Native American dream catcher. The chimes were different shapes of feathers. It was so foreign to anything she knew, she couldn't imagine why she would be hallucinating about it, and wondered if she was dead.

The man lifted his hand, and as he did, she had the

strongest urge to wave back, but she couldn't seem to move. She couldn't see his face clearly, yet she knew that he was crying. A sad, empty feeling hit her belly and then swallowed her whole.

By the time she realized she wasn't dead, only facedown in the dirt, the vision was gone. If that wasn't enough humiliation, her perp was nowhere in sight.

"Oh, crap," she muttered, then breathed easier when she saw Agent Dave Wills coming back with the perp she'd been chasing. Garcia was handcuffed and cursing at the top of his voice.

"Can it, Garcia," Wills snapped, then saw Sonora on the ground. "Jordan! Are you all right? Are you hit?"

"No…no, I'm okay," Sonora said as she got up, picked up her gun, then began brushing at the dust on her face and clothes.

"What happened?" he asked, as he shoved Garcia into the back of his car and slammed the door.

She didn't know what to say. "I guess I tripped." It was lame, but it was better than the truth.

He frowned. Sonora Jordan wasn't the tripping kind. He reached for her shoulder, intent on brushing a streak of dirt from her face when movement caught the corner of his eye. He turned just as the other Garcia brother appeared.

"Look out!" he yelled, shoving Sonora aside as he reached for his gun.

Sonora reacted without thinking. Her gun was still in her hand and she was falling again. Only this time, she got off four shots. Two of them connected.

Juanito Garcia died before he hit the ground.

Enrique saw the whole thing from Wills's car and began to scream, cursing Sonora and Wills and the DEA in general.

Wills waved his arm at another agent and yelled, "Get him out of here!"

As he was being driven away, Enrique looked back at Sonora, mouthing the words, "You're dead."

It wasn't anything she hadn't heard before, but it never failed to give her the creeps.

Wills eyed the muscle jerking in her jaw but shrugged it off. She was tough, no need getting bent out of shape on her behalf. Still, this bust hadn't gone as they'd planned.

"They made you too early," he said. "What happened?"

She spun, eyeing him angrily. "Oh, hell, Wills, I hate to venture a guess, but it might have been your ugly mug showing up a good ten minutes too soon. I wasn't through making my play when you came flying around the corner."

Wills shrugged. "But we got 'em."

"No, we got two. Miguel Garcia is the boss man and he wasn't here...yet."

This time Wills frowned. "So, it's not my fault he didn't show. You said he would."

"Yeah...at three-fifteen."

"So, what time is it now?" Wills asked.

"Three-fifteen," Sonora snapped, then strode to her car and got in, slamming the door behind her. When Wills still hadn't moved, she leaned out the window and yelled, "You plan on buying a house down here?"

Wills glanced down at what was left of Juanito Garcia and then at the faces peering out at them from windows above the street.

"Hell, no," he said.

Within minutes, they were gone, leaving the aftermath and cleanup to others. There was a border to cross and reports to be written before anyone slept tonight.

Sonora typed the last word in her report and then hit Print. She gathered up the pages with one eye on the clock and the other on the scowl her boss was wearing.

Gerald Mynton wasn't any happier than she'd been about

letting Miguel Garcia get away. Capturing two out of three wasn't the kind of odds Mynton operated on. He was an all-or-nothing kind of man. Added to that, Sonora Jordan was no longer a viable agent in this case. He knew Wills was partly responsible for missing the last Garcia brother, but there was nothing they could do about it now except pick up where they left off—minus Jordan.

When he saw Sonora get up from her desk, he motioned for her to come in. She gathered up what was obviously her report and strode across the floor.

Even though he was a happily married man and totally insulted by the thought of sexual harassment among his agents, he couldn't ignore what a beautiful woman Sonora was. She was over five feet nine inches tall and could bench-press double her weight. Her hair was long and dark and her features exotically beautiful. In all the years he'd known her, he'd only seen her smile a few times.

But it wasn't her looks that made her a valuable agent. Besides her skill, there was an asset Sonora had that made her a perfect agent. She had no relatives and no boyfriends. She was as alone in this world as a person could be, which meant that her loyalties were 100 percent with the job.

Unfortunately, killing Juanito Garcia had temporarily put an end to her usefulness, and until Miguel Garcia was brought to justice, she needed to lay low. Miguel was the kind of man who dealt in revenge.

Gerald Mynton hated to be in corners, but he was in one now. If he put Sonora back to work on anything new, Garcia could dog her until he got a chance to kill her. Mynton's only option was for her to drop out of sight until Garcia was brought in and she could live to solve another case.

He squinted thoughtfully as Sonora entered his office. Now he had to convince her that it was in her best interest to hide when he knew her instincts would be to confront and overcome.

"My report," Sonora said as she laid the file on his desk.

He nodded. "Close the door, then please sit down."

Sonora stood her ground with the door wide-open. "I'm not hiding."

Mynton sighed. "Did I say you should?"

"Not yet, but you're going to, aren't you?"

"There's a contract out on your life."

Sonora's chin jutted. "I heard."

"So...do you have a death wish?"

"No, but—"

"Garcia won't take what happened without payback. No matter what case I put you on, your presence could put everyone else in danger, not to mention yourself."

Sonora's shoulders slumped. "I hate this."

"I'm not all that excited about it myself," Mynton said.

Sonora nodded. She wasn't the kind of person who let herself be down for long. If this was the way it was going to play out, then so be it.

"I'm sorry, sir. I'll do as you ask," she said.

Mynton stood up and then walked around his desk until they were standing face-to-face.

"You don't apologize," he said shortly. "You don't ever apologize for doing your job and doing it well. Do you hear me?"

"Yes, sir."

"Is there anyplace special you can go?"

She thought of the hallucination she'd had in Mexico— of the house surrounded by a forest of green and the wind chime hanging on the porch. It had seemed so perfect. If only it had been real, she'd already be there.

"Not really. I'll think of something, though."

"Find a different mode of transportation. We don't think Garcia is in Phoenix yet, but once here, it won't take him long to find out where you live. I don't want you to be there when he arrives. As for leaving Phoenix, you can be traced too easily by credit card. Also, I'd skip the airports and bus stations."

"Well, damn it, sir, since my broom is also in the shop, what the hell else do you suggest?"

Mynton's frown deepened. "Use your imagination."

"This is a nightmare," Sonora muttered. "Just do me one favor."

"If I can," Mynton said.

"Find Miguel Garcia," she added.

"And you stay safe and keep in touch," he added.

A few minutes later, she was gone.

By the time she got home, she was exhausted. However, there were plans to be made. Mynton wanted her to get lost. He didn't know it, but she'd been lost all her life. Dumped on the doorstep of a Texas orphanage when she was only hours old, Sonora had grown up without a sense of who she was or where she was from. When she was young, she used to pretend that her mother would suddenly appear and whisk her away, but it had never happened. Life for Sonora was nothing but one kick in the teeth after another. She didn't believe in luck, had never believed in Santa Claus or the Easter Bunny and trusted no one. What had happened on their last case had been unexpected, but she could handle it. All she needed to do was get out of town.

Transportation was no problem. She knew exactly how she would travel. All she needed to do was call her old boyfriend, Buddy Allen, and have him bring back her Harley.

She stripped down to a bra and panties before she sat down on the side of the bed. She rubbed the back of her neck with both hands, wishing she had time for a massage, but that was too public for someone who needed to lay low.

She picked up the phone and dialed Buddy's number. Although it had been more than six months since they'd quit seeing each other, they were still on good terms. Sonora had been gone too much to commit herself to anyone, and

Buddy wanted more than a once-a-month lay. The decision to quit trying had been mutual.

Still, as she waited for Buddy to pick up, she couldn't help but wish she had a little backup in her personal life.

Buddy answered on the third ring. "Heelloo, good lookin'."

"Did you know it was me, or is that the way you always answer your phone?" Sonora said.

Buddy laughed. "Caller ID and yes."

This time it was Sonora who chuckled. "Some things never change...you being one of them," she said.

Buddy sighed. "Did you call to chastise me for being male, or can I talk you into a round of good sex for old times sake?"

"No on both counts. I called because I need my bike."

Buddy groaned. "Aw, man...not the Harley."

"Sorry, but I need it," Sonora said shortly.

The smile disappeared from Buddy's voice. "Are you in trouble?"

"Not if I get out of town quick enough."

"Damn it, Sonora, why do you do it?"

"Do what?" she asked.

"You know what. There are a hundred careers you could have picked besides the one that you chose, and none of them would have been dangerous."

"Can you bring it over?" she asked. "I'd come get it, but I don't want to advertise my presence any more than necessary."

Buddy sighed. "Hell, yes, I'll bring the Harley, serviced, gassed up and clean. When do you need it?" he asked.

"Yesterday."

Buddy cursed and asked, "Do you need to leave before morning?"

"No. It can wait until then, but early...please."

"Thanks for nothing," he muttered. "I'll be there before 7:00 a.m. Will you make me some coffee?"

"Yes."

"And maybe some of your biscuits and gravy?"

"No."

He sighed. "Can't blame a guy for trying."

"I'm not blaming you for anything," she said. "Never have. Never will."

"I know," Buddy said, and knew that she was no longer talking about the bike. "See you in the morning."

"Okay, Buddy, and thanks."

"It's okay, honey," Buddy said, and hung up.

With that job over, Sonora walked to the closet, then grabbed her travel bag and quickly packed. She thought about where she might go and then went into the living room, found an atlas and carried it to the kitchen.

She opened the pages to the map of the U.S. and then just sat and stared. One line seemed to stand out from all the others. She fumbled in a drawer for a yellow highlighter, then popped the cap. Her fingers where shaking as she held it over the map. Something rattled behind her, like pebbles in a can. She ignored it and began to mark.

Without a thought in her head, she began drawing a line north out of Phoenix toward Flagstaff, then across the country until she came to Oklahoma. The line ended there.

She paused, frowned, then shook her head, certain she'd just lost her mind. Still, she left the atlas on the counter as she went into her bedroom.

She showered quickly, afraid that the vision would come back. Even after she crawled into bed and closed her eyes, she was reluctant to sleep. Finally, she rolled onto her side, bunched her pillow under her neck, then grabbed the extra one and hugged it to her. It was an old habit from childhood, and one she rarely indulged in anymore. The simple act made her feel childish and helpless and Sonora was neither of those.

Somehow she slept, and woke up just after six. Time enough for a quick shower.

True to his promise, Buddy showed up right before seven. She met him at the door with a to-go cup of coffee.

"Good morning," she said, eyeing his tousled hair and unshaven face. "Thanks for bringing the Harley."

"You're welcome," he said, then dropped the keys in her hands, handed her the helmet and took the coffee, downing a good portion of it before he spoke again. "I don't suppose you'd like to tell me what's going on?"

She shrugged. "Someone wants me dead."

"Son of a bitch," Buddy muttered.

"Yes, he is," Sonora said. "A real bad one. I don't think anyone knows about you and me, but just to be on the safe side, don't mention my name to anyone."

"There is no more you and me," Buddy reminded her. "And don't worry about me. I'm not the one with the death wish."

Sonora frowned. "I don't have a death wish. I just do my job and do it well." Then she kissed him on the cheek, as much as a thank-you as for old times' sake, as well as for bringing back her bike, then pointed at the cab in the street. "I suppose that's your ride. Don't keep him waiting."

She watched him get into the cab before checking the area for someone who didn't belong. All was well. When he looked back, she waved goodbye, then quickly closed the door.

She walked through her home one last time, making sure everything was as it should be, then shouldered her bag, picked up the helmet and turned off the lights. She opened the door, hesitating briefly to scan the neighborhood once more, and saw nothing amiss. The black and shiny Harley was at the curb.

She hurried outside, opened the storage compartment
and dropped her handgun inside, then lowered the lid and
tied her bag down on top. When she stuck the key in the
ignition, she could tell Buddy had been good for his word.
Not only was the bike clean, but the gas gauge registered
full. She checked to make sure her toolbox was in place,
then put on the helmet and slung her leg over the bike as if
she was mounting a horse.

The engine roared to life, then settled down to a soft
rumble as she released the kickstand and gave it the gas.
As the rumble changed to a full-throttle blast, she put it in
gear and rode away without looking back.

It wasn't until she was on the highway that she remembered the path she'd highlighted on the atlas. There was no
reason for her to have chosen that direction, and a couple
of times she even considered turning around and heading
for Las Vegas or points farther west. But something more
than instinct was guiding her trip.

Chapter 3

Miguel Garcia was in Juarez, trying to figure out how to get over the border. The Mexican police had staked out his hotel and would have already had him in custody if it hadn't been for Jorge Diaz, one of his dealers, who'd sent his own child into the restaurant where Miguel was having breakfast to warn him.

Now he was in a dingy room over what must be the oldest cantina in the city, without his clothes, and without access to his bank. Even though he hadn't been born to it, Miguel had been in the drug business long enough that he'd become accustomed to fine dining, elegant surroundings. Being forced to hide in a room like this was like a slap in the face—a degradation that only added to the grief of losing his brothers.

Enrique was incarcerated somewhere in the States, and Juanito was on a slab in a Tijuana morgue. He'd promised his mother on her deathbed that he would take care of Juanito. He was the baby of their family, the last of eight children, but now, because of that DEA bitch, Juanito was dead.

Before he'd gone into hiding, Miguel had made a promise at his mother's grave that he would avenge Juanito's death. He'd also let it be known that he would pay big money for the name and location of the agent who'd killed his brother, with the warning to leave her alone. He wanted to end her life—personally.

And so he waited. And waited. A day passed in this hell, then a second, then a third before everything changed.

The *puta* Miguel had just paid for a blow job was in the bathroom brushing her teeth when someone knocked on his door. He reached for his gun, grabbed the woman who was just coming out of the bathroom and put his finger to his mouth to indicate she be quiet. His grip on her arm was so painful that she stifled a screech and covered her mouth with both hands. Tears ran down her face, but she didn't move.

Once he was satisfied that she understood what he meant, he whispered in her ear, "Ask who is there."

She nodded, then called out as he told her.

There was a long stretch of silence, then a man spoke. "I have news for Miguel."

Miguel recognized the voice of Jorge, the dealer who'd helped him escape. He pulled the woman away from the door, opened it enough to make sure Jorge was alone and then shoved her out.

"Get lost," he said.

She scurried away, glad to be leaving in one piece.

"Come in," Miguel said.

Jorge nodded quickly, looked over his shoulder, then stepped inside. He didn't waste time or words. "You wanted the name of the agent who killed your brother."

Miguel's heart skipped a beat. "Yes."

"Her name is Sonora Jordan. She lives in Phoenix, Arizona."

Miguel stifled the urge to clap his hands. This was the best news he'd had in days. "You are sure."

"*Sí,* Patron."

Miguel put a hand on Jorge's shoulder to explain why he couldn't pay him yet. "They are watching my home and my bank."

Jorge nodded again. No further explanation was needed. "I know," he said, reaching into his pocket for a roll of hundred dollar bills, which he handed to Miguel. "For you, Patron, and if you're ready, I can get you across the border tonight."

Miguel was not only surprised, he was shocked. He had greatly underestimated this man's loyalty. "When this is over, you will be greatly rewarded."

Jorge shrugged. "I expect nothing, Patron. It is my honor to help. At eleven o'clock, there will be one knock on your door. The man who comes will take you to a hacienda outside of Juarez where a private plane will be waiting. The pilot has already gotten clearance for his trip, but it does not include landing in Juarez, so the timing will be crucial. You must not be late because he will not wait. Once across the border, he will touch down briefly at a small airstrip outside of Houston. More money and a car will be waiting for you there. The man who brought it has been instructed to stay until he sees that you're safely on the ground."

Miguel threw his arms around Jorge. "*Gracias,* Jorge… *gracias.* I will never forget this."

Jorge nodded and smiled. "*Vaya con Dios,* Patron." And then he was gone.

Miguel glanced at his watch. It was just after nine. Within two hours, he would be gone from this place and on his way to fulfilling the promise he'd made at his mother's grave.

As soon as Jorge reached the street, he took out his cell

phone and made a call. "Tony, this is Jorge Diaz. I need you to do something for me."

Tony Freely was one of Jorge's mules. He traveled back and forth regularly from his ranch outside of Houston to Juarez, doing his part to make sure that the drug market continued to thrive and being nicely reimbursed for his troubles.

"Yeah, sure, Jorge. Just name it."

"You remember the old runway where I had you pick up a load about three months back?"

"Yeah, but I thought you didn't want to use it anymore."

"I don't. It's something else," Jorge said. "What I want you to do is go to that runway at an hour before midnight tonight and wait for a small plane to land there. A man will get off. You let him see you. Let him see your face, but don't talk to him. Just get in your car and drive away."

Tony frowned. This didn't sound right, but he knew better than to question Jorge.

"Sure. No problem."

"Thank you," Jorge said. "I'll make it worth your while."

Tony's frown disappeared. Money talked loud and clear to him. "Consider it done," he said, and hung up the phone.

Jorge did the same, smiling as he disconnected. Before he was through, the Garcia brothers' reign of power would be over and he would be the one in charge.

As promised, Miguel's ride appeared on time. He didn't recognize the short, fat man who came to get him, and the man didn't offer a name. They got to the airstrip without incident. Soon the lights of Juarez were swiftly disappearing below them. Miguel was already making plans as to how to find Sonora Jordan and make her pay for the death of his brother.

In about an hour, the plane began to lose altitude and

Miguel's heartbeat accelerated. He leaned over and peered out the window to the sea of lights that was Houston.

The pilot banked suddenly to the west and began descending. Minutes later, the small plane landed, taking a couple of hard bounces before rolling to an easy stop.

Miguel saw a small hangar and a man standing beneath a single light mounted above the door. In the shadows nearby, he could see the outline of a car.

He owed Jorge big-time.

"You get out now," the pilot said shortly.

Miguel frowned. It was the most the man had said to him since they took off. Still, he grabbed his bag and jumped out of the plane. Even as he was walking away, the plane turned around and took off the same way it had landed.

Caught in the back draft, Miguel ducked his head and closed his eyes while dust and grit swirled around him. When he opened his eyes, the plane was off the ground and the man he'd seen under the lights was gone.

The unexpected solitude and quiet made him a little uneasy, and when a chorus of coyotes suddenly tuned up from somewhere beyond the hangar, he headed for the car in a run.

Only after he was inside with the doors locked and his hand on the keys dangling from the ignition did he relax. He started the engine and checked the gauges. The car was full of gas, and two maps were on the seat beside him—one of Texas and one of Arizona. After a quick check of the briefcase in the passenger seat, he knew he would have plenty of money to do what had to be done. He backed away from the hangar and followed the dirt road until he hit blacktop. Gauging his directions by the digital compass on the rearview mirror, he turned north and drove until daylight. The first town he came to, he stopped and ate breakfast, then got a room at the local motel. It was ten minutes after

nine in the morning when he crawled between the sheets.
Within seconds, he was out.

Even though Sonora had started out with an indefinite
direction in mind, the farther she went, the more certain
she became that, whatever her future held, she would find
it somewhere east.

Near the Arizona border, it started to rain. Sonora
stopped and took a room at a chain motel. She tossed her
bag onto the bed before heading to the restaurant on-site.

Once she finished her meal, she started back to her room
on the second floor. She was halfway up the stairs when she
pulled an Alice and, once again, fell down the rabbit hole.

*It was raining. The kind of rain that some people called
a toad strangler—a hard, pounding downpour with little
to no wind. She'd never stood in the rain and not been wet
before. It was an eerie sensation. And it was night again.
Why did insanity keep yanking her around in the dark? It
was bad enough she was hallucinating.*

*She didn't have to look twice to know that she was back
at the Native American man's house. Water was running off
the roof and down between her feet, following the slope of
the ground. All of a sudden, lightning struck with a loud,
frightening crack. She flinched, then relaxed. There was
no need to panic. She wasn't really here. This was just a
dream.*

*She looked toward the house, then felt herself moving
closer, although she knew for a fact that her feet never
shifted. Now she was standing beneath the porch and looking into the window. At first, she saw nothing. Then she
saw the Native American man lying on the floor near a
doorway.*

*She gasped and started toward the door when she real-
ized that, again, she had no power here. She was nothing*

*but a witness. Dread hit her belly high. Why was she see-
ing this if she could do nothing about it?*

*Then, as she was watching through the window, she
realized there was a light in the window that hadn't been
there before. It took a few moments before she could tell
it was a reflection from a vehicle coming down the driveway behind her.*

*She turned, wanting to call out—willing herself to
scream out "please hurry," but as before, she was nothing but an observer.*

Adam Two Eagles drove recklessly through the storm.
The phone call he'd gotten a short time ago from Franklin
had frightened him. Even now as he was turning up Franklin's driveway, the knot in his gut tightened.

Franklin had sounded confused—even fatalistic. Adam
didn't think Franklin would do anything crazy, like do himself in, but he couldn't be sure. And when he'd tried to call
him back, there had been no answer.

He could have called an ambulance. The people in Broken Bow knew Franklin. They knew he had leukemia. They
would send an ambulance, but if it was unwarranted—
if Adam had misread the situation—it would embarrass
Franklin, and that he didn't want to do. So here he was,
driving like a madman in the dark, pouring rain, just to
make sure his friend was still of this earth.

As he came around the curve, he saw that the lights
were still on in Franklin's house. That was good. At least
he wouldn't be waking him up to make sure he was okay.

Lightning struck a tree about a hundred yards in front
of him. Even in the rain, sparks flew. Right before the
flash disappeared, Adam saw branches exploding, then
flying through the air. He swerved as one flew past the
hood of his truck, then sped past the site just before the
tree burst into flames. It wouldn't burn long in this down-

pour, but the sooner Adam got out of this rain, the better off he would feel.

He slid to a halt near the porch, jumped out in a run, vaulted up the steps and had his fist ready to knock when he realized he wasn't alone. He let his hand drop as he slowly turned, staring down the length of the porch to the small square of light coming through the window from inside.

The porch was empty, yet he knew he was being watched. Drawn by an urge he couldn't explain, he moved forward, and when he reached the window, stared out into the night, into the curtain of rain.

"Who's there?" he called, and then for a reason he couldn't explain, reached out and touched the air in front of him.

No one answered, and he felt only the rain.

Shrugging off the feeling as nothing but nerves, he turned back toward the door, and as he did, glanced through the window. Within seconds, he'd spied Franklin's body lying on the floor.

"Oh, no," he cried, and ran to the door.

It was locked, but not for long.

Adam kicked the door inward, then ran to his friend.

Sonora's heart was pounding so hard she thought it would burst. Every breath she took was painful, and she felt like she was going to be sick.

The man who'd come out of the storm onto the porch was unbelievable—like some knight in shining armor she might have conjured up during her teenage years.

His skin was the color of burnished copper. His hair was long, black and plastered to his head and neck from the storm. He was tall and lean, without an ounce of fat on him—a fact made obvious by the wet clothes molded to his body. But it was his face that intrigued her. His nose was hawklike, his chin stubborn and strong. His lips were full and his eyes were dark and impossible to read.

And he was looking straight at her.

Sonora shivered.

This wasn't supposed to be happening.

He wasn't part of the dream.

And it was a dream. It had to be.

When he started toward her, she screamed, or at least she thought she screamed. The sound was going off inside her head like the bells of an alarm, but the man kept coming.

All of a sudden, she fell off the porch. When she came to, she was on her hands and knees on the stairs of the motel.

"Hey, lady! Are you okay? I saw you trip and fall but I was all the way down at the end of the walkway. Couldn't get here fast enough to do you much good."

Sonora shuddered, then brushed at the knees of her pants and dusted off her hands as she looked up at the man standing at the head of the stairs. He was short and stocky with a bald head and a red beard. An odd combination of features for the guy, but he seemed harmless.

"I'm okay," she said. "I guess I wasn't paying attention to where I was going. I'm fine, but thanks."

The guy nodded, then took a couple steps backward before turning around and going back down the hall to his room.

Sonora unlocked her door and went inside, hung a do-not-disturb sign on the outside of the doorknob, and then carefully locked the doors. It took even less time to undress, and moments later, she fell into bed.

The hallucination she'd just had was still in her mind, but she shrugged it off. She couldn't be bothered with worrying about some stupid daydream with Miguel Garcia still on the loose. With those thoughts in her mind, she fell asleep.

Chapter 4

Sonora crossed the Arizona border into New Mexico just before noon the next day. Traffic was already thicker on I-40, as well as on the access roads. A digital message on a bank near the interstate gave a temperature reading of 98 degrees. With the amount of traffic and exhaust fumes heating up the pavement, Sonora could add another ten degrees of heat to that reading and know she wasn't off by much.

She'd already made a decision that traveling in the heat of the day in this part of the country wasn't smart. So she took the next exit off the interstate and found a motel.

Within minutes she had a room on the ground floor. She left the office and rode her bike to the parking place in front of her room. When she dismounted, she realized her hands and legs were shaking. Too much heat and not enough water, but she was about to fix that. She locked up her bike, shouldered her bag and unlocked the door to her room, gratefully inhaling the artificially cooled air inside as she entered.

She went to the bathroom to wash up, and drank a big glass of water while she was there. There was a café on the other side of the parking lot, which she planned to visit, but not in this hot biker leather. When she came out of the bathroom, she took off her pants and vest, tossed her shirt aside as well as her biker boots for some cooler clothes and tennis shoes.

She stretched and then bounced once on the bed, testing it for comfort. She scooted all the way up on the mattress, then stretched out—but only for a minute. She noticed the red LED light on the smoke detector was working and closed her eyes.

When she woke up, it was after 10:00 p.m. She groaned as she rolled over and swung her legs off the bed.

"Oh, great, I didn't mean to sleep so long."

She stood up and went to the window. It was pouring. She probably wouldn't sleep tonight, but she could eat, and her belly was protesting the fact that she hadn't eaten since breakfast.

Grabbing a clean T-shirt and jeans from her bag, she dressed quickly and slipped her wallet in a fanny pack before she left.

Despite the rain, the smell of charcoal and cooking meat was heavy in the air. Her mouth watered as she made a dash across the parking lot and into the café.

"Ooh, honey, come in out of that rain," the hostess said as Sonora dashed inside. "Are you by yourself?" she added.

Sonora nodded.

The hostess picked up a menu. "This way," she said, and led the way across the floor to a booth in the back. "This okay?"

"Perfect," Sonora said, and meant it. Being at the far end of the room with a clear view of the door was a good thing.

The fact that she was close to the kitchen didn't bother her. She wasn't looking for ambiance, just food.

She ordered iced tea, salad and chicken alfredo, then opened a package of crackers and began nibbling on them while she waited for her food to arrive. Lightning flashed outside, momentarily lighting the parking lot. Lights flickered, then went out. A communal groan of dismay sounded throughout the seating area while cursing could be heard in the kitchen.

Sonora automatically felt for her fanny pack, making sure her wallet was in place. Before she could relax, there was the sound of falling furniture, then a woman's shrill scream.

"Help! Help! Someone just stole my purse!"

Sonora was on her feet without thinking. She heard running footsteps coming toward her. The way she figured it, the only person running in the dark would be the perp.

She moved instinctively and heard, more than saw, him coming. What she did see was that the shadow coming toward her was well over six feet tall. Using one of her kickboxing moves, she caught the running man belly high. She heard him grunt, then heard him stagger into a table and some chairs. She spun on one foot and came back around with another kick that caught him in the chest and ended up on his chin.

He went down like a felled ox.

Lights flickered, then fully came on as power was restored.

The woman who'd been robbed was still screaming and crying.

The hostess who'd seated Sonora saw the man on the floor, then eyed the tall, dark woman she'd just put in the back of the room and pointed. "Lord have mercy, honey! Did you do that?"

"Call the cops," Sonora said.

The man on the floor moaned and started to roll over.

Sonora put her foot in the middle of the man's back and pushed. "Uh-uh," she warned. "You stay right where you are, buddy, or I'll snap your spine faster than you can blink."

"Damn, lady. My belly hurts bad. I think you broke my ribs." The man moaned.

Soon the squall of approaching sirens could be heard. The perp moaned again.

The police came in the door, followed by a pair of EMTs.

The hostess waved them over. "Here! He's here!" she yelled.

Sonora quickly exited the café through the kitchen, looking wistfully at the food as she ran through. The last thing she needed was to call attention to herself, and she'd done that big time by stopping the perp. The police would have wanted to see her name and ID. Having them identify her as DEA was completely opposite to what she was trying to do—which was get lost.

She hunched her shoulders against the rain and walked out into the parking lot. Quickly she crossed the street to a pizza place on the corner.

"One more time," she muttered as she hurried inside.

"Sit anywhere," a waitress said as she hurried by with an order. "I'll be right with you."

This time, Sonora settled in at a booth near the front door and then leaned her head against the glass as she looked out into the night. She was alternating between sausage or mushroom pizza when another flash of lightning sent her back into the black hole that had become part of her mind.

The older Native American man was sitting at a table with his back to Sonora. She wanted to go around him and see what he was doing, but she found herself unable to move.

"Why am I here? What the hell do you want?" she yelled.

Either he didn't hear her, or he was ignoring her.

The man stood up slowly, then walked away, revealing a small piece of wood and a pile of wood curls.

He was carving something, but whatever it was, it was little more than an outline in the wood. Her gaze slid from the wood to the man. He was shaking pills from a bottle into his hand. There was a strange expression on his face as he tossed them down the back of his throat and chased them with water.

He's dying.

The moment Sonora thought it, she flinched. A deep sadness came over her. "What am I supposed to do?" she cried. "Why are you haunting me?"

"Hey, lady!"

Sonora jerked.

"What?"

"I asked you...what do you want?"

Sonora blinked. Traveling from insanity to the real world was confusing, but she was getting better at it. It didn't take her but a moment to answer.

"A medium sausage-and-mushroom pizza and a large Pepsi."

The waitress nodded and left Sonora on her own again, only this time, Sonora focused her interests on the people at the other tables as she waited for her food to arrive.

She was both frustrated and confused by these recurring hallucinations. Talking to a shrink was a possibility and probably wise, but she wouldn't risk it. The first time the precinct got wind of an agent in "therapy," that agent would wind up doing desk duty until pronounced fit for duty again. Sonora didn't want that on her record, so she was relying on instinct to get her through this. She couldn't help but feel as if she was seeing this man for a reason.

Maybe if he was real, and maybe if she found him, she'd discover for herself what this all meant.

Then the waitress came, delivered the pizza, refilled Sonora's drink and left her to dine alone. By the time she had finished eating and paid for her meal, the rain had stopped. Reflections from the streetlights were mirrored in the puddles as she crossed the street to get to her room.

She was wide-awake and itching to be on the move. Despite an old fear of the dark, she handled it better outside. When she thought about it, which was rarely, it always made sense. She'd gotten her fear of the dark from being locked in a closet, so if she wasn't bound by four walls, the fear never quite manifested into a full-blown panic attack. Glad to be on the move again, she packed her bag quickly, dropped her room key off at the office and mounted up. Within the hour, she was gone.

Miguel Garcia had been in Phoenix less than six hours when he'd gotten his first good lead on Sonora Jordan's whereabouts. He had a name and an address, only it wasn't Sonora's address. It belonged to her ex-boyfriend, Buddy Allen.

It was just after 10:00 p.m. when Buddy pulled into the driveway of his apartment building. It was the first time he'd been home since this morning when he'd left for work. With his mind on a shower and bed, he got off the elevator, carrying a six-pack of beer and a bag of groceries. He set down the six-pack, then toed it into his apartment after he opened the door. The door locked as it swung shut. Buddy was halfway across the living room when it dawned on him that all the lights were on, but he distinctly remembered turning them off when he'd left.

The hair rose on the back of his arms. He set down the

sack and the six-pack and stepped backward, intent on leaving the apartment to call the police.

Then a man walked out of the bedroom holding a gun. "You're not going anywhere," he said, and motioned for Buddy to sit down on the sofa.

Buddy measured the distance to the door against the gun and cursed silently. The man didn't look like the kind to be making idle threats.

"Who the hell are you?" Buddy asked.

"My name is of no importance," he said.

"Then what are you doing here?" Buddy countered.

"Looking for a friend of yours."

"Who?" Buddy asked.

"Sonora Jordan."

Buddy's stomach rolled. Suddenly, it hit him how much danger he was in. Sonora didn't deal with lightweights, and she'd been spooked enough to leave Phoenix. There was every possibility that he might not live to see another day.

"I don't know where she is," Buddy said.

The man frowned. "Wrong answer," he said, and swung the butt of his gun up under Buddy's chin.

Buddy dropped, then didn't move.

DEA agent Gerald Mynton was pouring his second cup of coffee of the day when the phone rang. He set down his cup and reached across the desk to answer it. "Mynton."

"Agent Mynton, I'm Detective Broyles with Phoenix Homicide."

"Detective, what can I do for you?" Mynton asked.

"I'm not sure, but we're working a murder and the name of one of your agents came up."

Mynton frowned. "Who?"

"Sonora Jordan."

Mynton sat down in his chair with a thump. "What about her?"

"Do you know a man by the name of Robert Allen... goes by the name of Buddy?"

"Not that I— Wait! Did you say Buddy Allen?"

"Yes."

"Oh, hell," Mynton said.

"Then you do know him?" Broyles asked.

"Not personally, but I do know that Agent Jordan used to date a Buddy Allen. Is he the one who's dead?"

"Yes."

"And you say it was murder?"

"Beat all to hell and back," Broyles said. "Died in E.R. about two hours ago."

"And you're looking for Agent Jordan because?"

"Mr. Allen had a message for her. It was the last thing he said before he died. He said to tell her that 'he didn't tell.' Do you know what that means?"

Mynton felt sick. "Maybe. Do you have any leads?"

Broyles shuffled his notes.

"Uh,...here's what we know so far. Around two in the morning, a neighbor was coming home when she saw a stranger get out of the elevator and leave the building. She said he had blood on the front of his clothes. She got into her apartment and went to bed. But she said she couldn't sleep because she kept hearing an intermittent thump from the apartment above her. She knew it belonged to Buddy Allen, and said it wasn't like him to make noise of any kind, so she called the super. He went up and checked... found Mr. Allen in a pool of blood and called an ambulance. When he died, we were called in. After questioning the other occupants of the building, we're leaning toward the theory that the man the neighbor saw might be our man."

"Got a name?" Mynton asked.

"No, just a description."

"Was he Latino?"

There was a long moment of silence, then Broyles spoke. "Yes, and I want to know how you know that."

"We got word a few days ago that there was a hit out on Agent Jordan." Mynton sighed. "God…we never thought about warning any of her friends. She's going to be sick about this."

"That's all fine, but I want to know about the Latino."

"Of course," Mynton said. "I can't guarantee that the man who killed Allen is the one who's after Sonora Jordan, but just in case…you might be looking for a man named Miguel Garcia, or one of his hired goons."

"We would like to talk to Ms. Jordan."

"Yeah, so would I, but she's gone," Mynton said.

"What do you mean, gone?"

"We knew Garcia was after her. I told her to get lost for a while, but I haven't heard anything from her since she left."

"How long ago was that?"

"Uh…three, maybe four days, I'm not sure."

"Do you have a cell phone number?"

"Yes, but would you allow me to get in contact with her first? She's going to take the news about Allen hard. She'll blame herself for his death and she's already under a load."

"Yes, all right," Broyles said. "But as soon as you contact her, please have her call us."

"Will do," Mynton said.

He hung up the phone, then flipped through his Rolodex for Sonora's cell phone number.

By noon, Mynton had left three messages on Sonora's cell without receiving a call back. He was worried and frustrated by his inability to reach her, but he knew that, if she was okay, she would eventually return his call. It was fifteen minutes to one when he left the office for a lunch meeting.

* * *

After riding all night and stopping for a few hours at a motel, it was close to sunset when Sonora mounted the Harley and got back on the road. The setting sun was at her back as she rolled out onto the interstate.

The night promised to be clear. The first star of evening was already out and although the air was swiftly cooling, the heat of the pavement was still a force with which to be reckoned.

The power of the Harley carried Sonora swiftly down the highway. She rode with the confidence of a seasoned biker. Just before the last of the light faded away, Sonora signaled to change lanes, then glanced in the rearview mirror. The last thing she expected to see was the outline of a horse and rider up in the sky, following at her back.

Startled by the sight, the bike swerved slightly. She quickly regained control and then ventured another glance. This time, she saw nothing but a scattering of clouds.

Rattled, she curled her fingers tighter around the handlebars and focused on the road ahead.

It was nothing but clouds in an odd formation—no way had she seen a ghost rider.

No way, indeed.

Miguel Garcia was ticked off. He'd beaten Buddy Allen senseless and still wasn't any better off than he'd been when he'd walked into the apartment. Either the man didn't know, or he'd rather die than tell where Sonora Jordan had gone. All he'd gotten from his visit to Allen's apartment was a photo of Sonora. He'd seen her driver's license photo, but it did not hold a candle to the one Buddy had in a frame. Miguel stared at the image, eyeing the copper-colored skin and straight black hair. Her eyes were dark and almond shaped, her lips full with a twist that could be read as sensual or sarcastic.

Miguel had to admit that Sonora Jordan was beautiful. But beautiful or not, she'd killed Juanito and helped put Enrique in prison and for that she would pay.

Before he'd left the neighborhood, he'd done a little investigating, spread a little money around and learned that Buddy Allen used to have a Harley parked near his pickup truck, but that he'd ridden away on it about five days ago and come back in a cab. After that, he'd drawn a blank.

Once he got back to his hotel room, Miguel made a call to Jorge Diaz to see if he had any contacts in Phoenix who could hack into computer systems. Jorge had given him a name. Toke Hopper. It turned out to be a good one.

At Miguel's instructions, Toke hacked into the Arizona DMV and discovered that the missing Harley actually belonged to Sonora Jordan, not Robert Allen.

Since Miguel had already been to her apartment and seen the amount of accumulating mail dropped through the slot in her door, he was guessing that she'd already been gone for a few days. He'd been puzzled by the fact that her car was still in its parking place, and assumed she'd taken a plane or a bus out of Phoenix.

Just to make sure his guess had been right, he had Toke check the passenger lists of airlines and buses for the past week. To his surprise, Sonora Jordan had not used either to leave the city. The only thing missing besides Sonora herself was the Harley. If she left town on it, he had no way of knowing a destination.

He decided to go back to her apartment and look again. Maybe he'd missed something before that would make sense to him now.

He paid off the hacker and drove back to Sonora's apartment building, then walked in like he owned the place. It was quarter to eleven in the morning and most of the residents were at work. No one challenged him as he rode the elevator up to her floor and picked the lock on her door as he'd done before.

Once inside, he began going through papers, looking for something—anything—that would give him a clue as to where she'd gone. Thirty minutes later he was no closer to an answer than he had been when he came in, and was ready to give up. He was on his way out of the kitchen when he accidentally dropped his car keys. As he was picking them up, he noticed something on the floor underneath the island. He got down on his hands and knees and pulled it out.

It was nothing but a book. He had a difficult time speaking English and couldn't read it at all, so he was definitely disappointed. He didn't get interested until he realized the book wasn't just a book, it was an atlas—a book of maps.

He was looking for a woman who'd obviously gone on a trip, so he started at the beginning and began turning pages one by one. About six pages in, he came to the page showing the map of the United States and found his first clue.

Someone had taken a highlighter and traced a path north out of Phoenix and into Oklahoma. The yellow line ended near a small town on the interstate called Henryetta.

He didn't know how old the atlas was, or if the yellow line was from a previous trip, but it was simple enough to check out. Within minutes he was gone.

He made Flagstaff around four o'clock and immediately began flashing her picture around at gas stations and eating establishments. It took a couple of hours before he hit pay dirt.

He found an employee at a gas station who remembered a pretty woman wearing black leather and riding a Harley. When Miguel showed him Sonora's picture, he confirmed it was her that he'd seen.

Miguel was congratulating himself on his detective

work and thought about driving on through the night, but
when he saw the gathering thunderstorms, he changed his
mind. He got a room for the night and settled in, satisfied
that he was on the right track.

Sonora was still rattled by her latest hallucination as she
rode through Amarillo, Texas, but kept going.

She never knew when she crossed the Oklahoma border,
but when the sun finally came up, she saw a sign on the side
of the road indicating Clinton and Weatherford were only a
few miles ahead. She'd never heard of Clinton, but for some
reason, she knew Weatherford was in Oklahoma.

Just knowing that she was in the state fueled a sense of
urgency she didn't understand, but she was too weary to
go any farther until she'd gotten some food and some sleep.

Adam Two Eagles had watched the sun rise, then fed his
cat before making himself sit down and write checks to pay
his bills. Some time today he was going to have to go into
town and get groceries, but not for a while. The day was
too nice to waste and he'd promised some families he'd go
visit and make medicine for them.

And so the day passed as Adam made visits and answered a couple of phone calls for help from his cell phone.
He worked without thought of what waited for him back
home until it was getting late and he had yet to go to town
and get his groceries. In a few hours it would be dark. He
thought about waiting until tomorrow to go shopping and
started to go inside his house, when suddenly the front door
swung shut in front of him.

Startled, he stopped, opened it, then stood on the threshold and waited, expecting to feel a draft from an open window somewhere in the house.

He felt nothing.

The skin crawled on the back of his neck.

He turned and looked toward the horizon.
The sense of imminency was still with him.
"Okay," he said softly. "I will go to town."

Chapter 5

A man was in the motel parking lot cursing the flat he'd found on his car as a police siren sounded a few blocks over.

Sonora heard none of it. The air-conditioning unit near her bed was a buffer against the heat outside, as well as the noise. She slept deeply and without moving, until she began to dream.

She was surrounded by trees. The wind was rustling the leaves overhead. In the distance, she could hear coyotes. She was lost, and yet she wasn't afraid. Something flew past her—most likely an owl. They were night hunters—like her. As soon as she thought that, she frowned. Why had she referred to herself as a night hunter? That made no sense.

A twig snapped off to her right.

Sonora froze. Something—or someone—was out there.

"Who's there?" she asked, and then feared the answer.

Another twig snapped. This time from behind her. She wanted to turn around, but as always, she couldn't move.

"Stop it," she yelled. "Either speak up or get the hell away from me. This isn't funny!"

Wind lifted the hair from the back of her neck as she curled her fingers into fists. It took a few moments for it to sink in that the gust of wind was past, but that her hair was still up.

She heard a sigh, then felt something brush the skin above her collar.

"No, no, no," she moaned. "I want to wake up."

"Not yet," someone whispered.

Sonora shuddered.

"Shh, pretty woman...you are safe."

"Oh, God, oh, God, I need this to stop. I'm waking up now. Do you hear me? I'm waking up now!"

She closed her eyes, counted to ten and then opened them, expecting to be anywhere but in a forest, in the dark, with a stranger at her back.

"Why am I not awake?" she moaned.

"Because we are not done," he said softly.

"Then show yourself, damn it!"

There was a long moment of silence. Sonora waited— uncertain what would happen first. Either he would disappear, or she would wake up. Then suddenly, her hair was laying against her neck once more, and she thought she heard him whisper something near her ear. She wasn't sure. It could have been the wind, but she thought she heard him say, "As you wish."

She closed her eyes.

"Look at me."

Panic hit her like a blow to the gut. Be careful of what you ask for, she thought.

"Woman. Look. At. Me."

His voice was firm, but she was no longer afraid.

She took a deep breath and then opened her eyes just as

*a cloud blew over the moon. In the dark, all she could see
were his eyes, looking down at her and glittering like a wolf.*

So he was tall.

*She felt his breath upon her face, or maybe it was just
the wind.*

"Do you see me?" he asked.

*The wind blew the last of the cloud away from the face
of the moon, and he was revealed to her in the moonlight.*

*It was a stunning face—a face that appeared to have
been carved out of rock—all angles and hard planes—
except for his mouth. It was full and curved in just a hint
of a smile. When he saw that she was looking at his lips,
she saw his nostrils flare.*

"I see you," she said.

"Then come to me," he demanded.

Sonora woke up just as someone fell against the outside door of her motel room. She heard a burst of muffled
laughter and then the sounds faded away.

"Oh, God, what is happening to me?" she whispered.
"Am I going insane?"

She swung her legs over the side of the bed and looked
for the digital clock. It was either broken or unplugged, because the digital readout was dark. She turned on a light,
then glanced around for her watch. She didn't see it, tried
to remember when she'd looked at it last and failed.

"Great," she muttered, then stumbled to the window. It
was still daylight outside.

She glanced back at the bed and then frowned. There
was no way she was going back to bed and chance resuming that dream. It was too unsettling. Without giving herself
time to rethink the decision, she hurried to the bathroom.
The sooner she got cleaned up and dressed, the sooner she
could leave.

She didn't know for sure where she was going, but that

hadn't stopped her yet. If she admitted the truth, she hadn't been in control of her life since that day in Tijuana when she'd fallen flat on her face and into what she could only describe as a parallel world. From the time she'd left Phoenix to right now in this strange motel room in a state named for the Native Americans who peopled it, she'd been led by something more powerful than anything she'd ever known before. As confused as she felt, she had come to believe that something—or someone would continue to lead her in the right direction.

As she was dressing, she remembered she'd been going to call her boss. She took the phone off the charger and made the call to the Arizona headquarters of the DEA, but when she was put through to Mynton's office, he was gone. Frustrated, she left him a message saying that she was okay and she'd call him later.

Within an hour, she was back on the Harley with the sun at her back, trusting in a force she could not see.

Franklin Blue Cat was asleep in his favorite lounge chair on the back porch. The disease he was battling and the medications he was taking to fight it often left his body feeling chilled and old beyond his years. Shaded from the sun and with the breeze in his face, he reveled in the heat of summer.

Although he was still, his sleep was restless, as if his mind refused to waste what little time he had left. In the middle of a breath, pain plowed through his body, bringing him to an immediate upright position and gasping for air. He struggled against panic, wondering if he would be afraid like this when his last breath had come and gone, then shoved the thought aside.

He believed in a higher power and he believed that when his body quit, his spirit did not. It was enough.

He glanced at his work in progress and then pushed

himself up from the chair. For whatever odd reason, he had a compulsion to finish this piece before he was too weak to work.

Once up, he decided to get something to drink before he resumed carving. He was in the kitchen when he heard a commotion outside in the front yard. He hurried onto the porch. At first, he saw nothing, although he still heard the sound. Puzzled, he stepped off the porch, then looked up.

High above the house, an eagle was circling. Every now and then it would let out a cry, and each time it did, it raised goose bumps on Franklin's arms.

"I see you, brother," Franklin said.

The eagle seemed to dip his wings, as if to answer, "I see you, too."

Franklin shaded his eyes with his hand, watching in disbelief as the eagle flew lower and lower.

Was this it? Was this how it would happen? Brother Eagle would come down and take his spirit back to the heavens?

His heart began to pound. His knees began to shake.

Lower and lower, the eagle flew, still circling—still giving out the occasional, intermittent cry. And each time it cried out, Franklin assured Brother Eagle that he was seen.

Franklin didn't realize that he'd been holding his breath until the eagle suddenly folded its wings against its body and began to plummet.

Down, down, down, it came, like a meteor falling to earth.

Franklin couldn't move as the great bird came toward him at unbelievable speed. Just when he thought there was no way they would not collide, the eagle opened his wings, leveled off his flight and sailed straight past Franklin with amazing grace.

Franklin felt the wind from the wings against his face,

saw the golden glint of the eagle's eye, and knew without being told that the Old Ones had sent him a sign.

Staggered by the shock of what had just happened, Franklin took two steps backward, then sat down. The dirt was warm against his palms. A ladybug flew, then lit on the collar of his shirt.

He smelled the earth.

He felt the sun.

He heard the wind.

He saw the eagle fly straight up into the air and disappear.

It was then he knew. A change was coming. He didn't know how it would be manifested, but he knew that it would be.

Gerald Mynton got back in the office around three in the afternoon. When he heard Sonora's voice on the answering machine, he groaned. He needed to talk to her and she'd given him no idea whatsoever of where she was or how she could be reached. It was obvious to Mynton that she kept her phone turned off unless she was physically using it, and had to be satisfied with leaving her another message that it was urgent he talk to her. All he could do was hope she called in again soon.

Sonora passed through Oklahoma City in a haze of heat and fumes from the exhausts of passing trucks and cars. Sweat poured from her hair and into her eyes until she could no longer bear the sting. She pulled over to the shoulder of the road long enough to take off her helmet and get a drink. She emptied a bottle of water that had long since lost its chill, then tossed it back into her pack to be discarded later. There was some wind, but it did nothing to cool her body against the midsummer heat of Oklahoma. In the distance, she could see storm clouds building on the hori-

zon and guessed that it might rain before morning. Maybe
it was just as well that she'd taken to the highway this day.
She knew Oklahoma weather had a predilection for tornadoes. Riding tonight would probably not be a good idea.

Reluctantly, she replaced the helmet, swung the Harley
back into traffic and resumed her eastward trek, passing
Oklahoma City, then the exit road to Choctaw and then
exits to Harrah and then Shawnee. It dawned on her as she
continued her race with the heat that nearly every other
town she passed had some sort of connection with the Native Americans.

It wasn't until she came up on Henryetta, once a coal-
mining town and now a town claiming rights to being the
home of World Champion Cowboys Troy Aikman and Jim
Shoulders, that she felt something go wrong.

She flew past an exit marked Indian Nation Turnpike.
Within seconds after passing it, a car came out of nowhere
and cut in front of her so quickly that she almost wrecked.
It took a few moments for her to get the Harley under control, and when she did, she pulled off the highway onto the
shoulder of the road.

Her heart was hammering against her chest and she was
drenched in sweat inside the leather she was wearing. She
sat until she could breathe without thinking she was going
to throw up, and got off the bike.

She took off her helmet, then removed her leather vest.
Despite the passing traffic, she removed her shirt, leaving
her in nothing but a sports bra. Without paying any attention to the honks she was getting from the passing cars,
she put her vest back on. Then she wound her hair back up
under her helmet, jammed it on her head and swung her
leg over the seat of the bike.

The engine beneath her roared to life, then settled into
a throaty rumble as she took off.

Less than a mile down the highway, a deer came bounding out of the trees at the side of the road. Sonora had to swerve to keep from hitting it. This time, when she got the Harley under control, she began to look for a safe place to cross.

She might be hardheaded, but she wasn't stupid. For whatever reason, she'd gone too far east. She thought of the exit she'd just passed, and the odd feeling that had come over her as she'd read the words.

Indian Nation Turnpike.

For the same reason that had taken her this far east, she felt she was now supposed to go south. She waited until there was a break in the traffic, and rode across the east-bound lanes and into the wide stretch of grass in the center median. She paused there until she caught an opening in the westbound lanes and accelerated.

It didn't take her long to find the southbound exit to the Indian Nation Turnpike, and when she took it, it felt right. Pausing at the stop sign at the end of the exit ramp, she took a deep breath and then accelerated.

The moment she did, it felt as if the wheels on the Harley had turned to wings. The wind cooled her body and she felt lighter than air.

Adam loaded the last sack of groceries into the seat of his pickup truck and then slid behind the wheel. As soon as he turned it on, he noticed his fuel gauge registered low. He lived too far up into the mountains to risk running out of gas, so he backed up and drove to the gas station at the end of the street.

As he pumped the gas, a sweat bee zipped past his nose, then took a second run back at his arm. He took out his handkerchief and wiped the sweat from his brow. As he did, he heard the deep, throaty growl of a motorcycle engine and, out of nothing but curiosity, turned and found himself staring into the simmering fires of a setting sun.

For a moment he was blinded by the glare, unable to see the rider or the bike. Quickly, he looked away, then shaded his face and looked again.

His breath caught at the back of his throat.

The bike and the rider were silhouetted against the heat and the sun as it paused on the horizon of an ending day. Despite the heat, Adam shivered. Although he knew it was an optical illusion, both rider and bike appeared to be on fire.

He was still staring when the illusion faded and the rider wheeled the bike into the empty space beside Adam's truck. He heard the pump kick off, signaling that his tank was full, and still he couldn't bring himself to move.

He didn't know when he realized that the rider was a woman, but he knew the moment she took off her helmet and turned to face him that he'd been waiting for her all of his life.

When their gazes connected, she gasped, then staggered backward. If Adam hadn't reacted so swiftly, she would have fallen over her bike. And the moment he touched her, he flinched as if he'd been burned.

"You came," he said softly.

Sonora looked down at his fingers that were curled around her bare arms. She could feel him. She could see him. But that had happened before. The test would now be if she could move.

She took a step back. To her surprise, her feet moved. In a panic, she wrenched away from his grasp.

"I'm awake," she muttered, more to herself than to him. She rubbed her arms where he'd been holding her, then looked up.

"Do you see me?"

He looked at her face as if trying to imprint every line and curve into his mind forever. There was no mistaking who she was, or why she was here. But from the little bit she'd just said, he suspected she was not in on the deal.

"Yes, I see you," he said softly.

Sonora exhaled a shaky breath. She didn't know what to say next.

"Do you know why you're here?" he asked.

She shook her head.

"And yet you came?" he asked.

She thought of the nights and days of hallucinations and was halfway convinced that this was nothing but a repeat of the same.

"It seemed I had no choice," she muttered.

"Your father waits for you," he said.

Sonora jerked as if he'd just slapped her. She was disgusted with herself for being so gullible. Whatever had been happening to her, now she knew it was a dream.

"I don't have a father," she said angrily.

"But you do," Adam said. "Have you ever heard your mother mention a man by the name of Franklin Blue Cat?"

She snorted in a very unladylike manner, and added a succinct curse word to boot.

"Mother? I don't have one of those, either," she said. "I was dumped on the doorstep of a Texas orphanage. The details of the ensuing years are hardly worth repeating. And now that this little mystery is over with, I'm out of here."

Adam winced. Franklin would be devastated by this news, and he couldn't let her leave. Not until they'd met face-to-face.

"You've come all this way. Don't you at least want to talk to him?"

"Why? He never bothered to look me up."

Adam heard old anger in her voice. The story wasn't his to explain, but if he didn't convince her of something, she would be gone before Franklin got a chance to state his case.

"Franklin didn't know about you. He still doesn't."

Sonora shook her head. "You're not making sense. And by the way, who the hell are you?"

"Adam Two Eagles."

She tried not to stare, but it was surreal to be standing here having this conversation with a specter from her dreams.

"So, Mr. Two Eagles, what do you do for a living... besides haunt people's dreams?"

Adam stifled a gasp of surprise. He'd been in her dreams? This he hadn't known. The Old Ones had really done a job on her.

"I haunt nothing," he said quietly. "I used to be in the army. Now I'm a healer for my people, the Kiowa. I know you're Franklin's daughter, but I don't know your name or what you do."

"Sonora Jordan is my name. I'm an agent with the DEA." Then she turned the focus back on him. "So...Adam Two Eagles. You call yourself a healer."

He nodded once.

She reached behind her, felt the seat of her Harley and clung to it as the only recognizable thing on which she could focus.

"Healer...as in medicine man or shaman, or whatever it is you people call your style of voodoo?" she asked.

"Healer, as in healer," he said. "And my people are your people, too. Whether you accept it or not, you are half Kiowa."

The words hit Sonora where it hurt—deep in the old memories of childhood taunts about being a throwaway child with no family and no name. She'd lived her entire life branded by two words that a priest and a nun had chosen out of thin air and given to the latest addition to their orphanage. Sonora because it was the priest's hometown, and Jordan for no reason that she knew other than that they felt by not giving her a Latino name, she might have a better chance at a decent life. A quixotic thought for two devout Catholics who believed that everyone was equal in the eyes of God.

"You can't prove that," she muttered.

"Well…actually, I can," he said. "You've come all this way. You don't have to believe me. Follow me if you dare, and see for yourself."

Sonora thought of the handgun tucked into the storage behind the seat and then of how far she'd let herself be guided by a whim. What could it hurt? If she had to, she could take him. Besides, maybe this would finally put an end to being a walking nightmare just waiting to happen.

Adam watched her eyes, only guessing at the jumble of thoughts that must be going through her head.

"I won't hurt you," he added.

She fixed her gaze on his face, remembered the last thing he'd said to her in her dream, and then sighed. "I know that," she said.

Her assurance was startling.

"Why do you say that with such confidence?" Adam asked.

"I'm here because I fell into some sort of twilight zone. I'm here because I keep dreaming of a man who's either sick or dying. And I'm here because you keep haunting my dreams."

Again she mentioned seeing him in her dreams. Intrigued, he had to ask. "What am I doing in your dreams?"

"Trying to seduce me…I think."

He wondered if he looked as startled as he felt.

"Indeed," he drawled. "And did I succeed?"

Thunder rumbled in the distance.

Sonora glanced up at the sky. Either she holed up in another motel until this storm passed, or she followed this man. Despite the fact that she'd seen his face in her dreams, she didn't know him. For all she knew, he might try to harm her. Then she sighed. Miguel Garcia wanted her dead. So what was new? It was either the devil she knew or the one she didn't.

"I have one question to ask you," she said, ignoring the fact that she had not answered his.

He shrugged. "Then ask."

"This man you claim to be my father. Does he have a wind chime on his front porch that looks like a dream catcher?"

Despite the depth of his tribal beliefs, Adam was taken aback by the question.

"Yes."

"And does he have a hobby of carving things out of wood?"

Adam thought of his friend's fame that was known all over the world by those who indulged in his particular brand of art.

"Yes, you could say that," he said.

"And…a few days ago, was he taken ill?"

Now Adam was feeling off-kilter.

"You have seen all of this…in dreams?"

She shrugged, then nodded.

"The Old Ones have been playing with you," he said softly.

"Who?"

"Never mind," he said. "If you want to meet your father, then follow me."

"I need gas."

"I will wait."

She reached for the nozzle to the pump, quickly filled the tank and then dashed into the station to pay.

Adam saw Franklin in every movement she made, from the cut of her features to the way she moved when she walked—with her toes pointed inward just the tiniest bit and with the grace of a young filly at one with the world. She was a woman with copper-colored skin and long legs that life had saddled with a hefty portion of defiance. She and Franklin would get along just fine.

When she came out and mounted her bike, Adam was already rolling out of the station and onto the street.

She stuffed her hair back beneath her helmet, then fired up the engine. She was on Adam Two Eagles's tail before he passed the city-limits sign.

Chapter 6

Sonora was still trying to wrap her mind around the fact that not only was the man she'd dreamed of actually real but that she was following him up a mountain without knowing where she was going. It was against every safeguard she'd been taught, and against every instinct she had. And yet she was doing it.

It was the first time in her life that she'd questioned the wisdom of having no personal ties. Before, it had been not only convenient but wise. Without family, bad guys had no leverage against agents like her. But she'd never been faced with this particular situation. She wanted someone to know where she was and what she was doing, if for no other reason than to have a place to start looking for her should she suddenly disappear.

Even as she was thinking the thoughts, something told her she was overstating the obvious. Adam Two Eagles had made no threats toward her. She didn't feel uneasy around him and she was a good judge of character. She wasn't afraid of Adam Two Eagles, but she was uncomfortable with what he represented.

Frustrated by thoughts that just kept going in circles, she began to focus on the beauty of the mountain, instead. Pine and cedar trees grew in great abundance, as well as knobby-barked blackjack trees—a cousin of the oak. Every so often she would see a bird fly out from among the branches of a tree and then disappear into another.

She thought of what it would be like to live up here, so far away from the conveniences of city living. One would have to be very secure to live so alone. Then it occurred to her that she lived in a city among thousands and was as alone as anyone could be. It was an eye-opening realization to know that it wasn't where you lived, but how you lived, that made lonely people.

Obviously, Franklin Blue Cat was alone, but if he was as secure within himself as Adam, she doubted that he was very lonely.

Just when she thought they would never arrive at their destination, Adam began to slow down, then came to a complete stop.

Sonora was forced to stop daydreaming and focus on the immediate. Up to now, the road had been blacktop, but she saw that at the fork it became dirt. She realized she was about to eat dust.

When Adam leaned his head out of the window and waved her over, it became apparent he was concerned with the same thing.

"If you follow me too closely, you will be covered in dust."

She flipped up the visor on the helmet so that she could more easily be heard. "I'll manage," she said.

"Still, if you want to lay back a little, I thought I'd tell you where we're going so that you don't miss a turn."

Sonora thought about it and decided that a serial killer

probably wouldn't give her a chance to get away like this. His offer went a long way toward easing her already suspicious mind.

"Yeah, okay, I see your point," she said.

"Good," Adam said, then pointed to the left. "Four miles down this way, you'll come to another fork in the road. Take the right fork, which goes up the mountain, and follow it. Franklin's home is at the end of the road. You'll see a couple of signs along the way that say Blue Cat Sculptures."

Sonora frowned. "Really? Does he sell arts and crafts from his home or something?"

"No." Then he grinned. "I think there are a few more surprises in store for you. Your father is world renowned for his carvings."

"The bird," Sonora muttered.

Adam frowned. "I'm sorry, what did you say?" he asked.

"Oh, nothing," she said. "Let's go. I need to get this over with. I don't want to have to find my way off this mountain in the dark."

Adam's frown deepened. "There is no need for that to happen," he said. "Your father will welcome you."

"How could he when he didn't know I existed?"

Adam eyed the woman, accepting her defensiveness as understandable, yet wondering how much of the spiritual world of the Kiowa she would be able to accept.

"It is your father's story to tell," Adam said. "So, are you ready?"

"As I'll ever be," she muttered, and waited for him to drive away. As soon as he'd gone about a half mile down the road, she revved up the engine and followed.

Franklin was sitting on the porch when he heard the sound of a car coming up the road. It wasn't out of the ordinary for people to come unannounced, but he wasn't in the mood to cater to strangers. Still, his good manners bade him to deal with it, just as he was dealing with the leukemia ravaging his body.

When the truck appeared at the curve in the road, he breathed a sign of relief. It was Adam. He was always welcome.

Franklin stood, then lifted his arm in a greeting as Adam pulled up to the yard and stopped. He was partway off the steps when he realized that someone had been following Adam's truck.

Stifling a frown, he took a deep breath and put on his game face. When he saw that it was a rider on a motorcycle, he paused politely.

"Adam, it's good to see you," Franklin said, and then pointed down the road with his chin. "He with you?"

Adam stifled a smile, and then nodded.

Franklin sighed. "This has not been a good day."

Adam put a hand on his old friend's arm. "I'm sorry to hear that, old friend, but I have good news. That's about to change."

Franklin flinched. The eagle had warned him a change was coming. Was it already here?

The rider pulled up beside Adam's truck and then parked. It was when he started to dismount that Franklin realized the he was a she. Even in black leather, the body was definitely feminine.

He glanced at Adam, but Adam only smiled at him, then shrugged as if to say wait and see. Franklin sighed. These days, he was not so good at waiting for anything.

The rider leaned slightly forward as she took off the helmet, and as she lifted her head, a long, black sweep of hair fanned out, then fell loosely down the back of her neck. Even though she had yet to face him, Franklin felt an odd sense of familiarity.

"Adam?"

"Just wait," Adam said.

In that moment, Sonora Jordan turned, and for the second time today, found herself face-to-face with the other man from her dreams.

"This is too weird," she muttered, and refused to let herself be overwhelmed by the fact that this man claimed he was her father.

Franklin was shaking. He couldn't quit staring at her face.

"Who are you?" he asked.

Sonora looked at Adam, then frowned. "I thought you said he knew I was coming."

Adam decided it was time for him to intervene. "Franklin, the Old Ones have delivered what you asked for. This is Sonora Jordan. She's an agent with the DEA."

Sonora frowned. "What Old Ones? What are you talking about?" She backed up and laid her hand on the storage compartment behind the seat of the Harley. It made her feel safer to be close to the gun. "Is this some trick Garcia has pulled to get me alone, because I warn you, if it is, I won't—"

"No. No," Franklin whispered. "It's no trick. It's a miracle. I asked Adam to find my child. And you have come."

Sonora looked at Adam. "I don't get it. You didn't find me. I found you."

"Actually, it was neither," Adam said. "The Old Ones found you. They are the ones who have guided your path. They are the ones who have brought you to this place."

"What are you talking about? Who are these Old Ones you keep talking about?"

Franklin waved her question away as he took her by the hand.

"Forgive me, but I just had to touch you. You are so beautiful. My heart is full of joy."

"Look," Sonora said. "I appreciate your kindness, but how can you be certain that—"

"Come into my house. I'll prove it to you," Franklin said, and then turned and strode to the porch and up the steps without waiting to see if she was behind him.

Sonora glared at Adam. "I'm not falling for all this ghost and spirit crap."

"Suit yourself," he said. "But consider this…how else did you come to be in this place?"

She flashed on the hallucinations and dreams she'd been having and glared even harder.

"My boss told me to get lost for a while. That's how. I've got one man already on my back trying to kill me. So if you're in mind of doing anything similar, you need to get in line."

Adam froze. His voice deepened as his eyes went cold. "You are in danger?"

"Oh, Lord…I don't know…. Yes, probably. At least enough that my boss told me to leave Phoenix."

"Come, come," Franklin called from the doorway. "You must see to believe."

Sonora gave Adam one last warning glance. "Just don't mess with me, okay?"

Adam didn't answer.

Sonora exhaled angrily, took her gun out of the compartment and put it in the back waistband of her pants, beneath her leather vest, then stomped into the house.

"So what do you have to show me?" Sonora said.

Franklin handed her a photo that he'd taken from the mantel over the fireplace.

Sonora eyed it casually, then stifled a gasp.

"Who is she?" she asked, pointing at the woman in the photo.

"My mother, and he is my father. It was taken on their wedding day."

"Good Lord," Sonora whispered, then carried it to a table in the hall and the mirror that hung above it.

She kept looking from the photo to her face and then back again until Adam took it from her hands and held it up beside her. Were it not for old-fashioned hair and clothing, and the man in the picture, she would have sworn the picture was of her.

"I look like her," Sonora said, and then bit her lip to keep from weeping. In all of her twenty-nine years, she'd never had the luxury of saying that before.

Franklin walked up behind her. Adam stepped back. Now Sonora was seeing herself, and Franklin Blue Cat, and seeing the similarities in their features. Her emotions were out of control. They went from jubilation, knowing she'd found a family, to hurt and anger that he'd never come looking for her. She wanted to cry, and settled for anger.

"Why?" she muttered.

"Why what?" Franklin asked.

"Why am I just learning you existed?"

Franklin took her by the hand. "Please, may we sit down? I'm not feeling very well."

"What's wrong?" she asked as he led her to a sofa.

Franklin shrugged. "I have leukemia and the medicines have quit working. I am dying."

Sonora reeled from the news. She'd known he wasn't well, and had even had the thought that he was dying, but to hear her suspicions were actually true made her sick to her stomach. This wasn't fair. She'd spent her entire life alone. Why would she be reunited with her only living family only to have him snatched away? How cruel was this?

"I'm so sorry," she mumbled, and bit her lip to keep from wailing.

Franklin nodded. "Such is life," he said, then brushed the topic aside. "Did your mother ever mention my name?"

Sonora smiled bitterly. "My mother, as you put it, dumped me on the doorstep of a Texas orphanage when I was less than a day old. I was named by a priest and a nun and dumped in a baby bed with two other babies. My earliest memory is of sitting in the corner of the bed and bawling because one of the bigger kids had taken my bottle and drank my milk."

Franklin reeled as if he'd been slapped. "You're not serious?"

She laughed to keep from crying. "Oh, but I am. She didn't want me and that's okay. I can take care of myself."

Franklin shook his head as tears unashamedly ran down his face. When she would have moved away, he took her hands, then held them fast against his chest.

"No. No. That is never okay. I am sorrier than I can tell you, but it's not okay. I didn't know until a few weeks ago that you might even exist. That's when I asked Adam for help."

Sonora shook her head. "That's what I still don't get. How did you come to believe you had a child? Who told you?"

"I had a dream," he said. "I have it often. It's always of your mother, whom I loved more than life. It's a repeat of our last day together, and how sad I am that she's moving away, even though I begged her to stay. Only this time the dream was diffcrent and it made me believe that your mother's spirit was trying to tell me to search for you."

"You're serious."

"Very."

Sonora pointed to Adam. "So, where does he come in?"

"He's the healer for our tribe. I am full-blood Kiowa. I have no brothers or sisters, and after your mother left, I never had another woman. I am the last of my people, or at least I was, until Adam sent for you."

"Both of you keep saying that, but I don't understand. How did he send for me when he didn't even know if I existed?"

"I made medicine," Adam said. "I told the Old Ones

what Franklin wanted. They are the ones who looked for you. They are the ones who found you. They are the ones who have given you your dreams that led you to us."

"Oh...oh, whatever," Sonora muttered. "I can't deal with all that hocus-pocus right now."

"It doesn't matter," Franklin said. "All that matters is that you are here."

Outside, there was a quick flash of lightning.

"It is going to rain. Will you stay?" Franklin asked. "I have many rooms in this house and yet I live in it all alone. I would welcome your company for as long as you can be here."

She thought about the danger her presence might cause, and then decided there was no way on earth that Miguel Garcia would ever find her here. Besides, she wasn't just curious, she ached to know this man who was claiming her. She wanted to know everything there was to know about the people whose blood ran through her veins.

"Yes, I'll stay, and thank you," she said. "I'll just go get my bag off the Harley."

"I'll get it," Adam said, "but then I must be going. I have animals to feed before dark."

He hurried outside, untied the bag from the back of the Harley and carried it into the house where Franklin was waiting.

"How can I ever thank you?" Franklin said, and then threw his arms around Adam and hugged him fiercely.

"It's the Old Ones you must thank," Adam said, then added, "Call if you need me."

Sonora was standing behind an easy chair, watching the two men part company. She felt like the outsider she really was, and had a sudden urge to jump on her bike and leave before she became too involved to let go. Then Adam turned his attention to her.

"Franklin has my number. Call me if you need me."

She made no comment, unwilling to admit that she didn't want him to leave.

Adam refrained from looking at her again. It was difficult enough not to let what he was thinking show through. Somehow he didn't think Franklin would thank him for lusting after his newfound daughter.

"Come tomorrow," Franklin said. "I'll make breakfast."

Adam arched an eyebrow. Franklin's fry bread was famous on the mountain.

"Fry bread, too?"

Franklin smiled. "Sure."

"What's fry bread?" Sonora asked.

Both men looked at her and then shook their heads.

"It won't look good if word gets out that Franklin Blue Cat's daughter has never had fry bread," Adam said.

Franklin smiled. "You are right," he said. "So…my first duty as a father will be to introduce her to it."

Sonora caught herself smiling back. "Am I being the butt of a big joke?"

"Oh, no," they said in unison. Then Adam added. "Your father often makes fry bread at the stomp dances."

"Stomp dances?"

They looked at her and then smiled again.

"You have a lot to learn about your people," Franklin said, then his smile went sideways. "I will teach you what I can with the time I have left."

Sonora nodded, then looked away. "Maybe you could tell me where you want me to sleep. I would like to wash off some of the dust before we talk any more."

"I'll be going now," Adam said. "See you for breakfast."

Sonora picked up her bag as Franklin led the way down a hall.

"These rooms are cool and catch plenty of breeze. However, there is an air-conditioning unit if you wish to be cooler. The medicine I take makes me cold, so I don't often use the main one in the house anymore."

"This is beautiful," Sonora said, overwhelmed by the subdued elegance. There were royal-blue sheers at the windows, as well as vertical blinds. A matching blue-and-gold tapestry covered a king-size bed and there was a large Navajo rug on the floor in front of it. But it was the carving of a small kitten that caught her eye. It was lying on its back with its feet up in the air, batting at a dragonfly that had landed on its nose.

She moved toward it, touched it lightly, then picked it up. "I can't believe this is wood. It looks real."

Franklin smiled. It was praise of the highest kind. "Thank you. It would honor me if you would accept it as a gift."

Sonora's eyes widened. "Oh. I didn't mean to suggest... I couldn't possibly..."

Franklin put a hand on her shoulder. "Please. You're my daughter. Of course you must have this."

Sonora ran a thumb along one of the paws, tracing each tiny cut that gave the appearance of fine hair.

"This is magnificent," she whispered.

"I call the piece Friends," Franklin said.

"It's perfect," Sonora said, and then held it close as she looked up into his face—a face so like her own. "Today has been overwhelming," she said. "There is so much I don't understand—so much I don't know how to explain. I've never had family of my own, so if I do something wrong, I beg your forgiveness ahead of time."

"You can do no wrong," Franklin said. "You're the one who's been wronged. I don't understand how this happened, but if I'd known about you, I would have moved heaven and earth to bring you home."

Threatened by overwhelming emotions, Sonora shuddered. "If this is a dream, I don't want to wake up."

Franklin shook his head. "It is no dream. Now, I have one request to ask of you."

"If I can. What do you need?"

"To hold my daughter."

Sonora hesitated long enough to put down the sculpture, then turned and walked into his arms.

Franklin stifled a sob as she laid her cheek against his chest. For the first time since he'd received the news of his death sentence, he was angry all over again. This wasn't fair. Why should they be reunited like this only to know it would soon come to an end?

It was almost dark by the time Adam got home. He finished his chores in the dark and then hurried inside, reaching shelter only moments before the heavens turned loose of the rain.

Wind blew. Thunder rumbled. Lightning flashed.

He ate a lonely meal and thought of the breakfast tomorrow, knowing that, for a short time, he would be with Sonora again

He didn't know what was going to happen between them, but he didn't want the relationship to end before they had a chance to know one another.

He thought of Franklin, wondering how he was going to take finding a daughter and losing his life.

Rain blew against the kitchen window as he washed the dishes from his evening meal. Lightning flashed, momentarily revealing the wildly thrashing trees and limbs and the flow of rainfall funneling through the yard to the creek below his house.

Then another, more sinister thought reared its head.

Sonora had said she was in danger.

He feared she was understating the issue. The soldier in him wanted to take her to a place of safety and guard her against the world. But the healer in him knew there was another way.

His eyes narrowed as he dried his hands and moved from the kitchen to the medicine room.

He paused in the doorway, thinking of a stranger on Sonora's trail, and then moved with purpose to the shelves. Without hesitation, he chose the items he needed, then carried them outside onto the porch. Sheltered from the rain, he lit a swatch of dried sweetgrass, then purified the air with the smoke.

He fell into the old language as easily as he breathed, turned to the north and began to chant, telling the Old Ones of the danger to one of their own, beseeching them to protect her when he could not. Then he repeated the request to the east, then the south and finally the west.

A wild crack of lightning hit the ground only yards away from his house. Adam staggered backward from the force of the strike. The scent of sulfur was heavy in the air. As he stood, the wind suddenly changed and blew rain up under the eaves of the porch and into Adam's face.

He took it as a sign that they'd heard.

It was done.

Chapter 7

Sonora spent the rest of the evening in a daze. It was difficult to wrap her mind around the fact that she not only had a father, but that she was actually in his house. While the premise was far-fetched and almost too good to be true, whatever doubts she might have had about being his daughter ended the moment she'd seen her grandmother's picture.

Thinking about how she got here could make her crazy if she dwelled on it, so she didn't. For a woman who'd spent all of her adult life dealing in truth and facts, accepting the notion of being guided by what amounted to ghosts seemed ridiculous. Still, however it had happened, she was grateful to be here.

And Franklin, who was normally shy and reticent toward strangers, was struggling to give her space. The last thing he wanted was to scare her off, but he felt a constant need to be with her. With his life span already limited, he was resentful that their time together was destined to be short.

So, while they wrestled to find comfort with each other,

the thunderstorm that threatened earlier had come full force. Sonora and Franklin ate their evening meal with an accompaniment of thunder and lightning, then washed dishes with rain splattering against the windows. After that, Franklin had taken her on a tour of the house, only to have it interrupted by a power failure. Sonora had embarrassed herself by panicking when the lights had gone out. By the time Franklin found flashlights and lit a few candles, the power was on.

Now they sat in front of a television without paying any attention to the programming, trying to find points of connection between their separate lives.

Sonora was fascinated with his artistic skills and was going through a photo album that represented a complete set of his work once he'd turned a hobby into a profession. She was in awe of where he'd been, and the heads of states he'd met in faraway countries.

Franklin, on the other hand, was trying to hide his dismay at the profession his only child had chosen.

"So, when did you begin working with the DEA?" he asked.

Sonora turned a page in the album, then looked up.

"It seems like forever, but I guess it's been about seven or eight years now. I had just turned twenty-one. I'm twenty-nine now. I'll be thirty in September."

Franklin's nostrils flared. It was the only indication he gave of realizing there was another slot to be filled.

"Your birthday," he said softly.

Sonora nodded, then stopped.

"Oh. Yes. Another gap in our knowledge of each other, which I can quickly fix. My birthday is September 12. I'm five feet ten inches tall in my bare feet. I wear a size ten in clothes, and I love chocolate."

He tried to smile and hugged her, thankful that she was

trying to make light of the vast gap between them, because the truth of it broke his heart.

"You are tall, like me," he said. "Your mother, Leila, was a small woman, but she had a big laugh." His smile faded. "It was the first thing I loved about her." Then he shook his head. "But that's for another time. I was born on June 4 in a storm cellar while a tornado blew away the house that was here. This is the one they built to replace it, so it is the only home I've ever known."

Sonora nodded as she listened to him talk, but she wasn't listening as intently as she should have been. Instead, she was marking the way his left eyebrow arched as he told something funny, noticing his slim hands and long fingers, hands of an artist. His skin was darker than hers, but not by much, and she suspected part of the washed-out color of his skin was due to his illness. She thought of seeing him unconscious on the floor and not knowing the connection between them, and how blessed she was to be sitting here now.

Then she thought of Adam coming to his rescue.

"Tell me about Adam Two Eagles," she said.

Franklin had sensed what seemed to be interest between the two and could only hope something came of it.

"His father was my best friend," he said. "His mother was a distant cousin on my mother's side."

"We're related?" she asked, unaware that she was frowning.

This time, Franklin allowed himself a grin. "Only in the most distant sense of the word. Probably what would amount to a sixth or seventh cousin."

"Oh. Well. That hardly counts, does it?"

Franklin's grin spread. "Definitely does not count."

Sonora realized he was having fun at her expense and made a face at him. "It's not what you think. I was asking only because I would want to know of any relatives."

Franklin sighed, and then took her hand in his. "I'm afraid, when it comes to close family, we're it." Then Franklin shifted gears to Sonora's life. "Have you ever been married?"

"No." She thought of Buddy and smiled. "Not even close, although I've had a couple of relationships and gotten a good friend from one of them."

"Friends are good," Franklin said.

Sonora thought of the dream she'd had of Adam, of the whisper of his breath on the back of her neck and the challenge he'd given her right before she'd awakened.

"Come to me," he'd said.

And she would have done it—willingly. However, faced with the real man and not one out of some dream, she was far more discerning. As intriguing as he was—as handsome and compelling as he was—he was still a stranger.

Unaware of the places her mind had taken her, Franklin had shifted a few mental gears of his own.

"In the morning, I'll show you the boundaries of our land," Franklin said.

Sonora was so taken aback by the fact that he'd referred to the property as "ours" that she could hardly speak. Still, she felt a need to slow him down from committing to things he might later come to regret.

"Franklin…wait. Please. You don't need to do this," she said.

"Do what?" Franklin asked.

"Include me in your life so quickly. It's not 'our' land, it's yours."

Franklin frowned, then shook his head.

"That's where you're wrong," he said. "Everything I do these days is done quickly. I don't have the luxury of assuming there will be a tomorrow. And knowing you exist and that you are of my flesh is a joy you don't understand. To the Native American, family is everything, and my family has lived in this area for generations. The last four generations are buried here, and until your arrival, that heritage was going to end with my death. Now I can die with peace. Even if you choose not to live here, it will always be yours, and hopefully, the generations that come after."

Sonora was too moved to speak. All she managed to do was nod and then look away.

Franklin sighed. "I did not mean to upset you, but these are things you must know."

Sonora's voice was shaking, but she looked him square in the eyes. "And by the same token, you cannot know what this means to me. I have lived twenty-nine years without belonging anywhere or to anyone. Now to have been given both at the same time is almost more than I can comprehend. I'm not upset. I'm overwhelmed."

Franklin relaxed, then patted her hand. "Then this is good, yes?"

Sonora sighed. "Yes, this is good."

"So…would you mind very much if, from time to time, I called you daughter?"

Sonora blinked away tears. "I would be honored. And for the same reasons, it would be wonderful to know I could call you Dad."

There was a time in Franklin's life when he would have hesitated to let someone see him cry, but that time had long since passed. His eyes filled with tears as he took her in his arms and held her.

They might have stayed there longer, but Sonora felt his body trembling and knew it was from fatigue. Without calling attention to his weakness, she claimed exhaustion on her own.

"I hate to be the party pooper, but this has been a long day. If you don't mind, I think I'd like to go to bed."

"Of course," Franklin said, and got up as she stood.

"So…you invited Adam for breakfast, didn't you?"

Franklin grinned.

"Quit that," she muttered. "I'm just asking so I won't oversleep. That would be rude."

"Oh, definitely, that would be rude," Franklin said, and then they both laughed out loud. "He'll probably show up around nine. He knows I don't get up as early as I used to."

"I'm a pretty good cook," Sonora said. "If you show me where stuff is, I'd love to make the meal."

Franklin took a slow breath, and then touched her face with the back of his hand. "And I would love to eat your cooking," he said, then puffed out his chest in an exaggerated manner. "My daughter cooks for me tomorrow. If someone had told me I would be saying these words tonight, I would have called them crazy."

"So it's a deal?" Sonora asked, and held out her hand.

Franklin shook it. "It's a deal," he said.

Sonora nodded and started to leave the room, then she paused and looked back.

Franklin was watching her go.

She bit her lip, then took a slow breath. Revealing her vulnerability was more difficult than she'd imagined it would be. Still, she'd waited a lifetime to say these words and she wasn't going to cheat herself out of the opportunity because she was afraid.

"Night…Dad."

Franklin smiled.

"Good night…daughter. Sleep well."

Soon the house went dark, and both father and daughter slept with a peace in their hearts they'd never known before.

Adam, on the other hand, didn't get much sleep. His dreams were troubled with a faceless enemy stalking Franklin's daughter. Finally, he woke up in a sweat, and abandoned his bed for the swing on his front porch.

The air was cooler and rain washed. Bullfrogs sang from

the overflowing creek while their tinier cousins, the tree frogs, contributed to the chorus. The quarter moon hung low in the sky, shyly showing its face from behind the swiftly moving clouds.

Adam walked to the edge of the steps and then looked up, inhaling deeply as he combed his fingers through his hair.

There was a power in the dark that daylight didn't share. He'd known it since childhood, and it had saved his life more than once during his years with the military. Night was a shield for those who needed it, and kept secrets better than a best friend ever could. It protected but at the same time left the weak more vulnerable.

Adam thought about the creek running out its banks down the hill below. If it wasn't for the copperheads between him and the water, he'd chance a midnight dip. However, his foolish days were long gone, and he would gladly settle for a cold shower.

He was about to go back inside when he heard a coyote yip. Within seconds, another answered, and then another and another, until the night was alive with their calls. He smiled. It was one of the sounds of the Kiamichi Mountains that he loved most.

He thought of the years he'd spent in foreign countries, living his life for the American government instead of for himself, and said a quiet prayer of thanks that he'd lived to make it home.

He stood on the porch and gave the coyotes their due by waiting until the chorus had ended.

"Good job, boys," he said softly, then started into the house. He was crossing the threshold when his cat, Charlie, slipped between his legs and darted beneath a chair.

He closed the door, then got down on his hands and knees and grinned at the cat who was peering at him from beneath the small space.

"What's wrong, old man? Coyotes make you a little nervous?"

"Rowrrr."

"I feel your pain," Adam said.

"Rrrpp?"

"Yeah, sure…why not?" Adam said. "I don't have anyone else fighting you for the space."

Since he'd been given permission, Charlie abandoned the space beneath the chair for a spot at the foot of Adam's bed.

Both males were soon sound asleep, taking comfort in the knowledge that, for tonight, they were not alone.

Miguel Garcia was in Amarillo, Texas, pacing the room of his motel with his cell phone up to his ear. He'd trailed Sonora Jordan this far and then had lost her. At this point, he knew he needed help, and had been trying to contact some of his men in Juarez. But no matter who he called, he got no answer. That alone was enough to make him nervous.

And if he'd known the truth, nervous would have been an understatement. He didn't know that there was already a big upheaval in his organization that had nothing to do with Enrique and Juanito's absences. He didn't know that Jorge was moving in on territory that had been under Garcia control for years. And, he didn't know that Jorge had given the DEA the description and tag number of the car Miguel was driving. Miguel thought he was the hunter, but in truth, he was also the prey.

Gerald Mynton was beside himself with frustration. Twice he'd missed phone calls from Sonora. He didn't know what she was trying to pull, dropping out of sight like this without staying in touch.

Yes, he knew he'd told her to get lost. But he hadn't expected her to actually do it. As far as he knew, she was in imminent danger and he had no way of warning her about it. So, in order to offset the chance that they might miss connecting again, he was having all of his calls, both personal and professional, forwarded to his cell phone. No matter what time of day or night a call came in, he would get it. With this small assurance set in place, Mynton finally gave up and went to bed. And while he wasn't a praying kind of man, he still said a prayer of safekeeping for Sonora before he could fall asleep.

Sonora woke abruptly, and for a moment couldn't remember where she was. Then her gaze fell on the carving of the kitten and the dragonfly and breath caught in her throat.

Home.

She was home.

She glanced at the clock, then her eyes widened. It was already seven-thirty and Adam was coming for breakfast. She flew out of bed and raced into the bathroom. It was the quickest shower she'd ever had. She dressed in a pair of old jeans and a red sleeveless T-shirt, and as an afterthought pocketed her cell phone. Then she pulled her hair up on top of her head, securing it with an elastic band. She started to put on her tennis shoes, then decided against it and left the room in bare feet.

As she started down the hall, she could hear Franklin moving around in his room, so she knew he was up, but she was going to do her own investigating into what was available in the kitchen without bothering him.

Before she started looking in the fridge, she made a big pot of coffee, hoping that the men liked it strong. Soon the enticing aroma of freshly brewing coffee filled the air as she began looking to see what was available to cook.

It was easy to spot the bacon and eggs, and she found half a loaf of bread and two kinds of jelly in the refrigerator, as well. A set of canisters on the cabinet revealed flour and sugar. After digging through the pantry, she found a partially used bag of self-rising flour, a can of vegetable shortening and a small bottle of sorghum molasses. She was in business.

She turned on the oven to preheat, laid her cell phone on the counter out of the way, then dug through the cabinets and drawers until she found the rest of what she needed. It wasn't long until the smell of baking bread was added to the aromas drifting through the house.

Sonora was frying bacon when she sensed she was no longer alone. She looked up. Franklin was standing in the doorway to the kitchen. She smiled.

"Good morning. How did you sleep?" she asked as he moved toward her.

Franklin touched her shoulder in a gentle, hesitant manner, then kissed the side of her cheek.

Sonora leaned against him for a fraction of a second, then made herself smile when all she wanted to do was cry. This family stuff was harder than she would have thought.

"I slept well," Franklin said. "And you?"

"Like a baby," Sonora said. "How are you feeling?"

He shrugged. "Some mornings are better than others."

She eyed the food she was making. "Does this bother you…I mean, the smells of food cooking? I didn't think that you might not be—"

Franklin held up a hand to silence her. "It smells wonderful. I will drink some coffee and take my meds and maybe steal a piece of that bacon when it's done before Adam comes and eats all my food."

Sonora nodded and made herself smile, but she could tell he wasn't right. Either he was weak, or in pain, or possibly both. It broke her heart to think that she had just met this wonderful man and might lose him before they got to know each other the way father and daughter should.

She pretended not to notice his hand shaking as he

poured coffee into a cup, and she busied herself making gravy when he counted out more than a dozen pills and swallowed them one by one.

Biscuits had just come out of the oven when someone knocked on the front door.

Franklin looked up at the clock and grinned.

"Adam already? It's barely eight-thirty. I'm thinking he must really be hungry…or something."

Sonora heard the sarcasm in his voice and laughed in spite of herself. Franklin was obviously a big tease and she may as well face the fact that he wasn't going to give up alluding to Adam's interest in her.

"Probably smelled the biscuits," she said. "Want me to let him in?"

Franklin's smile widened. "Someone has to. Might as well be you."

She threw a pot holder at him.

Surprise lit his face as he caught it. This daughter of his had fire in her soul. But he should have known that. No one did what she did for a living without having a large amount of faith in herself. It made him sick at heart to think of her growing up so alone. It was a good thing that she'd had a strong belief in herself, because there had been no one else to do it for her.

He heard Adam's deep voice, then the sound of Sonora laughing. He smiled. It had been years since such joy had filled this house. His blessing was that he'd lived long enough to hear it.

"Good morning, Franklin," Adam said as he followed Sonora into the kitchen. Then he eyed the stove and the pan of biscuits. "You outdid yourself this morning, didn't you?"

Franklin beamed. "I did nothing but oversleep. My daughter has cooked our food this morning."

Sonora bit her lip to keep it from trembling as she cracked eggs into the hot skillet. This was nothing short of a miracle, and she was frying eggs in this kitchen as if it was no big deal.

"I like mine over easy," Adam said.

Sonora jumped. She hadn't known he'd come up behind her.

"How many?" she asked.

"Two, please."

She grabbed another egg and broke it into the skillet beside the three that were already beginning to cook.

"What about you, Dad? How many eggs for you?"

"Oh…maybe one. My appetite isn't what it used to be."

Sonora turned around and frowned at Franklin. His color was ashen, and there was a bead of sweat on his upper lip. She took a piece of bacon from the platter, handed it to him and pointed toward the table.

"Sit."

Franklin took the bacon and sat without argument. Adam looked startled by Sonora's perception, and without comment, poured himself a cup of coffee and sat down by Franklin.

Sonora noticed the way Adam cared for Franklin, subtly checking the older man's pulse, then shaking out two painkillers for him from a bottle in the cabinet. By the time the eggs were done, Franklin appeared to be feeling better.

Sonora carried the plates to the table, then added the biscuits, bacon and jelly. She poured the gravy and refilled the coffee cups, then finally sat down.

Franklin eyed the table, then Adam, then Sonora.

"Today, I am truly blessed," he said softly. "And so I ask blessings for the food we are about to eat, and for the company of my daughter and my best friend."

"I am the one who's honored. Are those biscuits home-made?"

Sonora eyed Franklin, who appeared ready to offer another comment regarding her expertise in a kitchen, and headed him off.

"Yes, and before we get all carried away with praise for the cook, you should know that the eggs are getting cold," she said.

With that, she passed the biscuits down the table, trying not to appear too pleased when both men took two apiece to start with.

For a few minutes, little was said other than a request for something to be passed. It wasn't until Franklin was finishing his second biscuit that it occurred to him the food tasted good.

"Sonora, this food is very good," Franklin said. "Who taught you to cook like this?"

"Betty Crocker."

Adam grinned.

Franklin's eyebrow arched.

"*The* Betty Crocker?"

"The one and only," Sonora added.

Adam snagged another biscuit, slathered it with butter and jelly, then toasted Sonora with it.

"Then…my compliments to the cook," he said.

But Franklin wasn't satisfied.

"You learned to cook like this from a book?"

Sonora shrugged.

"Pretty much. I got tired of eating out all the time, bought myself an old Betty Crocker cookbook from a library sale when I was…oh…probably eighteen or nineteen. After that, it was largely a case of trial and error. I did get a few pointers from an elderly woman who was my neighbor at the time."

Franklin lifted his head and then stared off into the distance. Sonora could tell that he was troubled, but she didn't understand.

"What's wrong? Are you feeling bad again? Maybe you should go lie down for a—"

"I'm sick, but not like you mean. I am sick at heart that you have marked every step in your life alone."

Sonora got up and put her arms around her father's neck and hugged him.

"You worry too much," she said. "I'm fine. I'm strong. And if you're feeling all that good, you can do dishes."

Franklin looked startled, then he laughed and pointed at Adam.

"Two Eagles will do the dishes."

Adam grinned. "It would be my pleasure. However, I hope you know that there's a house rule about the dishwasher getting to take home the leftovers."

Sonora frowned.

"There's nothing left but biscuits."

"Exactly," Adam said, and then grabbed the bread plate and headed for the cabinet.

"We will be outside on the back porch for a while," Franklin said. "When you've finished, please join us."

"Hmmpf? Oh…shurr," Adam mumbled.

Sonora wasn't sure, but she thought he'd just stuffed another biscuit in his mouth, then Franklin took her hand and led her outside.

"Let's sit here," he said, and pointed to a couple of wicker chairs at the north end of the porch.

They sat. Franklin took a deep breath, folded his hands in his lap and then stared straight into Sonora's eyes.

"Now we ask questions of each other, and the answers must be honest."

Before they could start, Sonora heard the familiar ring of her cell phone that she'd left on the cabinet. At the same time, Adam called out.

"Sonora, your phone is ringing."

"The only person it could be is my boss," Sonora said. "I'd better get it."

Adam met her at the door and handed it to her as she came inside.

"Thanks," she said, glanced at the caller ID, then smiled. "I was right. It's my boss. This won't take a minute, okay?"

Franklin nodded, and then leaned back in the chair as Sonora answered.

"Hello."

Gerald Mynton breathed a huge sigh of relief.

"Thank God," he muttered. "You've been harder to find than the Loch Ness monster."

Sonora frowned. "What's wrong?"

Mynton sighed. There was no easy way to say this. "I'm afraid I have some bad news."

Sonora stilled. "How bad?"

"Your friend Buddy Allen is dead. We think Garcia got to him, trying to find you."

Sonora moaned. She didn't know it, but her face had gone white as a sheet.

"What happened to him?" she asked.

"It doesn't matter how. I don't know what this means, but before he died, Buddy said to tell you that 'he didn't tell'."

Sonora choked on a sob. Buddy the joker, the life of the party who could never shut up, yet he'd wanted her to know that he didn't tell Garcia anything about how she'd left town.

She took a deep breath and then made herself calm when all she wanted to do was start screaming. She compromised by shouting. "I asked you a question and I need an answer. What did Garcia do to him?"

Startled by her outburst, Franklin started to get up and go to her, but Adam beat him to it. Adam walked up behind her and put an arm around her waist, just to let her know she wasn't alone. To his surprise, her legs all but gave way.

"Easy, girl," Adam said softly. "We're here for you."

Sonora's knuckles were white from the grip she had on the phone and she was struggling to keep focused as she repeated herself one last time. "Please, boss. I have to know."

Mynton was sick to his stomach to have to be the one to tell her. "He beat him, honey…bad. He beat him real bad."

She bent over and grabbed her stomach, certain that her breakfast was about to come up.

"Oh, God, oh, God. It's my fault. I shouldn't have—"

"No, damn it. It's Miguel Garcia's fault," Mynton said. "And just so you know, he's on your trail."

Sonora straightened up with a jerk and cast a frantic glance at her father, and then at Adam. What evil had she brought to this beautiful place?

"How? How could he know where I am?" Sonora asked. "Nobody knew. Buddy sure as hell didn't. Even I didn't know where I was going and I'll bet my life I didn't leave a trail."

"Well, that's just it. You are betting your life and I don't like it. I want you to come in. We'll put you in protective custody and—"

"No. I will not hide from the bastard. Besides, how do you know he's following me?"

"He was last seen in Flagstaff. Did you go through there?"

Sonora shuddered.

"Yes, but so what? There are four different ways to leave that city."

"He's moving east."

"Shit."

Mynton heard her muffled curse.

"I'm sorry."

"Yeah," she said, swiping tears from her face even as she pulled herself out of Adam's arms. "I'm sorry, too, but not nearly as sorry as Garcia is going to be when I find him."

Mynton nearly dropped the phone. "What the hell do you mean...when you find him?"

"I'm not going to sit here like a Judas goat and let everyone else—"

Adam didn't know what was happening, but he could tell that it was bad. And he could tell that Sonora was in trouble.

He grabbed her arm and mouthed the words *what's wrong?*

She frowned and waved him away.

He grabbed her arm again, and this time, said it out loud.

"What's wrong?"

Sonora rolled her eyes.

"Boss...hang on just a minute, okay?" Then she turned her pain into anger and lit into Adam. "It's business, Adam, my business, which means it's none of yours. I'm a big girl and I can take care of myself."

"Who's Buddy?"

Her face crumpled like a used napkin.

"My friend. He is...was...my friend. The man who wants me dead beat him to death, trying to find out where I was."

Franklin took the phone from Sonora's hands.

She was so surprised by his actions that she let him do it.

"Excuse me," Franklin said. "I'm Sonora's father, and whatever trouble she is in, we will help her deal with it."

Sonora grabbed the phone away. "Boss! It's me! Don't pay any attention to him. I'll be leaving here as soon as I can pack. I'm not going to have Garcia come looking for me here."

Mynton was too stunned to follow her conversation.

"I thought you were raised in an orphanage."

"I was, damn it, but—"

"Then how did you find your father?"

"It's a long story," she muttered.

"I don't know what's going on there," Mynton said. "But

think a minute. No one knows you have family, so there's no one to look for. However, if you leave, how are you going to be sure that Garcia doesn't find them in his quest to look for you?"

"Because I'll find him first," she snapped.

"Yeah, well, Buddy Allen might have given you an argument with that thought."

Sonora reeled as if she'd been slapped.

"That's not fair," she mumbled, then swiped a shaky hand across her face. "I can't think right now. I'll call you later, okay?"

"Promise?" Mynton asked. "Oh. Wait. You're supposed to call a detective named Broyles with the Phoenix P.D. He's working Buddy's case."

"Yes, all right," she said, and then hung up.

For a moment, she stood with her head down and her shoulders shaking. Tears were rolling out of her eyes and down her face, but she wasn't making a sound.

Adam waited silently until he could take no more.

"You're not alone."

She put a hand over her eyes and then turned away.

Franklin put a hand on her shoulder.

"You're not alone," he said, repeating Adam's words.

She lifted her head, looking first at her father, then at Adam. Whatever might have been between them was over before it began.

"I can't be here," she said softly. "I will bring death to this place if I stay."

Franklin waved his hand as if he was shooing a fly.

"Death is already here, daughter. It's been here for months waiting for me to notice. Please, whatever is wrong, you must let us help you."

"It's DEA business," she muttered. "I can't get civilians involved in—"

Adam interrupted. "I spent twelve years with the army

rangers. I was good at what I did. You'll stay. We will help."

"It is settled," Franklin said.

Sonora was too overwhelmed to argue, and when they came to her and held her, she didn't say no.

Chapter 8

Once the shock of the call and the trauma of the morning had been dealt with, Franklin went inside to rest, leaving Adam and Sonora alone. Normally, she would have been defensive with a man she hardly knew, but she wasn't with Adam. She didn't bother with trying to figure out why. She just took his presence as the comfort she desperately needed, and finally let herself grieve.

Her eyes were shiny with unshed tears, and the sight hurt Adam's heart. As they walked beyond the yard into the shade of the forest, little by little Adam drew out details of the relationship that had been between her and Buddy Allen. He wouldn't let himself think about the spurts of jealousy that came and went as he listened to her talking about a man with whom she'd once been intimate. He didn't want to admit, not even to himself, that he was envious of a dead man.

"So you dated Buddy for nine months. You must have some really good memories," Adam said gently.

Tears finally spilled over and rolled down her face as she paused beneath a large oak.

"You'd think so, wouldn't you? But all I can remember was constantly disappointing him. I was gone so much and he wanted more from the relationship than I was ever able to give."

"He wanted to marry you?" Adam asked.

"Something like that," Sonora said, then her voice broke. "And now he's dead…he's dead because of me. I told him my life was too complicated for commitments, but he wouldn't listen." She choked on a sob and then covered her face with her hands. "Oh, God, Adam, Garcia beat him to death. I can't get that out of my head."

Adam put his arms around her. Sonora stiffened. Accepting sympathy was as difficult for her to deal with as accepting advice. But he didn't turn her loose and she didn't pull away, and slowly, slowly, she began to relax. When that happened, the wall of her emotions crumbled. Before she knew it, she was sobbing.

"Yes, pretty lady…cry for your friend…and for yourself. Cry it all out," Adam whispered.

And she did.

A day passed, and then another, until an entire week had come and gone since Sonora's arrival. As per her father's wishes, she'd checked in every day with Mynton, just so she would stay up-to-date on the investigations. She'd called the Phoenix detective as she'd been asked to do but had been unable to give him any information he didn't already have.

She knew that after a possible sighting of Garcia in Amarillo, Wills and the task force had left Flagstaff to check it out, and upon arrival had gotten a positive ID. Problem was, by the time all of that had been confirmed, Garcia was long gone—destination unknown.

* * *

As for Miguel Garcia, it had taken big money and calling in some favors from an old friend of his father before he'd finally gotten some help. Now four of the drug cartel's finest were combing the highways and the states bordering Texas and Oklahoma, trying to get a fix on the whereabouts of the missing DEA agent. Miguel had let it be known that it was worth a half million dollars to him to find Sonora Jordan.

While the men were searching, Garcia was forced to lay low. He now knew he had agents on his tail. He'd been assured by Emilio Rojas, the man who'd been his father's right hand, that not only did the DEA have agents on his trail, but they knew the make, model and tag number of the car he was driving. Once the significance of this news sank in, he felt sick. The only way that could have happened was if he'd been betrayed.

Time and time again, he went over a mental list of people who'd helped get him across the border. There were any number who could have tipped off the DEA, but he kept remembering the man at the airport outside of Houston who'd brought him a car and money and then so abruptly disappeared.

It stood to reason that this man could be the one who betrayed him. But then he would skip to the fact that Jorge Diaz had set everything up. Diaz was entirely responsible for successfully getting Miguel out of Mexico. He would have had access to the same information.

To go there in his mind, Miguel had to accept that Diaz would betray him, and he couldn't believe it, even though he had been unable to contact Diaz for days.

To be on the safe side, he'd sold his car at a used car dealer in Oklahoma City, bought a four-year-old Jeep from a different car lot, driven thirty minutes east on I-40 to Shawnee, Oklahoma and had the Jeep painted black.

Before he left town, he'd stolen a Native American license plate from a member of the Muscogee Nation while the car was parked outside the Firelake Casino south of Shawnee. He'd driven off with no one the wiser, traveling as far as Tulsa, Oklahoma before going to ground.

There, he'd begun the business of disguising his appearance. He'd shaved his head and mustache, bought himself some Western-style clothes, including a pair of ostrich skin boots and a big black hat. By the time he added a large silver belt buckle to his wardrobe, his own mother would not have recognized him.

Feeling fairly safe about getting back out in the world, he thought about resuming his own search for Sonora, but decided to err on the side of caution. If his men didn't find her within the week, he was going to go back to Phoenix. Sonora Jordan couldn't stay gone forever, and he was a patient man.

Adam had not been to Franklin's house or seen Sonora since the morning she'd received the news of her old friend's death. He relived their last moments together in his dreams—holding her close against his body—feeling the thrust of her breasts against his chest as she cried for another man. But in his dreams, her tears somehow turned to passion. They would lie down together beneath the sheltering limbs of the old oak. There would be whispers and promises and an ache so deep that it took Adam's breath away. What was driving him crazy was that he kept waking up before they could make love. He was sick and tired of cold showers and aches that wouldn't go away.

She and Franklin didn't have a lot of time to play catch-up, and he didn't want to intrude. But he wasn't a fool. He also didn't want to lose the small foothold he'd gained with her by staying gone too long. She was a stranger in every way that it mattered, and yet there was a part of him that knew he couldn't bear to let her go. He didn't know how much time she would give herself to stay on the mountain, but he wanted his share of it. The way he looked at it, he'd given them a week. His streak of generosity was over.

Franklin was having a bad day and, after breakfast, had gone back to bed. Sonora had quickly learned that on these days, the best thing she could do for him was give him space and quiet. So when he went back to his room, she took his fishing pole and straw hat and headed for the pond at the back of the property.

She caught a few grasshoppers on the way and put them in a jar to use for bait just like Franklin had shown her. The wide brim on his old hat shaded her face while the sun had its way with the rest of her body. Even though it was hot, she knew she wouldn't burn. By the time she got to the pond, her T-shirt was stuck to the sweat on her back and she had some kind of weird-looking burrs in her socks. Still, she was happier than she could ever remember being.

On the second day of her arrival, Franklin had saddled up two of his horses and they'd ridden from one corner of the property to the other until she knew where Blue Cat land began and ended. It had given her a sense of identity that she'd never known.

So, today, as she baited her hook, she had the satisfaction of knowing that she was standing on Blue Cat land— about to fish in a Blue Cat pond.

She wrinkled her nose and asked an apology of the poor grasshopper that was still kicking on the hook as she tossed it in the water. The red-and-white bobber bounced a few times within the spreading ripples. After that, it was a case of sit and wait.

For Sonora, it was like living out a dream. As a child, she used to imagine the innocence of a life like this, with people who loved her sitting beside her. There would be a picnic and laughter and playing barefoot in the water. It wouldn't matter if anyone caught fish because they were together.

The sun was hot. Sonora's eyelids were drooping. The bobber was riding high in the still water like an empty ship, and she couldn't bring herself to care that she wasn't getting any nibbles.

Something tickled her arm. She brushed at it without looking. Then something tickled the back of her neck. She brushed at it as absently as she had her arm.

"If I was a bad guy, you'd be in trouble."

Sonora choked on a squeak and fell backward. For a second, the sun was in her eyes, and then a tall shadow fell across her face and she could see.

It was Adam.

"Darn you," she muttered as she sat up, then yanked the pole from the water and flung it on the ground. "You scared me."

"Sorry," he said, but he was smiling as he sat down beside her.

"No, you're not," she said, and then pointed a finger in his face. "I didn't even hear you coming. How did you do that?"

"I'm Indian."

She rolled her eyes and then punched him lightly on the arm.

"You're full of it, that's what you are."

His smile widened. "Well, there is that, too."

She wanted to stay indignant, but it didn't work.

Adam brushed his hand against the curve of her cheek. "Forgive me?"

His dark eyes were glittering with laughter and his mouth was curved up in a smile. There was a small bead of sweat at the edge of his hairline as well as a sheen from the heat on his face. He smelled good—like the outdoors with a hint of musk, and the look in his eyes was on the broad side of dangerous.

At that moment, Sonora knew if she let it happen, they would be lovers. Part of her wanted to know him in that way. He was kind and generous. She could only imagine what kind of a lover he would be. But she had to remember there was danger in giving too much of herself away, and danger to whomever she let get too close. Buddy's death was evidence of that.

Adam watched the playfulness come and go on her face and wondered what she was thinking, although he doubted she was the kind of woman who gave away her secrets.

"Hey," he said, and playfully bumped his shoulder against hers.

She managed a halfhearted smile and then looked away.

"You're forgiven," she said.

She was slipping away from him and he couldn't let that happen.

"Hey," he said again, and cupped her face with the palm of his hand, pulling gently until she was looking at him. "What just happened here?"

Sonora met his gaze straight on. "I'm not who you need to be hanging out with."

He inhaled sharply. She was thinking of Buddy Allen.

"I don't run from anything," he said. "Not even you."

Sonora frowned. "I don't know what you think you want, but I'm not it."

"I don't think. I know what I want," Adam said. "I'm just not sure you're ready to hear it."

Sonora's heart skipped a beat.

"I don't run from anything…or anyone…either," she said. "I left Phoenix only because I was ordered to do so."

Adam turned until he was facing her. His legs were crossed, his gaze steady upon her face.

"I know," he said gently. "You are fierce and you are

strong. You wouldn't be your father's daughter if you were not. But it's not your job to protect me or Franklin. We've faced our own troubles and dealt with them just fine."

"You've never had troubles like the kind Miguel Garcia can bring."

Adam shook his head, then ran the tip of his finger down her nose, tapping the end like punctuating a sentence.

"Again you forget I was an army ranger. I've been in the middle of things the American public never knew happened. I am not afraid of a drug dealer, and you should trust me when I tell you this."

He was no longer smiling, and the tone of his voice was as dark as his eyes. Sonora took a deep breath and then nodded.

"Okay."

Adam hated the expression in her eyes. It was a combination of distrust and fear. When he reached for her, she looked away.

"Don't do that," Adam said.

There was a frown on her forehead as she cast him a sideways glance.

"I don't know what you are talking about," she said

"Are you afraid of what you're feeling?"

Her nostrils flared as she raised her chin. "I still don't know what you're talking about."

It was a defensive motion Adam knew only too well. He shook his head, leaned forward, slid a hand behind her neck and pulled her into a kiss.

She sighed, then she moaned. She'd known this man would be different. This man could hurt her in a way like no other. She knew it and still clung to the urgency in his kiss.

Adam had no sense of self. He'd lost it the moment he'd covered her mouth with his. He'd known it would be like this. She was sweet as wild honey, but the kiss was no longer enough. He rose up on his knees without breaking their kiss, then pulled her up to meet him. Now they were body to body, clinging to each other in quiet desperation.

The kiss lengthened—deepened.

Sonora lost focus when he took down her hair and ran his fingers through the length. She swayed weakly, then grabbed his shoulders to steady herself, but it was too little, too late.

Adam took her in his arms and laid her down, cradling the back of her head with his hand as he leaned over her, and as he did, saw a moment of panic on her face. Regretfully, he leaned down and rubbed his cheek against her face. Her skin was warm against his lips, and he could feel the rocket of her pulse against his fingers.

"I will never hurt you," he whispered.

A tear rolled out of Sonora's eye.

"You will break my heart."

The poignancy in her words was a red light to what had been about to happen. Adam didn't know what to say to make her believe it wasn't true. But he couldn't— wouldn't—make love to her without her complete faith and trust.

"Never," he said softly, then wrapped his arms around her and rolled them both until she was the one on top. They lay without moving or talking while the passion cooled.

Sonora didn't know what to think. She'd thought they were going to make love and she'd wanted it. God knew how badly she'd wanted it. She still ached for the weight of him—for that promise in his eyes of things to come. And she still couldn't believe what she'd said—that he would break her heart. It was as good as admitting that she already cared for him, which seemed ridiculous. They'd spent less than twenty-four hours together, but she felt as if she'd known him forever. He was a healer. Maybe he was a wizard, as well.

"Adam?"

He shifted to allow the weight of her head against his shoulder.

"Hmm?"

"Did you really make magic to get me here?"

He sighed. How did you explain the Native American way to someone who had not been raised in the culture?

"It's not magic...exactly."

"Did you put a spell on me, too?"

He grinned. "Honey, I didn't even know you were you until I saw you at the gas station with the fire of a setting sun behind your back. How could I put a spell on someone I'd never met?"

"I don't know...maybe the same way you sent for me. What did you call those...those...?"

"The Old Ones?"

"Yes, the Old Ones."

"Do you believe in them?" he asked.

Sonora rose up on her elbows to look down at his face.

"I don't know what to believe, but I'm here, and that in itself is a miracle. So if I accept your truth of how I got here, then it's not reaching much further to assume you've put a spell on me." She looked embarrassed, but she kept talking, intent on making her point. "It's the only explanation for this...this...thing that's between us."

Adam's eyes narrowed. "It's called sexual attraction."

Her eyes widened. She almost smiled.

"Is that what you call it?"

"Well, woman...it's what we Indians call it. Is there another name for hot and heavy in the white man's world?"

She grinned, then lightly punched his shoulder. "You're teasing me."

He grinned back. "Not about the sex part."

"Okay, so there's something between us."

He arched an eyebrow and rocked his pelvis against her belly. "Yeah, but don't worry. Eventually, it will go away."

This time she laughed out loud then rolled off him and grabbed her fishing pole. "Shut up, Two Eagles. I have fish to catch."

"Can I watch?"

She eyed him cautiously. "Are you capable of keeping your hands to yourself?"

"Oh, yes," he said, and then proceeded to kiss her one more time.

"Hey," Sonora said. "I thought you said—"

"You asked me if I was capable of keeping my hands to myself. I told you the truth. I am capable. But I didn't promise I would."

Sonora cast the line in the water, then propped the pole against a rock. Without saying a word, she turned around, grabbed Adam by the collar with both hands and yanked him forward.

They'd kissed before, but never like this. Sonora set him on fire. He'd thought about dying plenty of times, but never thought it would be like this.

"Sonora…God…let me—"

She turned him loose as fast as she grabbed him.

"I've got a bite," she said calmly, bent down and picked up her fishing pole and landed a fish.

Adam was still shaking when she took it off the hook and put it on the stringer.

"You'll stay for lunch, won't you?"

Adam took a deep breath and jammed his hands through his hair, but wouldn't answer.

That didn't stop the conversation.

"Good," Sonora said. "How hungry are you…one fish or two?"

"Starving," he muttered, and pulled his T-shirt over his head.

When he sat down and pulled off his boots, then got up and started unbuckling his belt, Sonora's lips went slack.

"Um…uh…"

He glared. "What? Don't tell me you've never seen a naked man before?"

Sonora's mouth went dry. She'd seen naked men before, but never one so remarkably built or so remarkably aroused.

She glared back. "I've seen plenty," she snapped.

"So what's your problem, then?" he asked.

She kept trying to look at his face, or at the trees under which they were standing —at anything and everything but the obvious.

"Uh…you're…you're…"

"I'm what?" he said, and then turned his back on her and dived into the water.

She watched the perfect dive with undue appreciation, both for his form and his perfect backside.

He came up with a whoosh, sending a shower of water into the air. The frustration and anger were gone from his face. To add insult to injury, he was treading water and grinning.

Sonora wanted to scream.

"I'm sorry," he said. "I think I was in the water when you answered. You were saying I was…?"

Sonora hadn't grown up alone and tough for nothing.

"I was about to say…you're scaring the fish."

Chapter 9

Sonora made Adam clean the fish. He considered it only fair since he'd come to the meal uninvited. Franklin woke up just as Sonora was taking the last fish from the skillet and followed the scent of his favorite food into the kitchen.

His delight in knowing there was fish for lunch doubled when he realized they would be having company.

"Adam! It's good to see you. I was beginning to think you'd found something better to do than visit a sick old man."

"You're not old," Adam said.

"Maybe not, but today I am not so sick that I can't eat some of this wonderful fish. Daughter! It seems you have been busy while I was sleeping."

"You have no idea," Sonora muttered, then made herself smile.

She was still shocked at herself for letting Adam push all her buttons. Her lack of self-control was so out of character she felt off-center with the world.

Franklin paused. There was something different in her tone of voice, and now that he was looking, there was something different about her appearance, as well. This morning her hair had been up. Now it was down, and her face was flushed. The flush on her cheeks could have been from the heat of the kitchen, but the fact that she was studiously avoiding looking at Adam seemed more likely. And there was no explanation forthcoming as to why Adam's hair was damp.

"Has something been going on in my house that I should know about?" he asked.

Sonora looked guilty.

Adam looked up. "Of course not, Franklin. I would never disrespect you or your home in that manner. The pond, however, is neutral territory, right?"

Sonora gasped, and then glared at Adam all over again.

Adam's eyes were twinkling, but his expression was completely calm as he awaited Franklin's answer.

Franklin grinned. "Yes. You are right. The pond is neutral territory."

"Oh…I'm so laughing my head off," Sonora muttered, then pointed at Adam. "You. Put some ice in the glasses, please."

Adam knew better than to say anything else. He was still reeling from the kiss she'd laid on him down at the pond.

"Hey, Franklin…I was looking at that new piece you're working on. It's really something. What kind of bird is that…a wren?"

"Yes. I thought it was going to be a barn swallow, but when I began carving, the wren is what began to emerge."

Sonora was listening to their conversation with interest as she put a small bowl of quartered lemons on the table, along with a bottle of tartar sauce.

"You mean, you don't know what the sculpture is going to be before you begin?" Sonora asked.

Franklin smiled. It was something people often asked him once they found out his process.

"How can I know until I remove the excess wood?"

Sonora's eyes widened with amazement. "The excess?"

"Yes, you know—the part that doesn't belong."

"That's just amazing," she said.

Franklin shrugged. "It's not so much. It's just the way it works."

A timer went off.

"I'll get it," Adam said.

"It's the corn bread," Sonora said, and pointed to a platter on the counter. "After you cut it, would you put it on that plate?"

Already absorbed in his task, he nodded absently.

Sonora caught herself staring, and when she finally came to herself and turned around, her father was grinning at her.

"Don't say a word," she warned him.

Franklin could tell she was interested in Adam. He just didn't know how much.

It was all Sonora could do to sit down at the table with Adam and get past the memory of his naked body enough to pass him the fried potatoes.

Adam knew she was bothered. It served her right. Yes, he'd kissed her first, but it hadn't been the toe-curling, mind-blowing lip lock that she'd laid on him. She was dangerous to mess around with.

Still, he couldn't keep his eyes off her. There was tension in her shoulders and her back was too straight. She was bothered, all right. He smiled as he passed her the bowl of potatoes.

"Want some?" he asked.

Her eyes narrowed. He wasn't asking about potatoes, and they both knew it. She snatched the bowl from him and spooned a large helping onto her plate, then passed it to her father.

Adam managed to pretend disinterest as the meal progressed, but the truth was, he could have used another cold dip in the pond.

It wasn't until they were doing the dishes that Franklin decided to stir the pot simmering between his daughter and friend.

"Hey, Adam, isn't there a powwow coming up in a couple of weeks at the campgrounds?"

Adam was drying the last plate and answered before he thought. "Yes."

"You gonna go?" Franklin asked.

"What's a powwow?" Sonora asked.

"Kind of like a family reunion. There will be food and both men and women's dancing."

Sonora frowned. "What do you mean…men and women's? Don't they dance together?"

"No."

"Isn't that sort of antisocial?"

"Not when you see it," Franklin said.

"Then show me," she said.

Franklin sighed. "I'm sorry, Sonora. I would like to, but I'm afraid I will have to wait and see how I feel when the time comes."

"I could take her," Adam said.

Franklin pretended to think about it, when in fact it was his plan all along.

"Yes, that might be best," he said. "If I feel well, I can come with you, but if I don't, then you two can go on alone. Would you like to do that, daughter?"

Sonora wanted to know this side of her heritage, but she wasn't sure she'd learn a damn thing with Adam Two Eagles except how much restraint she had left. Still, she wasn't about to let either one of them know how much she wanted to be with Adam.

"Sure. Why not?" she said, then added, "But I hope you can come, too."

"As do I," Franklin said. "It would give me great pleasure to introduce you to some of our clan."

"Clan? You mean the Kiowa?"

"The People are Kiowa, but we are of different clans. We belong to the Snake clan, as does Adam and his family."

Sonora felt the blood draining from her face and thought she would pass out. There was a roaring in her ears and her legs suddenly went weak.

"Oh, God…oh, God," she whispered, and staggered backward. Adam caught her, steadying her until she could sit down in a chair.

"Sonora? What's wrong? Are you ill?" Franklin asked.

Adam knelt down in front of her, then looked up into her face. "Sonora? Sonora?"

She saw Adam's lips moving, but she couldn't hear anything but the thunder of her own heartbeat.

Franklin pulled up a chair and sat down beside her as Adam bolted from the room.

"Daughter…what did I say? If I offended you, it was unintentional."

Adam came back with a wet washcloth and pressed it to Sonora's forehead.

"Here, honey, see if this helps," he said.

She grabbed it with both hands, and then swiped it across her face.

"This just keeps getting crazier and crazier," she muttered. "Half the time I feel like the luckiest woman in the world, and the other half of the time like I've fallen into the Twilight Zone."

She handed the washcloth to Adam, and then stood abruptly.

"You said you belong to the Snake clan?"

Both men nodded.

"What does that mean?"

Franklin frowned, then looked to Adam for support.

"Think of it like this," Adam said. "You are an American, from the state of Arizona, right?"

"Right."

"So then transpose that same identification process to your ethnicity. You are Kiowa, from the Snake clan."

"So, what does the snake mean to people from the same clan?"

"It's like our totem…what the white man might consider a mascot. But we believe it is like a conduit between us and the spirit world. That's a little simplistic, and it means much more, but it's the best way that I can describe it."

"I see," she said, and began rubbing her hands together nervously. "This is so weird," she kept saying.

"What is it that is weird to you?" Franklin asked.

She shrugged and tried to laugh, but it sounded more like a sob.

"Wait until you see this," she said, and stood up, then turned her back on the men.

Before they knew what was happening, she'd pulled her T-shirt over her head, revealing the tattoo of an elongated snake that traced the length of her spine. The snake's tail was somewhere below the waistband of her jeans, while the head marked the bottom of her shoulder blades and was twisted toward the viewer with fangs showing and the forked tongue extended. It was so perfectly depicted that neither man would have been surprised if it had suddenly hissed and struck.

Franklin's eyes widened in disbelief.

Adam inhaled sharply.

"This is strong medicine," he said softly.

"Daughter, how long has this been on your body?"

"Since I was sixteen," she said.

"Your parents let you do this?" Adam asked.

"I didn't have parents, remember? At sixteen, I'd just run away from my third foster home in the same year. I think I was on the streets in San Francisco when I had it done," she said, and pulled her shirt back down before she turned around. "Cost me a whole week's worth of tips, too."

Franklin stifled a moan. There were times when the plight of her childhood took his breath away.

"I'm so sorry," he said softly.

She frowned. "About the tattoo?"

"No, no, that's not what I meant," Franklin said. "When I hear you speaking of your growing-up years, it always saddens me. You should have been with family, learning the ways of The People and growing up knowing you were always safe and always loved."

Adam was momentarily stunned to silence. That this woman, who knew nothing of her heritage, should choose such a mark for her body made her powerful. He suspected the Old Ones had always known where she was and were just waiting for the right time to show her the way home.

"Sonora."

She hesitated, then shifted her gaze from her father to Adam. "What?"

"Why the snake?"

"You mean, as opposed to any other tattoo I might have chosen?"

He nodded.

"The reason just sounds silly," she said.

"Try me," he asked.

"Have you ever been in a tattoo parlor?"

He nodded.

"So…you know how they have all these photos and drawings of different tattoos? Well, I was with a couple of friends. We'd been in there for a good hour, looking at photos and daring each other to go first, but no one could decide on what they wanted. I was flipping through this book of drawings and when I got to the page that had this snake on it, I felt like I was going to pass out. The room started spinning around me and I began hearing a rattle in my head…like the kind a rattlesnake makes."

The skin crawled on the back of Adam's neck. The Old Ones had been with her all along and she'd never recognized the signs.

"The tattoo on your back…it's a rattlesnake?" Adam asked.

"Yes. You can't see the rattles unless I'm—"

"Naked," he said, and felt like he'd been punched in the gut.

She nodded, then glanced at her father.

His face was expressionless. She didn't know what he was thinking, but it surely had nothing to do with the tattoo. She'd had the tattoo for so long that she often forgot it was there. Slightly embarrassed, she pulled her shirt back over her head moments before Franklin laid his hand on the top of her head.

"You are blessed among women," he said softly.

She was uncomfortable with what she considered Native American voodoo and tried to make light of it.

"Couldn't prove it by me," she said. "My life has been anything but blessed and pure."

"Not in that way," Adam said. "The snake has power not often given to a woman."

"I don't get it," she said. "I wasn't born with this. It's not a birthmark. It's a tattoo I picked out of a book, compliments of a man named Stumpy."

"You didn't pick it. It chose you," Adam said.

"I don't—"

"You said you heard it rattle?"

"Yes, but Stumpy was smoking weed. We were all probably suffering the effects of his secondhand smoke."

Adam stifled a frown. "Believe what you must."

"Yeah, okay...whatever," she said, a little embarrassed by the seriousness of the conversation.

Franklin kissed the side of her cheek and gave her a quick hug.

"If you don't mind being left on your own again, I think I will go work on my little bird for a while. He's anxious to be free."

"And I need to go check on Linda Billy's little girl," Adam said.

"I hope she hasn't been ill. She's a sweet child," Franklin said.

"Not exactly ill," Adam said. "She overheard her grandmothers talking about someone dying in their sleep. By the time Johnny called me, she'd been awake almost three days."

"Poor baby," Sonora said.

Adam eyed her curiously. "So, Sonora, what are you going to do this afternoon?"

"It's too hot to be outside," Sonora said. "I'm thinking about a nap under the air conditioner in my room."

"Come with me," he said.

"Uh..."

"It's not far. I'll have you back in a couple of hours."

Sonora glanced at her father. "Dad?"

He smiled. "You'll like them."

She still wasn't convinced. "So...what are you going to do there?" she asked.

Adam grinned. "Well, I won't be killing any chickens and slinging the blood about the house or praying to the sun gods today, if that's what you're worried about."

Franklin snorted softly, then grinned.

She glared. "You're making fun of me."

Adam jammed his hands in his pockets and grinned. Payback was fine. "Yeah, I am," he drawled.

"Fine! Laugh your head off while I go change my clothes. I smell like fish."

"Okay, but don't dress up," Adam warned. "The Billy family is a fine family, but somewhat distressed when it comes to money."

"Well, damn, and I had my heart set on wearing the Versace," she snapped, as she strode out of the room.

Adam figured he'd aggravated the situation even more by telling her what to do. The last thing he heard her say was something about "…making me nuts."

He frowned, then let go of regret. He had all afternoon to get her in a good mood.

"I'm going to the studio while I have the energy to work," Franklin said. "It was good to see you. Come back soon."

Adam grinned. "You know I will."

Franklin turned to leave, then paused. "I wish you well," he said softly.

Adam stilled. "Thank you. You honor me with your trust."

Franklin nodded.

"She doesn't need my permission to do anything, but I ask only that you don't hurt her. She's been hurt far too many times already."

"I would sooner hurt myself," Adam promised.

"Then it is done," Franklin said, and walked away, leaving Adam on his own.

He didn't quite know how he felt, but he knew he was more than attracted to Sonora. She did things to him— made him feel things that he'd never felt for another woman.

And there was that tattoo. It had to be more than coincidence that a lost child of the Kiowa would choose the sign of her clan purely by accident. Adam was certain that there was more at work here than either he or Franklin first believed, and he didn't know where he fit in at all. What he did know was that he didn't want to lose the tenuous connection that they had.

"Is this all right?" Sonora said.

Adam turned around, surprised that she had changed clothes so quickly. She was wearing a pair of clean, but well-worn jeans with a denim shirt hanging loose against her hips. It was sleeveless and nearly white from countless washings, but both the jeans and the shirt were clean and crisp. She'd brushed the tangles out of her hair and left it hanging. It swung against her neck as she walked, teasing Adam with its silky sheen.

"Where's Dad?" she asked.

"In the studio."

"Wait. I need to talk to him." She dashed from the room before Adam could answer.

Franklin was already bent over the worktable when Sonora hurried inside.

"Dad...I need a favor."

He smiled as he looked up. "After that fine fish dinner... you have but to ask."

"This little girl that we're going to see. How old is she?"

"Not sure... Four or five...maybe six. Why?"

"I would like to take her a gift, but I don't have anything. What would you suggest?"

He looked up, quickly scanning the pieces of the shelves of his studio as he moved toward them.

"How about this?" he asked, and lifted a small carving from the end of a shelf, then put it in the palm of her hand.

"Oh, Dad...it's perfect. Do you mind?"

He shook his head as he smiled. "Mind? It is my joy to be able to share my work with you."

She threw her arms around his neck and gave him a quick kiss on the cheek.

"Thank you again," she said, then added, "Don't work too long."

"I'm fine," he said. "I've been taking care of myself for years. I can do it for a while longer, I think."

Sonora frowned as she watched him return to his work-table. What he'd said was an unwanted reminder of the limits with which he was living.

"We'll be back soon," she said.

"Take your time," he said, already immersed in his work.

Sonora dropped the carving into her shirt pocket and then ran back into the living room.

"Okay, I'm back," she said. "Are you ready?"

"Oh, yeah. I stay ready," Adam answered.

Words stuck in the back of her throat as her mind went right to the memory of him brown and bare as the day he was born. Despite the knot in her belly, she straightened her shoulders and tossed her hair.

"Shut up, Two Eagles, and just so you know…I'm a black belt in karate."

"Well, now…isn't that interesting? I had no idea that we have so much in common."

"What are you talking about?" she asked.

"I'm a black belt, too."

She rolled her eyes.

"Weren't we going somewhere?"

He opened the door and then stepped aside.

"After you, Ms. Jordan."

The ride to the Billy home started out awkwardly, but it wasn't long before Adam had Sonora laughing about an incident from his childhood.

"I can't believe you and your cousin thought up such an intricate revenge."

He laughed as they sped down the road, leaving a cloud of dust behind them to settle on the trees and bushes along the way.

"We were ten. What can I say? Kenny was like a brother

to me, and Douglas Winston told all the kids at school that Kenny still wet the bed. We just figured to give him a dose of his own medicine."

"Yes, but how did you get the plastic tube under him while he was sitting at the desk?"

"Douglas had a habit of breaking the lead in his pencils, so he was always having to get up to sharpen it. Kenny sat right behind him and I was on Kenny's right with the aisle between us. We waited until Douglas got up to sharpen his pencil. When he was on the way back, we pretended to be working, and as soon as he turned around and began sitting down, Kenny slipped the tube directly under him. It was so small and pliable that he never felt it. As soon as he began writing again, I handed Kenny the water bottle. He poked the tube in the place where the straw would go, then squeezed. Water went up and through that tube as slick as butter."

"Didn't the other kids see you?"

"Yeah, but Douglas was something of a bully, so they figured he had it coming."

"Then what happened?"

"The bell rang. Kenny yanked the tube out from under him as he leaned over to get his backpack out from under the seat. I stuffed the water bottle in my backpack while Kenny stuffed the tubing in his, and we ran like hell out of the classroom."

"What about Douglas?"

"Well, it looked like he'd peed his pants and then sat in it. We were halfway up the hall when we heard him squall. He bellowed and bawled and then refused to come out of the room. The principal had to call his mama, who had to take off work to bring him some dry underwear and pants. She was so mad. He begged to go home, but she made him change his clothes and stay."

"Did he ever know it was you and Kenny?"

"Probably, but he didn't have the guts to confront us and everyone was so busy teasing him that they forgot all about Kenny. It was fifth-grade justice at its best."

"Remind me never to get on the wrong side of you," Sonora said.

Adam tapped the brakes as he took a sharp turn, then glanced sideways.

"I'll never be your enemy, Sonora. Trust that. Remember that."

Sonora felt branded by the glitter in his eyes, but it was the promise of his words that soothed the fire. Even after he turned his attention back to the road, she kept watching him time and time again. She knew he was right. They'd never be enemies, but they would be lovers. Of that she was certain.

Chapter 10

Clouds were beginning to gather as Adam pulled up in front of Johnny Billy's home. He eyed the sky, remembering that there were thunderstorms predicted for this part of the state later today. From the way they were building, it appeared that they would be here sooner. Still, he believed they had time for him to check on Patricia.

"Do they know you're coming?" Sonora asked.

He nodded.

"Are you sure it's okay that I'm with you?" she added.

He took her by the hand and gave it a tug.

"Yes, I'm sure, and don't try to make me think you're scared of an ordinary family and one little girl...not after I know what you do for a living."

"There's scared and there's scared," she said. "It's far more scary to face rejection than it is to face danger or pain."

Adam was silenced by the simplicity of her words, and at the same time shamed. He'd grown up so confident of his sense of worth. He couldn't imagine what it had taken for Sonora to become the self-possessed woman she was today.

She was a true beauty. Her hair was thick and dark. He liked it when she chose to wear it down as she was today. Her eyes were brown, just like Franklin's, and she had a jut to her chin, just like Franklin, when she was about to defy propriety. Still, he knew that the jut to her chin was also part of the armor she wore to protect her heart. He didn't know what it was going to take to make her trust him, but he was willing to wait.

"So let's get this show on the road," he said. "The weather doesn't look as promising as it did when we left. We probably won't stay very long."

"I'm lost when it comes to Oklahoma weather, so I bow to your greater understanding," she said.

Adam smiled as he opened the door and got out. Sonora slid out behind him, then followed him to the house. Just as they were walking up the steps, the front door opened. It was Linda Billy.

Adam smiled easily as he gave Sonora's hand a comforting squeeze.

"Hello, Linda."

"Hey, Adam." She glanced shyly at Sonora. "Welcome. Come in, please. It's so hot this afternoon."

Adam put a hand at the small of Sonora's back, and as he did, remembered the snake tattoo. The urge to jerk his hand back was instinctive, even though it was just a picture on her skin and not the real thing, the power of its presence was not lost on him.

"Johnny still at work?" Adam asked as they followed Linda into the living room and sat down.

"Yes. He took Eldon Farmer's route for him this morning. Eldon broke his arm last night feeding cows, which means Johnny won't be home until after midnight." Then she gestured toward the sofa. "Please, sit down."

Adam cupped Sonora's elbow. "Thanks, but there's someone I want you to meet first. Linda, this is Franklin Blue Cat's daughter, Sonora Jordan. She's visiting him for a while."

Linda's mouth dropped open. "Uh…I didn't know… I mean…it's very nice to meet you."

"It's nice to meet you, too," Sonora said.

Before Linda had time to say anything about Franklin's bachelor status that might be embarrassing to Sonora, Adam changed the subject.

"How has Patricia been since I made medicine?"

"Good," Linda said.

"Any residual problems with her sleep pattern?" he asked.

"No, and we buried the little pot the next morning as you suggested." The somberness of her expression changed with a soft, easy smile. "She visits the 'grave' every day with fresh flowers, and was so taken with the burial process that she's since buried a dead beetle, a couple of grasshoppers, one of which was unfortunately, still kicking, and a mole that the dogs dug up and killed. I'll be glad when this fixation with death passes."

She looked at Sonora.

"Do you have children?"

"No," Sonora said. "I've never been married."

Linda giggled. "These days that doesn't mean a thing."

Sonora laughed. She liked the young woman with the round face and happy eyes.

"You're right," Sonora said. "Maybe my answer should have been no, I've never had the urge. However, my dad and Adam are so taken with your daughter, I can't wait to meet her." She touched her pocket, making sure that the piece Franklin had given her was still there. "I brought her a little gift. I hope you don't mind."

Linda's eyes widened with delight. "Of course not, although I warn you, she might be a little shy at first."

"That's okay," Sonora said. "I know how that feels."

There was the sound of running footsteps on the porch, then a squeak as the screen door opened, then banged shut.

"Mama, Mama, is the magic man here?"

Adam grinned.

Linda rolled her eyes in silent apology as her little girl came running into the room.

In one quick scan, Patricia Billy saw Adam, then the stranger, and came to an abrupt stop. The smile disappeared from her face as she ducked her head and scooted to her mother's side.

Adam held out a hand. "Come talk to me a minute," he asked.

The little girl hesitated, but only a moment. She was too curious to stay still. Timidly, she moved to Adam, making sure to keep on the far side of the strange woman.

Adam put an arm around her. "Patricia, you remember Franklin Blue Cat, don't you?"

She frowned. "The man who finds animals in the wood?"

Adam smiled. "Yes, the man who finds animals in the wood. This is his daughter. Her name is Sonora." Then he looked at Sonora. "Sonora, this is my friend Patricia."

Sonora had little experience with children, but she instinctively knew what not to do, which was overwhelm them by being too loud and too friendly.

"Hello, Patricia. I am happy to meet you."

Patricia scooted a little closer to Adam, but managed to smile.

Sonora dug into her pocket, and pulled out her gift. "I asked my father for a gift to bring to you. He gave me this and said you might like it."

"Wow," Adam said, and meant it, because the small,

perfect horse Sonora was holding in the palm of her hand was so lifelike, the mane and tail appeared to be in motion.

"Oh, Sonora, that is a gift far too expensive for a little girl to have," Linda protested.

"No gift is too expensive if it's given in love," Sonora said, and then extended her hand.

The horse was as enticing as Franklin had predicted it would be. Patricia made a sudden switch in loyalties as she slid out from under Adam's arm and moved to stand in front of Sonora.

"He has no name," Sonora said, and set the horse in the little girl's outstretched hand.

Patricia took it, then turned it over and over, studying it until she seemed to come to some kind of conclusion.

"Yes, he does," she said. "He said it was Thunder."

Adam raised an eyebrow, then grinned at the expression on Linda's face.

"Don't panic," he said. "I once knew such things, too."

No sooner had it been said than a loud rumble of thunder sounded overhead.

"And, it appears as if the horse's namesake has arrived earlier than predicted. If you don't have any further concerns about Little Bit here, then I think Sonora and I will make a quick exit. Severe thunderstorms were predicted today, and I don't want to be out on the road when they hit."

"I hear you," Linda said. "My uncle Harmon…"

"…liked watermelon, didn't he?"

Adam knew the story about Harmon Marshall dying in a tornado and figured that was the last thing Patricia needed to hear.

Linda was slower on the uptake. "Yes…I guess, but I was going to—"

"Little ears, remember?" Adam said.

Linda's eyes widened, and then her shoulders slumped. "I'm sorry, Adam. I don't know what I was thinking."

He touched her arm, smiling as they walked out onto the porch. "It will take time to remember that she's grown up enough to hear what's being said, but not old enough to grasp the entire meaning."

"Yes, yes, of course," Linda said, and blushed as she looked at Sonora. "You must think I'm a terrible mother."

"On the contrary," Sonora said. "I can see what an amazing parent you are. Patricia is a very blessed child to have both parents in her life."

"Franklin didn't know about Sonora until only recently," Adam explained.

Linda's sympathy was immediate. Her dark brown eyes mirrored a quick rush of tears. "Your mother never told you?" she asked.

"My mother…" Sonora stopped. Patricia was staring intently at her. She knelt quickly until she was eye to eye with the little girl, then reached out and tickled her tummy. "My mother wasn't as nice or pretty as yours," she said.

Patricia giggled, and then saw the family cat coming out from under a bush beside the porch.

"Two Toes…look! We have a new friend," she cried, and held up the miniature carving as she bounded off the porch.

As soon as she was out of earshot, Linda turned back to Sonora. "I must apologize. I did not mean to cross-examine you."

Sonora shook her head.

"It's all right. There's no way you could have known," Sonora said. "Truth is, I never knew my mother. She left me on the doorstep of an orphanage."

"I'm sorry," Linda Billy said softly. Before anyone knew what she was doing, she put her arms around Sonora and hugged her, just as she would have any child who'd been hurt.

Sonora rarely allowed people into her personal space and was completely unprepared for being hugged. Still, the woman's touch was gentle and the tears in her eyes were genuine.

"Thanks," Sonora said, and realized that she meant it.

Linda stepped back and then folded her arms across her chest, as if embarrassed that she'd done something so impulsive.

"Welcome home," she said softly.

Sonora felt as if she'd been sucker punched. Her belly knotted. Welcome home? No one had ever said that to her before. She bit the inside of her mouth to keep from crying and then blinked rapidly to clear her vision.

"Yes...well...thank you," she said as another round of thunder, this one even closer, rippled through the clouds.

Adam cupped Sonora's elbow.

"Storm's getting closer. We'd better be going."

"Come back anytime," Linda said.

"Thank you," Sonora said as she followed Adam off the steps.

Patricia came running around the corner of the house.

"'Bye," she yelled, waving the horse in the air. "Thunder says goodbye, too."

Adam waved and laughed while Sonora got into the truck. He slid in beside her, then started the engine just as the first drops of rain began to fall. By the time they reached the main road again, it was pouring.

Adam glanced up at the dark, lowering clouds and then handed Sonora his cell phone.

"Call Franklin. Tell him we're going to my place. I'm thinking we'll need to take shelter soon, and it's closer."

She made the call. Franklin answered on the second ring.

"Dad, it's me. We're just now leaving the Billy residence and it's raining really hard. Adam said to tell you that we're going to go to his place to take shelter."

Franklin had been worrying about them ever since they'd begun forecasting weather warnings.

"Thank goodness," Franklin said. "Tell Adam that there are tornado warnings out for this entire area."

Sonora looked nervously up at the sky.

"Adam...Dad says there are tornado warnings for this area."

"I'm not surprised," Adam said. "The clouds don't look good."

The wind was growing stronger. Trees were bending to the force of the wind as rain fell harder. Sonora thought of her father, alone and unwell.

"Are you going to be all right?"

Franklin smiled to himself. He couldn't remember when someone had been concerned about his welfare.

"Yes, daughter. I will be fine. The storm cellar is right beneath the house, remember? I don't even have to go outside."

"Yes, yes, I just wasn't thinking," she said.

Franklin heard the uneasiness in her voice. "It's not easy getting used to worrying about someone else, is it?"

Sonora sighed. "No, it's not."

"I'll be fine. Call me after the storm passes so I'll know that you're both all right."

"Okay."

The line went dead in her ear. She disconnected, then laid the phone in the seat between them.

"Is he all right?" Adam asked.

"Yes. He told us to call after the storm passes."

"Definitely," Adam said, and then flinched when a limb broke off a tree and landed in the road just behind the truck bed. "That was close," he said.

Sonora was white knuckled and trying not to panic. "Are we in danger?" she asked.

"We're almost home. It'll be okay."

Breath caught in the back of her throat as a strong gust

of wind caused Adam's truck to lurch. She tightened her hold on the door handle, but didn't say a word.

Adam was tight-lipped and entirely focused on keeping the truck in the road and moving.

Thunder roared and thumped, reverberating inside the truck to the point that Sonora's ears popped. A second later, lightning struck just to their right, shattering a tree. Wood flew through the air like shrapnel.

"Look out!" Sonora screamed as a large shard of wood came toward the windshield.

Adam swerved. It hit the side of the truck, then ricocheted into the ditch.

"Okay...okay...I'm thinking this can't be good," Sonora mumbled.

"We're almost home," Adam said.

Moments later, he turned right.

Sonora couldn't see a thing but a solid sheet of horizontal rain and had to trust Adam knew what he was doing. Suddenly, she saw the outline of a house. When he drove around it then stopped, she guessed he'd been right.

"We're here," he said. "We're right beside the cellar. Get ready to get out on my side."

"I'm scared," she said, and then didn't believe that had come out of her mouth.

"Just trust me," Adam said, and jumped out of the truck.

Sonora didn't have time to do anything but gasp before he grabbed her hand and dragged her across the seat and out into the storm.

She couldn't see and didn't know where they were going, but she remembered what Adam had said. *Trust me.* The way she looked at it, she didn't have any choice.

Seconds later, he stopped.

"Hold on to my belt!" Adam yelled.

She grabbed the back of his belt as he reached for the door. The force of the wind nearly knocked her off her feet. If she hadn't been holding on to him, she would have been gone.

"Adam! Hurry!" she screamed.

She felt the muscles in his back tense, then ripple, as he pulled the door open against the wind.

"Down!" he shouted. "Come around to my right and get in. Eight steps down! Hurry!"

The wind had begun to whine. Sonora didn't hesitate. She ducked her head against the downpour and turned Adam's belt loose. Seconds later, she felt the first step beneath her feet and began counting as she moved down.

The rain was turning to hail. It peppered against her head and back as she went deeper and deeper into the hole. She could hear Adam coming down behind her and tried to hurry. Instead, she stumbled on the last two steps and fell belly down on the cellar floor just as the heavy wooden door fell shut with a loud, solid thunk.

The cellar was dry but dark. She couldn't see them, but she knew she'd made her arms bleed. They were stinging and burning as she rolled over on her back then sat up.

Adam had seen her falling, but hadn't been able to catch her.

"Sonora, honey, are you all right?" Adam cried.

"I think so," she said.

It was still hailing, but from where they were now, the sounds were muffled.

"Don't move," he said. "I have a lantern down here. I'll get us some light."

"Good," Sonora said.

"Don't tell me you're afraid of the dark," Adam said.

"Okay."

He chuckled as he felt along the shelves for the lantern he knew to be there. "Does that mean you are?" he asked.

"Somewhat," Sonora muttered. "Haven't you found that lantern yet?"

Adam frowned. Her voice was shaking.

"I'm sorry, honey," he said softly. "I'm hurrying." Just as he said it, he felt the base beneath his hands. "Here it is…just a second and I'll have it—"

Light bloomed in a corner of the cellar. It was small and yellow, but to Sonora, it was as good as the bright light of day.

At the same time she saw it, Adam saw her. Her elbows were scraped and her chin was trembling. He reached for her and pulled her up and into his arms.

For a moment, neither one of them moved or spoke. Finally, it was Adam who pulled back, and only then to check her injuries.

"I am so sorry," he said as he pulled her sleeves away from the scrapes on her elbows. "I think I have some first-aid stuff down here."

Sonora watched silently as he opened a small plastic box and then dug through the contents. Rainwater had plastered his shirt and jeans to his body. All it did was remind her of what he looked like nude, and that was a vision she didn't need. Not when they were alone and, for the time being, trapped by the storm.

Adam found a tube of antibiotic, but when he turned around, the look on her face stilled his intent. Every stitch of clothing she had on was soaked and molded to her body like a second layer of skin. When she lifted her arms above her head, then twisted her hair into a knot to wring out the excess water, he looked away. He didn't want to think of the thrust of her breasts against the fabric or the outline of her nipples showing through the thin, wet shirt. He didn't want her to feel trapped or threatened, but if she knew what he was thinking, she very likely would.

She moved into the circle of light, then pointed at the ointment.

"Did you find something?" she asked.

Adam looked at her, then sighed. He'd found something, all right. A woman capable of stealing his heart.

"Yes, some antibiotic ointment. Would you let me put some on your elbows?"

"Sure," she said. "Maybe it will make them quit stinging."

"I'm so sorry you were hurt," he said.

Sonora snorted softly as she folded her arms to allow him better access to the scrapes. "Getting shot hurts. These are nothing."

Adam's fingers stilled. He tried to form the words to what was running through his mind, but they just wouldn't come out. It wasn't until he'd put the ointment back into the first-aid box that he got it said.

"You've been shot?" he asked.

She nodded. "Once in the leg, once in the shoulder."

He'd been a soldier. He'd seen men shot. He'd seen men die. But for some reason, the thought of this woman in that kind of danger made him sick.

"Couldn't you have picked a safer job?"

"Of course I could have. But I didn't. What's your excuse?"

There was a challenge in her voice he hadn't expected.

"You're right. I'm sorry. It's none of my business."

The cellar door rattled on its hinges.

Both of them flinched and then turned.

"It's holding," Adam said.

Sonora moved to the back of the cellar, then stood against the wall.

"What if it doesn't?"

Adam sighed. He needed to keep his hands off her, but he could hardly deny the fear he heard in her voice. He followed her to the wall, then stopped, giving her time to adjust to the invasion of her space.

"Come here," he said, and opened his arms.

Sonora shivered. She wanted what he offered. But at what price? Still, when she walked into his arms, it felt right.

"At least I'm not going to be getting you wet," she said as his arms enfolded her.

"You're shivering," Adam said as he cupped her head with one hand and settled the other on the small of her back.

"So are you," she said, and wrapped her arms around his waist.

"That's not cold. That's a healthy physical reaction to a pretty woman."

She hid a smile. "You must be pretty hard up to be turned on by someone who looks like a wet rat."

"I'm not touching any part of that comment," Adam said.

Sonora shivered. "God…aren't you cold?" she asked.

But Adam didn't answer. He was listening to something else.

"Listen," he said softly.

Sonora tensed. "What? I don't hear anything."

"Exactly," Adam whispered.

"Is it over?" Sonora asked.

"I don't know. Stay here. I'm going to take a look."

Sonora grabbed his arm. "Adam! Wait! What if it's just a lull? You might get hurt!"

He stopped, then cupped her face and kissed her. The combination of wet skin and the hot blood beneath it made Sonora's knees go weak. When he finally pulled away, they were both breathing hard. He ran his thumb along the curve of her bottom lip as his eyes narrowed.

"Be right back," he promised.

Sonora's stomach knotted as he moved up the steps. When he put his shoulder against the heavy wooden door to push it up, she held her breath, watching as his head cleared the opening.

"Adam?"

"It's okay," he said. "The storm has passed."

She turned out the lantern, then followed him up the steps. Tree limbs were scattered all over the yard, but the house was still standing and except for slight hail damage, his truck was all right, too.

Adam helped her out, then lowered the cellar door before moving toward the house.

"Let's go inside. I need to check windows," Adam said.

Sonora followed him into the house, then stopped just inside the door. He turned around.

"I'll get everything wet," she said.

He held out his arms. "And I won't?"

She shrugged.

"Would you check the kitchen and laundry room while I take the back of the house?" Adam asked.

"Sure," she said, and after he aimed her in the right direction, they parted company.

Sonora heard his footsteps as he moved down the hall and into the bedrooms. She took off her shoes and then headed for the kitchen, dripping water from her clothes as she went.

The windows were closed, and none were broken, although the plants in his backyard had sadly been shredded. She walked out the back door and onto the porch for a better view and was met at the steps by a large cat.

Sonora knelt as the cat came up to her and rubbed his head against her outstretched hand.

"Hey, kitty, are you all right?"

Sensing a sympathetic hand, Charlie the cat butted his head against her leg.

"Rowr."

Sonora smiled as she reached down and rubbed him, but when her hand came away bloody, she gasped. "Oh, no! You're hurt!"

She picked him up and hurried back into the house with him, calling Adam's name as she went.

He came running. "What's wrong?" Then he saw Charlie. "Hey, I see you met Charlie."

"He's hurt," Sonora said, and held out her hand.

Adam saw the blood and frowned. "Hey, old fella…did you get caught in the storm?"

"Rowrp."

"So, let's see what's happened to you," he said as he took the cat out of Sonora's arms and carried him to a table by a window in the laundry room.

Sonora followed anxiously.

"His name is Charlie?"

"Yeah," Adam said as he rolled the old cat onto his back. "Here it is," he said as he quickly spied the cut. "It's not too deep, but it's jagged. Probably got caught trying to get out of the storm."

"Can you fix him?"

"Sure," he said gently, as he rubbed a thumb under the cat's chin, then scratched his head. "We'll get him fixed up. There's a blue box in that cabinet behind you. Hand it to me, will you?"

Sonora found it quickly and laid it on the table beside the cat, then opened the lid.

"Would you hold Charlie for me while I find what I need?"

Sonora looked anxious.

"Will he bite me?"

"I don't know. Let's ask him," Adam said.

Sonora thought Adam was joking until he bent down and stared right into the cat's face.

"Charlie, this is my friend Sonora. She's going to help me make you feel better, so no bites or scratches, okay?"

Sonora started to grin, but when the cat looked up at her as if assessing her worth, the smile died on her face.

"Rrrrp."

"Okay, then," Adam said. "Good boy."

"What?" Sonora asked.

"You're good to go. Oh…you might like to know that he loves to have his head scratched right behind his ears."

"I can't believe this just happened," she muttered, as she laid a hand on the big cat's head, then gently began to stroke.

Adam hid a smile. Poor Sonora. She had much to learn about the Native American way. Then he heard her crooning sweet words to his cat and sighed. First Charlie. Next it would be himself. It was only a matter of time before they both succumbed.

Chapter 11

The storm had passed just before sunset. Darkness came quickly, leaving the debris in the yard to be dealt with tomorrow. Sonora called Franklin to let him know they were okay.

"Dad…it's me."

Franklin's joy bubbled over into a delighted chuckle.

"What's so funny?" Sonora asked.

"I'm not laughing because anything's funny. I just couldn't hide my delight in hearing those words come out of your mouth."

"What words?"

"Those *Dad, it's me* words."

She grinned. "Oh. Yes." Her smile faded slightly. "What's really strange for me is that even though it's only been a short time since we found each other, it all seems so natural."

"We share blood, daughter."

Sonora bit the inside of her mouth, struggling with a sudden need to cry. She'd had a lot of moments like this lately, and was still unprepared for the feelings of vulnerability.

"So, did the storm pass you by?" she asked.

"Yes, I'm fine. How about you and Adam? Did his home suffer any damage?"

"Some, but I'm not sure how much. I'll let you ask him," she said, and handed Adam the phone.

Adam had changed out of his wet clothes earlier and had gone to get a towel to dry his hair when Sonora called Franklin. He came back into the kitchen in time to hear her side of the conversation.

"What is it?" he asked, as he took the phone.

"It's Dad, wanting to know how much damage you had."

"Oh. Okay," Adam said, then covered the phone so that Franklin couldn't hear.

"I laid out some dry clothes for you on my bed. They'll be too big, but they will feel better than what you have on. Bring your own stuff back with you when you come and we'll toss them in the dryer, okay?"

She mouthed a thank-you as she left the room.

At that point, Adam turned his attention to the phone. "Franklin...are you all right?"

"Yes. No damage here. Just a lot of water in the creek."

"We had a close call here. Part of the barn roof is gone but the house is still intact. Got a call from Mose and Sheila Roundtree. They said the road between their house and mine was blocked and probably wouldn't be open until morning."

Startled by the news that she'd overheard, Sonora paused in the doorway and turned around, watching Adam's face. As best she could tell, there was no deception in his voice, but if what he was saying was true, then the good news was she'd be staying overnight. The bad news was that she was secretly pleased.

"Don't try to take that old back road," Franklin said. "It's most likely underwater."

"Yeah, I agree," Adam said. "I was going to suggest Sonora stay here for the night, then when daylight comes, we'll see where we are with the roads."

"Good," Franklin said. "Have a good evening and tell Sonora I said good-night and I'll see you both tomorrow."

"All right. Take care," Adam said, then hung up. When he turned around, Sonora was standing in the doorway—still in her wet clothes. "Is there something wrong with the clothes I laid out?"

"I don't know. I haven't seen them yet," she said, then added, "I heard what you told Dad."

"Yes?"

"I didn't know the roads were blocked."

"Neither did I until I called Mose and Sheila to make sure they were okay. Sheila said there were about four big trees in the road that would have to be cut up and moved before we could pass."

"Oh."

"Franklin said to tell you good-night and that he'd see us tomorrow," he added.

"So...I'm spending the night."

Adam grinned. Now he understood what was on her mind.

"Yes, but through no fault of mine, so you can get that look off your face."

"What look?" Sonora said.

"The one where you slit my throat as soon as I close my eyes tonight."

Sonora's eyes narrowed as she eyed him up and down. "That's not murder you see on my face...it's lust."

At the same time Adam's grin died, his belly knotted. "Damn, woman."

"What?" Sonora asked.

"You don't mince words, do you?"

Sonora shrugged. "Waste of time."

"Yeah. Right," Adam said, and then glanced at the clock. "Are you hungry?"

Sonora thought about the next few hours and shivered. Eating seemed like a good idea, but she wasn't sure that she'd be able to swallow a bite.

"Maybe," she said. "But nothing difficult. Do you have stuff for sandwiches or some cans of soup?"

"I have both."

"You do soup. I'll make sandwiches," she offered.

"When do we get to the lust?" Adam asked.

Sonora laughed out loud.

Adam didn't.

She frowned. "You're not serious."

"Why not? You were," he said.

"But—"

Adam cupped her face with his hands. "Don't go all female on me. You spoke your mind. I love that about you."

Sonora felt the air go out of her lungs. "You love…?"

He sighed. "Ah, for Pete's sake, Sonora. Don't freak. Consider it a poor choice of words."

"What kind of soup do we have?"

"I am so out of my element here," Adam muttered as he turned around and strode to the pantry. He turned on the light, then stepped aside. "Get out of those wet clothes first before you make yourself sick. As for the pantry… Feel free to investigate," he said. "I'm going to feed Charlie." Then he took a small can of cat food from a sack beneath the shelves and left her alone in the kitchen.

Sonora stared at the soup cans as if her life depended on it, when in truth, all she could think about was Adam and the inevitability of sex. Still, the only decision she had to make at the moment was choosing what kind of soup they were going to have with their sandwiches.

She started into the pantry, then remembered she'd been going to change, so she hurried out of the room.

A short while later, Adam heard her banging around the pantry and gritted his teeth. He might not survive this woman, but he was falling under her spell. If he didn't survive, it would be one hell of a way to die. Meanwhile, he had a cat to feed.

Earlier, he'd padded a laundry basket with a handful of old towels to make a bed for the injured cat. He knelt down and pulled Charlie's makeshift bed from under a table, then peered over the side.

Charlie was looking up, somewhat the worse for wear.

"Hey, Charlie," Adam said as he leaned over and rubbed the old cat's head. "Feeling better now, aren't you?"

He could feel the lack of tension in the cat's muscles, which told him that the pain the cat had been in earlier was easing. Obviously, his medicine was working.

"How about some supper, fella?"

"Meowp."

"That's what I thought," Adam said, and emptied the can of cat food onto a paper plate before setting it inside Charlie's temporary bed.

He sat, watching Charlie eat and listening to the sounds of a woman in his kitchen. After a while, he decided he couldn't remember a time when he'd felt this peaceful.

Sonora cut the last sandwich into halves and then laid it on the plate with the others. She hadn't been able to find two cans of the same kind of soup, so she'd made potato soup on her own. It was being kept warm on the back burner while she finished the rest of their meal.

The clothes he'd laid out for her to wear were definitely roomy, but they were warm and dry and she couldn't ask for more. The sweatpants had a drawstring tie to help hold them up and the T-shirt he'd given her was soft from countless washings. He'd left her some socks as well, but she'd chosen to go barefoot instead, and was enjoying the cool surface of the vinyl flooring beneath her feet as she moved about the kitchen.

She knew she'd pushed more of Adam's buttons and wondered what it was about him that made her do that. Normally, she wasn't a confrontational kind of woman, except on the job, but there was something about him that made her nervous.

Maybe after they had sex and got it out of their systems, they wouldn't be so focused on pretending they weren't attracted to each other.

As she finished setting the table, she kept thinking about Miguel Garcia— wondering where the DEA was with regards to his capture and wondering what her life would be like if they never did get him. She didn't know what she thought about spending the rest of her life looking over her shoulder, or fearing what might happen to Franklin or Adam if Garcia knew how much they'd come to mean to her.

She set the last of the cutlery by the bowls and plates then stepped back, eyeing the table to see if there was something she'd missed. Confident that everything was in place, she glanced toward the closed door to the laundry room. Surely Adam was through feeding his cat.

She peered out a window into the darkness, absently hoping she hadn't aggravated him to the point of wishing she wasn't here. Still, he was the one who'd wanted her to go with him, and she wasn't responsible for the weather. The way she looked at it, he was the reason she'd gone, so he didn't have anything to complain about.

Just as she turned back toward the sink, the door to the laundry room opened.

"Something smells good," Adam said.

The fact that he seemed ready to call a truce made her smile.

"It's just potato soup," she said. "I hope you like it."

His eyes widened in delight. "You made soup?"

She nodded.

"From scratch?"

"Yes. You didn't have two cans of soup that were alike so rather than heat up two different kinds, I just—"

Adam hugged her. "After what I've put you through today, you're amazing. I bring you into my house as a guest, not to cook. Still, I confess that I'm looking forward to eating your soup. It's one of my favorites."

Sonora was still smiling when he moved to the kitchen sink to wash his hands. She carried the soup pot to the table and ladled soup into two bowls, then started back to the stove.

"Here, let me," Adam said, and took the pot from her hands and set it on the burner. "Anything else you need?"

Just you. Luckily for Sonora, Adam couldn't read her mind. "No. That's it," she said.

"Then we eat."

Adam seated her, then himself. Once seated, he looked across the table. The feeling of peace that was with him settled firmer. Seeing Sonora at his table seemed so right.

"Ham sandwich?" Sonora asked.

Adam blinked. She was holding the platter.

"Yes, please," he said, and so the meal began.

Sonora was still curious about Adam, and after a few bites of sandwich and part of her soup, she quit eating, put her elbows on the table, and leaned forward.

"Adam?"

He looked up, still chewing. "Hmm?"

"Are your parents still living?"

He nodded as he swallowed quickly. "Yes. They live in Anadarko."

"So, how did you wind up here after you left the army?"

"Oh. This is the family home. I bought it from Mom and Dad after I quit the military. My sister and her family live in Anadarko. Mom and Dad got lonesome for their grandchildren, said they didn't see them enough and moved. This house had been vacant almost a year when I came back."

"You didn't want to be close to them?" she asked.

He smiled. "It wasn't that. It was just that I knew what I wanted to do and the people who needed me most were here."

Her eyes narrowed as she tried to picture this brown-skinned man with a military haircut and a gun in his hand. He seemed more of a pacifist.

"How did you know… I mean…how did you go from the white man's army to the Native American world without complications?"

"I didn't. The complications were there. Sometimes they're still there, especially with the tribe elders. They see me as something of a contradiction. In my heart I am a healer, but my past is all mixed up with the white man's conflicts and war."

"Does your past trouble you?" she asked.

"No. It's something I did. It made me stronger, I think, but it didn't lessen my abilities as a healer."

Her eyes narrowed slightly. "How did you know?"

"Know what?" Adam asked.

"That you were supposed to be a healer?"

His expression softened and he almost smiled. "How did you come to law enforcement?"

Sonora frowned. "That's not fair. I asked first."

Adam stifled a grin. "That you did." Then he sighed. "I've always known what I was born to do. I just resisted it for a while."

Her eyes widened. "You knew? How did you know?"

"When I was a child, I got blood poisoning in my foot

from stepping on a rusty nail. I was sick for a long time. One night, I heard my parents talking with the doctor. He told them that I might die. I remember being scared…afraid to close my eyes for fear I wouldn't wake up. I think that's why I was so sympathetic with the little girl we went to see today. I remembered what it felt like to be afraid to close my eyes."

"So what happened?" Sonora asked.

He smiled. "Eventually, I slept, but when I did, the Old Ones came to me in my sleep and told me that I wouldn't die because when I grew up, I was going to be a healer."

Sonora's lips went slack as a shiver went up her spine. Even as Adam was speaking, her mind took her straight back to her childhood—to the countless nights she'd gone to bed lonely and afraid only to be visited by a repetitive dream that had both confused and comforted. Surely it couldn't be the same.

Adam saw her reaction and frowned. "What?"

Sonora thought of the tattoo on her back and shivered again.

"What did the Old Ones look like?" she asked.

Adam's frown deepened. There was more than curiosity in her questions, and because of that, he described something that, in another set of circumstances, he would never have revealed.

"They are four ancient warriors. One wears a long war bonnet. Another is wrapped in a bearskin and has the mark of a claw on his chest. The third—"

"What are they riding?" she asked.

He frowned. How did she know there were horses?

"They are riding—"

Sonora shuddered, closed her eyes and finished his sentence. "…ghost horses with red eyes and feathers tied in their manes. One has a black handprint on its left hip. Its rider has two white handprints on his face. The last rider is naked with hair so long that it's tangled up in the mane and tail of his horse."

The hair stood on the back of Adam's neck. "How do you know this?"

"I used to dream about them all the time," she whispered, and then covered her face with her hands. "I didn't know who they were."

Adam stared at her, absorbing the shock of what she was saying. From the time he'd learned of the snake tattoo on her back, he'd believed she was special. This only confirmed it for him. He didn't know what it was she'd been singled out to do, but it was obvious that the Old Ones had a hand in it.

He leaned across the table and pulled her hands from her face. "Sonora. Look at me."

She opened her eyes and found herself falling into the bottomless shadows in Adam's eyes. She felt humbled and at the same time strengthened by his presence.

"Don't be afraid of your blessings," Adam said.

"Is that what they are?"

Adam sighed. "Why is it so hard for you to understand?"

"If I was so damned special, then why was my childhood staged in the pit of hell? If these Indian…ghosts… were watching over me, as you suggest, then why didn't they help me?"

"How do you know they didn't?" Adam asked. "You're alive."

Sonora went still. Suddenly all the times she'd walked away from danger without a scratch seemed to be more than what she used to call luck. All the times growing up when she could have been hurt, when she might have been arrested or killed now took on a different tone. Her perceptions of her past took a one-eighty turn. Could this be? Had she been looking at a half-empty glass instead of one that was half-full? It was something to consider.

"You're right. I am," she said. "And my soup is getting cold."

Adam didn't push her into any more conversation. It was obvious that, for the moment, more had been said than she could handle.

"That soup is also wonderful," Adam said softly. "My mother always puts grated carrot with the celery and onion, too. She says that, without it, potato soup is too white."

Sonora laughed.

"You should do that more often," Adam said, then downed his last bite of sandwich.

"Do what?" Sonora asked.

"Laugh," Adam said, talking around a mouthful. He got up from the table, refilled his glass with iced tea and then took a big drink. "Want a refill?" he asked, as he pointed at her glass.

"No. I'm good."

He grinned. "You sure are."

She laughed again. "Are you flirting with me?"

"Yes," Adam said, then took another drink.

Sonora swallowed nervously and then began gathering up the dirty dishes and carried them to the sink.

Adam helped her clean up the kitchen, making small talk when the silence in the room grew noticeable. Finally, he pronounced the room clean.

"That's good enough," Adam said as he took the dish-cloth from Sonora's hands and hung it up to dry. "Don't get it too clean or you'll make my efforts at housekeeping look bad."

"But I just—"

"Sonora."

She sighed, then grew quiet before asking, "It's time, isn't it."

Adam slid his hands around her waist, then stopped

without pulling her close. "You're calling the shots," he said softly.

She was still thinking about the power he'd given her when the lights flickered then went out.

"Damn," Adam muttered. "I wondered when that would happen."

Sonora clutched his forearms, telling herself it was okay, that there was nothing in the dark that hadn't been there in the light. Still, her heartbeat accelerated and her knees went weak.

"When what would happen?" Sonora asked. "Aren't they coming back on?"

"Not for a while, honey. Maybe not until morning. Storms are always knocking out power around here. A tree probably fell over on a line somewhere. It will take the power crews a while to find it, then fix it."

"Oh, Lord," Sonora muttered.

It was then Adam remembered she was afraid of the dark. He pulled her close beneath the shelter of his arm.

"Honey...I'm sorry. You'll be okay, I promise."

An encroaching panic left her breathless. "Do you have a candle or a flashlight? We need to make light. Please, Adam, we need to make light."

He frowned at the fear in her voice and wondered what had happened to her to make her this afraid.

"And we will. Take hold of my hand. There's a flashlight in my bedroom."

She clung to his hand as if it was her lifeline to sanity. Even though she knew it was Adam who was beside her, her mind wouldn't turn loose from the past—to the foster parent who'd locked her in a closet every time her men friends came calling.

Adam was hurrying. He could tell she was bordering on panic, and while he didn't understand what drove it, he understood fear.

"I've got you, honey. Just hang on to me. We're almost there. I've got a great big flashlight in the table by the bed and there are some candles all around the house. We'll light the place up like a church on Christmas, okay?"

"Okay…okay, just like Christmas."

She tried to laugh, but it sounded more like a sob. God, she hated herself for this weakness. All these years and it was the one thing she'd never been able to get over.

"We're in the bedroom now. Here…feel the bedpost. I want you to sit on the bed while I find the flashlight, okay?"

"Yes. I'm sorry that I'm such a nutcase," Sonora said as she sat down on the end of the bed, clutching the bedpost for security.

"You're nothing of the kind," Adam said as he scrambled for the table. Within seconds, his fingers curled around the handle of the battery-powered lantern. "Bingo," he said, and flipped on the light.

Once again, Sonora's world centered.

"Thank God," she muttered, then shook the hair back from her face and stood. "What can I help you do?"

Adam was already pulling a smaller flashlight from a dresser drawer. "I'm going to light a few candles so that we can move around as needed. You can either come with me or wait for me to come back. I won't be long."

"I'll wait."

Adam's cursory glance was meant to appear casual, but he was, in fact, assessing her condition. Even in the poor lighting, the pallor in her face was still evident, but he could tell she was breathing easier from the rise and fall of her breasts.

"I'll be right back."

He took the other flashlight and made a run through the house, lighting candles and moving them about so that there was at least one light in every room in the house. He checked on his cat one last time, satisfied that Charlie was comfortable and sleeping, then locked up as he moved back through the house.

When he got back to his bedroom, Sonora was right where he'd left her, clutching the flashlight and staring into the shadows about the room.

He pulled a couple of Yankee candles from a cupboard and lit them, putting one on the dresser and the other in the adjoining bathroom, then sat down on the bed beside her.

"Sonora...honey..."

"What?"

He put his arm around her shoulders. "I want you to do something for me."

She looked up, then into his eyes and wondered when she'd come to trust him. "What is it?" she asked.

He put his hands on either side of her face and held her until her gaze was locked into his, then he took one of her hands and laid it on his chest. "Do you feel that?" he asked.

"What...your heartbeat?"

"Yes."

"Yes, I feel it."

Then he put his hand behind her head and pulled until the side of her face was against his chest. "Do you hear it?"

Sonora sighed. The rock-steady rhythm of his heart was impossible to miss. "I hear it," she whispered.

"Then remember, because even if you can't see me, you need to know that even if the batteries go dead and the candles burn out, I'll be your light in the dark. All you have to do is reach out and I'll be there. Can you remember to do that? Can you remember not to be afraid?"

She nodded.

Long silent moments passed. Moments in which they grew easier with each other's presence. Moments in which Sonora's last hesitation for what was about to occur finally died.

She pulled back from Adam's embrace and then stood.

As he watched, she stepped back from the bed and then pulled the borrowed T-shirt over her head.

Adam grunted softly, as if he'd been kicked in the gut, but he never moved.

Sonora untied the drawstring on the sweatpants. They slid from her slender hips into a puddle of fabric at her feet, leaving her completely naked.

It was obvious to Adam that she was comfortable with her body, as she should have been. She was all lean muscle with a soft, womanly shape. When she lifted her arms to take down her hair, he stood.

"Wait," he begged. "Let me."

Without thinking, she turned around, giving him easier access to the ponytail. But it wasn't her hair that caught Adam's eye. It was the snake tattoo that ran the length of her spine.

He knew she was waiting, but he was unable to move. The snake's eyes seemed to be watching him—marking the distance between them.

Without warning, Adam heard a distant rumble and for a moment thought another round of thunderstorms were coming. When he realized it was drums he was hearing, the room in which they were standing began to fade and another image soon took its place.

They were standing in a desert with nothing in sight but a distant cloud of dust. Sonora seemed to be swaying to a rhythm only she could hear, while the snake on her back came alive. As Adam watched, the snake slithered off her skin and onto the earth. Then it raised its head toward the dust cloud and began to grow tall. It grew in size until it was standing taller than a tree, directly between them and the approaching cloud of dust.

As the snake grew tall, Sonora seemed to waver, then fell. Adam tried to move, but when he looked down, roots were growing out of his feet into the earth, rendering him immobile.

The dust cloud was closer now, and Adam thought he heard screams coming out of the mass. He didn't know what it was in the cloud, but he knew it meant danger to Sonora. Sweat broke out on his skin as he struggled to get free, but the roots had gone too deep.

Just before the cloud enveloped them, he screamed out her name, and as he did, the snake opened its mouth. In the same moment, Sonora rose up from the ground. There was a split second in Adam's mind when Sonora and the snake seemed to be one. The snake, or Sonora—or maybe it was both—inhaled for what seemed like forever, until they had swallowed the dust cloud whole.

When Adam looked again, the roots were gone from his feet and Sonora was lying motionless on the ground. His heart seemed to stop as fear enveloped him. It couldn't be. He couldn't lose her this way. The snake's rattles were loud in his ear as he called out her name.

Sonora turned around.

"Adam?"

Between one heartbeat and the next, the desert disappeared and Adam was back in his bedroom.

He gasped as if he'd been drowning, and then staggered backward and sat down on a bench without taking his gaze from her face.

Sonora frowned. "Are you all right?" she asked.

For the moment, speech was impossible. He managed a nod.

"Look, if this isn't the right—"

He pulled her to him, and then buried his face against her belly. Even as he was wrapping his arms around her waist, the sound of rattles was fading from his mind.

She was real. Not the vision. Just her. But as he was mapping the contours of her hips with the palms of his hands, he was certain of one thing. Sonora was in danger, and he wasn't going to be able to do a damned thing about it. Only the power within her was going to keep her alive.

Chapter 12

Sonora knew something had happened. She could tell by the look on Adam's face that it had undone him, but she didn't know what or why. So, when he wrapped his arms around her, she took it as the opening she'd been waiting for, combed her fingers through his hair, then arched her back.

"Come to bed with me, Adam. Make the dark in my world go away."

It was exactly what Adam needed to get the picture of her in danger out of his head. With one motion, she was in his arms and then he was carrying her to the bed. He laid her down, then stripped without word or explanation for what he'd seen. She'd asked him to bed and he wasn't about to refuse.

Once his clothes were off, he paused to look at her, naked in his bed and wanting him. It was something out of a dream.

When she reached for him, he reacted instantly by lying down beside her and taking her in his arms.

When she began to run her hands upon his body, he didn't trust his self-control enough to allow her the freedom. Instead, he swung a leg over the lower half of her body, then straddled her, pinning her to the bed.

"Who do you see?" he asked.

His hair had fallen down on either side of his neck, partially hiding his face from view, and even though they'd never been this close or this intimate, it seemed that she'd known him forever.

"I see you," she whispered, and spread her legs.

Adam's pulse shifted into a higher gear. Her invitation was impossible to misunderstand. He slid into the valley between her thighs, rocking against her a couple of times without penetration, testing his own willpower while waiting for a positive invitation.

"Who am I?" he asked.

"The man I want."

She locked her legs around his back, caught him on a downward thrust and pulled him in.

The joining was immediate, and at the same time, Sonora felt a physical shock, as if she'd touched a live electric wire. She shuddered as she closed her eyes, and still she saw Adam's face, silhouetted against a shower of sparks.

"Don't close your eyes."

His demand seemed impossible to heed and yet somehow Sonora managed to focus. She saw him, and she saw herself. In a way, it seemed as if time stopped and she was outside her own body, watching them make love. They rocked and writhed in perfect unison, while the shadows from the lamplight flickered upon the walls. Soft whispers, coupled with a moan and the occasional sigh played an accompaniment to the dance.

Sonora was caught up in the act of making love in a way she'd never known before. Her sense of self was gone, leaving her at the mercy of this man and his skill at bringing her to a frenzy.

She wanted, needed, begged.

He heard her, felt her desperation, matched it with need of his own. Being inside her was like being caught in the storm they'd endured earlier. It was happening, and they were in it together, but without any control.

One moment she was caught up in the power between them and the next she was coming apart. The wave of the climax washed through her so hard that she heard herself scream.

The sound ripped through Adam like a bullet through flesh, shattering mind and body alike as he climaxed along with her.

Coming down from the high they'd created left them both exhausted and breathless, but there was a peace inside Adam that he hadn't felt since he'd come home from the army. Whatever there was between him and Sonora, he wasn't willing to lose it. Gently, he wrapped his arms around her and rolled, so that she was now the one on top.

Sonora lay sprawled across his chest, her long legs entwined with his, her fingers tangled in his hair. There were unashamed tears on her cheeks and a flush to her skin. She felt as if she'd been in a flash fire and cleansed by the heat.

All of the ugliness and the loneliness of her past had been reduced to ashes by this man and what they'd done together.

Slowly, she raised up on her elbows and looked down at him, marveling at the gentleness in his eyes and remembering the passion with which they'd made love. Somewhere between the bed and the moment he'd taken her, the act of sex had been replaced by something more. There had been men in her life before Adam, but there would never be another after him. She didn't know what he hoped to gain from being with her, but she knew what she wanted from it.

She wanted him.

Gently, she traced the dark wings of his eyebrows with her fingertips and kissed the shadows his lashes left on his cheeks. She could feel the faint ebb and flow of his breath from his slightly parted lips and shivered, remembering that he'd actually made her scream.

"Adam…"

His nostrils flared.

"Don't say it," he said. "No promises are needed. Not now. Later, when you come to know and accept that you are forever safe with me, there will be promises made. But not now. Just know that you are in my heart and in my blood."

Sonora's lips parted and she started to speak, then stopped. He was right. For now, all they needed to do was savor the magic they made together.

"All right. But…I have one thing to say."

He smiled. "Of course you do. You're a woman, aren't you? Women always have to have the last word."

"Then let me have it," she said, and when he grinned, she laid her hand on his chest. "I see you, Adam Two Eagles. Do you see me?"

Adam was shocked by quick tears that blurred his own vision. Showing emotion, let alone feeling it like this, was foreign to him. He groaned beneath his breath as he reached for her.

"See you? Woman…I am numb to everything but your touch. I don't know what's happening between us, but I am forever changed by what we've done."

Sonora raised up and then sat, straddling his thighs. Adam lay silently, watching the play of light and shadows flickering upon her body from the candles.

Slowly, he watched her as she rocked back on her heels and began stroking him, gently at first and then faster and faster until he was rock hard and aching for a release. It was then that she raised up and took him inside her.

Time ceased. Life shrank to a pinpoint of promised ec-
stasy as she swung her hair away from her face, arched
her back, then bore down, racing with Adam to the end
of the dance.

Later, when they could move without shaking, Sonora
rolled over onto her side. Adam curled up behind her, pulled
the covers over them and held her while she slept.

He watched the shadows lengthen throughout the night
as the candles finally burned out, and daylight was only
a whisper away. He watched her sleeping while morning
broke and drowned the darkness in a fine display of pale
light. He watched and remembered his vision and knew that
there would come a day when she would need him and he
would be helpless to come to her aid. It was the worst thing
he'd ever faced—worse than anything the army had ever
thrown at him, worse than believing his own life might
end. He didn't know the face that danger would wear for
her, but he knew it was coming.

Miguel Garcia was, as the cowboys used to say, lying
low. The men who'd been sent out to search for Sonora Jordan were making progress, but mostly by elimination. He
didn't know where Sonora Jordan was, but he knew where
she wasn't, and he knew where she'd been.

There had been two separate sightings of women they
thought were the female agent, but both had proved to be
mistaken identities. He was frustrated at having to hide in
a country that was not his own, and absolutely convinced
that he'd been betrayed by someone he trusted. There was
no other explanation for how the DEA knew what he was
driving and how long he'd been in the States. He'd thought
about it long and hard, and the only name that kept coming
to mind was Jorge Diaz. It seemed impossible to believe
that the man who'd helped him escape was the same man

who'd betrayed him. There was, however, one way to find out, and it meant another call to Emilio Rojas.

Rojas was sitting in a lounge chair under a pair of palm trees, holding his newest grandson. The day was hot and sunny in Juarez, just the way he liked it. The baby was his twelfth grandchild, but the first one who had been named for him. Family had gathered for a Sunday meal after church and Emilio was counting his blessings as he held the month-old baby boy.

A peacock was perched on a low limb nearby, emitting intermittent squawks of disapproval for the fact that the yard it normally occupied was full of running, squealing children.

Emilio was laughing and urging on the games that the children were playing when he looked up and saw his eldest daughter, Pia, coming toward him carrying the phone.

"Papa, it is for you," she said, then handed him the phone and took the grandchild out of his arms. With a few quick words, she ushered the children to another part of the yard to give Emilio some privacy to take his call.

Emilio was not all that happy with the interruption, and after he recognized the caller, even more displeased.

"Miguel, why are you calling?" he asked abruptly.

Miguel frowned. "I have another favor to ask of you."

Emilio stifled a curse. He was old. He was tired. He didn't want anything more to do with the drug world, but it was easier said than done.

"And what would that be?" Emilio asked.

"I have reason to believe that Jorge Diaz is the one responsible for betraying me to the authorities."

Emilio sighed. He knew what was coming, even before Miguel got it said.

"So, how do you know this?" he asked.

"Process of elimination," Miguel said.

"And what do you want me to do about it?" Emilio asked.

"I want Diaz confronted and I want the truth. I don't care what has to be done to make him talk, but if I'm right and he does confess. I want him to pay."

A tiny, dark-eyed, dark-haired toddler crawled up in Emilio's lap just as Miguel was still talking. Emilio's expression darkened. How dare that man talk about such things on a Sunday, and when his family was here! It made Emilio feel obscene to have this precious little face looking up at him with love, completely unaware of what was being said in her presence.

"I am too old for such things," Emilio said.

Miguel cursed. "I need this done," he said. "I can't let it become common knowledge that I was betrayed and let it pass. I want justice. I want him dead."

"Papa…Papa…a candy, *por favor?*"

Emilio stared down at his little granddaughter. She wanted a piece of candy and Miguel Garcia wanted him to kill. If he could have put his hands on Garcia, it would be him who'd be dead.

"Una momento, chica," he said gently, then gripped the phone a little tighter. "Miguel! You know this is no longer my life and yet you ask it anyway?"

Miguel could tell his father's old friend was angry, but he didn't much care. He was the one with problems.

"You know what I'm going through," Miguel said. "I need you to do this for me."

"And what if you're wrong? What if Diaz is not your enemy?"

"Then you find out who is and deal with it!" Miguel demanded.

Emilio gritted his teeth. He knew who needed to be dealt with, but even he didn't have the guts to make an enemy of Miguel. It was his private opinion that Miguel's father had catered to his sons to the point of ruination, but since his old friend was dead and Miguel was the last of the seed, he didn't want the bad karma of being the one who ended the lineage.

"I will do what I can," Emilio said, and hung up before Miguel could argue further, then made a call to his eldest son.

"Benecio, I need a favor."

Benecio Rojas smiled to himself. His father always prefaced his calls with those words.

"What can I do for you, Papa?"

"Find Jorge Diaz and confirm that he's the one who betrayed Miguel."

Benecio frowned. "Then what?"

"You know what," Emilio said.

"Papa, why are we involving ourselves with Miguel's business? You know what he's like."

"Yes, I do," Emilio said. "And for that reason alone, I do it. I don't want a member of my family to go missing because I displeased him in some way."

Benecio cursed beneath his breath, but he understood. "I will do it, Papa, but only for you. Not because I care what happens to Miguel Garcia."

"Thank you, my son. Go with God."

"And you, too, Papa."

Emilio heard his son disconnect, then sighed. He looked down into the little girl's smiling face, laid down the phone, picked her up in his arms and then stood.

"Now, *niña,* let's go find that candy, okay?"

It was Monday, which was why Ming, the Chinese manicurist, was massaging Jorge's right hand while the left hand was still soaking. Ming had fastened a hot-pink cape around his neck to protect his clothes and rolled his pants up to his knees while his feet were soaking in a footbath attached to the massage/manicure chair. The chair was a little cheesy, but Jorge secretly loved the fact that he got a quickie back massage without getting naked.

Actually, Jorge got a manicure and pedicure at Ming's shop every Monday and a haircut every other week at her salon next door. His eyes were closed as Ming turned off the footbath and wrapped his feet in a warm towel. Part of his mind was savoring his time with Ming while he was giving himself a mental pat on the back for enlarging his territory and at the same time getting rid of Miguel.

He heard the little bell jingling over the front door of the shop but didn't bother to look up. People came and went in here constantly, and besides that, he was operating on the theory that if he didn't see who'd come in, then he wouldn't have to acknowledge them.

There was also a part of him that thought getting manicures was effeminate, so he didn't want to see judgment in their eyes. The only men he knew who did it were wealthy, thus the reason for his habit. He wanted the world to know how he'd risen in society. Thanks to the nation's desire for drugs, he was, by anyone's measure, an immensely wealthy man. It suited him to flaunt that, but only to a degree. Too much attention could get a man in his business killed.

However, once Garcia was completely out of the picture, his wealth would most likely triple. It was only a matter of time before the DEA found Garcia, and when they did, he would bet his own life that Miguel would die before being taken alive—which was exactly what he was hoping for.

"Mr. D…do you want clear polish on your nails?"

"Sure…why not?" he said.

Ming picked up a bottle of clear polish, tapped it a few times in the palm of her hand, unscrewed the lid and then sat it down beside her. She picked up a towel then dried Jorge's hands thoroughly before loading her nailbrush with polish.

Jorge was pleasantly aware of the scent of sandalwood

as Ming bent her head to her task. He was not aware of the man with the gun until he felt the barrel in his ear.

"Don't move," the man said softly. "I have a question for you."

Ming started to quietly weep.

To Jorge, it was more frightening than if she'd been screaming her head off. Even though he was shocked, it wasn't entirely unexpected. The lifestyle had its drawbacks and this was one of them. Only this time he was wearing Ming's hot-pink cape. It was perfect protection as he opened his eyes and slid his hand inside his jacket.

"Who sent you?" Jorge asked.

The man leaned over and whispered a name in Jorge's ear.

Jorge's face paled. He didn't even need to ask—he already knew the answer. Obviously, Miguel Garcia had figured out who'd betrayed him. Then he reassured himself that it didn't matter. He was here. Miguel was stranded in the States with the American Federales on his trail.

"So…when you get to hell, say hello to his brother for me," Jorge said.

The man's eyes widened in sudden understanding as the protruding bulge beneath the cape around Jorge Diaz's neck suddenly bloomed before he could get off a shot.

The bullet caught Emilio Rojas's eldest son right between the eyes. His blood splattered all over the glass partition behind him, as well as on Jorge and Ming.

Customers were screaming and running with hot-pink capes, flying and stringing wet nail polish as they went. Ming's hands were over her face and she was wailing in Chinese.

Jorge sighed. Damn. He was probably going to have to find another manicurist. Chances were Ming wouldn't let him in the front door after this. Still, there were things to be done. He grabbed Ming by the shoulder and shook her.

"Ming! Stop crying and call the police. Someone just tried to kill us and I saved our lives."

Even in her shock and fear, she got the message. By the time the Mexican police came, she was all about the man coming in threatening to kill everyone in sight and praising Mr. Diaz for saving their lives.

The police weren't stupid. They recognized Emilio Rojas's eldest son lying dead on the floor, and they knew Jorge Diaz's reputation well. But it was to their advantage not to make waves in this case. The way they figured it, the cartel was just taking care of their own business.

However, no one had taken Emilio Rojas's reaction into account. Before the sun set on the day, every member of Jorge Diaz's family was dead, including Diaz, except his mother, Amelia, who now lived in a sanatorium and hadn't known her own name for the past five years.

Retribution had been met for Miguel Garcia, but at a terrible expense to the Rojas family. And Emilio had vowed to his family and to himself that if Garcia somehow escaped the talons of the American DEA, he would not escape Rojas himself.

Miguel continued to live low-key in a Tulsa motel, completely unaware of what had happened, or that Rojas had called in the men who'd been helping him. He didn't know it yet, but he was as alone in the world as he'd ever been. It would be the first time in his life that money wouldn't buy him what he wanted.

Dave Wills was eating breakfast in an IHOP restaurant after an all-night stakeout to nab Garcia. Unfortunately, their tip was wonky. A man named Miguel Garcia had recently arrived in Amarillo flashing a big bankroll, but when Garcia finally showed up at his motel, they discovered it was the wrong man.

The DEA agents were decidedly disgusted with the

motel owner who'd called in the tip. After further questioning, he finally admitted that all Mexicans looked alike to him.

Dave had resisted the urge to punch the man out and settled for treating himself to a real, sit-down breakfast instead of sausage, egg and biscuits on the go. He was down to his last few bites of blueberry pancakes and last piece of bacon when his cell phone rang.

He glanced at the caller ID and then answered quickly. "Good morning, sir."

Gerald Mynton grunted a response. After the news he'd just received, it was all he could manage.

Dave could tell something was wrong and glanced down at his plate, guessing his appetite was about to change. "Sir, do we have a problem?"

"You might say that," Mynton said. "I've got a call in to Sonora, but she has yet to return it. I'm not sure how she's involved in what's happened, but I can guarantee I won't rest easy until I hear her voice."

Now Dave was really concerned. "Sir?"

"There was a bloodbath down in Juarez. Jorge Diaz killed Emilio Rojas's eldest son and Rojas's contingent retaliated by destroying everyone related to Diaz, including Diaz himself. The only member still living is an old woman in the last stages of Alzheimer's. I guess Rojas decided she was already as good as dead."

"How does Sonora figure in this?" Dave asked.

"Not sure, but Jorge Diaz was one of the top men in the Garcia cartel. What you don't know is that the tips we've had on Garcia's whereabouts in the States came directly from Diaz himself, and Rojas used to be old man Garcia's right-hand man. We're thinking that Diaz figured out who ratted him out and sent word to do him in."

"Talk about overkill," Dave said. "So, what do you want us to do?"

"As soon as Sonora calls, I'll let her know what's happened. I still want her to come in. We can't protect her if we don't know where she is, but I don't think she's going to change her mind. So…I'm sending out another half dozen men. They'll rendezvous with your team sometime this afternoon. Fill them in on everything you know so far and step up the search for Garcia. I wouldn't have thought it was possible, but whatever's going on with him has gotten uglier."

"Yes, sir. Will do."

Mynton disconnected just as a waitress came by Dave's table.

"More coffee?" she asked.

"Yeah, why not?" Dave muttered. "May be my last chance to get the good stuff for some time to come."

Chapter 13

Sonora woke up to a room filled with sunlight, a cup of hot coffee on the table beside the bed and Charlie curled up on her feet.

She stretched, careful not to dislodge Charlie's comfort zone, and then scooted backward until she could feel the headboard against her spine. Once she was settled, she crossed her feet, pulled the sheet up to her waist and reached for the coffee.

Sensing the possibility of a good head scratch, Charlie abandoned his spot at the foot of the bed for Sonora's lap.

"Hey, baby," she said softly. She started to pick him up, then remembered his wounds and allowed him to find his own place.

Once the cat was through moving, she took a grateful sip of coffee and laid her hand on Charlie's head. At that point, he started to purr. It sounded a little bit like an old man's snore, which made her smile. Then Adam walked into the room wearing a pair of red gym shorts and nothing else, and her smile got even wider.

"Good morning, Adam."

"Good morning to you, too, sunshine," he said softly, then frowned at his cat. "Hey, Charlie, so this is where you got off to, and here I thought you were my friend."

Adam was carrying a cup of coffee and a plate of sweet rolls. He sat down at the foot of the bed beside Sonora and then laid the plate between them.

"Help yourself," he offered, as he took a big bite of a bear claw, eyeing his cat as he chewed. "So. I let you in because I feel sorry for you, and this is how you repay me? By getting into bed with my woman?"

Sonora was grinning and couldn't stop. Not only was it charming the way Adam and Charlie communicated, but he'd referred to her as *his* woman. If someone would have asked her before she ever met Adam Two Eagles, she would have said she didn't like possessive men, but hearing those words coming out of his mouth had changed her tune. When it came to him, she liked being claimed.

She eyed the plate he'd put down, then reached for a jelly doughnut.

"Mmm, my kind of man," she said as she took a big bite.

Adam grinned. "Besides knowing how to rock your world, exactly what kind of man would that be?"

Sonora arched an eyebrow then threw back her head and laughed. Out loud. Until she gave herself the hiccups.

Hic.

"The kind of man who thinks breakfast consists of sugar," she said.

Hic.

"Take a drink of coffee," Adam suggested.

Hic.

"I didn't know coffee would cure hiccups."

Hic. Sip.

"I don't know that it will. It was just the first thing that came to my mind," he said, and took another bite of his bear claw.

Hic. Sip.

"You're a piece of work, Two Eagles," Sonora said, then began to hold her breath.

"That won't work, either," Adam said, stuffed the rest of his bear claw in his mouth, chewed, then swallowed.

He was considering a second sweet roll when he saw Charlie look toward the window. A pair of robins lit on the bird feeder outside and began to feed.

Adam saw Charlie's eyes suddenly cross and his tail twitch. He recognized the signs of an imminent attack.

"Uh...Sonora, watch out. I think Charlie—"

Charlie launched himself from her lap, which meant digging in to her legs with his back claws for better leverage.

Sonora gasped in pain. Coffee lurched from one side of the cup to the other. And since her fingers had tightened instinctively on the cup handle, the fingers on her other hand—the one holding the jelly doughnut—tightened, as well. Jelly squished out both ends of the roll. The south end of the doughnut squirted onto her breasts while the north end ran between her fingers and started down her elbow.

"Oh, Lord," she cried, and looked to Adam for help, which was a mistake.

Adam was laughing so hard he couldn't move, let alone help. So she sat there in disgust with jelly running down between her breasts as well as down the inside of her forearm while Charlie hit the window with a thud.

It was the surprised look on the cat's face as he got up from the floor that sent them both into a second wave of hysteria. Meanwhile, Charlie stalked out of the room with his tail in the air and his ears flat to his head, indicating his total disgust with a pair of tricky birds and two humans.

"Oh, my God...that was funny," Sonora said as she tried

to catch her breath. "Did you see Charlie's face when the birds flew away? It was such a…so close and yet so far away…look."

Adam's laughter had come and gone far quicker than hers. The moment he'd seen that jelly begin to slide past her breasts, he'd been unable to think of anything else but tasting it. He took the doughnut from her hand, then moved it along with the plate of sweet rolls to the floor, took the coffee cup out of her hands and set it aside, then grabbed her by the ankles and pulled until she was flat on her back.

"Adam, I'm going to get jelly all over the—"

He licked the jelly from her arm, then from between her fingers with slow, deep strokes until her toes curled.

"Uh, um…" Her body went weak. "Have mercy," she whispered.

Now he was on his hands and knees above her. Sonora saw his head dip, felt his hair brushing against her skin as his tongue licked the jelly trail between her breasts. When he started up her body to the point of impact, her eyes rolled back in her head.

"Oh. My. God."

It was her last conscious thought.

After a shower and then dressing in yesterday's clothes, which were now clean and dry, Sonora had to face the fact that her time with Adam was coming to an end. She didn't know what to think about how quickly he'd gotten under her skin. She was way more than in lust and it made her nervous.

She'd followed Adam outside and was watching him load up his pickup truck with an assortment of tools. The yard was covered with leaves and small bits of tree limbs. There was a corner of the roof off the barn and a tree had fallen across a fence. The blessing of it all was that the house had weathered it well.

"Don't you want me to help clean all this up?" she asked as she followed him into a shed.

"No, honey. I'll tend to this after I get back." Then he picked up a chain saw and a plastic fuel can with fuel for the saw and carried them out.

"Why do you need this chain saw?" she asked as he set it in the truck bed up against the cab.

"In case there are still some trees blocking roads."

"Oh."

"I called Franklin while you were in the shower," Adam said. "Told him we'd be there before noon."

"Is he all right?" Sonora asked.

Adam hesitated, then nodded. "Yes, although his voice sounded weak. He may be having a bad day."

Sonora looked away. It still broke her heart to think that her time with her father was going to be so short. They were being cheated and there was nothing either one could do about it.

"So, are you ready to go?" she asked.

Adam glanced up. Sonora's eyes were shimmering with tears. That was something he couldn't bear.

"Come here, honey," he said softly, and opened his arms. She walked into them willingly and selfishly let herself be held.

"I'm so sorry that your reunion with your father has to be colored with his health crisis."

"Me, too," she said, then lifted her head and took the kiss that he offered, savoring the smell of soap on his skin.

Finally, it was Sonora who pulled back.

"We'd better go. I've left Dad alone too long as it is."

"He's used to coping alone. He's been alone all his life," Adam said.

"As have I," she said.

"Yes, but you're not anymore. Remember that," Adam said.

"Only I don't know how long I'll have him, Adam. That's what makes me sad."

Adam combed his fingers through her hair, then cupped the backside of her hips and pulled her close against him. "I'm still here," he said. "And I'm not going anywhere."

Sonora looked at him then, accepting his quiet reminder as truth. "I'm just beginning to realize what that means," she said, and then looked away. "So, we'd better get going, okay?"

Adam watched her climb into the truck and then followed her into the cab. Once she'd settled, he patted her on the leg.

"It's going to be all right."

Then he started the engine.

Sonora watched as he backed up and then started down the driveway to the main road.

"Adam?"

"Yeah?"

"When you said that it was going to be all right..."

"Yeah?"

"Well, did you know that because it's something you... uh...'know,' or did you say that because it was a kind thing to say?"

He was surprised by her perception and had to think about it for a bit.

"You know what, honey?"

"What?" Sonora asked.

"I'm not really sure."

She sighed, then nodded. "Yeah. Me, either," she said, then added, "But I want it to be true. I so want it to be true."

The wren Franklin had been freeing from the chunk of wood had flown out last night and landed on a nest with two tiny eggs in it.

Franklin was more than pleased with the finished prod-

uct and had carried it around the house all morning, studying it for flaws. So far, he'd found none.

Finally, he'd set it on the table in front of him while
he'd eaten breakfast, admiring the cocky tilt to the little
bird's head.

"Little Mother," he said softly, and rubbed the curve
of her tiny head, feeling the grooves where he'd given her
feathers, and imagined he could almost feel a heartbeat.
"That's what I'm going to call you. Little Mother."

Even though he knew it couldn't happen, he thought he
heard the beginnings of a pleased chirp.

He ate his breakfast without tasting it, knowing it was
important so that he could keep up his strength, and was
glad for the diversion when he heard the sound of a vehicle
coming down the drive.

He got up quickly and carried his dirty dishes to the
sink, then started toward the front door. Before he could
get there, the door opened and Sonora and Adam entered.
His heart quickened at the sight of her face. If he could live
one hundred years, it would still not be long enough to take
her presence for granted.

He shook Adam's hand and hugged his daughter.

"So glad you're both all right. That storm was a nasty
one. I'm so glad no one got hurt."

"Oh, Charlie did, but he survived," Sonora said.

Franklin frowned. "Who's Charlie?"

Adam's eyes were twinkling, although he managed not
to grin. "My cat," he said.

Franklin nodded. "Oh, yes. The big one with gray-and-
black stripes."

"That's the one," Adam said.

"But he's all right?" Franklin asked.

"He had some cuts on his side and he was so cold and
wet, but Adam doctored him and he was obviously well
enough to attack a window this morning, trying to catch

two birds at the feeder outside," Sonora said, and then grinned, remembering the sight.

Franklin chuckled, and resisted the urge to hug Sonora again. He didn't want to put her off by smothering her with attention, but she filled his heart with such joy.

As they were talking, Sonora heard the sound of her cell phone ringing down the hall.

"Oh, yes," Franklin said. "Your phone. It's been ringing off and on since last night."

Sonora frowned. That didn't sound good.

"I'll check the messages," she said. "Be right back."

"Go ahead," Adam said. "I'll still be here. I want to talk to Franklin a bit."

Sonora nodded, then flew down the hall toward her room.

Once she was gone, Adam straightened his shoulders and looked Franklin in the face.

"I'm falling in love with her," he said quietly.

Franklin was not unhappy to hear it.

"What about her feelings?" Franklin asked.

Adam shrugged. "I can't tell for sure. She holds everything back."

Franklin sat down on the sofa. Adam followed.

"She's been so hurt by life," Franklin said.

Adam hesitated, then realized that Franklin needed to know what he'd seen in his vision.

"She's in danger," Adam said softly.

Franklin stilled. "And you know this because?"

"I saw it," Adam said.

Franklin's shoulders slumped. He didn't have Adam's gifts, but he knew enough to trust them.

"Does she know?" Franklin asked.

"No, I didn't tell her about the vision, but it's nothing she doesn't already know. Remember...she's the one who told us when her friend was murdered."

"What can we do?" Franklin asked.

Adam thought of the vision again, and of the helplessness he'd felt at not being able to help her.

"I don't think there's anything we can do, except trust Sonora to be able to take care of herself. There is a great power within her. More than even she knows about herself."

Franklin nodded. "Then so be it," he said.

Unaware that she'd become the topic of their conversation, Sonora burst into her room and grabbed her cell phone from the charger just as it rang again.

She answered, a little breathless and a little nervous. "Hello."

Gerald Mynton stopped pacing and dropped into his chair with a huge sigh of relief. "Thank God," he muttered. "Where the hell have you been? I told you to stay in touch."

"Good to hear from you, too," Sonora said. "As for where I've been…in a cellar dodging tornadoes, then at a friend's house until daylight."

"Good Lord!" Mynton said. "Real tornadoes…as in on the ground and sucking up everything in its path?"

"As in," Sonora said, and then quickly changed the subject. "What's happened?"

"A big mess down in Juarez. Don't know how Garcia figures into it, and not sure how it impacts you, but I'm guessing it does."

She dropped down onto the side of the bed and leaned forward with her head in her hand. "Talk to me," she said.

"You know who Emilio Rojas is?"

She thought a minute, then remembered the background info on the Garcia clan. "Wasn't he the old man Garcia's right-hand man?"

"That's the one," Mynton said.

"So, what does he have to do with all of this?"

"Okay, here's what we know so far. Jorge Diaz is the

man who leaked info to the DEA regarding Garcia's whereabouts. We're guessing that he wanted Garcia out of the way to take over the cartel's business. With Juanito dead and Enrique already in jail awaiting trial, Miguel was the only one left in his way."

"But how did Rojas and Diaz connect?"

"We're guessing that Miguel called in a marker, talked Rojas into doing a little payback for him and it all backfired. Diaz killed Rojas's eldest son. Rojas retaliated by decimating the entire Diaz family, except for an old woman with Alzheimer's disease."

"Oh, Lord," Sonora said. "What a mess."

"That's an understatement, Jordan."

"So, how does this affect me?"

"Not sure, but there is the possibility that when Garcia finds out what's happened, he's going to freak and blame you for the entire incident, since Juanito's death was what started this whole thing."

"Crap."

Mynton sighed. "And then some. Please. Reconsider. Come back to Phoenix where we can protect you."

Sonora thought of all that had happened to her since she'd begun this journey: the visions she'd had, the dreams of her childhood, the tattoo on her back and Adam Two Eagles's power to heal. She didn't know what was going to happen, but she knew that whatever came, she would be safer within the boundaries of this world.

"No. I'm not leaving. I'm safe here."

"But for how long?" Mynton argued.

"Until I'm not, I guess. And when that happens, I'll deal with it, just like I've dealt with everything else. I'm not helpless, sir. The government trained me well."

Mynton leaned back in his chair and closed his eyes. "I never said you were helpless, Sonora. You're a good agent. I just don't want to lose you, that's all."

"Agents are a dime a dozen, sir, but there's only one of me."

Mynton flinched. She'd put him in his place and rightly so.

"I didn't mean that you were valuable only as an agent, and I'm sorry it came out like that."

"I have a father, sir. I have never been able to say that before. He's not well and I'm not leaving him. With him, I have found where I came from, and to whom I belong. I'm not Latino, I'm Native American. I never knew that before. Can you understand what that means to me?"

"Coming from a huge Irish family, I can only imagine what it must have been like to grow up like you did. I'm happy for you, Sonora, but at the same time, you need to remember the caliber of the man who's looking for you. He's scum. Be careful...and stay in touch."

"Yes, I will, and thank you for the update."

"I don't suppose you'd be willing to meet with Dave Wills?"

She frowned. "We have nothing to talk about. Just tell him to get Garcia off my tail. In a way, it's his fault this whole mess even happened."

"Yes. I'm well aware of his foul-up in Mexico. However, what's done is done. I'll pass on your message."

"Thank you," Sonora said, and disconnected.

She sat for a few moments, absorbing the ramifications of what she'd just learned. While it was a terrible disaster for those two families, she couldn't see how it changed her situation. Garcia was still out there, looking for her. She needed to get her mind back on that and quit worrying about her new feelings for Adam. Still, as she got up to leave the room, she knew that was going to be easier said than done.

It wasn't until she reached the end of the hall that she realized her dad and Adam had moved into the kitchen.

Just hearing the deep rumble of Adam's voice put a knot in her stomach. The man was magic, all right, especially in bed. She was out-of-her-mind crazy about him and unsure what to do about it.

She was still smiling as she started into the kitchen, but the smile quickly ended when she overheard the end of their conversation.

"Still no word on any donors?" Adam asked.

Franklin shook his head. "No, and they warned me early on that there probably wouldn't be. It's difficult to find a match. For whatever reasons, there are not a lot of Native Americans in the donor system and some of the markers needed for a match are confined to that specific ethnicity."

Sonora had stopped in the doorway, and now grabbed on to the wall for support. She was stunned and so mad she was shaking.

"What the hell are you two talking about?" she asked.

Both men wore equally guilty expressions as they looked up.

Adam frowned. She was angry and he couldn't blame her, but it hadn't been his story to tell.

Franklin held out his hands. "Come here, daughter. Sit with us a bit."

"I'm not sitting anywhere until you start talking. Did I hear you correctly? Are you waiting for some kind of organ donation?"

"Not an organ, exactly," Franklin said.

"Then what?"

"Bone marrow."

She reeled as if she'd been slapped. "And why wasn't I told of this? I'm your daughter. What if I'm a match?"

"This is between you two," Adam said.

For once, Sonora agreed and fixed Franklin with an angry glare. "I'm waiting," she said.

"Look. I didn't even know you existed. It was just a dream and a gut feeling that even led me to believe your mother had been pregnant with my child when she left. I was so stunned when you showed up that it never even entered my mind. Then later, when I did think of it, it didn't matter."

"Didn't matter? Didn't matter? What? You don't think it's important that I have my father around?"

Franklin sighed, then sat down. "I'm sorry. I didn't think of it like that."

Sonora's shoulders slumped. Her anger dissipated as quickly as it had come. She crossed the room and then put her arms around his neck and hugged him.

"Dad...Daddy...for God's sake. Let me be tested. Maybe this is why all of this is happening, you know? You needed me as much as I've needed you."

Franklin looked up at Adam. "If I called my doctor, could you get her to Tulsa to the cancer center to be tested?"

"Of course," Adam said.

Sonora unwound herself from Franklin's neck and stepped back. "Then it's settled?" she asked.

"Yes. It's settled," Franklin said.

"Good."

Adam could tell she was satisfied with the end result of the conversation, but he could tell there was still something wrong. Then he remembered the phone calls.

"Sonora."

"Yes?"

"What's happened? Is there news about the man who killed your friend?"

She looked pale, but her voice never wavered. "In a roundabout fashion, I guess there is."

"So?" Franklin asked, urging her to tell.

"It's sort of complicated, but the short version of what's happened is that two Mexican families that sort of belong to the Garcia cartel went to war. A man named Rojas was killed by another named Diaz. The old man of the Rojas family retaliated by destroying every single member of the Diaz family, including women and children."

"Dear Lord," Franklin said, and stared at Sonora in disbelief. That she could talk about this so dispassionately told him how hardened she'd become by that world.

"How does this affect you?" Adam asked.

She shrugged. "Maybe it does. Maybe it doesn't."

"What did your boss say?" he asked.

She looked up then, meeting his gaze straight on. "That everything began to come undone for Miguel Garcia when I killed his brother Juanito, and that if he blames me for that, then he might blame me for the implosion that's occurring within the cartel now."

"Which means you're in more danger than ever?" Franklin asked.

"Don't worry, Dad," Sonora said. "I'm well trained in protecting myself. I'll make sure this ugly part of my world does not infringe upon you."

"That's not what I'm worrying about," Franklin said.

"Me, either," Adam added.

"I can take care of myself," she said, and then turned around and walked out of the room.

Adam saw the stiff set to her shoulders and the quick, angry motion in her stride, then remembered the tattoo on her spine and knew she was right. She had even more power than she knew.

Chapter 14

The drive to Tulsa went faster than Sonora would have believed. When Adam told her that it was at least a two-and-a-half-hour drive, she'd resigned herself to a long trip. But she hadn't counted on her growing connection to Adam. After the night of the storm and the passion of their lovemaking, she had been a little embarrassed about being alone with him again. However, instead of the stilted conversation she'd expected, she'd been at ease from the first. Adam even had her laughing about their passionate lovemaking by telling her that from now on, whenever he knew she was coming over, he was planning on blowing some fuses. But it was when he offered to have Charlie declawed if she would let him lick more jelly off her breasts that she lost it.

Adam knew Sonora was a little nervous about what being a bone-marrow donor entailed, so he'd done his best to keep her mind off the process, and at his own expense.

He grinned when she began to laugh, then returned his attention to the highway and the traffic.

She didn't know that he lived for the times he could make her happy.

He didn't know how he was going to live when the day came that she would leave.

After another hour of driving and talking, they began to approach the city.

"Is this Tulsa?" Sonora asked.

"No, it's Glenpool, but we're not far away."

"Okay," Sonora said, and then pulled at the hem of her shirt and flicked a bit of lint off her jeans.

"Are you afraid?" Adam asked.

"Not like you mean," she said. "I am afraid I won't be a match."

Adam sighed. There wasn't anything he could say to make her feel better about any of this. There was nothing to do but wait and see.

Miguel Garcia was sick of staying holed up in the Tulsa motel. He'd been trying to call the four men who'd been helping him search for the better part of thirty-six hours, but with no luck. He couldn't figure out what was going on and why they didn't answer. His only option was to call Rojas and see what the hell was going on. He knew Rojas was unhappy with what was happening, but it couldn't be helped. It was his duty as the eldest son to avenge his brother's death any way he could.

As he started toward the table to get his cell phone, someone knocked on his door.

"Maid service!" a woman called.

"Dios," he muttered. *"Una momento."*

He grabbed his leather vest and put it on over the sleeveless T-shirt he was wearing, buckled the Western-style belt around his waist, rubbed the dust off the toes of his boots, grabbed his phone and his hat and stepped out of the room.

The maid slipped in behind him carrying a handful of clean linens and began stripping the bed as he got into his car. As soon as he'd turned on the engine and started the air conditioner to cool off the car, he reached for his phone. Time to make that call.

He punched in the numbers by memory, then counted the rings. It wasn't until it had rung the sixth time with no answer that he began to be concerned. There was always someone at home at the Rojas estate. Maids, houseboys or any number of Emilio's large family were always coming or going. The house was never empty.

He disconnected, then tried again, thinking he might have hit a wrong number. Again, it began to ring, and again, the fifth, then sixth, then seventh ring came and went. Miguel was about to hang up when he heard someone pick up.

"*¡Hola! ¡Hola!* Hello? Hello?" Miguel said.

Emilio Rojas took a slow breath. "Yes. I am here," he said.

Miguel's concerns faded. "I've been calling and calling. Where the hell is everybody?"

"We've been to a funeral," Emilio said.

Miguel frowned. "Oh. Sorry. Anyone I know?"

"My eldest son, Emilio Jr."

Miguel grunted as if he'd been punched. "What happened? Was it an accident?"

"No. It was murder."

"Murder? Who did it? I will make them pay!"

Rage rose so fast and so high in Emilio's chest that he thought he would explode.

"Who did it? Who did it? I did it, that's who. I sent him to run your little…errand…and this was the result."

Rojas had never spoken to Miguel in this tone of voice—ever.

"I didn't think… I mean, I never intended for—"

"It is of no importance anymore," Emilio said softly. "They are dead. All of them."

Miguel stuttered, then choked.

"They?"

"The Diaz family. Who else?" Emilio said.

Miguel had visions of wives, mothers, children, brothers and sons. There had been a lot of them—at least twenty-five or thirty, and Rojas had—

Madre de Dios.

"I'm sorry," Miguel said. "I didn't know—"

"You are on your own," Emilio said. "I have called in my men. They are no longer doing your dirty work for you. Do not call me again. Ever. Do not come back to Juarez. Do not even come back to Mexico. If you do, I will know it, and I will kill you, myself."

The line went dead in Miguel's ear.

Time passed, but Miguel couldn't have attested to the fact. He still had the phone to his ear when someone wheeled into the parking space beside him and gunned the engine. As it revved, it backfired.

Miguel flinched and ducked. The phone went flying.

It was a few moments before he realized he was still breathing and that he hadn't been shot at. Just the victim of a car in need of new plugs and points.

He got up from the seat, muscles trembling and gasping for breath. Everything he knew was gone. It no longer mattered if Jorge Diaz was dead or not. With Emilio Rojas for an enemy, his days were numbered.

He rubbed the palms of his hands on top of his head, feeling the faint stubble of new growth, and realized he needed a shave. His fingers were trembling as he swiped them across his face. Then he doubled up his fists and began pounding the steering wheel. He didn't know he was crying until he felt the tears on his face, and even then couldn't think past the rage.

Everything was fine until the DEA had messed in his business. Sonora Jordan had been the agent who killed Juanito. She represented everything he hated, and if it was the last thing he did, he was going to wrap his hands around her neck and watch the life go out of her eyes.

Sonora was white-lipped and shaking when she came out of the doctor's office, but it wasn't entirely from pain. The stress of knowing she was her father's only chance to live was taking its toll. When she saw Adam stand up and start toward her, her eyes welled with tears. She hated this weak-kneed, sissy side of herself—hadn't even known it existed until she'd met Adam Two Eagles.

"Are you all right?" Adam asked.

"I'm just peachy," she said, and ducked her head to hide her tears.

"I already saw them, so get over it," Adam said as he handed her his handkerchief.

"God. Can't even shed a few tears without you getting all bossy about it."

Adam sighed. It figured she'd rather make an ass of herself than let someone see her cry. Damned if that didn't endear her to him even more.

"It's not about being bossy, Sonora. It's because I care about you and you know it."

She rolled her eyes, thumped him on the arm in frustration and then hugged him.

"You cheated," she muttered, wincing as she walked.

He smiled gently as he helped her out the door.

"How did I cheat?" he asked.

"You're too nice. It's impossible to be mad at nice."

He grinned. "Well, that's something I've never been

accused of before, and if it will make you feel any better, there's a whole company of army rangers who would disagree with you."

"So, tough guy, take me home."

Adam frowned as he watched her walk. Her normal stride was gone and she was moving gingerly, as if there was a pain in her back.

"Are you in much pain?"

"It wasn't great," she muttered, remembering the punch of bone marrow they'd taken from her right hip.

"Did they give you some pain medicine?"

"Yeah. Shot me full of the stuff and gave me some to take home."

"Then we should go before it wears off," Adam said. "You can eat as I drive, then sleep if you wish."

Miguel had made up his mind. He was going to go back to Phoenix and wait for Sonora Jordan to surface. She couldn't stay on the run forever. The way he figured it, when she walked in her front door, she'd get a welcome she never expected and he'd get the justice he deserved. Still, to be on the safe side, he was going back in a different car.

He'd been at the used car lot for almost an hour, waiting for the salesman to get the okay from his boss on the money Miguel wanted for his black Jeep.

The sun was hot, which matched his mood. It was long past noon and he wanted food and something cold to drink. Just as he was about to go into the office to look for the salesman, he saw him coming out. He was smiling, which bode well for Miguel. Miguel was guessing that he was about to get the price he'd wanted, which meant he would have more than enough money to buy the other car he intended to use for the trip back to Phoenix. Since his money sources had been cut off, he didn't have money to waste.

As he was standing in the lot, there was a sudden squeal

of tires and several horns began to honk. Someone cursed and another cursed back.

Miguel turned to look.

The driver of a car and the driver of a delivery truck had just had a fender bender. Traffic was stalling in both directions. He was thanking his lucky stars that he wasn't out on the street in the middle of the mess when he noticed a dark-colored pickup truck about three vehicles back.

He saw the long-haired, dark-skinned man behind the wheel and marked him as Native American, but it was the woman sitting in the seat beside him that made his heart skip a beat. He stared in disbelief.

It couldn't be.

He scrambled in his wallet for the photo of Sonora Jordan that he'd been carrying, then compared it to the woman in the truck. It was her! It had to be—either that or a double.

He stuffed the picture back in his wallet and then started to run.

"Hey! Hey, mister!" the salesman yelled. "What about your money?"

Miguel hesitated, then turned around.

"I'll be right back," he shouted, and then turned back toward the street.

The truck was still there, but a couple of police cars had arrived and traffic was beginning to move. He cleared the curb in a leap, and without care for the traffic, started running toward the truck.

"Do you think anyone was hurt?" Sonora asked as she scooted to the edge of the seat to get a better look at the wreck.

"I think they're yelling too loud to be very hurt," Adam said.

"Yeah, you're right, and for that I am glad. I hate this kind of stuff. Never would have made a good patrol cop."

"I disagree," Adam said. "I think you would be great at anything you set your mind to doing."

Joy settled in Sonora's heart. She could get spoiled with this positive affirmation Franklin and Adam seemed bent on giving her.

She saw movement from the corner of her eye as she leaned back in the seat and turned to look. Some bald-headed cowboy had come running out of a used-car lot and was headed toward the accident.

"Look at that nut," Sonora said. "He isn't paying any attention to the traffic."

No sooner had she said it than someone on a motorcycle, thinking he could bypass the traffic jam by winding through the stalled cars, came flying out from between two vehicles and hit the man in midstride.

"Oh, no!" Sonora gasped, and flinched as the man flew up into the air and then came down on his back. It was instinct that had her reaching for the door handle when Adam grabbed her arm.

"No, honey. Police are already on the scene, as are a couple of ambulances. If you get involved, then you'll have to identify yourself, and that might not be such a good idea."

She sighed, then let go of the door.

"You're right. I just wasn't thinking."

At that point, traffic started to move. Sonora stared out the window at the injured man and winced. She could see blood coming out of his nose and ears, which was never a good sign. Head injuries were tricky. She hoped that he would be all right.

Lunch had come and gone a few days later and Franklin was sitting in his favorite chair out on the back porch, watching a pair of bluebirds taking turns feeding the babies in their nest. In the middle of his meditation, he heard the phone ring. Frowning, he started to get up, then remembered Sonora was inside and sat back down.

The male bluebird seemed to be on watch duty as his mate darted from the nest up in the branches to the ground below, then back up again. He could just see the edge of the nest and the open beaks of her three babies, begging for whatever it was she brought back. It pleased him to see these tiny moments with Mother Earth and her children, and wouldn't let himself dwell on the fact that one day he would be gone and life would go on without him.

Sonora hadn't spoken one word about the bone-marrow testing since her return from Tulsa, and he hadn't asked her. He knew she was scared. He also knew that she feared she would fail him. He didn't have the words to comfort her, because the truth was, for the first time in months, he had hope, and it was because of her. In the beginning, even though he didn't want to die, he'd come to terms with it. But now that he knew he had a daughter, his acceptance of death had done a one-eighty change. Truth was, he didn't want to leave her or this earth.

The screen door opened behind him. He heard the hinges squeak, then the loud pop as it slammed shut. He turned around. Sonora was coming toward him, and she was crying.

His stomach rolled. Something terrible must have happened.

In a panic, he stood up and started toward her, then she started to laugh through her tears.

"Dad...I'm a match! Your doctor wants you in the hospital tomorrow before noon. Says they have to prepare you for the transplant...whatever that means."

Franklin was taken aback, both by the news and the suddenness. He'd been going to take Sonora and Adam to the powwow. Obviously, that was going to have to wait.

He wanted to laugh, to dance, to clap his hands and run in circles. Instead, he took her by the shoulders.

"It will not be pleasant. Are you sure you want to do this?"

"Absolutely positive," she said.

It was then that he laughed. "This is, indeed, the most wonderful news."

Sonora wrapped her arms around his waist. "It's going to work. I can feel it in my bones."

Franklin silently agreed. Considering the power that was within his daughter, he had no doubt that her healthy blood cells would not only heal him, but make him as good as new.

"Little woman of the snake," Franklin whispered.

Sonora heard and shivered. She hadn't considered the significance of her snake and the Kiowa beliefs in power and healing, but it was obvious Franklin did. She didn't care what they believed as long as her father got well.

"Do you mind if I leave for a bit? I want to tell Adam, but not over the phone."

"Of course, but you're welcome to take my car."

"Thanks, but I have a need to feel the wind in my hair."

Franklin eyed the dark wings of hair framing her face and recognized the restlessness of her spirit.

"Ride safely," he said.

She nodded absently, then looked up at Franklin. "Do you think he'll come with us tomorrow?"

"I think wild horses couldn't keep him away," Franklin said.

Adam had just returned home after a visit to an elderly couple from the tribe. Daisy, the wife, had a bad case of poison ivy from gathering mushrooms. While it was rare that Native American people contracted poison ivy, it did happen. The entire time he was treating her, she kept blam-

ing her grandmother's predilection for sleeping with white
men as the reason she had succumbed to the rash.

In her own words, "Indians don't get poison ivy. It's the
taint of white man's blood that weakens my body."

Adam knew she was miserable, and that her opinion of
white people was normally just fine. But it was the itching
and swelling all over her face and arms that had her in such
a bad mood. He'd left her with salve and kind words, and
a suggestion to her husband to do the cooking for a while
so Daisy wouldn't be exposed to the heat.

He'd been in the house long enough to put up his bag of
salves when he heard the familiar sound of a motorcycle
coming down the drive. He spun toward the sound.

Sonora!

He went out to the porch. The sound was getting louder.
Within moments he saw her flying toward him, barely out-
running the cloud of red dust behind her.

Sonora's heart jumped when she came around the bend
in the road and saw Adam waiting for her out on the porch.
She couldn't wait to tell him—to see the joy in his eyes.
She rode into the yard and then stopped abruptly, turning
the bike in a quick half circle before dropping the kickstand and killing the engine. She hung her helmet on the
handlebars then dismounted quickly, unaware of Adam's
silent admiration.

"What a nice surprise!" Adam said as he met her at the
steps.

"You have no idea," Sonora said. "I have news. Good
news. I'm a perfect match to be Dad's donor."

Adam grinned and picked her up in his arms and gave
her a ferocious hug.

Sonora laughed when he turned them both in a circle,
then did a little two-step.

"That's phenomenal!" he cried. "Come in. Come in. Tell me what the doctor said."

She followed him inside, then into the kitchen. She began to talk as he poured them both cold drinks. "I have to have Dad there in the morning before noon. The doctor said there are some things that must be done before surgery can occur. Something about isolation and irradiating him. They have to kill his bad cells and his good cells, too, before replacing them with some of mine, or something like that. I was just so excited at the news that only parts of it soaked in."

Adam handed her a glass of cold Pepsi, then sat down at the table across from her.

"Yes, I'm familiar with it. All of that must be done before they put your healthy bone marrow into his body."

"Yes...that's it," Sonora said.

"Would you let me drive the both of you back to Tulsa?"

Sonora smiled. "I was hoping you'd say that."

Adam reached across the table and took her hand. "We're in this together, okay?"

The smile on her face disappeared as she nodded and looked away.

"Did I say something wrong?" Adam asked.

She hesitated, then made herself look up. He was always honest with her. She could do no less.

"No. Quite the opposite."

He frowned. "I don't understand."

"I've never been part of a 'we'. It's always been a 'me', and I'm not complaining. It just touches me, that's all."

Adam's heart tugged. Over and over, he was struck by the loneliness that had been her life until now. Even though he was moved, knowing that she valued his presence in her life, he wanted her happy, not constantly reminded of her past.

"So...you like being touched, do you?" He pulled on her

fingers, spreading them wide, then threading his fingers through hers. "I'd be happy to oblige with more touching— in private."

Sonora grinned. "Subtlety is not one of your strong suits, is it?"

Adam pretended dismay. "Ah, lady...you wound me by doubting my intentions."

"Your intentions weren't to get me in bed?"

"Well...yes...but you would have enjoyed it, too."

This time when she laughed out loud, he grinned.

Chapter 15

Franklin's pulse was rapid. He knew it. The nurse knew it and gave him a studied look, as if trying to judge the reason.

"When did you take your last dose of medicine, Mr. Blue Cat?"

"This morning, as directed."

She nodded and made a note.

"Once we start the irradiating process, you will be in isolation, and will continue to be isolated after the transplant until you are released."

"Yes, I am aware of the restrictions," Franklin said. "However, the possibility of being cured far outweighs the aggravation."

She smiled. "Yes, sir. You are so right."

"May I see my daughter now?"

"Yes, of course. I'll send her in."

Franklin leaned back in the bed, grateful for a few moments of respite. The trip had been wearing, and the hustle and fuss of getting admitted, then changing out of his clothes and into hospital clothes, as well as all the lab work that occurred upon admission, had tired him.

He hadn't expected to be reluctant to leave home, but once the time had come, he realized there was a chance he might never come back. Surgery was a chancy thing at best, and Franklin was not at his best. He had accepted the possibility of not waking up once the transplant began, but still had pangs of sadness as he locked the door to his home and then left. However, once they'd begun the journey, his attitude had changed to one of hope. Now all he had to do was maintain positive thinking and trust the process.

His eyes were closed and his breathing was steady when he felt a touch on his hand. He looked up, then he smiled.

"Hello, daughter."

Sonora leaned over the bed and hugged, then kissed her father.

"I don't want you to stay alone at the house," he said.

"Of course I will. There's nothing—"

His fingers curled around her wrist.

"Please. Adam already suggested it and I completely agree. Your situation is not a normal one and you know it. How can I rest and heal knowing your life might be in danger? Besides, within a few days the surgery will happen and you do not need to try to heal from your part of it all alone."

Sonora hadn't thought this far ahead, but obviously Franklin and Adam had.

"All right, Dad. I promise."

"Good," he said, and when she would have pulled away, he still held her. "There's something else you need to know. I have changed my will. You are my sole heir. Even if I don't survive this illness, you still belong to the tribe and to our land."

Sonora's eyes teared. "I don't want to talk about—"

"I don't either, but one must face the inevitability of mortality. No one lives forever."

Sonora pulled up a chair and sat down, then leaned forward and laid her head on the bed near where Franklin lay. He reached for her, laying his hand on her head. They stayed that way until finally a nurse returned. After that, the visits were over.

"I'll see you in surgery," Franklin said.

"Count on it," Sonora said, and gave him a big thumbs up and a smile as she left.

She made it all the way down the hall to the waiting room, but when she saw Adam's face, she began to cry. He went to her, comforting her as best he could, but there was little he could do. Right now, everything was out of their hands.

Just twelve doors down the hall was Miguel Garcia. He'd been in a coma in Intensive Care ever since he'd been brought to St. Francis. His head injury had been severe, resulting in a considerable amount of swelling on his brain. For a few days it had been touch and go, but somewhere around midnight last night, he had started to turn a corner. He'd quit struggling for breath and had shown signs of increased brain activity. Garcia woke up slowly, uncertain of where he was or how he'd gotten there. The nurse who was checking his vitals noticed that he was coming around and quickly rang for the doctor.

Miguel groaned.

The nurse moved to his side. "Mr. Trujillio, don't move, okay?"

He groaned again. Who the hell was Trujillio?

"You're in a hospital. You were hit by a man on a motorcycle. Do you remember?"

Images came and went so fast he couldn't assimilate. He was in an English-speaking hospital, which meant he must be in the States, but he couldn't remember why or how he got here. He wanted to tell the nurse to call his brothers, but the words wouldn't come.

Moments later, a doctor strode into the room, but it was too late for questions. Miguel was out again.

Adam stopped by Franklin Blue Cat's home long enough for Sonora to pack her belongings. She didn't have much and it didn't take her long, but as she was going through the house to make sure everything was turned off and locked up, she saw the carving of her kitten and put it inside her bag.

"I think I have everything," Sonora said as she walked back into the living room where Adam waited. He'd already loaded her Harley into the back of his truck, and there was nothing to do now but leave.

"If not, you're welcome to anything that's mine," he said.

Sonora nodded as she started toward the door.

Suddenly, the room tilted and disappeared. The strap on her bag slid off her shoulder and hit the floor, but she didn't hear it, or Adam's sudden call of concern.

She was alone and in the dark and she didn't know what was wrong with her, but knew she was either sick or injured. She was weak and frightened, and at a level she'd never known. The air was filled with the sound of gourd rattles, from behind her, in front of her, on both sides of her, and there were voices. She'd never heard the voices before. They were speaking in a language she'd never heard, and yet somehow, she knew what was being said.

This was a warning of danger. Not imminent, but danger still the same.

Then just as quickly as it had come, it was gone. When she would have staggered backward, Adam caught her. The moment she felt his arms around her, she went weak.

"Sonora…what the hell just happened to you? Are you ill?"

"Just like before," she muttered, and covered her face with her hands.

Adam grabbed her hands and pulled them away. "Look at me!" he said.

She moaned.

"Sonora! Talk to me, damn it! What do you mean, just like before?"

She shuddered as she made herself focus. "It was some kind of…hallucination. I've been having them since the day the Garcia arrests went bust."

"It's not a hallucination…it's a vision. Tell me what you saw."

"Lord…I'm not sure what I saw and what's part of my imagination."

"Just talk to me," Adam said.

"Everything was dark. I was weak, either from an injury or illness, I couldn't tell, but I wasn't myself. I didn't see anything, but I knew I wasn't alone. Then the rattles started. The sound was all around me, and out of that, I heard voices, only they weren't speaking in English. It was a language I didn't understand, but I knew what they were telling me."

Despite the fact that Adam completely believed in what she was saying, it was unsettling to know what she was going through.

"You said they. There was more than one voice?"

She frowned. "I didn't realize it until you just pointed it out, but, yes, there was more than one voice, only they were telling me the same thing."

"The Old Ones," Adam muttered, more to himself than to her. "You said you knew what they were saying?"

"Sort of. I can't explain it, but somehow I did."

"What was it, honey? What were they telling you?"

"That my life is in danger—not imminent, but it's coming and I must be prepared."

Adam grabbed the bag that she dropped and then took her by the hand. "Come on. We're leaving now."

"What's the hurry?" she said. "I told you that the danger wasn't imminent...or at least I don't think so."

"I want to get you settled and then put you in protection."

"I'm not going to be locked up, so don't even go there," she said.

"I'm not talking about walls you can see."

In the back of her mind, she heard one last, distant rattle, as if reminding her to heed. She shivered.

"What kind of protection are you talking about, then, some spell like the one you say brought me here?"

"I'm not talking about anything. Just get in the truck," he said shortly.

She did.

Miguel Garcia had been suffering from a fever for the past two days. His sleep had been restless and broken, and when he did sleep, his dreams were crazy and disjointed. But the evening Franklin Blue Cat had been admitted to the hospital to begin the process that might give him a new chance at life, Garcia woke from his sleep with a cry of dismay. The fever had broken, and so had his heart. He'd dreamed his brother Juanito was dead, and when he woke, remembered that it wasn't a dream.

On the heels of that revelation, he also remembered why he was in the States.

Sonora Jordan.

He'd seen her.

She'd been right within his reach, and then the accident had happened. Once again, bad things had come to him because of her. Without thinking of the consequences, he sat up and started to swing his legs off the bed. It was fortunate for Miguel that the nurses always kept the guardrails up, because the moment his head came off the pillow and he tried to sit up, he had no sense of balance.

His upper body lolled sideways, then slid at an angle off the side of the bed. Pain lanced through his shoulders and up the back of his head. He was trying to grab hold of the guardrail when the door to his room flew open. Two nurses grabbed him just before he fell over the side of the bed.

"Get his arms!" one of the nurses shouted as she rang for more help.

Before Miguel knew what was happening, he was flat on his back in the bed with his arms strapped down.

"No! No!" he kept screaming. "You don't understand! I have to get up. I have to find her!"

He was still shouting when a nurse rushed in and shot a syringe full of sedative into his IV. He felt the rush of unconsciousness, even while he was still screaming.

Sonora's stay with Adam was strained. She kept jumping at shadows and was afraid to go to sleep at night. Adam had lights on all over the house for reassurance, which meant no one was getting much sleep. Charlie sensed the discord and abandoned the both of them for the peace and quiet under the back porch.

She'd called Mynton twice in the past two days to see if there was any news regarding Garcia's whereabouts, but all Mynton could tell her was that everything had gone quiet. The powers that be had even ordered Dave Wills and the other DEA agents to be called in and assigned to other, more pressing business.

Sonora had accepted the news without comment, but when she hung up the last time, she knew she wouldn't call again. They'd abandoned her to her fate.

Then the phone call came from Franklin's doctor at St. Francis. The transplant surgery was scheduled. Sonora was to come in before noon tomorrow and the surgery would be the day after that.

Adam gave her the news with a piece of pie and a Coke, then sat down beside her while she ate, waiting for her to say what she needed to get said.

"I'm going to miss you," he said.

Sonora was scared, and because she felt completely off kilter, she picked on the only person around who was on her side.

"You're either a masochist or a liar. I've been nothing but a problem to you and Dad ever since the day of my arrival. I'd think you'd be happy to get your life back," she snapped.

He frowned.

"Well…I'd tell you that I didn't have much of a life until you rode in on that damned Harley, but since I'm supposed to be a liar, I don't suppose you'd believe that."

His sarcasm wasn't lost on Sonora. She stared down at the plate and the half-eaten piece of pie, then sighed and set it aside.

"I'm sorry."

"You should be," he said shortly. "I don't know anything more to say to make you believe that I care for you." Then he laughed, but the sound wasn't happy, just resigned. "I can tell you for sure that loving you is a lonely damn job."

The words were like a slap in the face. She looked up at him as if she'd never seen him, then leaned back in the chair.

"You love me."

"Is that a question or a statement of disbelief?" he asked.

Her chin quivered, but she lifted her head proudly. "Why?" she asked.

"Damned if I know," Adam said. "I never thought of myself as a masochist, but I must be. Every time you throw another log onto the wall you keep between us, I keep knocking it down and climbing back over."

His words hurt. She'd never been on this side of his anger before, and it didn't feel good. The only problem was, she was the one who'd put herself here.

"I'm sorry," she muttered.

"Why? Because I love you, or because you don't love me? Either way, don't worry about it."

She reeled as if she'd been slapped. The room was filled with anger, and she didn't know where it had come from. One minute she'd been eating pie and the next thing she'd done was pick a fight with the only man she'd ever let herself care about.

She got up from the chair, walked out of the kitchen, got the keys to her Harley and walked out of the house.

She could hear Adam banging dishes in the kitchen as she threw her leg over the bike and picked up the helmet. Part of her wanted to ride with the wind in her hair and to hell with safeguards, but she had family to consider. If something happened to her, Franklin's second chance at life would be over before it began. So she pulled the helmet down onto her head and fastened the strap under her chin.

The engine turned over and then caught. Sonora revved the engine once, then twice, then shoved the kickstand up with the heel of her boot and took off.

Rocks and dust flew out behind her as she spun out of the yard and headed down the driveway. She didn't know where she was going, but she had to get away. Too much had happened in too short a time. She'd been alone too many years and had no idea of how to accept something freely given, like love.

Adam heard the engine start, and for a moment thought about racing out and stopping her. But he made himself stay, and when he heard her riding away, he threw the dishcloth into the sink and walked out of the house in the other direction. Either she'd come back or she wouldn't. Either she'd love him or she couldn't. There was no power on earth, or from the Old Ones, that could stop what was already turning.

Sonora rode with a stiff-lipped concentration that would have made Gerald Mynton proud. This was the agent he knew and counted on—the woman who was more machine than human. Only she wasn't running away any longer. She was riding back to Adam as fast as the bike would take her. She wouldn't let herself think of the oncoming night. She'd ridden in the dark plenty of times before. She'd had stakeouts in the dark, too. There was nothing in the dark that was so different from the day. Just less light to see it by. But coming in to a dark house was another thing altogether. That was where she'd been locked up as a child, and that was where the ghosts of her past still lived.

When she finally saw the dirt road leading from the highway up the mountain to Adam's house, she breathed easier. She hadn't meant to go so far so fast. She'd just needed some fresh air.

Now here she was, only minutes away from Adam, and she couldn't wait to get there. She only hoped that he could forgive her for being such an ass. She took the turn without slowing down and accelerated as the bike hit dirt. One mile, then a little bit more and she would be there.

She didn't realize until she took the last turn that she'd been holding her breath. But when she saw that every light in the house had been left on for her, she exhaled quickly, then choked on a sob.

She came to a sliding halt, then when she tried to stand all but fell on her face. Her legs were weak and shaking as she tore off the helmet and then tossed her hair, reveling in the night air blowing through the length. She hung her helmet on the handlebars and started toward the porch, her steps dragging. It wasn't until she reached the front door that she realized she wasn't alone.

Adam had been sitting on the porch, waiting for her to come back long before night had fallen. He couldn't believe that she was still out in the dark, and didn't know that for her there was a fine line between a dark house and a dark night. He didn't know about the closet or the men who'd paraded through her foster mother's life.

He hadn't realized until he'd heard the Harley's engine that he'd been bracing himself for a disappointment. The relief that came with the sound was huge, and as he sat in the dark, listening to her coming closer and closer, he fought the urge to cry. She made him weak in ways he would never have believed, and yet he loved her with a strength of passion that surprised him.

Then she was here, getting off the Harley and tossing that wild mane of hair that had been shoved up under the helmet. He saw her face in the faint lights coming through the windows and knew she was as lost as he felt. Her shoulders were slumped as she started up the steps. When he saw her wipe a weary hand across her face, he couldn't stand it any longer. He shoved the chair out from under him as he stood.

"Adam?"

He stepped into the light.

She paused.

He kept walking until they were face-to-face, then he took her in his arms.

"I'm sorry," he said softly.

"So am I," she countered.

"Come inside with me?"

"Yes," she whispered, and leaned against his strength.

He kissed her then, felt the tremble in her lips as he tasted dust and tears.

"Come lay with me, love. I will hold you while you sleep."

She let herself be led because she was too weary to remind him that he, too, had been missing sleep.

Later, she stood beneath the showerhead as warm water sprayed down upon her body and let him wash her as if she was a baby. Afterward, he dried her hair, then her skin, and pulled back the covers of the bed.

"Get in, honey," he said gently. "I'll be right back."

She crawled beneath the sheets, then rolled over on her side as Adam made a last check through the house to make sure everything was locked. Only after he crawled into bed beside her and pulled her safe against his body did she trust herself to close her eyes.

"Adam…"

"Shh," he said softly. "Go to sleep."

Silence filled the room, then Adam became aware of the sounds of the house. The slight drip of the showerhead, the sound of wind rising, the pop and creak of the older house as it, too, settled for the night.

Finally, he shut his eyes. Just between consciousness and exhaustion, he thought he heard Sonora speak, then he convinced himself he must have been dreaming, because he thought he heard her say that she loved him.

The surgery was successful.

It was the first thing the doctor told Adam when he entered the waiting room. Adam grabbed the doctor's hand and then shook it, from one healer to another, although the doctor would have argued the point.

"When can I see her?" Adam asked, referring to Sonora.

"As soon as she comes out of recovery. Franklin, of course, is already in isolation in ICU. He will not be having visitors."

"I understand," Adam said. "How soon will we know if the transplant worked?"

"Soon," the doctor said. "Blood tests will tell us a lot in the next few days. But you have to trust the process and that all takes time."

"If Ms. Jordan's recovery is normal, how soon before she can go home?" Adam asked.

"Will she be on her own?" the doctor asked.

"No. She'll be staying with me until she's back on her feet."

The doctor nodded. "Then I'd say probably tomorrow or the next day. We want to make sure she's in no danger of infection, and regaining her strength. As for the visit now, I'll have a nurse let you know when she's back in her room."

"Thank you," Adam said. "Thank you more than you will ever know."

The doctor smiled. "It's been my pleasure, believe me."

With that, he moved on to the next surgery awaiting him while Adam sat back down and waited to see Sonora.

About forty-five minutes later, a nurse came looking for him. "Adam Two Eagles?"

Adam stood. "Yes, ma'am?"

"Come with me," she said.

He followed anxiously.

Sonora was back in her bed when he entered her room. She was pale and too quiet for his peace of mind. He walked to the edge of the bed, then laid a hand on her forehead, instinctively feeling for fever. At his touch, she moaned.

"Adam?" she mumbled.

He leaned close and kissed the side of her face. "I'm here," he said softly. "It's over. You did well and so did Franklin. Close your eyes and sleep, love. I'll be here when you wake up."

She meant to ask him something else, but between one

breath and another, she forgot. The remnant of the anesthesia was still in her system and quietly pulled her under.

She woke three more times, but for less than a minute before falling back to sleep. It was some time in the night before she woke up for real, and when she did, saw Adam asleep in the chair beside her bed. His presence was proof of his faithfulness. He'd promised her he would be there for her, and he was. Satisfied that all was right with her world, she managed to roll over onto the side opposite the one where the bone marrow had been taken. Once she was at ease, she fell back to sleep.

Two days later, Miguel was out of restraints, but they kept him sedated more than he liked. Upon complaining, his doctor had explained the reasoning for the treatment and the problems of confusion that often came with head injuries. It made enough sense that Miguel hadn't argued, but he was counting the days until he could get out and resume the hunt. He'd seen her once. He would find her again.

He judged the time and the days by the number of times nurses changed shifts. He'd also learned that the nurses who came on in the afternoon and stayed until midnight were the ones who talked the most. This evening was no exception. One had carried in his food on a tray while another was administering medicine through his IV. He watched as the clear liquid left the syringe and went straight into the drip.

"Will this put me to sleep before I get a chance to eat my food?" he asked.

"It's not a sedative," the nurse said. "It was an antibiotic, but if they're serving meat loaf for dinner this evening, you might wish you'd slept through it."

Her laughter sounded like a cackling hen. When she slapped her leg and then added that she'd been teasing, he didn't smile. There was nothing funny about any of this.

The other nurse, who Miguel thought of as a busybody,

took the lid off the food tray and set it on the table, then swung it over Miguel's bed.

"Can you manage?" she asked.

"Yes," he said, and picked up the enclosed packet that held plastic cutlery and condiments.

The two nurses were talking to each other as they finished their work in his room. At first he paid no attention until he heard one of them mention a name.

"It's like something out of a Hollywood movie," Cackling Hen said. "Imagine, finding out you have a daughter and then having that daughter save your life."

"I know," Busybody said, then lowered her voice. "I heard she's some kind of government agent."

Cackling Hen nodded. "Yes, so did I." Then she frowned. "I wouldn't take that kind of job if you gave it to me. I mean…everyone knows that people whose jobs take them undercover have to do things with the bad guys to keep from being found out. Imagine having to have sex with some drug dealer or murderer?"

Busybody snorted. "Lord, Carleen, aren't those kind of people one and the same?"

Cackling Hen laughed and then shrugged. "Yes, I guess you're right."

However, Miguel wasn't laughing. When he'd heard the word *she,* then *government agent,* his attention had shifted. Still, there had to be plenty of people who worked for the government in Oklahoma. Just because he was looking for one didn't mean they had to be one and the same. Still, he couldn't help but ask.

"So…you say a woman saved her father's life by donating an organ?"

"Not an organ. Bone marrow," Cackling Hen said. "Quite a story. And the father's famous."

Miguel lost interest. To the best of his knowledge, Sonora Jordan had no family and he would certainly have known if she had famous parents.

"Hmm," he said, and salted the green beans on his plate.

"Ooh, really?" Busybody said. "I didn't know that."

"Apparently they didn't know each other existed until a short while ago. It's just like a movie, I tell you."

"What's he famous for?" Busybody asked.

"He carves things out of wood, but a lot of Native Americans are good at art and stuff."

Miguel stilled. Native American? The woman he was looking for could pass for a Native American.

Busybody wasn't through with her interrogation. "What's his name?" she asked.

"Franklin Blue Cat," Cackling Hen said. "He lives up in the Kiamichi Mountains. Has a studio there and ships his work all over. I heard some Japanese big shot even commissioned some work from his once."

"Never heard of him," Busybody said, then added, "I'll bet he's rich, though."

"Yeah, and can you imagine what the long-lost daughter must think? Not only has she found a family, but the family is rolling in dough. What are the odds of that?"

"So, this Blue Cat woman works for the government. They have good benefits and all. My Al tried to get on a government job, but he didn't have the right credentials," Busybody added.

"Her name isn't Blue Cat. Her last name is Jordan."

Miguel knocked over the glass of iced tea on his tray, which sent both nurses scrambling to mop up the spill. One left to get him a refill, the other went to get a clean sheet while Miguel accepted what fate had dropped into his lap. If he was to believe his luck, the woman he sought was here in this hospital. He already knew that this wasn't the time or the place to exact revenge, but at least he knew his search was over. He had a name and a place to start looking.

Chapter 16

Sonora was packed and ready to go, and none too soon for her. She'd had all of St. Francis Hospital that she cared to experience. Whoever said that a hospital was a good place to heal had never tried to sleep in one. Now all she had to do was wait for Adam to arrive. The drive home would be long and most likely uncomfortable for her, but the end of the line promised peace and quiet and Adam's loving arms, which was worth whatever it took to get there.

She glanced at the clock, and then out the window. It was too early for Adam to get here, but she didn't feel like sitting any longer. She got up and headed for the door. At least she could take a couple of turns around the floor. The sooner she recovered her strength, the better off she would be. She hadn't forgotten her last vision or the warning she'd had of coming danger, and she wanted to be on familiar ground if it happened.

Even as she was stepping into the hallway, the hair rose on the backs of her arms. It was a warning she'd heeded many times before, and to her advantage. But this time, although she was without her weapon, felt she was surely safe. After all, it was broad daylight and there were people everywhere. Her warning had been about darkness.

She stayed close to the handrail on the side of the walls in case she had a moment of lightheadedness or felt sick, but it didn't happen. In fact, the farther she walked, the better she felt. The doctor had assured her that as long as she didn't overdo it, she would be back to normal in no time.

She had walked all the way to the end of the hall and was about to turn the corner when she was awash in cold air. The faint sound of rattles sent her grabbing on to the handrail for fear another vision was imminent and that she might fall. But the world didn't shift and the hallway didn't disappear. And when she looked up, she realized she was standing beneath an air-conditioner vent.

Disgusted with herself for jumping to conclusions, she continued her walk, right past the half-open doorway where Miguel Garcia lay watching television. He didn't see her. She didn't see him, and even if she had, wouldn't have recognized him as anyone except the man she'd seen getting hit. Without his mustache and hair, he was a stranger.

By the time she circled the hall and was back to her room, she was shaky. She stretched out on her bed and closed her eyes, and when she next woke, Adam was standing beside her bed.

"Hey, pretty lady," he said softly, and kissed her on the cheek.

She smiled and then turned her face just enough so that the kiss settled on her lips instead.

"Mmm, good," she said softly when he pulled away. "I am so ready to go, but there's some paperwork that—"

"Already tended to," he said. "All you need is the wheelchair, and that's coming up."

"Then we can go?"

"Yes, honey, we can go."

"Did you see Dad?" Sonora asked.

"Only through a window. He's not allowed visitors, remember?"

She nodded. "Did he see you?"

"Yes. He waved…once for me, once for you."

A bright smile spread across her face. "He did that?" she asked.

"Yes, baby…he did that."

After that, Sonora was satisfied and within minutes, they were gone from the floor.

The trip home wore Sonora out. Adam had reclined her seat in the truck and within an hour of leaving Tulsa she was sound asleep. She slept all the way to Adam's home, then managed to get inside before she crawled into bed again. Adam helped her off with her clothes, and once she was comfortable, he pulled the covers up over her shoulders, pulled down the shades at the windows and left her alone so that she could sleep.

The phone rang several times during the rest of the day, but Sonora barely heard it. Adam was fielding requests from some of his patients, wanting everything from his advice to some kind of healing. Because he wouldn't leave Sonora alone, he dispensed advice over the phone and requested the sick to come to him. There was a room in his house that he had set aside for times such as this, and so he waited as they came and went.

And so the day went, and each ensuing day afterward until Sonora was almost 100 percent back to her old self and Adam wasn't so concerned about leaving her on her own from time to time.

Sonora talked on the phone to her father on a daily basis, and with each passing day it became evident that Franklin Blue Cat had a new lease on life.

It seemed to Sonora that the world was, once again,

spinning properly on its axis, and whatever danger that had once awaited her was gone. In her mind, she spun several scenarios, all of which had Miguel Garcia either dead or on the run. She hadn't thought past Franklin coming home from the hospital and had told Mynton that she was considering an early retirement. He was understanding, but regretted her decision and kept telling her not to make any hasty decisions.

However, it was Adam's constant and faithful presence in her life, and the family unit that he and Franklin represented, that appealed to her most. Bottom line, she was in love with Adam Two Eagles, and if there was a snowball's chance in hell that he returned the feelings enough to keep her around for the rest of her life, she wasn't going anywhere.

Miguel was being dismissed. Days earlier, when his memory had returned, he'd had the foresight to call the used-car dealer. The salesperson was relieved to hear Miguel's voice, assured him that they still wanted to buy his car, and that the money they had agreed upon earlier was still good. He'd come to the hospital that same day with the luggage that had been in Miguel's car, the papers Miguel needed to sign and a cashier's check for the car that he'd sold. Now he had just enough money from selling his car to pay for his hospital stay, which left him flat broke but upright and still determined to exact revenge.

The hell of it was, he had millions in a Mexican bank and even more in an offshore bank in the Cayman Islands. Any money he might request to be transferred from the Mexican bank would certainly pinpoint his presence to the authorities. But there was a chance that they didn't know about the Cayman accounts, and he needed money. It was a risk he was going to have to take.

Even though he felt weak and shaky, he was on his own.

He took a cab to a motel, got a room and dumped off his luggage, then headed for one of the larger downtown banks.

He filled out the necessary paperwork to access a transfer to the new account he'd just opened and asked how long it would take.

The banker, being the sympathetic man that he was, had already learned of Miguel's plight. He remembered hearing on the news of the incident where Miguel had been hurt, so he did all he could to facilitate a quick response. Within twenty minutes of a phone call, then a corroborating fax with the proper account numbers, over half a million dollars had been transferred into Miguel's new account.

He was all smiles and charm as he withdrew a hundred thousand with the explanation that he would be buying a new vehicle and didn't want to run short, then left the bank. He hailed another cab, went back to his motel and slept for the better part of eleven hours. When he woke up, he was starving and it was three o'clock in the morning.

He called a cab, which took him to an all-night diner. He ate ravenously, hailed another cab back to the motel and slept until after ten the next morning. It was then that he ventured out to the car dealers, paid cash for a brand-new car and drove off the lot feeling much better about himself.

After a few wrong turns, he found his way to the Tulsa library, parked and went in. Playing upon the sympathy of a middle-aged female librarian who obviously viewed his accent as romantic, she helped him get online and straight to a website devoted to wood carver and sculptor Franklin Blue Cat, which included the area in which he lived, as well as a business number.

He jotted them down and left while the librarian was busy tending to someone else, stopped to buy gas and an Oklahoma road map, then went back to his motel.

He studied the map for the better part of the day, located the Kiamichi Mountains and the town nearest where

Franklin Blue Cat supposedly lived and then took a long nap. He was conserving energy for the day when revenge would be his.

He was there for two days before he decided it was time to make his move. He longed for his native Mexico, but knew that as long as Emilio Rojas lived, he could never go home. However, there was always the Caymans. A large part of his money was there, and once in residence, he could have his account in the Mexican bank transferred, as well. Yes, it was a plan that suited him, and he longed to begin his new life. But there was a piece of his old one that had yet to be dealt with. Once he knew that Sonora Jordan was as dead as his Juanito, then he would start over and not a day before.

It was 103 degrees in the shade. Sonora knew because she could see the reading on the outdoor thermometer Adam had hung on the porch. It was cool in the house but confining, and Sonora itched to be outside doing something. She felt as if she was in hiding, even though most of her indoor activities had been in place because of the need for rest and healing rather than a reluctance to show herself.

Adam had gone to visit an elderly woman who wanted him to give her a potion to get a man for her granddaughter, who had been living with her for five years. She told Adam that her granddaughter was lazy and getting fat and if she didn't find a man and get married soon, no one would have her.

Adam had stifled a grin and told her that he would certainly stop by on his way into town. She didn't know it and he wasn't going to tell her as yet, but he wasn't going to pretend, like some healers he knew of, that there was such a thing that could be concocted. What it amounted to was a young woman with no self-confidence and a grandmother who wanted her little house back to herself.

He'd left Sonora with the number to his cell phone and a promise of bringing home some ice cream along with the groceries. He'd gone so far in planning ahead as to having an ice chest in the truck to keep the refrigerated and frozen items from spoiling on the way home.

Sonora thought of the shaded creek below the house and the cool running water. It wouldn't be much over her ankles, but it was out of the house and something different to do. Excited now that she had a plan, she went to change into some shorts instead of the jeans she was wearing, and tennis shoes instead of bare feet. She eyed the small, healed wound where the bone marrow had been removed. There was no more pain or stiffness at the site, and she deemed it to be fit. She thought about taking her cell phone, then discarded the notion, left Adam a note telling him where she'd gone and then hurried out the back door.

The heat was like a slap in the face. There was a moment when she thought about changing her mind and going back into the house, but the creek wasn't far and the thought of walking barefoot in the water was too enticing to ignore.

A few minutes later she was on the bank above the creek. She saw the sweat lodge but left it alone. It had nothing to do with her and she didn't want to intrude in a place where she didn't belong.

She looked down at the creek, and as she'd expected, the water was running free and clear. From where she was standing, she could see a crawdad as well as a couple of small frogs moving about in the water below. The trees on both sides of the bank leaned slightly toward the water, their branches forming an arch above it. Pleased with herself for thinking of this, she found a way down that wasn't too steep, and once on the narrow shore, took off her shoes and stepped in. Compared to the temperature of the day, the water was cold, but it felt wonderful.

There were small rocks along the sandy bottom that had

long ago lost their jagged edges by the constant flow of sand
and water. A squirrel immediately voiced its disgust at her
unexpected appearance and promptly dropped a couple of
acorns near where she was walking, as if to scare her away.
She looked up just in time to see a little red squirrel disappearing into the upper branches.

"Everyone's a critic," she said, and proceeded to wade
along the creek bed.

She came upon a small, deep pool about three feet in di-
ameter and paused to look down. As she did, a tiny green
snake that had been lying on some nearby rocks made a
quick getaway by slithering off into some leaves.

Sonora felt a moment of recognition with the little snake
as she thought of the one on her back. In a moment of abandon, she stripped off her shirt and shorts, leaving her in
nothing but a pair of bikini panties, then folded them up
and left them lying on a pair of flat rocks at the edge of the
shore. She checked her wound again to make sure it was
not getting dirty or wet, and then straightened.

The sway of hair hanging down her back and the air on
her body was a sensual experience she hadn't expected.
But for the narrow strip of turquoise silk that passed for
underwear, she was naked as the day she'd been born, and
loving it.

A pair of hummingbirds darted past her line of vision
on their way up from the creek where they'd been getting
a drink. She watched until they reached the top of the bank
then began drinking nectar from the red-orange trumpet
flowers hanging from their vines among the trees. For a
brief, fanciful moment, she could almost envision what life
had been like for her people many, many, years ago, when
their only concerns had been finding food and shelter from
one season to the next.

She lost all track of time down in her little Eden, and was

crouched down and staring into a round hole in the creek bank when she heard a twig snap on the banks above her.

Startled, she straightened, and for the first time, realized the danger of being down here alone and naked.

"Who's there?" she called out.

At that point, Adam appeared on the bank above. He'd been going to tease her for slipping off to the creek like a child, but when he saw her, the words died on his lips. There wasn't one childlike thing about the woman standing in the water.

She was golden-brown all over, with curves that could make a man weep. She was holding her hands over her breasts until she saw it was him. At that point she dropped them to wave a hello and he almost fell into the creek.

"You're a little overdressed," Sonora said, and then laughed softly, as if she knew a secret he didn't know.

"Yes, I can see that," he said, and then jumped from the bank down to the shore without bothering to find a good place to descend.

"Don't hurry on my account," Sonora said, and grinned.

But the smile slid off her face when Adam began to undress.

"Uh…"

He didn't take his gaze from her face as he came out of his shirt, pants and shoes. Unlike her, he didn't stop with the underwear. Before she knew what was happening, he was completely nude.

His long brown body and hair dark as night made him look like a savage, then her gaze shifted to his face. She took a deep breath, and then sighed.

"You are so beautiful," she said softly. "Did you know that?"

He walked into the water and came toward her.

Her eyes widened as she realized his intent. She laughed

as she spun and started to run, splashing diamond-like droplets of water as she went.

Adam hesitated only once when she turned her back. He saw the snake. It certainly wasn't the first time he'd seen her naked with the tattoo completely revealed, but it never failed to make his heart skip a beat. But after that, the hesitation was brief as he bolted after her.

He caught her in three strides, spun her around and yanked her close against his chest.

"You're supposed to be recuperating."

She leaned her head back against his forearm and stared straight into his eyes. She could feel every curve and muscle in his body, as well as his breath against her face. His eyes were dark and glittering with a warning she didn't mistake.

"Recuperating?" she repeated.

He nodded.

She slid her arms up around his neck. "So heal me," she challenged.

Before she knew what was happening, he had stripped the bit of silk from her hips, lifted her off her feet, and with his hands under her backside to guide the way, lowered her down onto his erection.

Sonora moaned beneath her breath as he slowly filled her, then closed her eyes.

"Does this hurt you?" he asked.

"Lord, no," Sonora said.

"Then open your eyes and know the man who loves you."

Sonora did as he asked, locked her legs around his waist and her arms around his neck, then held on as he took her for a ride.

At that point, everything seemed to happen in moments of slow motion.

A ray of sunlight coming down through an opening in the limbs that settled on the crown of his head.

The sound of flesh against flesh as Adam took her where they stood.

Droplets of water on Adam's face mingling with tiny beads of sweat.

His nostrils flaring.

Her breasts pressed against his chest as the ache between her legs blossomed, then exploded in a blinding white light of passion.

As she was coming down from the adrenaline rush of her climax, she felt Adam shudder. Before she knew what was happening, his hold on her tightened. One more thrust, then another and he suddenly threw back his head and let go with a groan.

It echoed up and down the creek bed, startling a small fox out of hiding and sending a pair of doves flying from the branches of a tree above them.

As the last bird took flight from the creek, Adam gently set her back down, then took his hands and proceeded to wash them both from the clear, running water of the little creek.

Sonora steadied herself by putting both hands on his shoulders as he knelt at her feet, washing her gently with water he cupped in his hands.

His hair was silky to the touch, his shoulders broad and strong. She said his name, just to hear it from her lips.

"Adam."

He paused, then looked up.

"I think there's something about me you should know," she said.

He straightened, then waited.

"I'm going to tell you something that I've never told another man. Ever."

His heart thudded once out of rhythm.

"I'm in love with you," she said. "And it scares me to death."

Relief hit him like a fist to the gut. He combed his fingers through her hair, then pulled her to him, his voice husky and full of emotion.

"I had begun to fear I would never hear those words from your lips. I love you back, Sonora, more than you can imagine. I want to know that I will see your smile each morning and feel your hands upon me every night. I can't even face the thought of a life without you."

"You don't have to," Sonora said, and gave herself up to his kiss.

Adam held her there, in the middle of the creek with the water running cool on their feet and the trees shading their bodies from the sun, and knew that for the rest of his life, he would forever associate this place with her.

Finally, he urged her out of the water, helped her dress, then dressed himself. He showed her an easy way up from the creek, then together they walked back to the house.

Sonora was so happy and at peace that she didn't even heed the faint sound of running horses or the distant gourd rattles in the back of her mind. She was too full of Adam and the love they'd just professed.

Miguel had been up and down every road within a fifteen-mile radius of Franklin Blue Cat's home and gallery, and that was after realizing that no one was home. He cursed himself for not thinking to check at the hospital before he left to see if anyone knew who'd taken Sonora Jordan home. It was obvious she was not in residence at her father's home, but considering the fact that she'd been part of some transplant procedure, he was assuming she might have needed aftercare. At that point, he remembered the Native American man she'd been with and the dark blue Ford truck he'd been driving and figured if he could find that man, he might find Sonora.

He'd thought about going back down the mountain to the

small town he'd passed through before going to the Blue
Cat gallery, then decided against it. He didn't want anyone
remembering later that a Latino man had been asking about
the woman, especially when she later turned up dead. He'd
given himself permission to do a little investigating on his
own, then worry about being recognized later.

He'd driven for what seemed like hours without seeing anything resembling that truck, and then he'd taken a
corner in the two-lane dirt road a little too wide and found
himself almost face-to-face with the truck and the driver
he'd been looking for.

He swerved immediately to the side to avoid the head-
on collision and shrugged and waved, hoping that it passed
for enough of an apology that the bastard didn't stop and
start a fight. He was feeling okay, but he definitely did not
want to take a blow to the face.

He saw the man nod and wave back and breathed a quick
sigh of relief. Noting the direction in which he was driving,
he waited until the dust was almost settled, then followed. It
didn't take long to see the little road leading up the mountain that the Native American had taken. He stopped for
a moment, trying to decide if he wanted to chance being
seen again, or wait until dark.

But the area was new to him, and the mountain was
heavily wooded. He didn't want to play detective in the dark
with a bunch of coyotes, so he took a chance and followed.

Within a couple of minutes, he realized this was a driveway, and not another main road. He parked and started
walking, taking care to stay within the edge of the trees.
Before long, he saw the roof of a house. After a couple more
minutes of walking, he saw a house, then the pickup itself,
although no one was in sight.

He was just about to go back to his car when he saw the
man come out of the house and head toward the backside
of the property. Miguel watched until he disappeared, then

proceeded the rest of the way up the drive. If someone else was in the house when he knocked, he would pretend he was looking for Blue Cat's gallery and got lost. And if no one else was there, it wouldn't take him long to check out the place, just in case.

When he reached the front door and knocked, no one answered. He smiled to himself and reached for the door-knob, thinking he might force the door, only to find out that it turned beneath his touch. His smile widened. Rural people who still didn't lock their doors. He couldn't believe his luck.

He glanced quickly toward the direction that the Native American had gone, and then stepped inside. He knew within seconds of entering that there was no one there. It felt empty, as if the energy of the place had departed with the occupants.

Careful of the time, he made a quick sweep through the house to reassure himself that he was alone, then did a second run-through of the bedrooms. Only one bedroom seemed to be occupied, but there were things belonging to two people. As he looked out a back window, he saw the back end of a motorcycle sticking out of a shed. He looked closer, and when he saw the Arizona tag, smiled to himself.

He remembered she'd owned the Harley Buddy Allen had once had. So that was how she'd gotten out of town.

He thought about hiding somewhere in the house and surprising them both when they came back, then decided against it. That Native American was big and Jordan was DEA. Neither one would be easy to take down. Besides that, he wanted the woman to suffer. She wasn't going to get off so easy with a quick bullet through her head.

Having settled all of that in his mind, he hurried out of the house the same way he came in, pausing long enough to make sure there was no one in sight, then made a run for the trees.

He was breathing hard and sweating when he reached them, and could feel the beginnings of a headache. He was used to heat, but there was something different about this Oklahoma heat that sapped the strength right out of him. He wouldn't have been interested in listening to someone speak about the humidity factor in the state, but if he had, it would have soon become apparent to him what the difference was. Oklahoma in the summer was a perpetual sauna.

He stopped for a few moments to rest, and as he was waiting, saw the man suddenly appear from below the crest of a hill, only this time he wasn't alone. He watched carefully, then started to smile.

He'd found Sonora Jordan.

Chapter 17

By sundown, what appeared to be a group of thunderclouds was gathering on the horizon. Another round of storms was evident—something they dealt with at this time of year. Adam stood out on the back porch, judging the possibility of its arrival before morning and figured it was likely.

Charlie was winding himself around Adam's legs, begging for supper.

"Okay, okay, I hear you loud and clear," Adam said, and headed toward a shelf on the back porch to get a can of cat food.

Charlie voiced his pleasure with a small, happy "mowrp," which made Adam grin.

Sonora was in the kitchen, finishing up the dishes that she'd insisted on doing since Adam had cooked the meal. As she was hanging the dish towel up to dry, the telephone rang.

"Adam! Phone!" she called.

"Get it for me, will you?" he called back. "I'm feeding Charlie."

Sonora took the wall phone off the receiver. "Adam Two Eagles residence."

There was a single second of shock that someone other than Adam had answered, then someone started talking—fast and loud—and in Kiowa.

Sonora didn't know what was going on, but she could tell something was wrong. "Adam! Come quick!"

He dropped the empty can into the trash as he hurried into the kitchen and took the phone she thrust into his hands. Within seconds of taking the phone, he began to talk, louder and firmer and in the same language.

Within seconds, he'd obviously gotten the caller's attention, because he began to ask questions and in English.

Finally, she heard Adam say, "I'll be right there."

Sonora could tell Adam was bothered when he hung up the phone, and when he turned around to face her, he was frowning.

"What's wrong?" she said.

"I have to go. A young man has been injured and he's also in trouble."

"I'll go with you," Sonora said.

Adam's frown deepened. "It's better if you don't."

"Why?"

"Because I'm pretty sure that the injuries he's suffered are from making meth. You're DEA. You don't want to be in the middle of this."

"Oh, crap," she muttered, immediately getting the message as to what her life would be like married to Adam if she became legally involved with the people he'd come home to help.

"I'm sorry," he said. "It sounds like he needs an ambulance and to be taken to a burn unit, but they won't do a thing until I tell them it's all right."

"Why are some of your...our people so distrustful of whites?"

He sighed, then held out his hands. "Let's just say that if you'd been raised Native, you would probably understand."

She flinched as if she'd been slapped. "Prejudice? In this day and age?"

"Lazy. Blanket ass. Living on tribal money and not working. I could go on and on, despite the fact that every bit of it is lies."

"Good Lord," she muttered, then waved him on. "Go. Go. Whatever has happened, they need help, but not mine. At least not yet."

Adam hugged her quickly, thanking her in the only way he knew how, then grabbed his bag, his car keys and headed out the door.

"Lock the door behind me!" he yelled as he bounded off the porch.

"Wait! You forgot your phone," Sonora said, and carried it out to the truck.

He tossed it in the seat beside him as he was starting the engine. By the time Sonora got back into the house and locked the door, he was already gone.

Miguel was coming up the mountain from the town below when a pickup truck appeared at the crest of a hill and quickly sped past. He had a quick glimpse of a dark truck and then nothing. He cursed softly, hoping that he hadn't waited too long and that upon his return to the house Sonora Jordan would be gone.

Still, he retraced the path that he'd taken earlier in the day and almost missed the turn in the dark. He stopped, backed up, then started up the dirt road that led to the big Native American's house. When he was almost there, he turned out his lights and drove the rest of the way in the dark, guided only by a faint bit of moonlight.

He saw the lights before he saw the house, and when he saw a light suddenly go off in the back part of the house, his spirits lifted. Someone was home, most likely her. When he drove up to the house and realized the pickup was gone, he smiled.

That had been the Native American he'd met coming up. She was home alone.

He grabbed his handgun from the glove box, then got out. As he stood there, the moonlight suddenly disappeared. He looked up. The stars were disappearing, as well. When a couple of raindrops suddenly splattered on his face, he realized a fast-moving storm was moving into the area.

He smiled.

Even better.

She wouldn't hear him coming in the wind and the rain.

He hurried up onto the porch, then did a quick check through the curtains at the windows. He couldn't see details, but he could tell there was someone inside moving around.

A loud clap of thunder suddenly slammed down upon the roof, followed by a swift flash of lightning. Miguel ducked in reflex, then swiped a shaky hand across his face. That had been close—too close.

He moved toward the front door, then gripped the knob, expecting it to turn as easily as it had earlier, and was surprised that it was locked. Cursing softly beneath his breath, he started to draw back and kick down the door when it suddenly opened.

He froze momentarily at the shock of suddenly seeing Sonora Jordan only inches away.

Sonora gasped. In the half-light and despite the bald head, she saw the family resemblance. Miguel Garcia had found her.

Lightning flashed again.

The lights went out!

Dark was the impetus Sonora needed to move. She pivoted sharply and darted toward the bedroom where she kept her gun. Before she'd gone two steps, she was hit from behind in a flying tackle. The impact of Garcia's weight against the place where the bone marrow had been taken left her screaming in pain and her legs almost too numb to move.

"I will kill you, bitch! Just like I killed your friend in Phoenix. Just like you killed my little brother."

It was the mention of Buddy having been beaten to death that gave her the will she needed. Still on her belly, she bucked her body violently, as if trying to unseat a rider, then kicked out with both bare feet. She knew she'd connected to something vital when she heard the pitch of the man's scream.

She didn't know that she'd just broken his nose, or that, for the time being, he was blind with pain. All she knew was that when she got up to run, no one was stopping her.

Thunder rocked the house as the squall line hit. Sonora heard the tinkle of breaking glass and guessed that the fiercely blowing winds had probably blown something through a window. She thought of the storm shelter only a few yards away from the house. She probably needed to be down there, but she wasn't going without her gun. The last place she wanted to be was cornered and helpless.

She reached Adam's bedroom in seconds. The dense blackness in the room was unnerving, but the fear of the man behind her was worse. She felt along the walls until she came to the closet, then yanked it open and dropped to her knees. Her bag was down here somewhere, and inside it was her gun.

She heard running footsteps now, and the wild, frantic screams and curses of a man in pain. Her fingers were shaking so badly that she couldn't even find the bag, then when she finally did, couldn't get a grip on the zipper.

The door to Adam's room hit the wall with a bang just as she found the zipper tab. She pulled frantically, then thrust her hand inside the opening. Within seconds, she had the gun. She felt along the bottom of the bag until she found the small magazine of bullets as well, and shoved it up into the grip. Under the cover of thunder, she jacked the barrel and loaded the first bullet into the chamber.

Slowly she stood with the gun in her hand, waiting for that flash of lightning to tell her where her enemy stood. Within seconds it came. She saw Garcia at the same time he saw her. Then the room was once again dark.

Sonora fired a shot in the direction of where he'd been standing, and then kicked the door hard. There was a loud cry of pain as she dived out of the closet and onto the bedroom floor. A half second later, a shot went over her head.

She felt the edge of the bedspread against her cheek and without thinking, slid under the bed, then out the other side, bringing her closer to the door. When lightning flashed again, she saw Garcia's boots facing an opposite wall. The moment the light was gone, she jumped up and ran.

Within seconds, he was once again in pursuit. Her legs were cramping and there was a spreading pain going down the back of her hip from where he'd landed on her. Sensing that he was only a step or two behind her, she spun, firing off two shots as she did, then fell backward into the kitchen as he ran past. With only seconds to spare, she rolled to her feet, made a dash for the kitchen door, then ran out into the storm.

Adam was within a mile of the family's residence when something moved in front of the headlights. He swerved to keep from hitting it as he slammed on the brakes. By the time he came to an abrupt halt, he was shaking.

At first, he thought it was a deer, but it had gotten away. As he started to take his foot off the brake, something began to materialize just beyond the lights. He watched in disbelief as a rider on horseback came out of the dark, then grunted, as if he'd been punched. Both rider and horse were transparent.

Nothing was said, but he heard the meaning just the same.

Go home. Go home.

Then one last word surfaced.

Hurry.

The hair rose on the back of his neck. Sonora!

He grabbed his cell phone as he turned the truck around, calling his own number. To his dismay, there was no answer, and when he began the trip home, realized he was driving into a storm.

He thought of the young man who awaited him, who was possibly dying of burns. There was nothing to do but get help. He dialed one more number—to the local fire and ambulance service.

The dispatcher answered on the first ring. "Fire and Rescue, what is your emergency?"

"Travis, this is Adam Two Eagles. I got a call from the Wapkinah family up on County Road 114. Their eldest boy got burned. They called me first, but I'm calling you. I can't get there and I don't want that boy to die."

Travis Younger immediately understood. "Thanks, Adam," Travis said. "We'll get 'em some help."

"Thanks," Adam said. "Talk to you later." He tossed the phone into the seat beside him, then stomped on the gas.

Miguel was blind with pain and choking on his own blood. She'd broken his nose for sure—once with her foot and the second time with the closet door. He kept trying to remember the layout of the rooms he'd seen earlier in the day, but with the pain and the dark, it was confusing.

The next time the lightning flashed, he realized he was in the room all alone. It occurred to him then that he might be in trouble. He pivoted abruptly and began to retrace his steps. After the second sweep through the house, he knew she was gone.

Cursing in both English and Spanish, he stumbled through the kitchen, wiped the blood off his face with a small towel, then shoved it up against his nose, hoping to stop the flow.

He moved out onto the porch just as another flash of lightning came and went. It was then he saw his car was missing. With a scream of rage, he ran out into the storm. It took another flash of lightning and the rain in his face to realize he wasn't at the front porch but the back.

He looked toward the shed and saw the faint outline of the Harley. She had to be somewhere nearby.

"Hear me, bitch!" he screamed. "Hear me good. I will make you wish you'd never been born before you die."

He heard the shot too late to duck. It was nothing but luck that he was still standing when the bullet hit the porch post right behind him. He hit the ground belly first, splattering water and mud in his mouth and up his still-bleeding nose.

The roar of his rage was so loud that Sonora heard it over the storm. If the storm didn't pass too quickly, and if Adam came back in time, she might have a chance of staying alive.

She'd already been in his car and tried to hot-wire it, but the new models and safeguards that were in place made that impossible. She had an added advantage of knowing the property far better than he did and thought about hiding out in the woods. He'd never find her, but there was a part of her that feared he would give up and leave, which meant she would be facing him again sometime, and the odds might not be in her favor.

She didn't know where he was until another strike of lightning came and went and she saw him moving toward the cellar. At that point, she was glad she wasn't in it, and ran to the front of the house.

It didn't take long for her to break the valve stems off the tires. She could hear the hiss of escaping air as she stood. Then she saw him, less than five yards away, with his gun pointed right at her face.

"Drop it!" he yelled, waving his gun in her face.

"Or what?" she screamed back and took aim with her own. "You're going to shoot me anyway. I'd rather take you with me."

They both fired.

Sonora was falling backward as the first bullet came out of her gun. It hit Garcia in the shoulder, spinning him around. The gun fell out of his hand into the mud while the bullet he'd fired plunged into the ground just beside Sonora's head. Mud and water flew into her eyes, momentarily blinding her.

For a few seconds, both Sonora and Garcia were out of commission. She struggled to get up while Garcia dealt with more pain and the loss of his gun. When he saw that she was down, he pounced. Bleeding from his shoulder and his nose, he went belly down on top of her. The impact knocked the wind out of Sonora's lungs and for a few frantic moments, she was paralyzed, unable to move.

In the fleeting breath between heartbeats, a gust of wind blew rain into Sonora's face. She gasped, and in doing so, drew sweet, life-giving oxygen into her body. At the same time, the air was suddenly filled with the sound of drums— and of gourd rattles—and voices chanting over and over in a language she did not know.

Garcia's hands slid around her throat.

She was fighting him and kicking and gouging at his eyes, pushing against his weight, but to no avail.

The drums grew louder, as did the rattles. Sonora wondered if this was what the Kiowa heard when they were going to die.

And then suddenly the weight was off her body. She struggled to get up and felt hands beneath her arms pulling her upright, but when she turned to look, there was no one there.

Garcia was standing a short distance away from her, holding his arms up across his face as if to ward off a blow, although there was nothing between them but the downpour of rain. He was screaming and praying as he'd never prayed before.

Sonora felt a great wind at her back and feared a tornado was about to drop down. She tried to move, to run for the cellar, but her feet wouldn't move. All around her, the air was filled with the beat of a thousand drums and the ground shook from the shock waves of gourd rattles and she thought that they were going to die.

Then, through the wind and the rain and the war drums hammering against her brain, she saw a flashing, bouncing light. Someone was coming up the driveway at great speed. When she recognized the pickup and the man who jumped out in a run, she screamed out his name.

"Adam!"

He launched himself at Garcia as he spun and fired. The bullet went wild as Adam hit him waist high and sent them both flying into the rain. At the moment of their impact, it was as if Sonora was suddenly released from a spell. Frantically, she began feeling about in the mud to find her gun, and just as suddenly, it was in her hand.

She turned.

Lightning flashed.

Garcia was getting away from Adam.

She fired into the air.

Then time seemed to stop.

Garcia froze with Adam still holding on to his leg.

The rain stopped.

The quiet was even more frightening than the storm.

Garcia was looking at something above Adam's head, and the look on his face was one of horror.

Sonora turned, following his line of vision, and that was when she saw them.

"Adam."

Her voice was barely above a whisper, and yet he heard it. As he turned to look, Garcia rolled away from him and grabbed his gun from the mud. He turned, firing as he rolled, willing to die if he could take her with him.

The bullets didn't find a target, but lightning did. It came out of nowhere and nailed Garcia to the ground. Fire came out of his ears and the bottoms of his feet. Within seconds he was gone.

Adam looked up.

There were four Native Americans above him, one naked and riding a pure white horse. One was wrapped in a bearskin, one wearing a war bonnet that trailed the ground and one had a white handprint on either side of his face. They were mounted on horses with fiery red eyes and stamping feet.

The one on the white horse waved a war shield as the horse reared up, then disappeared. Another shouted something into the wind, until one by one, they were gone.

"The Old Ones," Adam said.

Sonora stumbled, then sat flat.

Adam ran toward her, then picked her up in his arms.

"When I saw you two in the headlights, I thought I was going to be too late. He had his arms around your throat. I saw you fighting him, then suddenly he went flying. You must have landed quite a blow."

The war drums were silent, as were the gourd rattles. The fear that had been with her since the day she'd learned Buddy Allen was dead was no more. She felt empty and free and ready to be filled with Adam Two Eagles's love.

"It wasn't me," she said. "It was them. They saved me."

Adam shuddered, then held her closer. "Let's get in the house. You need to get cleaned up and into dry clothes, and I've got to make some calls."

Sonora suddenly remembered the boy who'd been burned. "What happened to the boy?" she asked.

"I don't know. I was almost there when one of the Old Ones stopped me. When I saw him in my headlights, I knew you were in some kind of danger. That's why I came back."

Sonora laid her head against his shoulder as he carried her inside. She'd seen them for herself; it still seemed impossible to believe. Still, Garcia was dead, which was good, and since he wasn't alive to tell what he'd seen, then she had nothing to worry about.

Once they were inside the house, Adam lit candles for her again. She was standing in the laundry room taking off her wet, muddy clothes when the power suddenly flickered, then returned.

Sonora breathed a sigh of relief, but not because she was no longer in the dark. She was pretty sure that the events of this night had cured what ailed her about darkness. Her greatest joy right now came from knowing she could get clean.

Adam came from the kitchen with a large bath towel. He wrapped it around her, then helped her to the bathroom.

"Need any help?" he asked.

"No. I can handle it," she said, and dropped the towel. As she turned to step into the shower, the tattoo of the snake rode the movement of her muscles, making it appear as if it was about to strike.

"You sure can," he said softly, and left her on her own.

A short while later, the front yard of Adam's house was crawling with all manner of authorities. The local sheriff, the county division of the DEA and someone from the Feds was supposed to be on the way.

Miguel Garcia had once been a big deal in this country, responsible for funneling billions of dollars worth of drugs up from Colombia, through Mexico and then into the States.

As far as the law was concerned, he'd attacked a DEA agent in a plot of revenge. She wounded him twice, before he succumbed to a lightning strike during a storm.

It was a good story, and Sonora Jordan was sticking to it.

Epilogue

Franklin Blue Cat was sitting in his favorite chair, watching the sunset from the screened-in back porch of his home. He could hear his daughter's laughter and the deep, rumbling voice of her husband, Adam, as he responded to something she'd said.

He heard her footsteps moving across the kitchen floor and smiled to himself. She was coming to check on him, when it was she who should be sitting with her feet in the air.

"Dad, need something cold to drink?"

He shook his head, and then held out his hand. "Come to me for a moment," he said, and pulled her down in his lap.

"I'll squash you," she argued, even as she was sitting.

"That tiny baby in your belly weighs nothing," Franklin said.

"Maybe so, but tiny baby's mother weighs plenty," she argued, then flinched. "Oh! Man! That was some kick."

She splayed her hand across her belly and then rubbed, as if trying to soothe the infant within.

"Already he is impatient to be born," Franklin said, and laid his hand ever so gently on the round swell of Sonora's stomach.

Adam came out onto the porch with two cold longneck bottles of beer. "Here, Grandpa, something to cool your throat."

Franklin took it with a smile and then lifted it to a toast to Adam. "To your son and my grandson," he said.

Sonora frowned. "Hey, I'm in this party, too."

"Yes, but you're not drinking, little mama," Adam said, then he lifted the bottle to her. "To Franklin Blue Cat's daughter, who just happens to be the woman of my dreams…and to Sonora, the light of my life and the mother of my son."

She beamed as both men lifted the bottles to their lips and took a long drink. She didn't care. She'd never liked beer much anyway.

Then Adam set his beer aside and lifted her out of Franklin's lap and into his arms. While Franklin watched and grinned, Adam waltzed her down the back porch and then up again.

Sonora had the world—and the men of her heart—at her feet. She'd never been happier or more fulfilled. Her days with the DEA seemed like they'd happened to someone else. Only rarely did she ever think of the department or the people she'd known, and only then with a distant fondness. She didn't miss anything or anyone, because here she was whole.

Franklin smiled, and then leaned back in his chair and closed his eyes, letting the sounds of their joy and laughter wash over him in healing waves.

It was amazing how good he felt these days.

Remission, they called it.

He knew better.
Because of his daughter, he knew he was cured.
Only time and the Old Ones would prove him right.

* * * * *

WHEN YOU CALL MY NAME

Once in the middle of the night, I heard my sister, Diane, call my name. I sat alone in the dark, listening for hours for the sound of her voice. It never came again.

I do not believe that death breaks the bonds of love. And because of that, sometimes I still listen, just to see if she will call for me again.

Diane, if you're listening, this book is dedicated to you, and to the love that we shared.

Chapter 1

It's all your fault. You let me down...let me down.

Wyatt Hatfield shifted in his seat and gripped the steering wheel a little tighter, trying to see through the falling snow to the road ahead, doing everything he could to ignore the memories of his ex-wife's accusations. Shirley and his years with the military were things of the past.

This soul-searching journey he'd embarked upon months earlier was for the sole purpose of finding a new direction for himself. He'd fixed what was wrong with Antonette's life with little more than a phone call. Why, he wondered, couldn't he find a way to fix his own? And then he grinned, remembering how mad his sister had been when he'd interfered.

"At least I'm in her good graces now," he muttered, then cursed beneath his breath when his car suddenly fishtailed.

His heartbeat was still on high as he reminded himself to concentrate on the more pressing issues at hand, namely the blizzard into which he'd driven. The windshield wipers scratched across the icy film covering the glass, scattering the snow in their paths like a dry, whirling flurry, while the heater and defroster did what they could to keep the interior of his car warm.

But as hard as he tried to concentrate on driving, her voice kept ringing in his ear, complaining that when she'd needed him, he was never there.

"Damn it, Shirley, give me a break," Wyatt muttered. "I was wrong. You were right. That should be enough satisfaction for you to let go of my mind."

The car skidded sideways on a patch of ice and Wyatt eased off on the gas, riding with the skid and sighing in relief as the car finally righted itself.

He'd made the wrong decision when he hadn't stopped back in the last town, and he knew it. Then the weather hadn't been this bad, and getting to Lexington, Kentucky, tonight had seemed more important then than it did now. To make things worse, because of the severity of the snowstorm, he wasn't even sure he was on the right road anymore. The weak yellow beam of the headlights did little to illuminate what was left of the road, leaving Wyatt with nothing more than instinct to keep him from driving off the side of the mountain.

And then out of nowhere, the dark, hulking shape of a truck came barreling around a curve and into the beam of light, slipping and sliding as Wyatt had done only moments before, and there was no more time to dwell upon past mistakes. It was too late to do anything but react.

Wyatt gripped the steering wheel, trying desperately to turn away from the truck gone out of control, but he knew before impact that they were going to crash.

"God help us all," Wyatt murmured, knowing there was no earthly way to prevent what was about to happen.

And then the truck's bumper and fender connected with the side of Wyatt's car. Bulk and weight superseded driving skill. Impact sent Wyatt and his car careening across the road and then down the side of the snowpacked mountain.

The last thing he saw was the picture-perfect beauty of lofty pines, heavy with snow and glistening in the headlights of his car. Blessedly, he never felt the car's impact into the first stand of trees...or the next...or the next, or knew when it rolled sideways, then end over end, coming to a steaming, hissing halt against a fifty-foot pine.

He didn't hear the frantic cries of the truck driver, standing at the edge of the road, calling down the mountain and praying for an answer that never came.

The wind from the blizzard whistled beneath the crack in the windowsill across the room. Even in her sleep, Glory heard the high-pitched moan and unconsciously pulled the covers a little higher around her neck. She could hear the warm, familiar grumble of her father, Rafe, snoring. It signified home, protection and family. Directly across from Glory's room, her brother, J.C., slept to the accompaniment of an all-night music station. Mixing with the wail of the wind and the low rumble of an old man's sleep, the melodies seemed somehow appropriate. Glory's long flannel gown added to the cocoon of warmth beneath the mound of covers under which she slept. She shifted, then sighed, and just as her subconscious slipped into dream sleep, she jerked. There was no escape for what came next, even in sleep.

Eyes! Wide, dark, shocked! Red shirt! No...white shirt covered in blood! Blood was everywhere. Pain sifted, filtering through unconsciousness, too terrible to be borne!

Glory's eyelids fluttered and then flew open as suddenly as if someone had thrown open shutters to the world. She sat straight up in bed, unaware of the familiarity of her room or the snow splattering against the windowpanes. Her gaze was wide, fixed, frozen to the picture inside her mind, seeing but not seeing...someone else's horror.

White. Cold, so cold! Snow everywhere...in everything. Can't breathe! Can't see! Can't feel! Oh, God, don't let me die!

Glory shuddered as her body went limp. She leaned forward and, covering her face with her hands, she began to sob. Suddenly the warmth of her room and the comfort of knowing she was safe seemed obscene in the face of what she'd just witnessed. And then as suddenly as the vision had come upon her, the knowledge followed of what she must do next.

She threw back the covers, stumbling on the tail of her nightgown as she crawled out of bed. As she flipped the switch, her bedroom was instantly bathed in the glow of a pale yellow light that gave off a false warmth.

The floor was cold beneath her bare feet as she ran down the hall to the room where her father lay sleeping. For a moment, she stood in his doorway in the dark, listening to the soft, even sound of his snore, and regretted what she was about to do. Yet ignoring her instinct was as impossible for Glory to do as denying the fact that she was a woman.

"Daddy..."

Rafe Dixon woke with a start. He'd heard that sound in his daughter's voice a thousand times before. He rolled over in bed like a hibernating bear coming out of a sleep and dug at his eyes with the heels of his hands.

"Glory, girl, what's wrong?"

"We've got to go, Daddy. He's dying...and I've got to help."

Rafe groaned. He knew better than to deny what Glory was telling him, but he also knew that there was a near blizzard in force, and getting down off this mountain and into Larner's Mill might prove deadly for them all.

"But honey...the storm."

"We'll make it, Daddy, but he won't."

The certainty in her voice was all Rafe Dixon needed to

hear. He rolled out of bed with a thump and started reaching for his clothes.

"Go wake your brother," he said.

"I'm here, Daddy. I heard."

J.C. slipped a comforting arm across his baby sister's shoulders and hugged her. "Was it bad, sis?"

The look on her face was all he needed to know. He headed back down the hall to his room, calling over his shoulder as he went. "I'll go start the truck."

"Dress warm, girl," Rafe growled. "It's a bitch outside."

Glory nodded and flew back to her room, pulling on clothes with wild abandon. The urgency within her made her shake, but her resolve was firm.

Minutes later, they walked out of the house into a blast of snow that stung their faces, but Glory didn't falter. As she was about to step off the porch, J.C. appeared out of nowhere and lifted her off her feet, carrying her through the snow to the waiting vehicle. She shuddered as she clung to his broad shoulders, still locked into the vision before her. And as she saw…she prayed.

"We're not gonna make it," the ambulance driver groaned as he fought the steering wheel and the vehicle's urge to slide.

"Damn it, Farley, just quit talking and drive. We have to make it! If we don't, this fellow sure won't."

Luke Dennis, the emergency medical technician whose fortune it had been to be on duty this night, was up to his elbows in blood. His clothes were soaking wet and his boots were filled to the tops with melting snow. The last thing he wanted to hear was another negative. They'd worked too long and too hard just getting this victim out of his car and up the side of the mountain to give up now.

"Come on, buddy, hang with me," Dennis muttered, as

he traded a fresh container of D5W for the one going empty on the other end of the IV.

An unceasing flow of blood ran out of the victim's dark hair and across his face, mapping his once-handsome features with a crazy quilt of red. It was impossible to guess how many bones this man had broken, and to be honest, those were the least of Dennis's worries. If they couldn't get him back to the hospital in time, it was the internal injuries that would kill him.

"I see lights!" Farley shouted.

Thank God, Dennis thought, and then grabbed his patient and the stretcher, holding on to it, and to him, as the ambulance took the street corner sideways. Moments later they were at the hospital, unloading a man whose chance of a future depended upon the skills of the people awaiting him inside.

Before he was a doctor, Amos Steading had been a medic in Vietnam. When he saw Wyatt Hatfield being wheeled into his E.R., he realized he might have been practicing medicine longer than this patient had been alive. It hurt to lose a patient, but the younger ones were much harder to accept.

"What have we got?" Amos growled, lowering his bushy eyebrows as his attention instantly focused upon the injuries.

"Trouble, Doc," Dennis said. "Thirty-four-year-old male. Recently discharged from the marines. He's still wearing his ID tags. He got sideswiped by a truck and went over the side of Tulley's Mountain. Didn't think we'd ever get him up and out. He's got head injuries, and from the feel of his belly, internal bleeding, as well. From external exam, I'd guess at least four broken ribs, and his right leg has quite a bit of damage, although it's hard to tell what, if anything, is broken. We had to saw a tree and move it off him to get him out of the car." He took a deep breath as the stretcher slid to a halt. As they transferred the victim to the gurney, he added, "This is his third bag of D5W."

Steading's eyebrows arched as he yanked his stethoscope from around his neck and slipped it into place. This man was bleeding to death before their eyes. Moments later, he began firing orders to the nurse and the other doctor on call.

"Get me a blood type," Steading shouted, and a nurse ran to do his bidding.

It was then that EMT Luke Dennis added the last bit of information about the victim, which made them all pause.

"According to his dog tags, he's AB negative," Dennis said.

A low curse slid out of Amos's mouth as he continued to work. Rare blood types didn't belong in this backwater town of eighteen hundred people. There was no way their blood bank was going to have anything like that, and the plasma they had on hand was sparse.

"Type it anyway," Steading ordered. "And get me some plasma, goddamn it! This man's going to die before I can get him stable enough for surgery."

The once quiet hospital instantly became a flurry of shouts, curses and noise. Luke Dennis stepped out of the way, aware that he'd done his job. The rest was up to the doc and his staff...and God.

He started back toward the door to restock the ambulance, aware that the night was far from over. It was entirely possible that more than one fool might decide to venture out in a storm like this. He just hoped that if they plowed themselves into the snow—or into someone else—they were nowhere near a mountain when it happened. But before he could leave, the outside door burst open right before him, and three people blew in, along with a blinding gust of snow.

Glory breathed a shaky sigh of relief. One hurdle crossed. Another yet to come. She burst free of her father's grasp and ran toward the EMT who'd stepped aside to let them pass.

"Mister! Please! Take me to the soldier's doctor."

Dennis couldn't quit staring at the young woman clutching his coat. Her voice was frantic, her behavior strange, but it was her request that startled him. How could she know that the man they'd just brought in was—or at least had been—a soldier?

"Are you a relative?" Dennis asked.

"No! Who I am doesn't matter, but he does," Glory cried, gripping his coat a little tighter. And then she felt her father's hand move across her shoulder.

"Ease up, Glory. You got to explain yourself a little, honey."

She blinked, and Dennis watched focus returning to her expression, thinking as he did that he'd never seen eyes quite that shade of blue. In a certain light, they almost looked silver...as silver as her hair, which clung to her face and coat like strands of wet taffy.

She took a deep breath and started over.

"Please," she said softly. "I came to give blood."

Dennis shook his head. "I don't know how you heard about the accident, but I'm afraid coming out in this storm was a waste of time for you. He's got a rare—"

Glory dug through her purse, her fingers shaking as she searched the contents of her wallet.

"Here," she said, thrusting a card into the man's hands. "Show the doctor. Tell him I can help—that it's urgent that he wait no longer. The man won't live through the night without me."

As Dennis looked down at the card, the hair crawled on the back of his neck. He glanced back up at the woman, then at the card again, and suddenly grabbed her by the arm, pulling her down the hall toward the room where Steading was working.

"Doc, we just got ourselves a miracle," Dennis shouted as he ran into the room.

Amos Steading frowned at the woman Dennis was dragging into their midst.

"Get her out of here, Dennis! You know better than to bring—"

"She's AB negative, Doc, and she's come to give blood."

Steading's hands froze above the tear in the flesh on Wyatt Hatfield's leg.

"You're full of bull," he growled.

Dennis shook his head. "No, I swear to God, Doc. Here's her donor card."

Steading's eyes narrowed and then he barked at a nurse on the other side of the room. "Get her typed and cross-matched. Now!"

She flew to do his bidding.

"And get me some more saline, damn it! This man's losing more fluids than I can pump in him." He cursed softly, then added beneath his breath, fully expecting someone to hear and obey, "And call down to X-ray and find out why his films aren't back!" As he leaned back over the patient, he began to mumble again, more to himself than to anyone else. "Now, where the hell is that bleeder?"

There was a moment, in the midst of all the doctor's orders, when Glory looked upon the injured man's face. It wasn't often that she had a physical connection to the people in her mind.

"What's his name?" she whispered as a nurse grabbed her by the arm and all but dragged her down the hall to the lab.

"Who, Dr. Steading?"

"No," Glory said. "The man who was hurt."

"Oh…uh…Hatfield. William…no, uh…Wyatt. Yes, that's right. Wyatt Hatfield. It's a shame, too," the nurse muttered, more to herself than to Glory. "He looks like he was real handsome…and so young. Just got out of the service. From his identification, some sort of special forces. It's sort of ironic, isn't it?"

"What's ironic?" Glory asked, and then they entered the lab, and the scents that assailed her threatened to overwhelm. She swayed on her feet, and the nurse quickly seated her in a chair.

The nurse grimaced. "Why, the fact that he could survive God knows what during his stint in the military, and then come to this, and all because of a snowstorm on a mountain road." Suddenly she was all business. "Stuart, type and cross-match this woman's blood, stat! If she comes up AB negative and a match to the man in E.R., then draw blood. She's a donor."

As the lab tech began, Glory relaxed. At least they were on the right track.

Three o'clock in the morning had come and gone, and the waiting room in E.R. was quiet. Rafe Dixon glanced at his son, then at his daughter, who seemed to be dozing beside him. How he'd fathered two such different children was beyond him, but his pride in each was unbounded. It just took more effort to keep up with Glory than it did J.C.

He understood his son and his love for their land. He didn't understand one thing about his daughter's gift, but he believed in it, and he believed in her. What worried him most was who would take care of Glory when he was gone? J.C. was nearly thirty and he couldn't be expected to watch over his sister for the rest of his life. Besides, if he was to marry, a wife might resent the attention J.C. unstintingly gave his baby sister. Although Glory was twenty-five, she looked little more than eighteen. Her delicate features and her fragile build often gave her the appearance of a child... until one looked into her eyes and saw the ancient soul looking back.

Glory, child...who will take care of you when I am gone?

Suddenly Glory stood and looked down the hall. Rafe stirred, expecting to see someone open and walk through the doors at the far end. But nothing happened, and no one came.

She slipped her fingers in the palm of her brother's hand and then stood. "We can go home now."

J.C. yawned and looked up at his father. Their eyes met in a moment of instant understanding. For whatever her reasons, Glory seemed satisfied within herself, and for them, that was all that mattered.

"Are you sure, girl?" Rafe asked as he helped Glory on with her coat.

She nodded, her head bobbing wearily upon her shoulders. "I'm sure, Daddy."

"You don't want to wait and talk to the doctor?"

She smiled. "There's no need."

As suddenly as they'd arrived, they were gone.

Within the hour, Amos Steading came out of surgery, tossing surgical gloves and blood-splattered clothing in their respective hampers. Later, when he went to look for the unexpected blood donor, to his surprise, she was nowhere to be found. And while he thought it strange that she'd not stayed to hear the results of the surgery, he was too tired and too elated to worry about her odd exodus. Tonight he'd fought the grim reaper and won. And while he knew his skill as a surgeon was nothing at which to scoff, his patient still lived because of a girl who'd come out of the storm.

Steading dropped into a chair at his desk and began working up Hatfield's chart, adding notes of the surgery to what had been done in E.R. A nurse entered, then gave him a cup of hot coffee and an understanding smile. As the heat from the cup warmed his hand, he sighed in satisfaction.

"Did you locate his next of kin?" Steading asked.

The nurse nodded. "Yes, sir, a sister. Her name is Antonette Monday. She said that she and her husband will come as soon as weather permits."

Steading nodded, and sipped the steaming brew. "It's good to have family."

High up on the mountain above Larner's Mill, Glory Dixon would have agreed with him. When they finally pulled into the yard of their home, it was only a few hours before daybreak, and yet she knew a sense of satisfaction for a job well done. It wasn't always that good came of what she *saw,* but tonight she'd been able to make a difference.

She reached over and patted her father's knee. "Thank you, Daddy," she said quietly.

"For what?" he asked.

"For believing me."

He slid a long arm across her shoulder, giving her a hug. There was nothing more that needed to be said.

"Looks like the snow's about stopped," he said, gauging the sparse spit of snowflakes dancing before the headlights of their truck.

"Who's hungry?" Glory asked.

J.C. grinned. "Wanna guess?"

She laughed. It was a perfect ending to a very bad beginning.

Back in recovery, Wyatt Hatfield wasn't laughing, but if he'd been conscious, he would have been counting his blessings. He had a cut on his cheek that would probably scar and had survived a lung that had collapsed, a concussion that should have put him into a coma and hadn't, five broken ribs and two cracked ones, more stitches in his left leg than he would be able to count and, had he been able to feel them, bruises in every joint.

He could thank a seat belt, a trucker who hadn't kept going after causing the wreck, a rescue crew that went above and beyond the call of duty to get him off the mountain and an EMT who didn't know the meaning of the word *quit.* And it was extremely good luck on Wyatt's part that, after all that, he wound up in the skilled hands of Amos Steading.

Yet it was fate that had delivered him to Glory Dixon. And had she not given of the blood from her body, the cold and simple fact was that he would have died. But Wyatt didn't know his good fortune. It would be days before he would know his own name.

All day long, the sun kept trying to shine. Wyatt paced the floor of his hospital room, ignoring the muscle twinges in his injured leg and the pull of sore muscles across his belly.

He didn't give a damn about pain. Today he was going home, or a reasonable facsimile thereof. While he didn't have a home of his own, he still had roots in the land on which he'd been raised. If he had refused to accompany his sister, Toni, back to Tennessee, he suspected that her husband, Lane Monday, would have slung him over his shoulder and taken him anyway. Few but Toni dared argue with Lane Monday. At six feet seven inches, he was a powerful, imposing man. As a United States marshal, he was formidable. In Wyatt's eyes, he'd come through for Toni like a real man should. There was little else to be said.

Outside his door, he could hear his sister's voice at the nurses' station while she signed the papers that would check him out. He leaned his forehead against the window, surprised that in spite of the sun's rays it felt cold, and then remembered that winter sun, at its best, was rarely warm.

"Are you ready, Wyatt?"

Wyatt turned. Lane filled the doorway with his size and his presence.

He shrugged. "I guess." He turned back to the window as Lane crossed the room.

For a while, both men were silent, and then Lane gave

Wyatt a quick pat on the back before he spoke. "I think maybe I know how you feel," Lane said.

Wyatt shrugged. "Then I wish to hell you'd tell me, because I don't understand. Don't get me wrong. I'm happy to be alive." He tried to grin. "Hell, and if truth be told, a little surprised. When I went over the mountain, in the space of time it took to hit the first stand of trees, I more or less made my peace with God. I never expected to wake up."

Lane listened without commenting, knowing that something was bothering Wyatt that he needed to get said.

"As for my family, I consider myself lucky to have people who are willing to take me in, but I feel so...so..."

"Rootless?"

For a moment Wyatt was silent, and then he nodded.

"Exactly. I feel rootless. And...I feel like leaving here will be taking a step backward in what I was searching for. I know it's weird, but I keep thinking that I was *this* close to the end of a journey, and now—"

Toni broke the moment of confiding as she came into the room.

"You're all checked out!" When Wyatt started toward the door, she held up her hand. "Don't get in too big a hurry. They're bringing a wheelchair. Lane, honey, why don't you pull the car up to the curb? Wyatt, are you all packed?"

Both men looked at each other and then grinned. "She was your sister before she was my wife," Lane warned him. "So you can't be surprised by all this."

Toni ignored them. It was her nature to organize. She'd spent too long on her own, running a farm and caring for aging parents, to wait for someone else to make a decision.

"Why don't I go get the car?" Lane said, and stole a kiss from his Toni as he passed.

"I'm packed," Wyatt said.

"I brought one of Justin's coats for you to wear. The clothes you had on were ruined," Toni said, her eyes tearing as she remembered his condition upon their arrival right after the accident. She held out the coat for him to put on. Wyatt slipped one arm in his brother's coat and then the other, then turned and hugged her, letting himself absorb the care…and the love.

"Now all I need is my ride," Wyatt teased, and pulled at a loose curl hanging across Toni's forehead.

On cue, a nurse came in pushing a wheelchair, and within minutes, Wyatt was on his way.

The air outside was a welcome respite from the recirculated air inside his room. And the cold, fresh scent of snow was infinitely better than the aroma of antiseptic. Wyatt gripped the arms of the wheelchair in anticipation of going home.

Just outside the doors, Toni turned away to speak to the nurse, and Lane had yet to arrive. For a brief moment, Wyatt was left to his own devices. He braced himself, angling his sore leg until he was able to stand, and then lifted his face and inhaled, letting the brisk draft of air circling the corner of the hospital have its way with the cobwebs in his mind. He'd been inside far too long.

A pharmacy across the street was doing a booming business, and Wyatt watched absently as customers came and went. As a van loaded with senior citizens backed up and drove away, a dark blue pickup truck pulled into the recently vacated parking space. He tried not to stare at the three people who got out, but they were such a range of sizes, he couldn't quit looking.

The older man was tall and broad beneath the heavy winter coat he wore. A red sock cap covered a thatch of thick graying hair, and the brush of mustache across his upper lip was several shades darker than the gray. The younger man was just as tall, and in spite of his own heavy clothing, obviously fit. His face was creased with laugh lines, and he moved with the grace and assurance of youth and good health.

It was the girl between them who caught Wyatt's eye. At first he thought she was little more than a child, and then the wind caught the front of her unbuttoned coat, and he got a glimpse of womanly breast and shapely hips before she pulled it together.

Her hair was the color of spun honey. Almost gold. Not quite white. Her lips were full and tilted in a grin at something one of the men just said, and Wyatt had a sudden wish that he'd been the one to make her smile.

No sooner had he thought it than she paused at the door, then stopped completely. He held his breath as she began to turn. When she caught his gaze, he imagined he felt her gasp, although he knew it was a foolish thing to consider. His mind wandered as he let himself feast upon her face.

So beautiful, Wyatt thought.

Why, thank you.

Wyatt was so locked into her gaze that he felt no surprise at the thoughts that suddenly drifted through his mind, or that he was answering them back in an unusual fashion.

You are welcome.

So, Wyatt Hatfield, you're going home?

Yes.

God be with you, soldier.

I'm no longer a soldier.

You will always fight for those you love.

"Here comes Lane!"

At the sound of Toni's voice, Wyatt blinked, then turned and stepped back as Lane pulled up to the curb. When he remembered to look up, the trio had disappeared into the store. He felt an odd sense of loss, as if he'd been disconnected from something he needed to know.

Bowing to the demands of his family's concerns, he let himself be plied with pillows and blankets. By the time they had him comfortable in the roomy backseat of their car, he was more than ready for the long journey home to begin.

They were past the boundary of Larner's Mill, heading out of Kentucky and toward Tennessee, when Wyatt's thoughts wandered back to the girl he'd seen on the street. And as suddenly as he remembered her, he froze. His heart began to hammer inside his chest as he slowly sat up and stared out the back window at the small mountain town that was swiftly disappearing from sight.

"Dear God," he whispered, and wiped a shaky hand across his face.

"Wyatt, darling, are you all right?"

His sister's tone of voice was worried, the touch of her hand upon his shoulder gentle and concerned. Lane began to ease off the accelerator, thinking that Wyatt might be getting sick.

"I'm fine. I'm fine," he muttered, and dropped back onto the bed they'd made for him in the backseat.

There was no way he could tell them what he'd suddenly realized. There wasn't even any way he could explain it to himself. But he knew, as well as he knew his own name, that the conversation he'd had with that girl had been real. And yet understanding how it had happened was another thing altogether. He'd heard of silent communication, but this…this…thing that just happened… It was impossible.

"Then how did she know my name?" he murmured.

"What did you say?" Toni asked.

Wyatt turned his head into the pillow and closed his eyes.

"Nothing, sis. Nothing at all."

Chapter 2

Clouds moved in wild, scattered patterns above the Hatfield homestead, giving way to the swift air current blasting through the upper atmosphere. The clouds looked as unsettled as Wyatt felt. In his mind, it had taken forever to get back his health, and then even longer to gain strength. But now, except for a scar on his cheek and a leg that would probably ache for the rest of his life every time it rained, he was fine.

Problem was, he'd been here too long. He leaned forward, bracing his hands upon the windowsill and gazing out at the yard that spilled toward the banks of Chaney Creek, while his blood stirred to be on the move.

"The grass is beginning to green."

The longing in Wyatt's voice was obvious, but for what, Toni didn't know. Was he missing the companionship of his ex-wife, or was there something missing from his own inner self that he didn't know how to find?

"I know," Toni said, and shifted Joy to her other hip, trying not to mind that Wyatt was restless. He was her brother, and this *was* his home, but he was no longer the boy who'd chased her through the woods. He'd been a man alone for a long, long time.

She could hear the longing in his voice and sensed his need to be on the move, but she feared that once gone, he would fall back into the depression in which they'd brought him home. Her mind whirled as she tried to think of something to cheer him up. Her daughter fidgeted in her arms, reaching for anything she could lay her hands on. Toni smiled and kissed Joy on her cheek, thinking what they'd been doing this time last year and the telegram that Wyatt had sent.

"Remember last year…when you sent the telegram? It came on Easter. Did you know that?"

Wyatt nodded, then grinned, also remembering how mad Toni had been at him when he'd interfered in her personal life.

"In a few weeks, it will be Easter again. Last year someone gave us a little jumpsuit for Joy, complete with long pink ears on the outside of the hood. It made her look like a baby rabbit. The kids carried her around all day, fussing over who was going to have their picture taken next with the Easter Bunny."

Wyatt smiled, and when Joy leaned over, trying to stick her hand in the pot on the stove, he took the toddler from his sister's arms, freeing her to finish the pudding she was stirring.

Joy instantly grabbed a fistful of his hair in each hand and began to pull. Wyatt winced, then laughed as he started to unwind her tiny hands from the grip they had on his head.

"Hey, puddin' face. Don't pull all of Uncle Wyatt's hair out. He's going to need it for when he's an old man."

Joy chortled gleefully as it quickly became a game, and

for a time, Wyatt's restlessness was forgotten in his delight with the child.

It was long into the night when the old, uneasy feelings began to return. Wyatt paced the floor beside his bed until he was sick of the room, then slipped out of the house to stand on the porch. The moonless night was so thick and dark that it seemed airless. Absorbing the quiet, he let it surround him. As a kind of peace began to settle, he sat down on the steps, listening to the night life that abounded in their woods.

He kept telling himself that it was the memories of the wreck and the lost days in between that kept him out of bed. If he lay down, he would sleep. If he slept, he would dream. Nightmares of snow and blood, of pain and confusion. But that wasn't exactly true. It was the memory of a woman's voice that wouldn't let go of his mind.

You will always fight for those you love.

Eliminating the obvious, which he took to mean his own family, exactly what did that mean? Even more important, how the hell had that…that thing…happened between them?

Toni had told him more than once that he'd survived the wreck for a reason, and that one day he'd know why. But Wyatt wanted answers to questions he didn't even know how to ask. In effect, he felt as though he were living in a vacuum, waiting for someone to break the seal.

Yet Wyatt Hatfield wasn't the only man that night at a breaking point. Back in Larner's Mill, Kentucky, a man named Carter Foster was at the point of no return, trying to hold on to his sanity and his wife, and doing a poor job of both.

Carter paced the space in front of their bed, watching with growing dismay as Betty Jo began to put on another layer of makeup. As if the dress she was wearing wasn't revealing enough, she was making herself look like a whore. Her actions of late seemed to dare him to complain.

"Now, sweetheart, I'm not trying to control you, but I think I have a right to know where you're going. How is it going to look to the townspeople if you keep going out at night without me?"

He hated the whine in his voice, but couldn't find another way to approach his wife of eleven years about her latest affair. That she was having them was no secret. That the people of Larner's Mill must never find out was of the utmost importance to him. In his profession, appearances were everything.

Betty Jo arched her perfectly painted eyebrows and then stabbed a hair pick into her hair, lifting the back-combed nest she'd made of her dark red tresses to add necessary inches to her height. Ignoring Carter's complaint, she stepped back from the full-length mirror, running her hands lightly down her buxom figure in silent appreciation. That white knit dress she'd bought yesterday looked even better on than it had on the hanger.

"Betty Jo, you didn't answer me," Carter said, unaware that his voice had risen a couple of notes.

Silence prevailed as she ran her little finger across her upper then lower lip, smoothing out the Dixie Red lipstick she'd applied with a flourish. When she rubbed her lips together to even out the color, Carter shuddered, hating himself for still wanting her. He couldn't remember the last time she'd put those lips anywhere on him.

"Carter, honey, you know a woman like me needs her space. With you stuck in that stuffy old courtroom all day, and in your office here at home all night, what am I to do?"

The pout on her lips made him furious. At this stage of their marriage, that baby-faced attitude would get her nowhere.

"But you're *my* wife," Carter argued. "It just isn't right

that you...that men..." He took a deep breath and then puffed out his cheeks in frustration, unaware that it made him look like a bullfrog.

Betty Jo pivoted toward him, then stepped into her shoes, relishing the power that the added height of the three-inch heels gave her. She knew that if she had college to do over again, she would have married the jock, not the brain. This poor excuse for a man was losing his hair and sporting a belly that disgusted her. When he walked, it swayed lightly from side to side like the big breasts of a woman who wore no support. She liked tight, firm bellies and hard muscles. There was nothing hard on Carter Foster. Not even periodically. To put it bluntly, Betty Jo Foster was an unsatisfied woman in the prime of her life.

Ignoring his petulant complaints as nothing but more of the same, she picked up her purse. To her surprise, he grabbed her by the forearm and all but shook her. The purse fell between them, lost in the unexpected shuffle of feet.

"Damn it, Betty Jo! You heard me! This just isn't right!"

"Hey!" she said, then frowned. She couldn't remember the last time Carter had raised his voice to her. She yanked, trying to pull herself free from his grasp, but to her dismay, his fingers tightened.

"Carter! You're hurting me!"

"So what?" he snarled, and shoved her backward onto their bed. "You're hurting me."

A slight panic began to surface. He never got angry. At least he never *used* to. Without thinking, she rolled over on her stomach to keep from messing up her hair and started to crawl off the bed. But turning her back on him was her first and last mistake. Before she could get up, Carter came down on top of her, pushing her into the mattress, calling her names she didn't even know he knew.

Betty Jo screamed, but the sound had nowhere to go. The weight of his body kept pushing her deeper and deeper into the mattress, and when the bulk of him settled across her hips, and his shoes began snagging runs in her panty hose, she realized that he was sitting on her. In shock, she began to fight.

Flailing helplessly, her hands clenched in the bedspread as she tried unsuccessfully to maneuver herself out from under him. Panic became horror as his hands suddenly circled her neck. The more she kicked and bounced, the tighter he squeezed.

A wayward thought crossed her mind that he'd messed up her hair and that Dixie Red lipstick would not wash out of the bedspread. It was the last of her worries as tiny bursts of lights began to go off behind her eyelids. Bright, bright, brighter they burned until they shattered into one great, blinding-white explosion.

As suddenly as it had come, the rage that had taken him into another dimension began to subside. Carter shuddered and shuddered as his hands slowly loosened, and when he went limp atop her body, guilt at his unexpected burst of temper began to surface. He'd never been a physical sort of man, and didn't quite know how to explain this side of himself.

"Damn it, Betty Jo, I'm real sorry this happened, but you've been driving me to it for years."

Oddly enough, Betty Jo had nothing to say about his emotional outburst, and he wondered as he crawled off her butt why he hadn't done this years earlier. Maybe if he'd asserted himself when all of her misbehaving began, brute force would never have been necessary.

He smoothed down his hair, then wiped his sweaty palms against the legs of his slacks. Even from here, he could still smell the scent of her perfume upon his skin.

"Get up, Betty Jo. There's no need to pout. You always get your way, whether I like it or not."

Again, she remained silent. Carter's gaze ran up then

down her body, noting as it did, that he'd ruined her hose
and smudged her dress. When she saw what he'd done to
the back of her skirt, she would be furious.

"Okay, fine," Carter said, and started to walk away.

As he passed the foot of the bed, one of her shoes suddenly popped off the end of her heel and stabbed itself into
the spread. He paused, starting to make an ugly comment
about the fact that she was undressing for the wrong man,
when something about her position struck him as odd. He
leaned over the bed frame and tentatively ran his forefinger across the bottom of her foot. Her immobility scared
the hell out of him. Betty Jo was as ticklish as they came.

"Oh, God," Carter muttered, and ran around to the edge
of the bed, grabbing her by the shoulder. "Betty Jo, this
isn't funny!"

He rolled her onto her back, and when he got a firsthand
look at the dark red smear of lipstick across her face and her
wide, sightless eyes staring up at him, he began to shake.

"Betty, honey…"

She didn't move.

He thumped her in the middle of the chest, noting absently that she was not wearing a bra, and then started to
sweat.

"Betty Jo, wake up!" he screamed, and pushed up and
down between her breasts, trying to emulate CPR tech-
niques he didn't actually know.

The only motion he got out of her was a lilt and a sway
from her buxom bosom as he hammered about her chest,
trying to make her breathe.

"No! God, no!"

Suddenly he jerked his hands to his stomach, as if he'd
been burned by the touch of her skin. To his utter dismay,
he felt bile rising, and barely made it to the bathroom before it spewed.

Several hours later, he heard the hall clock strike two

times, and realized that, in four hours, it would be time to get up. He giggled at the thought, then buried his face in his hands. That was silly. How could one get up when one had never been down? Betty Jo's body lay right where he'd left it, half on, half off the bed, as if he wasn't sure what to do next.

And therein lay Carter's problem. He *didn't* know what to do next. Twice since the deed, he'd reached for the phone to call the police, and each time he'd paused, remembering what would happen when they came. There was no way he could explain that it was really all her fault. That she'd ruined him and his reputation by tarnishing her own.

And that was when it struck him. It *was* her fault. And by God, he shouldn't have to pay!

Suddenly, a way out presented itself, and he bolted from the chair and began rolling her up in the stained bedspread, then fastening it in place with two of his belts. One he buckled just above her head, the other at her ankles. He stepped back to survey his work, and had an absent thought that Betty Jo would hate knowing that she was going to her maker looking like a tamale. Without giving himself time to reconsider, he threw her over his shoulder and carried her, fireman-style, out of the kitchen and into the attached garage, dumping her into the trunk of his car.

Grabbing a suitcase from the back of a closet, he raced to their bedroom and began throwing items of her clothing haphazardly into the bag before returning to the car. As he tossed the suitcase in the trunk with her body, he took great satisfaction in the fact that he had to lie on the trunk to get it closed.

As he backed from the garage and headed uptown toward an all-night money machine, the deviousness of his own thoughts surprised him. He would never have imagined himself being able to carry off something like this, yet it was happening just the same. If he was going to make this work, it had to look like Betty Jo took money with her when she ran. With this in mind, he continued toward the town's only ATM.

As he pulled up, the spotlight above the money machine glared in his eyes. He jumped out of the car, and with a sharp blow of his fist, knocked out the Plexiglas and the bulb, leaving himself in the bank drive-through in sudden darkness. Minutes later, with the cash in his pocket, he was back in the car and heading out of town toward the city dump.

Ever thankful that Larner's Mill was too small-town in its thinking to ever put up a gate or a lock, Carter drove right through and up to the pit without having to brake for anything more than a possum ambling across the road in the dark.

When he got out, he was shaking with a mixture of exertion and excitement. As he threw the suitcase over the edge, he took a deep breath, watching it bounce end over end, down the steep embankment. When he lifted his wife from the trunk and sent her after it, he started to grin. But the white bedspread in which she was wrapped stood out like a beacon in the night. He could just imagine what would hit the fan if Betty Jo turned up in this condition. He had to cover up the spread.

It was while he was turning in a circle, looking for something with which to shovel, that he saw the bulldozer off to the side.

That's it, he thought. All he needed to do was shove some dirt down on top. Tomorrow was trash day. By the time the trash trucks made the rounds and dumped the loads, she'd be right where she belonged, buried with the rest of the garbage.

It took a bit for him to figure out how to work the bulldozer's controls, but desperation was a shrewd taskmaster, and Carter Foster was as desperate as they came. Within the hour, a goodly portion of dirt had been pushed in on top of the latest addition to the city dump, and Betty Jo Foster's burial was slightly less dignified than she would have hoped.

Minutes later, Carter was on his way home to shower and change. As he pulled into his garage, he pressed the remote control and breathed a great sigh of satisfaction as the door dropped shut behind him.

It was over!

His feet were dragging as he went inside, but his lawyer mind was already preparing the case he would present to his coworkers. Exactly how much he would be willing to humble himself was still in the planning stage. If they made fun of him behind his back because he'd been dumped, he didn't think he would care. The last laugh would be his.

Days later, while Betty Jo rotted along with the rest of the garbage in Larner's Mill, Glory Dixon was making her second sweep through the house, looking behind chairs and under cushions, trying to find her keys. But the harder she looked, the more certain she was that someone else and not her carelessness was to blame.

Her brother came into the kitchen just as she dumped the trash onto the floor and began sorting through the papers.

"J.C., have you seen my keys? I can't find them anywhere."

"Nope." He pulled the long braid she'd made of her hair. "Why don't you just psych them out?"

Glory ignored the casual slander he made of her psychic ability and removed her braid from his hand. "You know it doesn't work like that. I never know what I'm going to *see*. If I did, I would have told on you years ago for filching Granny's blackberry pies."

He was still laughing as their father entered the house by the back door.

"Honey, are you ready to go?" Rafe asked. "We've got a full morning and then some before we're through in town."

She threw up her hands in frustration. "I can't find my keys."

Her father shrugged, then had a thought. "Did you let that pup in the house last night?"

The guilty expression on her face was answer enough.

"Then there's your answer," he muttered. "What that blamed pooch hasn't already chewed up, he's buried. You'll be lucky if you ever see them again."

"Shoot," Glory muttered, and started out the door in search of the dog.

"Let it wait until we come home," Rafe said. "I've got keys galore. If you don't find yours, we'll get copies made of mine. Now grab your grocery list. Time's a'wastin'."

"Don't forget my Twinkies," J.C. said, and slammed the kitchen door behind him as he exited the house.

Glory grinned at her brother's request, then did as her father asked. As she and Rafe drove out of the yard, they could see the back end of the John Deere tractor turning the corner in the lane. J.C. was on his way to the south forty. It was time to work ground for spring planting.

Carter was playing the abandoned husband to the hilt, and oddly enough, enjoying the unexpected sympathy he was receiving from the townspeople. It seemed that they'd known about Betty Jo's high jinks for years, and were not the least surprised by this latest stunt.

As he stood in line at the teller's window at the bank, he was congratulating himself on the brilliance of his latest plan. This would be the icing on the cake.

"I need to withdraw some money from my savings account and deposit it into checking," he told the teller. "Betty Jo nearly cleaned me out."

The teller clucked sympathetically. "I'll need your account numbers," she said.

Carter looked slightly appalled. "I forgot to bring them."

"Don't you worry," the teller said. "I can look them up on the computer. It won't take but a minute."

As the teller hurried away, Carter relaxed, gazing absently around the room, taking note of who was begging and who was borrowing, when he saw a woman across the lobby staring at him as if he'd suddenly grown horns and warts. So intent was her interest that he instinctively glanced down to see if his fly was unzipped, and then covertly brushed at his face, then his tie, checking for something that didn't belong. Except for her interest, all was as it should be.

Twice he looked away, thinking that when he would turn back, she'd surely be doing something else. To his dismay, her expression never wavered. By the time the teller came back, his impatience had turned to curiosity.

He leaned toward the teller, whispering in a low, urgent tone. "Who is that woman?"

The teller looked up as he pointed across the room at Glory.

"What woman?" she asked.

"The blonde beside that old man. The one who keeps staring this way."

The teller rolled her eyes and then snorted softly through her nostrils.

"Oh! Her! That's that crazy Glory Dixon and her father."

Dixon... I know that man. I hunted quail on his place last year with Tollet Faye and his boys.

The teller kept talking, unaware that Carter was turning pale. He was remembering the gossip he'd heard about the girl and imagined she could see blood on him that wasn't really there.

"She fancies herself some sort of psychic. Claims that

she can *see* into the future, or some such nonsense. Person-ally, I don't believe in that garbage. Now then…how much did you want to transfer?"

Carter was shaking. He told himself that he didn't be-lieve in such things either, but his guilty conscience and Betty Jo's rotting body were hard to get past. He had vi-sions of Glory Dixon standing up from her chair, pointing an accusing finger toward him and screaming "murderer" to all who cared to hear.

And no sooner had the thought come than Glory un-crossed her legs. Believing her to be on the verge of a rev-elation, he panicked.

"I just remembered an appointment," he told the teller. "I'll have to come back later."

With that, he bolted out of the bank and across the street into an alley, leaving the teller to think what she chose. Moments later, the Dixons came out of the bank and drove away. He watched until he saw them turn into the parking lot of the diner on the corner, and then relaxed.

Okay, okay, maybe I made a big deal out of nothing, he told himself, and brushed at the front of his suit coat as he started back to his office. But the farther he walked, the more convinced he became that he was playing with fire if he didn't tie up his loose ends. Before he gave himself time to reconsider, he got into his car and drove out of town. He had no plan in mind. Only a destination.

The small frame house was nestled against the backdrop of Pine Mountain. A black-and-white pup lay on the front porch, gnawing on a stick. Carter watched until the puppy ambled off toward the barn, and then he waited a while longer, just to make sure that there was no one in sight. Off in the distance, the sound of a tractor could be heard as it plowed up and down a field. As he started toward the house, a light breeze lifted the tail of his suit coat.

He didn't know what he was going to do, but he told himself that something *must* be done or all of his careful planning would be for nothing. If he was going to ignore the fact that Glory Dixon could reveal his secret, then he might as well have called the police the night of the crime instead of going to all the trouble to conceal it.

Planks creaked upon the porch as it gave beneath his weight. He knocked, then waited, wondering what on earth he would say if someone actually answered. Then he knocked again and again, but no one came. He looked around the yard, assuring himself that he was still unobserved, and then threw his weight against the door. It popped like a cork out of a bottle, and before Carter could think to brace himself, he fell through the doorway and onto the floor before scrambling to his feet.

Now that he was inside, his thoughts scattered. Betty Jo's death had been an accident. What he was thinking of doing was premeditated murder. Yet the problem remained, how to hide one without committing the other. He stood in place, letting himself absorb the thought of the deed. And as he gazed around the room, his attention caught and then focused on the small heating stove in the corner.

It was fueled with gas.

He began to smile.

An idea was forming as he headed for the kitchen. His hands were shaking as he began to investigate the inner workings of the Dixons' cookstove. It didn't take long to find and then blow out the pilot light. As he turned on all the jets, he held his breath. The unmistakable hiss of escaping gas filled the quiet room.

With a sharp turn of his wrist, he turned even harder until one of the controls broke off in his hands. Let them try to turn that baby off, he thought, and hurried out of the kitchen.

Carter wasn't stupid. He knew that almost anything

could ignite this—from a ringing telephone to the simple flick of a light switch when someone entered a room. And while he had no control over who came in the house first, he could at least make sure the house didn't blow with no one in it.

With his thumb and forefinger, he carefully lifted the receiver from the cradle and set it to one side. The loud, intermittent buzz of a phone off the hook mingled with the deadly hiss behind him.

Now that it was done, an anxiety to escape was overwhelming. Carter ran through the house and out onto the porch. Careful to pull the front door shut behind him, he jumped into his car and drove away while death filtered slowly throughout the rooms.

It was dusk. Dew was already settling upon the grass, and the sun, like Humpty-Dumpty, was about to fall beyond the horizon as Rafe Dixon drove into the yard and parked beneath the tree near the back door.

J.C. came out of the barn just as Rafe crawled out of the cab. Glory swung her legs out and then slid out of the seat, stretching wearily from the long ride. It felt good to be home. She couldn't wait to get in the house and trade her ropers for slippers, her blue jeans for shorts and the long-sleeved pink shirt she was wearing for one of J.C.'s old T-shirts. They went down past her knees and felt soft as butter against her skin. They were her favorite items of clothing.

Their errands had taken longer than she'd expected, and she'd told herself more than once during the day that if she'd known all her father had planned to do, she wouldn't have gone. She leaned over the side of the truck bed and lifted the nearest sack into her arms.

"Right on time," Rafe shouted, and motioned his son to

the sacks of groceries yet to be unloaded from the back of their truck. "Hey, boy, give us a hand."

J.C. came running. "Daddy! Look! I found another arrowhead today."

Both Rafe and Glory turned to admire his latest find. Collecting them had been J.C.'s passion since he'd found his first years ago. Now he was an avid collector and had more than one hundred of them mounted in frames and hanging on the walls of his room.

"That's a good one," Glory said, running her fingers over the hand-chipped edge and marveling at the skill of the one who had made it. In spite of its obvious age, it was perfectly symmetrical in form.

"Groceries are gonna melt," Rafe warned.

J.C. grinned and winked at his little sister, then dropped the arrowhead into his pocket. He obliged his father by picking up a sack, and then stopping to dig through the one Glory was holding.

"Hey, Morning Glory, did you remember my Twinkies?"

The childhood nickname made her smile as she took the package from her sack and dropped it into the one he was holding. But the urge to laugh faded as quickly as the world that began to slip out of focus.

Common sense told her that she was standing in the yard surrounded by those who loved her best, but it wasn't how she felt. She could barely hear her father's voice above the sound of her own heart breaking. Every breath that she took was a struggle, and although she tried over and over to talk, the words wouldn't come.

Struggling to come out of the fugue, she grabbed hold of the truck bed, desperate to regain her sense of self. Vaguely, she could hear her brother and father arguing over whose turn it was to do the dishes after supper. When sanity returned and she found the words to speak, they were at the back porch steps.

"Daddy! Wait," Glory shouted, as her father slipped the key in the lock.

Even from where she stood, she knew it was going to be too late.

"Hey, look! I think I just found your keys!" J.C. shouted, laughing and pointing at the puppy coming out of the barn behind them.

It was reflex that made Glory turn. Sure enough, keys dangled from the corner of the pup's mouth as he chewed on the braided leather strap dangling from the ring.

And then it seemed as if everything happened in slow motion. She spun, her father's name on her lips as she started toward the house. In a corner of her mind, she was vaguely aware of J.C.'s surprised shout, and then the back door flew off the hinges and into the bed of the truck. The impact of the explosion threw Glory across the yard where she lay, unconscious.

When reason returned, the first things she felt were heat on her back and the puppy licking her face. She groaned, unable to remember how she'd come to this position, and crawled to her knees before staggering to her feet. Something wet slid down her cheek, and when she touched it, her fingers came away covered in blood. And then she remembered the blast and spun.

She kept telling herself that this was all a bad dream, and that her brother would come out of the door with one Twinkie in his mouth and another in his hand. But it was impossible to ignore the thick black coils of smoke snaking up from the burning timbers, marking the spot that had once been home.

Still unable to believe her eyes, she took several shaky steps forward.

"Daddy?" He didn't answer. Her voice rose and trembled as she repeated the cry. "Daaddee! No! No! God, no! Somebody help me!"

Something inside the inferno exploded. A fire within a fire. It was then that she began to scream.

Terror. Horror. Despair.

There were no words for what she felt. Only the devastating knowledge that she'd *seen* the end of those she loved most and had not been able to stop it.

She fell to her knees as gut-wrenching tears tore up her throat and out into the night. Heat seared her skin and scorched her hair as she considered walking into what was left of the pyre. All of her life she'd been separated from the crowd by the fact that she was different, and the only people who'd accepted and loved her for herself had been her father and brother. If they were gone, who would love her now?

And while she stared blindly at the orange-and-yellow tongues licking at what was left of her home, another image superimposed itself over the flames, and Glory found herself straining toward it, unable to believe what she saw.

A man! Walking through their house, running from room to room. She saw the backs of his hands as they hovered above the stove. Saw them twist…saw them turn… saw them kill. And then he ran, and all that she saw was the silhouette of his back as he moved out the door. The hair crawled on the back of her neck as a reality only Glory understood suddenly surfaced.

Oh, my God! This wasn't an accident!

It was a gut reaction, but she spun in fear, searching for a place to hide. In the dark, she stumbled, falling to her knees. Still in a panic to hide, she crawled, then ran, aiming for the dark, yawning maw of the barn door. Only when she was inside did she turn to look behind her, imagining him still out there…somewhere.

Why would someone want us dead? And no sooner had

the thought come than her answer followed. *It wasn't them.
It was me who was supposed to die.*

She slipped even farther inside the barn, staring wide-
eyed out into the night, unable to believe what her mind already knew. The guilt that came with the knowledge could
have driven Glory over the edge of reason. But it didn't.
She couldn't let her father and brother's killer get away
with this.

But who...and why? Who could possibly care if she
lived or died?

Instinct told her that it wasn't a stranger. But instinct
was a poor substitute for facts, and Glory had none. The
only thing she knew for sure was that she needed a plan,
and she needed time.

There was no way of knowing how long she'd been unconscious, but neighbors were bound to see the fire and
could be arriving any minute. A sense of self-preservation
warned her that she must hide until she found someone
she could trust. Within a day or so, the killer would know
that two, not three people, had died in the fire, and then
whoever had tried to hurt her would come looking again.

"Oh, God, I need help," she moaned, and then jumped
with fright as something furry rubbed up against her leg.
She knelt, wrapping her arms around the puppy's neck and
sobbed. "You're not what I needed, but you're all I've got,
aren't you, fella?"

A wet tongue slid across her cheek, and Glory moaned
as the puppy instinctively licked at the blood on her face.
She pushed him away, then stood. Her eyes narrowed above
lashes spiked with tears, her lips firmed, her chin tilted as
she stared at the fire.

*Daddy....J.C....I swear on Mother's grave...and on yours,
that I will find him. All I need is a little help.*

No sooner had that thought come than an image followed. A man's face centered within her mind. A man

who had been a soldier. A man who understood killing. A stranger who, right now, Glory trusted more than friends.

If I knew where you were, Wyatt Hatfield, I would call in a debt.

But the fantasy of finding a stranger in a world full of people was more than she could cope with. Right now she had to hide, and there was no family left alive to help her.

Except...

She took a deep breath. "Granny."

The puppy heard the tone of her voice and whined softly from somewhere behind her, uncertain what it was that she wanted yet aware that a word had been uttered it did not understand.

Granny Dixon's house sat just across the hollow as it had for the past one hundred years, a small shelter carved out of a dense wilderness of trees and bush. As a child, Granny had been Glory's only link with another female, and she had often spent the day in her lap, lulled by the sound of her voice and the stories she would tell.

Glory took a deep breath and closed her eyes, imagining she could hear her granny's voice now.

When you tire of them menfolks, child, you just come to old Granny. We women hafta stick together, now, don't we?

Her saving grace was that Granny Dixon's cabin was just as she'd left it. Its presence could be the answer to her prayer. She was counting on the fact that few would remember its existence. Rafe had promised his mother that he wouldn't touch or change a single thing in her home until they put her in the ground. In a way, Glory was thankful that Granny's mind was almost gone. At least she would be spared the grief of knowing that her only son and grandson had beat her to heaven.

And while the cabin was there, food was not. Glory made a quick trip through the root cellar using the light from the fire as a guide; she ran her fingers along the jars until she found what she wanted. She came up and out with a jar of peaches in one hand and a quart of soup in the other. It would be enough to keep her going until she figured out what to do.

And then she and the puppy vanished into the darkness of the tree line. Minutes later, the sounds of cars and trucks could be heard grinding up the hill. Someone had seen the fire. Someone else would rescue what was left of her loved ones. Glory had disappeared.

Chapter 3

The scream came without warning. Right in the middle of a dream he could no longer remember. Wyatt sat straight up in bed, his instinct for survival working overtime as he imagined Toni or the baby in dire need of help. In seconds, he was pulling on a pair of jeans and running in an all-out sprint as he flew out of the door.

He slid to a stop in the hallway outside the baby's room and then looked inside. Nothing was amiss. He sighed with relief at the sight of the toddler asleep on her tummy with her blanket clutched tightly in one fist. She was fine, so Toni hadn't screamed about her. That meant...

Fearing the worst, he crept farther down the hall, praying that he wouldn't surprise a burglar in the act of murder, and wondering why on earth Lane Monday wasn't raising all kinds of hell in response to his wife's screams.

More than a year ago, Lane had taken down a man the size of a mountain to save his sister's life. He couldn't imagine Lane letting someone sneak up on them and do his family harm. Yet in Wyatt's mind, he knew that whatever had made Toni scream couldn't have been good.

The door was ajar so Lane or Toni could hear the baby if she cried. Wyatt pushed it aside and looked in. Lane was flat on his back and sound asleep, with Toni held gently but firmly within the shelter of one arm. Even from here, Wyatt could hear the soft, even sounds of their breathing.

"Thank God," he muttered, and eased out of their room the same way he'd come in, trying to convince himself that he'd been dreaming. *But it sounded so real.*

He made his way through the house, careful not to step on the boards that creaked, and headed for the kitchen to get a drink. He wasn't particularly thirsty, but at the moment, crawling back in that bed did not hold much interest. His heart was still pounding as he took a glass from the cabinet and ran water in the sink, letting it cool in the pipes before filling a glass.

The water tasted good going down, and panic was subsiding. If he stretched the facts, he could convince himself that his heart rate was almost back to normal. It was just a bad dream. That was all. Just a bad dream.

Wyatt.

"What?"

He spun toward the doorway, expecting Toni to be standing there with a worried expression on her face. There was nothing but a reflection of the outside security light glancing off the living room window and onto the floor.

Wyatt...Wyatt Hatfield.

His stomach muscles clenched and he took a deep breath. "Jesus Christ."

Help me.

He started to shake. "This isn't happening."

God... Oh, God...help. I need help.

He slammed the glass onto the cabinet and stalked out of the kitchen and onto the back porch, inhaling one after the other of deep, lung-chilling breaths of cool night air. When he could think without wanting to throw up, he sat down on the steps with a thump and buried his face in his hands, then instantly yanked them off his face, unable to believe what he'd felt.

His hands were cold…and they were wet. He lifted his fingers to his cheeks and traced the tracks of his tears.

"I'm crying? For God's sake, I'm crying? What's wrong with me? I don't cry, and when I do, I will sure as hell need a reason."

But anger could not replace the overwhelming sense of despair that was seeping into his system. He felt weak and drained, hopeless and helpless. The last time he'd felt this down had been the day he'd regained consciousness in a Kentucky hospital and seen the vague image of his sister's face hovering somewhere above his bed.

He remembered thinking that he'd known his sister was an angel to have put up with so many brothers all of her life, but he'd never imagined that all angels in heaven looked like her. It was the next day before he realized that he hadn't died, and by that time, worrying about the faces of angels had become secondary to the mind-bending pain that had come to stay.

Out of the silence of the night, a dog suddenly bugled in a hollow somewhere below Chaney Creek. The sound was familiar. He shuddered, trying to relax as his nerves began to settle. This was something to which he could relate. Someone was running hounds. Whether it was raccoon, bobcat or something else that they hunted, it rarely mattered. To the hunters, the dogs and the hunt were what counted.

He listened, remembering days far in his past when he and his brothers had done the same, nights when they'd sat around a campfire swapping lies that sounded good in the dark, drinking coffee made in a pot that they wouldn't have fed the pigs out of in the light of day and listening to their hounds running far and wide across the hills and in the deep valleys.

He sighed, then dropped his head in his hands, wishing for simpler times, saner times. He wondered where he'd gone wrong. He'd married Shirley full of good intent, then screwed up her life, as well as his own.

And now this!

He didn't know what to think. He'd survived a wreck that should have killed him. But if it had messed with his head in a way they hadn't expected, then making a new life for himself had suddenly become more complicated than he'd planned.

Help. I need help.

He lifted his head like an animal sniffing the air. His nostrils flared, his eyes narrowed to dark, gleaming slits. This time, he knew he wasn't dreaming. He was wide-awake and barefoot on his sister's back porch. And he knew what he heard. The voice was inside his head. He shivered, then shifted his gaze, looking out at the darkness, listening...waiting.

When the first weak rays of sunlight changed the sky from black to baby-blue, Wyatt got to his feet and walked into the house. It had taken all night, and more soul-searching than he'd realized he had in him, but he knew what he had to do.

Somewhere down the hall, Joy babbled and Toni laughed. Lane smiled to himself at the sound, buttoning his shirt on his way to the kitchen to start the coffee. He walked in just in time to see Wyatt closing the back door.

"Up kinda early, aren't you, buddy?" Lane asked, and then froze at the expression on Wyatt's face, grabbing him by the arm. "What's wrong?"

Wyatt tried to explain, but it just wouldn't come. "I need to borrow one of your cars."

Lane headed for the coffeepot, giving himself time to absorb the unexpected request and wondering about the intensity of Wyatt's voice. Yet refusing him was not a consideration.

"It's yours," he said.

Measuring his words, along with coffee and water, Lane turned on the coffeemaker before taking Wyatt to task. "Mind telling me where you're going so early in the morning? This isn't exactly Memphis, and to my knowledge there's no McDonald's on the next corner cooking up sausage biscuits."

"I've got to go," Wyatt repeated. "Someone needs me."

Lane's posture went from easy to erect. "Why didn't you say so? I'll help."

Wyatt shook his head. "No, you don't understand. Hell, for that matter, I don't understand. All I know is, last night while I was wide-awake and watching dark turn to day, someone kept calling my name."

The oddity of the remark was not lost on Lane, but trespassing on another man's business was not his way.

"Do you know where you're going?" Lane asked.

Wyatt eyed his brother-in-law, wondering if he would understand what he was about to say.

"I think back to where it all started," Wyatt said quietly, remembering the woman outside of the hospital and the way he'd heard her voice…and she, his. He'd ignored it then. He couldn't ignore it any longer.

"Back to Kentucky?" Lane asked, unable to keep surprise out of his voice.

Wyatt nodded.

Wisely, Lane stifled the rest of his concerns. While he didn't understand what Wyatt was trying to say, he trusted the man implicitly. He swung a wide hand across his shoulder and thumped him lightly on the back.

"Then let's get you packed," Lane said. "It's an all-day drive."

Wyatt had been on this road before. Last winter. And with no destination in mind. This time, he knew where he was going. He even knew why. What he didn't understand was the pull that drew him down the road. The closer he came to the great Pine Mountain, the more certain he became that he was on the right track. He drove relentlessly, stopping only when necessary, compelled to reach Larner's Mill before nightfall. He couldn't get past the increasing panic he felt, or the fact that he was listening for a voice that had suddenly gone silent.

The sun was halfway between zenith and horizon when he pulled into Larner's Mill, but the relief he imagined he would feel was not there. In fact, the urgency of his quest seemed to have taken on darker overtones. An unsettled feeling had taken root in his belly, and try as he might, there was no rational explanation for the emotion, other than the uncertainty of his quest.

When he pulled into the parking lot of the small community hospital and got out, he found himself wanting to run. But to where? Instead, he took a deep breath and entered through the emergency room doors.

A nurse glanced up from a desk near the door. "May I help you, sir?"

"I want to talk to one of your doctors," Wyatt said.

She slipped a fresh page on a clipboard and held a pen poised above the lines.

"Your name?" she asked.

"Wyatt Hatfield," he said.

"And what are your symptoms?"

"I'm not sick. But I was here before. Last winter, in fact. I had a car wreck during a blizzard. I was…"

"I remember you," she cried, and jumped to her feet. "Dr. Steading was your doctor. You were the talk of the hospital for some time."

"Why was that?" Wyatt asked.

"You know," she said. "About how lucky you were to have had that donor show up when she did. With such a rare blood type, and the blizzard and all, there was no way we could access the blood banks in the bigger cities as we normally might have done."

The expression on Wyatt's face stilled as he absorbed the nurse's unwitting revelation.

"Yes, I suppose you're right. I am one lucky man." He gave her a smile he didn't feel. "So, could I talk to Dr. Steading? There are some things about the accident that I don't remember. I thought maybe he could give me some help."

"I'll see," she said, and shortly thereafter, Wyatt found himself on the way through the corridors to an office in the other wing. When he saw the name on the door, his pulse accelerated. He knocked and then entered.

"Dr. Steading?"

Amos Steading arched one bushy eyebrow, and then stood and reached over his desk, his hand outstretched.

"You, sir, look a damn sight healthier than the last time I saw you," he said, his gravelly voice booming within the small confines of the office.

Wyatt caught the handshake and grinned. "I suppose I feel better, too," he said.

Steading frowned. "Suppose?"

Wyatt took the chair offered him and tried not to show his uneasiness, but it seemed it was impossible to hide anything, including an emotion, from the grizzled veteran.

Steading persisted. "So, did you come all this way just to shake my hand, or are you going to spit it out?"

Wyatt took a deep breath, and then started talking.

"I know I was in serious condition when I was brought in here," he said.

"No," Steading interrupted. "You were dying, boy."

Wyatt paled, but persisted. "The reason I came is…I need to know if, in your opinion, I could have suffered any residual brain damage."

Steading frowned. That was the last thing he expected to hear this man say. His eyes were clear and bright, his manner straightforward and he'd walked into his office like a man with a purpose. None of this hinted at any sort of mental disability.

"Why?" Steading asked. "Are you suffering memory loss, or…"

Wyatt shook his head. "No, nothing like that."

"So…?"

"So, I want to know what exactly happened to my head," Wyatt growled.

"You had one hell of a concussion. I wouldn't have been surprised if you'd gone into a coma."

Wyatt started to relax. Maybe this would explain what he thought he'd heard. Maybe his head was still lost in some sort of fugue.

"But you didn't," Steading added. "After surgery, you pretty much sailed through recovery. There's a lot to be said for a young, healthy body."

"Damn," Wyatt muttered beneath his breath. One theory shot to hell.

This time both of Steading's eyebrows arched. "You're disappointed?"

Wyatt shrugged. "It would have explained a lot."

"Like what?" Steading persisted.

The last thing he intended to admit, especially to a doctor, was that he was hearing voices. They'd lock him up in a New York minute. He changed the subject.

"I understand that I was given transfusions."

"Transfusion," Steading corrected. "And damned lucky to have that one. Whole blood made the difference. I'm good, but I don't think I could have pulled you through surgery without it, and that's the gospel truth."

"I'd like to thank the person who cared enough to come out in such a storm. If it wouldn't be against hospital policy, could you give me a name?"

Amos Steading's face fell. He rocked backward in his chair, and gazed at a corner of the ceiling, trying to find the right way to say the words.

"If that's a problem," Wyatt said, "I'll understand. It's just that I'm trying to make sense of some things in my life, and I thought that retracing my steps through that night might help."

"It isn't that," Steading finally said. "It's just that you're about a day too late."

Wyatt straightened. An inner warning was going off that told him he wasn't going to like this.

"That young woman…the one who gave you blood… she, along with her family, died sometime last night. I heard about it when I came in to work this morning."

Oh, God! Oh, no! Was that what I heard…the sound of someone crying out for help?

Wyatt's voice broke, and he had to clear his throat to get out the words. "How did it happen? Was it a car accident?"

"No, a fire at the home."

Wyatt shuddered, trying not to think of the horror of burning alive.

"Yes, and a real shame, too, what with her and her brother so young and all. That night when the EMT dragged her into the room where I was working on you, I remember thinking she was just a kid. Wasn't any bigger than a minute, and all that white-blond hair and those big blue eyes, it's no wonder I misjudged her age."

It was the description that caught Wyatt's attention. He'd seen a woman who looked like that. A woman with hair like angel's wings, whom *he'd* mistaken for a girl until an errant wind had moved her coat, revealing a womanly figure.

He blanched and covered his face in his hands. There was something else about that woman that had been unique, and only Wyatt was privy to the fact.

Somehow, when his guard had been down and his defenses weak, she'd insinuated herself within his thoughts. He didn't know how it had happened, but after what he'd just heard, he was firmly convinced that she'd done it again last night, presumably at the point of her death.

"My God," he muttered. Leaning forward, he rested his elbows upon his knees and stared at a pattern on the carpet until the colors all ran together.

"Sorry to be the bearer of such bad news," Steading said. "Are you all right?"

Wyatt shrugged. "I didn't really know her. It was her kindness that I wanted to acknowledge. It's a damn shame I came too late." And then he had a thought. "I'd like to see. Where she lived, I mean. Do you know?"

"Nope, I can't say that I do. But you could ask at the police department. Anders Conway could tell you."

Wyatt stood. "I've taken up enough of your time, Dr. Steading. Thanks for your help."

Steading shrugged.

Wyatt was at the door, when he paused and then turned. "Doctor?"

"Yes?"

"What was her name?"

"Dixon. Glory Dixon."

A twist of pain spiked and then centered in the region of

Wyatt's heart. "Glory," he repeated, more to himself than to the doctor, then closed the door behind him.

"Damn," Steading muttered. "In fact...damn it all to hell."

Wyatt navigated the winding road with absentminded skill. He'd gone over the side of one Kentucky mountain. It was enough. Remembering the directions he'd been given, he kept a sharp watch for a twisted pine, aware that he was to turn left just beyond it. As he rounded a bend, the last rays of the setting sun suddenly spiked through a cloud and the waning light hit the top of a tree. Wyatt eased off the gas. It was the pine. He began looking for the road, and sure enough, a few yards beyond, a narrow, one-laned dirt road took a sharp turn to the left. Wyatt followed it to its destination.

The clearing came without warning. One minute the road was shadowed and tree lined, and then suddenly he was braking to a sliding halt as his fingers tightened upon the steering wheel, and his breath came in short, painful gasps.

"Dear God."

There was little else to say as he got out of the car and walked toward the blackened timbers. Yellow police tape was tied from tree to tree and then from fence post to the bumper of what was left of a pickup truck—a vivid reminder that death had occurred here.

The fact that the shell of a washing machine and dryer still stood while a house was gone seemed obscene, too vivid a reminder of how frail human life truly was. Smoke continued to rise from several locations as cross beams and a stack of something no longer identifiable smoldered. An unnatural heat lingered in the cooler evening air.

Wyatt stuffed his hands in his pockets and hunched his shoulders against the weight of despair that hung over the area. Last night he'd heard a cry for help and had been unable to respond, and yet when *he'd* needed help most, she had come. The burden of his guilt was almost more than he could bear.

"Ah, God, Glory Dixon. It *was* you, wasn't it? I am so, so sorry. If I had known, I would have helped."

"Do you swear?"

Wyatt spun. This time the voice he just heard had been behind him, not in his head. And when a young woman walked out of the trees, he thought he was seeing a ghost. It was her! The woman from the street!

He looked over his shoulder at the ruins, and then back at her, unable to believe his own eyes. Suddenly, a puppy darted out of the woods behind her and began pouncing around her feet. Wyatt stared. He'd never heard of a ghost with a dog.

He stood his ground, fighting the urge to run. "Are you real?"

Glory sighed, and Wyatt imagined he felt the air stir from her breath. And then she was standing before him, and he looked down and got lost in a silver-blue gaze. An errant breeze lifted the hair from her neck and shoulders, and for a moment, it seemed to float on the air like wings. Once again, Wyatt was reminded of angels.

"Why did you come?" Glory whispered. "How did you know?"

The sound of her voice broke the spell, and Wyatt blinked, trying to regain a true focus on the world around him. Unable to believe his eyes, he grasped a portion of her hair between his fingers. Although it was silken in texture, there was nothing unearthly about it.

"I heard you call my name," he muttered as he watched the hair curl around his finger.

Glory gasped, startled by what he'd revealed, and

stepped back. *Dear God, did I give him more than my blood? Have I given away part of myself?*

Then, drawn by the horror she couldn't ignore, her gaze shifted to the pile of blackened timbers, and without warning, tears pooled and then tracked down her cheeks in silent misery. Wyatt groaned and opened his arms, and to his surprise, she walked into his embrace with no hesitation.

In his mind, holding her was like trying to hold sunshine. She was light, fragile and seemed to sway within his arms with every beat of his heart. Her shoulders shook with grief, and yet her sobs were silent, as if the agony just wouldn't let go.

"I'm so sorry about your family," Wyatt said softly, and closed the gap between his hands until she stood locked firmly within his grasp. "But everyone's going to be so happy to learn that you survived. As soon as you're able, I'll take you back to town."

She went limp, and for a moment, he thought she was going to faint. Instead, it seemed more of a physical retreat. Sensing her uneasiness, he immediately turned her loose.

"I can't go back. Not yet," Glory said quietly.

Wyatt couldn't hide his surprise. "Whyever not?"

"Because this wasn't an accident. Because someone tried to kill me, and my daddy and brother suffered for it."

Before he thought, Wyatt had her by the arms. "What the hell do you mean, 'someone tried to kill me'? Are you saying that this fire was set?"

"At first it wasn't a fire, it was an explosion. The fire came afterward."

Unable to look at him, she turned away. He was bound to doubt. Everyone always did.

"Well, hell," Wyatt muttered. "Then you need to tell the police chief. He'll know what to do."

Glory spun, and for the first time since she'd walked

out of the woods, Wyatt saw a light in her eyes and heard fire in her voice.

"No! You don't understand! They'll come tomorrow… or the next day…to go through the ruins. When they do, they're only going to find two bodies, not three. And then whoever it was that did this will try again. I need time to try to figure out what to do."

Wyatt frowned. "What do you mean, whoever did this? I thought you knew."

She shook her head.

"Then how do you know it wasn't an accident?"

Glory lifted her chin, silencing his argument with a piercing look he couldn't ignore.

"I *see* things. Sometimes I know things before they happen, sometimes I see them happen. But however my knowledge comes…I know what I know."

Wyatt took a deep breath. He knew for a fact that he'd been hearing some things of his own. Right now, it wasn't in him to doubt that she might…just might…be able to do more than hear. What if she could see? What if she was for real?

"Are you telling me that you're psychic?"

"Some people call it that."

Wyatt went quiet as he considered the ramifications of her admission.

"Why did you come to the hospital to help me?"

Her chin trembled, but her words were sure. "I *saw* your accident as it happened. I heard your cry for help…and because I could come, I did."

Daring the risk of rejection, Wyatt reached out and cupped her face with his hand. To his joy, she withstood his familiarity, in fact, even seemed to take strength from the comfort.

"How can I thank you, Glory Dixon?"

"By not giving me away. By helping me stay alive until I can figure out why…and who…and…"

"It's done. Tell me what to do first."

Again, she swayed on her feet. Wyatt reached out, but she pushed him away. Her gaze searched the boundary of trees around the rubble, constantly on the lookout for a hidden menace. Fear that she would be found before it was time was a constant companion.

"You need to hide your car. Maybe drive it around behind the barn, out in the pasture."

"Where are you…uh…?"

"Hiding?"

He nodded.

"When you've parked your car, I'll show you, but we need to hurry. There'll be no moon tonight, and the woods are dense and dark."

Wyatt headed for his car, and as he followed her directions through the narrow lanes he wondered what on earth he'd let himself in for. Yet as the beam of his headlights caught and then held on the beauty of her face and the pain he saw hidden in her eyes, he knew he didn't give a damn. She'd helped him. The least he could do was repay the debt.

A few minutes later, they walked away from the site, following what was left of a road overgrown with bushes and weeds. The air was already damp. Dew was heavy on the grass, blotching the legs of their jeans and seeping into the soles of their shoes. The bag Wyatt was carrying kept getting caught on low-hanging limbs, but Glory seemed to pass through the brush without leaving a trace. It would seem that her fragile, delicate appearance was deceiving. He suspected that she moved through life as she did through these trees—with purpose.

The pup ran between their legs, barking once from the delight of just being alive. He ran with his nose to the

ground and his long, puppy ears flopping, yet a single word
from Glory and he hushed.

Something silent and dark came out of a tree overhead
and sailed across their line of vision. Instinctively, Glory
threw up her hands and gasped. Wyatt caught her as she
started to run.

"I think it was an owl," he said gently, and held her until
she had calmed.

"Sorry," she said. "I'm not usually so jumpy. It's just
that…" Tears were thick in her voice as she pushed herself
out of his arms and resumed their trek.

Visibility was nearly zero, yet Glory moved with a sure
sense of direction and Wyatt followed without question.
Night creatures hid as the pair walked past, then scurried
back into their holes, suddenly unsure of their world. Wyatt
heard the rustling in the deep, thick grass, and even though
he knew what it was that he heard, he couldn't prevent a
shiver of anxiety. This was a far cry from the safety and
comfort of the Tennessee home where he'd been recuperating. It reminded him too much of secret maneuvers he'd
been on in places he'd rather forget.

He clutched at the bag over his shoulder and caught
himself wishing it was a gun in his hands, not a duffel bag.
Twice, Glory paused, listening carefully to the sounds of
the woods through which they walked, judging what she
heard against what she knew should be there. After a time,
she would resume the trek without looking back, trusting
that because Wyatt had come, he would still follow.

Just when he was wondering if they would walk all
night, they entered a clearing. Again Glory paused, this
time clutching the sleeve of his shirt as she stared through
the darkness, searching for something that would feel out
of place.

The instinct that had carried Wyatt safely through several tours of duty told him that all was well.

"It's okay," he said, and this time he took her by the hand and led the way toward the cabin on the other side of the yard.

The night could not disguise the humble quality of the tiny abode. It was no more than four walls and a slanted, shingle roof, a rock chimney that angled up from the corner of the roof, with two narrow windows at the front of the cabin that stared back at them like a pair of dark, accusing eyes.

Glory shivered apprehensively, then slipped the key from her jeans. As her fingers closed around it, she was thankful that her daddy had kept this one hidden at the cabin, or she would have been unable to get inside the night before.

Wyatt listened to the woods around them as she worked the lock, and when the door swung open with a slight, warning squeak, she took his hand and led him through with an odd little welcome.

"We're home," she said.

As he followed her inside, he had the oddest sensation that what she said was true.

Chapter 4

"Don't turn on the light."

Wyatt's fingers paused on the edge of the switch. The panic in her voice was too real to ignore.

"You're serious about this, aren't you?"

Glory nodded, then realized that in the dark, Wyatt Hatfield couldn't see her face.

"Yes, I'm serious. Please wait here. I have a candle."

Wyatt did as he was told. He set down his duffel bag and then closed the door behind him, thinking that the dark in here was as thick as the woods through which they'd just walked. Moments later, he heard the rasp of a match to wood, focused on the swift flare of light and watched a wick catch and burn. And then she turned, bathed in the gentle glow of candlelight. Once again, Wyatt was struck by her fragile beauty.

"Will the pup be all right outside?"

"Yes," Glory said. "Follow me." Wyatt picked up his bag. "This is where you'll sleep," she said, and held the candle above her head, giving him a dim view of the tiny room and the single bed. "I'm just across the hall in Granny's bed."

"Granny?"

"My father's mother. This was her cabin. She's all the family I have left." And then her face crumpled as tears shimmered in her eyes. "The only problem is, she's ninety-one years old and in a nursing home. Half the time she doesn't remember her name, let alone me."

As she turned away, Wyatt set his bag inside the room and followed her across the hall, watching as she set the candle on a bedside table, then ran across the room to check the curtains, making sure that no light would be visible from outside.

"Glory?"

She stilled, then slowly turned. "What?"

"Talk to me."

She understood his confusion, but wasn't sure she could make him understand. With a defeated sigh, she dropped to the corner of the bed, running her fingers lightly across the stitching on the handmade quilt, drawing strength from the woman who'd sewn it, and then bent over to pull off her boots. She tugged once, then twice, and without warning, started to cry quiet tears of heartbreak.

Wyatt flinched as her misery filled the tiny space. Without thinking, he knelt at her feet. Grasping her foot, he pulled one boot off and then the other before turning back the bed upon which she sat.

"Lie down."

The gentleness in his voice was her undoing. Glory rolled over, then into a ball, and when the weight of the covers fell upon her shoulders, she began to sob.

"He was laughing," she whispered.

Wyatt frowned. "Who was laughing, honey?"

"My brother, J.C. One minute he was digging through the grocery sack for Twinkies and laughing at something the pup had done, and then everything exploded." She took a deep, shaky breath, trying to talk past the sobs. "I should have been with them."

Wyatt cursed beneath his breath. Her pain was more than he could bear. He wanted to hold her, yet the unfamiliarity of their odd connection held him back. Slowly, she rolled over, looking at him through those silver-blue eyes while the skin crawled on the back of his neck.

"I was the first female born to the Dixon family in more than five generations. They say that my eyes were open when I was born, and that when Granny laid me on my mother's stomach, I lifted my head, looked at my mother's face and smiled. An hour later, my mother suddenly hemorrhaged, then died, and although I was in another room, Granny says that the moment she took her last breath, I started to cry. Granny called it 'the sight.' I consider it more of a curse."

Wyatt brushed the tangle of hair from her eyes, smoothing it from her forehead and off her shoulders. "It saved me," he said quietly.

She closed her eyes. A tear slipped out of each corner and ran down her temples and into her hair.

"I know." Her mouth twisted as she tried to talk around the pain. "But why couldn't I save Daddy and J.C.? Why, Wyatt Hatfield? Tell me why."

Unable to stay unattached from her pain, Wyatt slid his hands beneath her shoulders and lifted her from the covers, then into his lap. As he nestled his chin in her hair, he held her against him.

"I don't know the whys of the world, Glory Dixon. I only know the hows. And I swear to you, I will keep you safe until they find the man responsible."

It was the promise he made and the honesty with which it was said that gave her hope. Maybe together they could get it done.

I'm so glad he's here, Glory thought.

"I'm glad I came, too," Wyatt whispered.

Glory froze. Without realizing it, he'd read her thoughts and answered. And as she let herself draw from his strength, she faced the fact that she'd given more than just blood to this man. It seemed impossible, and it shouldn't have happened, but it was the only explanation that made sense.

A dog ran across the street in front of the car as Wyatt turned a corner in Larner's Mill, aiming for the local police department down the street. He knew where it was. He'd been there yesterday when asking directions to the Dixon home. The people were friendly enough, but he wasn't sure if one small-town police chief and two part-time deputies were going to be up to finding a killer. When they'd driven out of the yard earlier that morning, no one had even bothered to stop them and ask why they were near the scene. On the surface, they seemed geared more toward drunks and traffic violations than tracking criminals. He hoped he was wrong. As he pulled to the curb and parked, Glory's nervousness was impossible to ignore any longer.

"It's going to be all right," he said.

Her eyes were wide and on the verge of tears, her mouth set. He could tell she was hovering on the edge of panic.

"They're not going to believe me," she said, but when Wyatt slipped his hand over hers and squeezed, the fear receded.

"It doesn't really matter whether they believe you or not, as long as they proceed with some kind of investigation. Besides, don't forget Lane's coming."

Glory nodded, remembering their earlier phone call to Wyatt's brother-in-law.

"Having a U.S. marshal on our side isn't going to hurt," Wyatt added, then glanced down at his watch. "In fact, I'd lay odds that he'll be here before dark."

Glory bit her lip and then looked away.

"You have to trust me, girl."

She turned, and Wyatt found himself looking into her eyes and fighting the sensation of falling deeper and deeper into a place with no way out. And then she blinked, and he realized he'd been holding his breath. Muttering to himself, he helped her out of the car.

Glory took heart in the fact that as they walked through the door, he was right beside her all the way.

"God Almighty!"

Anders Conway jumped to his feet and stumbled backward as the couple came in the door. He'd been police chief of Larner's Mill for twenty-nine years, but it was his first time seeing a ghost.

Wyatt felt Glory flinch, and instinctively slipped a hand across her shoulder, just to remind her that he was there.

"Chief Conway, I came to report a murder," Glory said softly.

He was so shocked by her appearance that her remark went right over his head. "We thought you were dead," he said. "Where on earth have you been, girl?"

"Hiding."

"Whatever for? No one's gonna hurt you."

Glory looked to Wyatt for reassurance. The glint in his eye was enough to keep her going.

"The fire at my house was not an accident. Someone deliberately turned on the gas jets. I saw them. When Daddy and J.C. walked in the back door with our groceries, it was nearly dusk and the house must have been full of gas. Wyatt says that one of them probably turned on the light, and that was what sparked the explosion."

Conway frowned. Apparently, none of this was making much sense. "If you saw someone turning on the gas, why didn't you tell your family? Why would your father knowingly go into a house set to blow?"

This was where it got rough. Glory braced herself, readying for the derision that was bound to come.

"I didn't actually *see* what had been done until the house was already burning, I just knew that something was wrong. I tried to stop them from going inside. I called out, but it was too late. They were already there."

The look on Conway's face was changing from shock to confusion. Afraid that he'd run her out before she got a chance to explain, she started talking faster, anxious to get it all said.

"I know it was a man who did it. I could see him in my mind. I saw the back of his hands as he turned on the jets on the stove. He even broke one of them so that it couldn't be turned off. I saw the back of his pant legs as he ran through the other rooms, doing the same to our heat stoves. One in the living room…and one in the bathroom, too."

"In your mind. You saw this *in your mind*."

She nodded.

Conway made no attempt to hide his disbelief. "Exactly *who* did you see? In your mind, of course."

Glory wanted to hide. The simple fact of her father's presence in her life had prevented most people from displaying any out-and-out derision they might have felt. This was the first time that she'd experienced it alone. Suddenly, Wyatt's hand slid under her hair and cupped the back of her neck. She relaxed. *I forgot. I'm not alone.*

"No, honey, you're not," Wyatt said, still unaware that he was reading her thoughts and answering them aloud.

Glory looked startled, but not as surprised as Anders Conway, who turned his focus to the man at her side.

"You're the fellow who was asking directions to the Dixon place yesterday, aren't you?"

Wyatt nodded.

"Are you kin?"

Wyatt glanced down at Glory and winked, then gave the policeman a look he couldn't ignore.

"I'm a friend. Miss Dixon saved my life last year. I'm simply returning a favor."

"How did…?"

"None of that matters," Wyatt said. "The point is, Glory Dixon knows that someone tried to kill her. And, obviously, they did not succeed. The fact remains that when it's made known that she's still alive, he will obviously try again." And then he added, as if it were an afterthought, although he knew what an impact his announcement would make, "You should also know that there's a U.S. marshal on his way here to help with the investigation. He's my brother-in-law. I called him this morning."

Conway's jaw dropped as Wyatt continued. "And I suppose you've already called the state fire marshal about the incident. When is he coming?"

Conway started to fidget. "Well, I… Uh, I mean…" Then he slapped his hand on the desk, trying to regain control of the situation. "Look! Everyone knows that fire was an accident. A terrible accident. The coroner should be on his way out there by now to recover the bodies. They tried once yesterday and the wreckage was still too hot."

He ran a hand through his thinning hair and tried to make them see his point.

"I'm real sorry that Miss Dixon lost her family. It has to be a shock, and that's probably what's making her imagine all of this. What you need to do is get her to a doctor and…"

"You didn't answer my question," Wyatt said. "When is the fire marshal coming?"

"I didn't call him…yet," Conway added.

Wyatt gave a pointed look toward the phone and then back at the lawman's face. "We'll wait," he said shortly.

Before they had time to sit down, a dispatcher came in from the back of the department with a note in his hand.

"Chief, you won't believe this. They just radioed in from the site of the Dixon fire and said they only found two bodies in the…" At this point, he noticed the couple seated across the room and froze. The note fluttered from his fingers to the floor. "Well, my Gawd! No wonder they didn't find a third body. There you are!"

Glory felt like a bug on a pin, displayed for everyone to see, and listening to them speak of her father and brother as mere "bodies" was almost more than she could bear. She bit her lip and looked away, fighting the urge to scream. And then Wyatt unexpectedly clasped her hand and wouldn't let go. Hysteria settled as she absorbed his warmth.

"Tell them to get on back here with what they've got," Conway growled. "I'm dealing with the rest. And tell them not to do any more than remove the remains. The fire marshal is going to come out and investigate the site."

"Yes, sir!" the dispatcher said, and hurried out of the room.

Wyatt stood. "I guess we'll be going now," he said.

"How can I reach you?" Conway said.

Wyatt heard Glory's swift intake of breath, and knew that while her whereabouts wouldn't be a secret for long, she wasn't ready to reveal them just now.

"We'll be in touch," Wyatt said. "For now, I think the fewer who know where she is, the better. Don't you agree?"

Conway's face turned red. The man had all but accused him of not being able to maintain confidentiality in his own department. And then he relented. If they wanted to make a big deal out of this, he wasn't going to stop them. Everyone knew that Rafe Dixon's girl was a little bit nuts. This so-called friend of the family would learn the truth soon enough, or turn out to be just like them. Either way, it didn't matter to him.

"Yeah. Right," Conway said. "Keep in touch."

The smirk in his voice was impossible to ignore. When

they walked outside, Glory wilted. "He doesn't believe me, you know," she whispered.

"I know," Wyatt said. "But I do."

His words were an anchor in Glory's unsettled world, and the touch of his hand was balm to her broken heart.

"Are you up to some shopping?" Wyatt asked. "I expect you would like some changes of clothing, and we definitely need to buy food. Is there anything else you can think of?"

Glory's lip trembled as she worked up the nerve to say it aloud.

"Funeral arrangements. I need to see about..." Her voice caught, and she knew this time she wasn't going to be able to stop the tears.

Wyatt pulled her into his arms, cupping the back of her head as she buried her face against the front of his shirt.

"I'm sorry, Glory. I'm so sorry you're having to go through this, but you need to remember something. It's *we*, honey, not *I*. Don't forget, you're not alone in this anymore. We'll do whatever it is you want. You're calling the shots."

He seated her in the car and then slid behind the steering wheel, waiting for her to settle.

Oh, God, I don't want to be in charge. I just want this to be over, Glory thought.

Wyatt raked her pale face with a dark, brooding look. "It will be, and sooner than you think. Now then, I don't know about you, but I'm hungry as hell. Where's the best place to eat?"

"How do you do that?" Glory asked.

Wyatt grinned as he began to back out of the parking space. "Do what?"

"You're reading my thoughts, and then answering my questions, even though I haven't said them aloud."

The smile on his face stilled. "No, I'm not."

Yes, you are.

He braked in the middle of the street. Fortunately, no

one was behind them. He went as pale as the shirt on his back as he looked at her face.

"What did you say?"

I said...you are reading my thoughts.

"Oh, Lord." His belly began to turn, and he could feel the muscles in his face tightening. He gripped the steering wheel until his knuckles turned white, and try as he might, he couldn't make himself move.

"You didn't know it was happening, did you?" Glory asked.

He shook his head. "It just seemed so..."

"Natural?"

His breath escaped in one long sigh. Finally he nodded. "Yes, natural. That's exactly what it feels like."

Glory nodded. "I know." Suddenly, she smiled. "You're the first person I've ever known who can understand my gift."

It wasn't much, but it was the first time he'd seen what a hint of joy could do to her face. And in that moment, before she redirected his attention to a restaurant down the street, Wyatt Hatfield feared he might be falling in love. It wasn't planned. And it definitely wasn't what he'd had in mind when he started this journey.

In the same instant that he had the revelation, he shut it out of his mind, afraid that she'd be able to see what was in his thoughts. He reminded himself that it was too soon in their relationship for anything like this. Besides, he needed to focus on keeping her alive, not finding ways to steal, then break her heart.

Carter Foster was trying to concentrate on the legal brief on which he was working, but his mind kept wandering to the different scenarios he might use to bring up his next lie. Should he say that Betty Jo had *called* and asked for a divorce, or should he just say she'd *written?* His legal mind instantly settled on the call. That way he would never be asked to show proof of a letter. And then the moment he thought it, he scoffed. Why should he worry about ever having to show proof? There was no one left to question his story. Not since the Dixon family had perished in that terrible fire.

He'd commiserated along with the rest of the town about the tragedy and listened to the different explanations circulating. They ranged from a faulty water heater to a leaking gas connection beneath the house. Carter didn't care what people thought. He had done what he'd intended. Glory Dixon was dead and his secret was safe, and…he had few regrets. The fact that he hadn't actually pulled a trigger kept his conscience clear enough to bear.

He had reminded himself that it wasn't his fault the Dixons hadn't detected the scent of gas in time to open some windows. It wasn't his fault that they'd come home so late that it was almost dark and automatically turned on a light upon entering the house. None of that was his fault. All he'd done was twist a few knobs. The results had been in the hands of fate. Obviously, fate was on his side.

"Oh, Mr. Carter! Did you hear?"

He frowned as his secretary flew into his office, clutching the burger and fries that he'd asked her to get.

"Hear what?" he asked, snatching the sack from her arms before she flattened the food beyond description. As he opened it, he sniffed the enticing aroma and then began unwrapping the paper from around the bun.

"Some man found that Dixon girl! She's alive!"

Mustard squeezed out from between his fingers and dripped onto the pad on his desk. A hot, burning pain shot across his chest and then down into his belly, and for a minute he thought he was going to faint.

"What do you mean…alive? How could she survive such a fire?"

"Oh, that's the best part! She wasn't inside after all. Someone said she'd spent the night in the woods, although I don't know why in the world she didn't come home with the firemen when it was over." Then she added, "Of course, you know what they say."

Carter shook his head, anxious to hear what *they* said.

"They say," the secretary said, "that she's a little off in the head. That she claims to be able to 'see things' and 'hear voices,' or some such garbage. It's a shame, too, what with her folks dead and all. Who's going to look after a grown woman whose mind is off plumb?"

Carter shrugged, pretending he didn't know and couldn't care less, and began wiping the mustard from between his fingers and then off his desk.

"I'm sure it will all work out," he said, and handed her the notes he'd been making on the brief. "Here. Type these up, please. I'll probably be out of the office for the rest of the afternoon."

"Yes, sir. Is there some place you can be reached?"

"Home. I'm going home."

She nodded, then left.

Carter stared down at the grease congealing on the paper beneath his burger and then down at the mustard that had dropped on his pants. Cursing beneath his breath, he swiped at it angrily, knowing that he'd have to take these to the cleaners again when they'd just come out. The mustard came away on the napkin, leaving behind an even darker stain on the dark fabric of his slacks.

Suddenly, another stain popped into his mind. The smear of Dixie Red lipstick across Betty Jo's face, and a matching one on the bedspread in which he'd wrapped her. His stomach rolled, and he closed his eyes and leaned back in his chair, telling himself not to panic.

Without taking a bite, he dumped his food in the sack and grabbed his briefcase. Moments later, he was on the street, inhaling the warm, spring air and telling himself to calm down. Just because one plan had failed, didn't mean he couldn't try again. He tossed the sack into a garbage can on the corner and ran across the street to the parking lot to get his car. There were things he needed to do, and they required privacy…and solitude, and a more criminal frame of mind.

A whip-poor-will called from across the small clearing in front of Granny's cabin. The pup whined in its sleep, and then was silenced when Glory leaned over and gently patted it on the head.

"It will be dark in an hour or so," Glory said.

"He'll be here," Wyatt said.

"Granny's cabin is hard to find unless you know that it's here."

"Don't forget that they were still digging through the ashes when we came back from town. Chances are there will be someone at the site who Lane can ask. If not, I gave him pretty good directions over the phone." Then he smiled. "You don't know Lane Monday. If he says he'll be here, then he will, and God help the man who gets in his way."

Glory stood up, suddenly restless in the face of nothing to do, and started to go inside.

"I think I'll start supper," she said.

Wyatt caught her at the door. "Glory…"

She looked up, shocked at herself that she was aware of his thumb pressing against the side of her breast. She waited for him to finish.

Suddenly the pup began to bark. Wyatt dropped Glory's arm and thrust her behind him as he spun. In the space of a heartbeat, Glory saw him as the soldier that he'd been. His posture was defensive, his eyes raking the dense line of trees beyond the small yard, and as quickly as he stiffened, he began to relax.

"It's Lane."

Glory took a step sideways, giving herself a better view of the man who was coming out of the trees, and then gasped. *He's a giant.*

Wyatt grinned at her. "Yeah, squirt, from where you stand, I guess he is."

"You're doing it again," she muttered, and punched him on the arm. "What I'd like to know is, if I'm the psychic, why is it you're the one who keeps reading my mind? Why can't I see into yours?"

He shrugged. "Maybe it's the soldier in me. I was trained not to let down my guard." *And the day I let you into my head, I'm in trouble,* he thought, and then focused on the big man who was coming their way.

Glory held her breath, watching the motion of man and muscle, and wondered who on earth would be brave enough to live with a man of that size.

"My sister," Wyatt answered, and then grinned. "Sorry. That slipped."

Ignoring him, Glory stepped forward and extended her hand as if welcoming Lane into a fine home, instead of a tiny cabin lost among the trees.

"Mr. Monday, I'm Glory Dixon. I thank you for coming." Then she watched as her hand disappeared in his palm.

Lane smiled, and Glory saw the gentleness in him in spite of his size.

"Well, I sort of owe old Wyatt here," he said. "And from what he said, you're outnumbered. I thought I'd come even the odds."

"I was about to put supper on the table," she said.

"We'll help," Wyatt said, and took Lane's bag from his hand. "Follow me, and duck when you enter."

A coyote howled far in the distance and a night owl hooted from a tree in the yard, sending the puppy into a frenzy of barking that made Wyatt nervous. He knew within reason that the night sounds had set the dog off, but visions of an attacker creeping through the forest would not go away.

"Want me to check it out?" Lane asked.

"Glory says it's just the night. That if it was a man, the pup wouldn't bother to bark at all and would probably lick him to death."

Lane accepted his explanation without comment, watching intently as Wyatt paced the floor between window and chair while Glory was down the hall, taking a bath.

"Do you think she's on the up-and-up?" Lane asked.

Wyatt froze, then turned. "Yes."

"Just like that?"

"Just like that," Wyatt said.

Lane shrugged. "So tell me what you know."

Wyatt's eyes darkened, and the scar across his cheek turned red.

"She says that someone turned on the gas in her house on purpose. I know her father and brother are dead. I hear what she's thinking and I don't know how to explain it."

Lane's mouth dropped, but only slightly. "You're telling me that you can read her mind?"

"Don't look at me like that!" Wyatt growled. "I know how that sounds. But I know what I know. Blame it on the fact that I nearly died. Blame it on the fact that her blood runs in my veins. Just believe me!"

"Wyatt, don't be mad at him."

Both men turned. Glory stood in the doorway to the living room, holding a towel clutched to her breasts while her granny's nightgown lightly dusted the floor. At first glance, she looked like a child, until one noticed the swell of breast beneath the white flannel and the curve of her hip beneath the fabric as she walked across the room.

"Your feet will get cold," Wyatt muttered, and wanted

to bury his fists in the silver-blond sway of her hair brushing close to her waist.

Glory paused, then looked up at both men. The plea in her eyes was impossible to deny.

"We're not fighting, honey," Lane said gently, and watched how she moved toward Wyatt, settling within the shelter of his arms as if she'd done it countless times before. He didn't think he'd ever seen a more gentle, trusting woman in his life.

"It's not his fault he doesn't understand," Glory continued, as if Lane had not even spoken.

"I don't have to understand to help," Lane said. "And I will help. Tomorrow, I'm going to do some investigating of my own at the fire site. One of the men I talked to earlier said the fire marshal was due around nine in the morning. You can come if you want to."

Glory's voice shook, but she managed to maintain her poise. "Tomorrow I bury my family. Maybe later." And then she gave them a smile that didn't quite reach her eyes. "If you don't mind, I think I'll go on to bed. Do you have everything you need?"

Unable to let her go without touching her one last time, Wyatt brushed at a stray strand of hair that was too near her eye. "We'll manage. Just sleep. Remember, whatever happens tomorrow, you won't be alone."

She nodded, and then went into her room and shut the door.

For several minutes, neither man spoke, and when the silence was broken, it was by Lane.

"I hope you don't think that I'm sleeping with *you*," he muttered.

Wyatt grinned. "I hope you don't think that I'm giving up my bed."

Lane grinned back. "Do you know if there are any extra quilts? I'm thinking that floor looks better all the time."

The tension of the moment was past, and by the time Lane's pallet was made and Wyatt was in the shower, there was nothing to do but watch and wait to see what tomorrow would bring.

Meanwhile, Carter Foster was at home, racking his brain for a solution. Before he'd gone two blocks from the office, he'd heard enough gossip on the street to choke a horse. The fact that Glory Dixon had brought an ex-marine with her to the police department, and that a U.S. marshal was on his way, made him nervous. He was out of his element. What he needed was muscle. Hired muscle. He wondered which, if any, of his ex-clients would be capable of murder, and then wondered what the going rate on hit men was these days.

He slumped into an easy chair, contemplating the rug beneath his toes, fearing that the cost of Betty Jo's burial was bound to increase, and cursed the day he'd ever said "I do."

Chapter 5

The scent of the bacon they'd had for breakfast still lin-gered in the air of the cabin as Wyatt watched Lane disap-pear into the trees beyond the small yard, already on his way to the site of the fire. Through the dense growth of leaves overhead, sunlight dappled the ground in uneven patterns, giving an effect similar to the crazy quilt that covered his bed. The pup was in a patch of sunshine wor-rying a bone, while a blue jay sat on a tree branch above the pup's head, scolding it for its mere presence.

To the eye, it would seem an idyllic day, and yet today Glory was to put to rest her entire family, leaving her vir-tually alone on the face of the earth.

He could hear her moving about in her room, presumably getting dressed for the memorial services later that morn-ing. He knew it couldn't possibly take her long to decide what to wear. She only had the one dress that she'd bought yesterday. His own clothing choices were limited, as well. When he'd left Tennessee, he'd had no inkling of what he would find. If he had, he might have planned accordingly. As it was, boots, clean jeans, a white shirt and his jacket would have to serve as proper dress. His only suit was on a hanger back at the farm above Chaney Creek.

Blindly, he looked through the window without seeing, concentrating instead on the woman he'd found at the end of his search. What was happening between them didn't make sense. It was as crazy as the fact that, seemingly, and for no apparent reason, two people had been murdered. She knew of nothing that would warrant the elimination of everyone she held dear, and yet all was gone. And she said it wasn't over.

Wyatt shuddered. Gut feeling told him she wasn't wrong, and he'd relied too many years on his instinct to ignore it now.

"Wyatt, I'm ready."

He pivoted, a half-voiced thought hanging at the edge of his lips, and then froze, forgetting what he'd been about to say as he beheld the woman before him. All images of the childlike waif were gone, hidden beneath the soft blue folds of the dress she was wearing. The bodice molded itself to the fullness of her breasts, and the narrowness of her waist only accentuated the gentle flare of hips beneath the ankle length of her skirt. Even her hair had undergone a transformation. Forgoing her normal style of letting it fall where it may, Glory had pulled it away from her face and then anchored it all on top in a white-gold spiral. Escaping strands fell around her face and down her neck, weeping from the silky crown atop her head.

"I know it's not the standard black dress," she said. "But it was Daddy's favorite color. I did it for him, not for tradition."

Wyatt cleared his throat, moved by her beauty as well as her grace.

"I saw them once," he said softly.

"Who?"

"Your father…and your brother."

Her eyebrows arched with surprise.

"Remember, outside the hospital, the day I was being released?"

Understanding dawned, and she almost smiled. "That's right! You did."

It gave her an odd sort of pleasure to know that in this, her day of greatest sorrow, he had faces to go with the names of those she loved best.

"I think they would be proud of you," he said.

She nodded, and then her chin trembled, but her voice was firm. "I wish this was over."

Her pain was so thick that he imagined he could feel it. He crossed the room and then stood before her, wanting to touch her in so many places, to test the new waters of Glory Dixon, but this wasn't the time. Today she must mourn. Tomorrow was another day.

He offered her his arm instead, and when her fingers moved across the fabric of his shirt and then locked into the bend of his elbow, Wyatt paused, savoring the contact, as well as her trust.

"Are you ready to go?" he asked.

She nodded, and together they walked out the door. It was only after she shut it behind her that Wyatt realized they were going to have to walk the quarter of a mile up the overgrown path to where his car was parked. He looked down at her shoes, worrying if she would be able to make it. The narrow strap that held the two-inch heels on her feet seemed too delicate for the rough underbrush that had overtaken the unused road.

No sooner had the worry occurred than a tall, dark-haired young man emerged from the woods, leading a horse behind him. His freshly starched and ironed overalls were shiny, and every button on his long-sleeved white shirt was fastened right up to the collar. Before Wyatt had time to ask, Glory gasped, her voice shaking as she quickly explained.

"Oh…oh, my! It's Edward Lee."

"He's a friend?" Wyatt asked sharply.

Glory nodded. "He lives about two miles from our house, as the crow flies. J.C. always took him fishing. He's shy of strangers, so don't expect much conversation. He's simple, you see."

"He's wh…?" And then suddenly Wyatt understood, although it had been years since he'd heard the old hill name for mental retardation.

Glory patted his arm. "Don't worry. Edward Lee knows he's different. He won't embarrass you."

That wasn't what Wyatt had been thinking, but it was too late to explain himself now. The young man was nearly at their feet.

"Hey, Mornin' Glory, I brought you my horse. You shouldn't be walkin' in the brush today."

The black gelding stood quietly at the end of the reins, as if it understood the limitations of its master quite well. The old saddle on its back was gleaming with polish, the metal studs on the halter glittered in the sunlight like polished silver. For Edward Lee, the work had been a labor of love.

Glory touched his arm in a gentle, easy manner. "Why, Edward Lee. How did you know?"

He ducked his head as tears ran unashamedly down his face. "I know that your pa and J.C. got burned up. Ma said the buryin' is today and I knew where you was stayin', and that the old road is all grown up with weeds and such." And then he lifted his head, as if proud of the assumption he had made, and continued, "I knew you'd be all pretty today, Mornin' Glory. I wanted to help you."

Morning Glory. Somehow that fits her, Wyatt thought, and suddenly resented Edward Lee for sharing a past with Glory that he had not. He saw the sweetness of Glory's expression as she accepted the young man's gift, recognized the adoration in Edward Lee's eyes and knew that but for a quirk of fate that had rendered Edward Lee less than other men, he would have been a fierce suitor for Glory Dixon's hand. Jealousy came without warning, and the moment he recognized it for what it was, he was ashamed of having felt it.

"Edward Lee, I want you to meet my friend, Wyatt."

Edward Lee glanced at Wyatt, his expression suddenly strained, his behavior nervous, as if expecting a negative reaction that must have happened all too many times before.

As Wyatt watched, he realized how special the bond was between Edward Lee and Glory. In their own way, they'd each experienced the judgment of a prejudiced and uneducated society. A society that seemed bound to ridicule that which it did not understand. Edward Lee was as different in his own right as Glory was in hers.

Wyatt smiled and extended his hand. "Any friend of Glory's is a friend of mine."

The grin that broke across Edward Lee's face was magnificent. He grabbed Wyatt's hand and pumped it fiercely as he started to explain.

"You can leave Rabbit in Mr. Dixon's barn," Edward Lee offered. "Then when you come home, you can ride him back here. When you don't need him no more, just lay the reins across the saddle and turn him loose. He'll come home."

Wyatt's smile widened. "Rabbit?"

Edward Lee nodded. "'Cause he runs like one."

Glory's small laugh broke the peace of the glade, and both men turned, each wearing a different expression as they gazed at the woman before them. Edward Lee's was one of devotion. Wyatt's was one of pure want.

Glory saw neither. All she knew was that two people

who meant something to her seemed at ease with each other. It gave her joy in this day of distress.

"I can't thank you enough for your kindness, Edward Lee. Tell your mother I said hello," she said.

He nodded, and then turned and walked away, moving with unnatural grace for one with so crippled a mind.

"Can you ride?" Glory asked, eyeing the saddle and remembering her dress, and wondering how she was going to accomplish this feat with any amount of dignity.

Wyatt grinned, then lifted her off her feet and set her sideways in the saddle, leaving her legs to dangle off to one side.

"That's almost an insult, honey. I'm a Tennessee boy, born and bred, remember."

And with one smooth motion, he swung up on the horse, settling just behind the saddle on which Glory was perched and slipped his long legs into the stirrups.

Glory shivered as Wyatt's breath moved across her cheek, and his arms fenced her close against his chest.

"Glory?"

"What?"

"Why did he call you Morning Glory?"

A sharp pain pierced and then settled around the region of her heart. She took a deep breath, knowing that it was something to which she must become accustomed.

"It was J.C.'s nickname for me…and they were Daddy's favorite flowers. They grow—" her breath caught on another pain as she amended "—grew on trellises on both sides of our front porch. That's how I got my name. Daddy said when I was born my eyes were as blue as the morning glory."

Impulsively, Wyatt hugged her, and feathered a kiss near her eyebrow.

"I'm sorry. I didn't know it would cause you pain."

She looked up at him, her eyes filling with unshed tears.

"It wasn't so bad," she said quietly. "In fact, it almost felt good to remember."

Wyatt watched her mouth forming around the words, and wanted to bend just a little bit closer and taste that pearly sheen of lip gloss painted on her mouth. But he couldn't, and he didn't, and the urge slowly passed. The horse moved sideways beneath them, ready for a command. He gripped the reins firmly and settled Glory a little bit closer to his chest.

"Can you hold on?" he asked.

"As long as you're behind me," she warned, trying to find an easy way to sit without sliding too far backward or forward.

As long as I'm behind you. The words hung in Wyatt's mind, fostering another set of hopes that he didn't dare acknowledge. *What if I never left you, little Morning Glory? How would you feel about that? Even more to the point, how do I feel? Are you what I was looking for when I started on this journey last fall...or am I just kidding myself, looking for easy answers to the emptiness inside myself?*

He shrugged off the thoughts, unwilling to pursue them while she was this up close and personal. He had to be careful. The last thing he wanted to do was ruin another woman's life as he'd ruined his and Shirley's. If he ever took a woman again, it would be forever. Wyatt Hatfield didn't make the same mistake twice.

The trip up the overgrown road was much easier on a horse, and done in the bright light of day. As they passed through the woods, Wyatt wondered how on earth they'd managed to get through it the other night without tearing their clothing to shreds.

For an old horse, Rabbit pranced, as if aware of his fine appearance and the precious cargo that he carried. In spite of the seriousness of the day, Glory smiled more than once at what they saw as they rode.

Once, her hand suddenly clutched at Wyatt's thigh and then she pointed into the trees. He followed the direction of her finger and saw the disappearing tail of a tiny red fox. And then a few minutes later, she pointed upward, watching as a hawk rode the air currents high above their heads.

"This is a fine place to live," Wyatt said.

The words gave solace to Glory's pain. It was a sentiment she'd heard her father offer more than once.

Wyatt felt some of the tension slipping out of her body, and she almost relaxed against him as they rode. Almost... until her homesite came into view, and the scent of something having been burned replaced the fresh mountain air.

Death seemed to hover above the spot where her house once stood. As they passed the ruins on their way to the barn to get his car, Wyatt noticed she turned away. In spite of the unusual activity taking place there, she was unable to look at the place she'd once lived.

Men hard at work paused at the sight of the pair's arrival on horseback. When they realized who it was, to a man, they took off their hats, standing with eyes down, sharing her sorrow and her loss.

Glory's breath caught on a sob.

"I'm sorry, honey," Wyatt said softly.

Tears were thick in her voice as she answered. "Oh, God, Wyatt Hatfield. So am I. So am I."

A short time later, as they passed the boundary sign on the north edge of town, Wyatt began easing up on the gas. It wouldn't do to get a ticket for speeding on the way to a funeral, but he'd been lost in thought.

While Glory had been unwilling to look at the men on her property, Wyatt had looked long and hard. Satisfied that Lane was right in the middle of what was being done, he'd left with an easy conscience. Whatever was found there today, whatever conclusion they came to, it would be fair, or Lane Monday would know the reason why.

"Are you all right?" Wyatt asked.

She nodded, her eyes wide and fixed upon the road before them. And then she asked, "Do you remember the turnoff to the cemetery we took to pick out grave sites yesterday?"

"I remember."

"I thought graveside services were appropriate for Daddy and J.C., considering their…uh…their condition." And then she hesitated, suddenly unsure of the decision she'd made yesterday. "Don't you?"

"I think whatever you decided is right. They were your family. Remember?"

She sighed and covered her face with her hands. Her voice was shaky, her fingers trembling as she let them drop in her lap.

"Oh, God, just let me get through this with my dignity."

"To hell with dignity, Glory. Grief is healthy. It's what you hold back that will eat you alive. Believe me, I'm the ultimate stiff upper lip, and look what a mess I've made of my life."

"I don't see it as such a mess," she offered.

He grimaced. "Yeah, right! I got married to a perfectly good woman, and then gave my heart, and attention, to the military instead of her. It took me years to figure out why."

She listened quietly, afraid to speak for fear he'd stop the confidences he'd suddenly begun to share.

"The military didn't demand anything from me except loyalty and a strong back. What my wife wanted from me was something I didn't know how to share."

And that was…

Wyatt answered her thought before he realized it had just been a thought.

"Me. I was too big and strong and tough to let someone see inside *my* soul. I suppose I thought it wasn't manly." A corner of his mouth turned up in a wry, self-effacing grin.

"I think that idiot notion came from having too many older brothers. They used to beat the hell out of me just to see how long it would take me to bleed, and then laugh. But let anyone else try the same stunt and they'd take them apart." He shrugged as the cemetery gates came into view. "Brotherly love is a strange, strange thing. It doesn't always lay the best of groundwork for making a good husband out of a strong man."

Glory shook her head. "You're wrong," she said quietly. "It wasn't that you were the wrong kind of man. I think it was the wrong time for you to have married. Maybe if you'd waited…" She shrugged, and then unbuckled her seat belt as he pulled to a stop.

For you?

The thought came and went so quickly that Wyatt almost didn't know it had been there. But the feeling it left behind was enough to keep him close at her side as they circled tombstones, walking across the close-clipped grass toward a tent in the distance.

When they were almost there, Glory paused in midstep and stared. Wyatt followed her gaze. Realizing that she'd spotted the single casket bearing what was left of both men, he reached down and clasped her hand in his.

Her chin lifted, her eyes glittering in the midmorning sunlight as she looked up at Wyatt. A slight breeze teased the thick dark hair above his forehead, scattering it with the temerity of an unabashed flirt. His dark eyes were filled with concern, his strong, handsome features solemn in the face of what she was about to endure. The scar on his cheek was a vivid reminder of what he'd endured, and as Glory saw, she remembered, and took hope from the fact that he'd survived…. So, then, could she.

Glory made it through the service with composure that would have made her father proud. Not once did she give way to the angry shrieks of denial that threatened to boil over. The only signs of her pain were the tears, constant and silent, that fell from her eyes and down her cheeks as the minister spoke.

It was afterward, when the people who'd come to pay their respects started to file past the chairs in which she and Wyatt were sitting, that she realized she wasn't as alone in this world as she'd thought.

The first woman who came was elderly. Her voice shook more than her hands, but her intention was plain as she paused at Glory's chair, resting her weight on the cane in one hand, while she laid a small picture in Glory's lap.

"I'm eighty-nine years old," she said. "I been burned out once and flooded out twice in my lifetime. In all them times, I never lost no family, and in that I reckon I was lucky. But I remembered the thing that I missed most of all that I'd lost, and it was my pictures. We talked about it at church last night. We've all knowed your family long before you was born, girl. The ones of us who had these have decided to give 'em you."

Glory stared at the picture, dumbfounded. It was an old black-and-white print of a young dark-haired woman with a baby on her hip.

"It's your granny," the old woman said. "And that there's your daddy, when he was just a young'un. I don't remember how I come by it, but me and Faith Dixon are near the same age."

Glory ran her finger lightly across the surface, absorbing the joy caught on their faces. Her voice was shaking when she looked up.

"I don't know how to thank you," she whispered.

"No need…no need," the old woman said. "Just don't you ever be so scairt that you go and hide in no woods alone again. That plumb near broke my heart. We won't hurt you, girl. You're one of us."

And one after the other, people filed past, giving their

condolences for her loss, along with another piece of her family to treasure. A girl from her high-school class gave her an annual of their senior year of school.

The man who owned the feed store had two photographs of J.C., taken years ago at a livestock show.

The newspaperman had old photos on file of the year her father had bagged a twelve-point buck.

And so they came, people and pictures of times she'd forgotten, and places to which she'd forgotten they'd been. And when they were gone, Glory sat in silence, clutching the mementos to her breast, unable to speak.

"They've made a dinner for you and your man at the church," the minister said as he started to take his leave. "I know it's hard, Miss Dixon, but letting them help you grieve will help you, as well."

"I don't know if I can," she whispered, then turned her face to Wyatt's shoulder and wept.

"Just give us a bit," Wyatt said. "We'll be along."

The minister nodded. "That's fine. Real fine. I'll let them know you're coming."

And finally, except for the casket waiting to be lowered, they were alone.

"Oh, Wyatt. I knew that people thought a lot of Daddy and J.C., but I didn't think they liked me."

Her pain broke his heart. "Cry, Glory. Cry it all out, and then let it go." With that, he pulled her a little bit closer to his chest and held her as she mourned for all that she'd lost…and rejoiced for what she had gained.

Food was everywhere inside the tiny cabin. On the small cabinet space, overflowing in the refrigerator, stacked two deep in aluminum-foil dishes on the table and waiting to be eaten.

It had been impossible to refuse the kindness of the ladies who'd prepared the meal, because when it was over, as was the custom of the country, the bereaved family had always to take home the leftover food.

Insisting that she could never use it up, Glory succumbed to their admonition that she had company to feed. They'd declared that, at the very least, she shouldn't have to cook for others in her time of grief.

Wyatt had been fully prepared to make several trips through the woods with the leftovers, because he had no intention of getting on Rabbit while trying to hold on to Glory and a handful of pies.

But when they drove into the yard, expecting Rabbit to be the next ride, they saw that while they were gone, someone had cleared the old road between their houses.

Thankful for the unexpected reprieve, Wyatt turned Rabbit loose as Edward Lee had instructed, and he and Glory drove up to Granny Dixon's cabin in comfort. It wasn't until later when Lane was helping them unload the food from the car that they learned one of Glory's neighbors had taken his tractor and front-end loader and done in two hours what would have taken a road crew two days to accomplish.

Glory disappeared into her room to change, and Lane dug happily through the covered dishes, eating his fill of the homemade food as he filled Wyatt in on all that had occurred while they were gone.

"She was right, you know," Lane said, as he took a second helping of scalloped potatoes. "Every gas jet in that house was opened wide. And one of the controls on the kitchen stove had been broken off. Short of turning off the gas at the propane tank, there would have been no way to stop its escape."

Wyatt shrugged. "I'm not surprised."

Lane grinned. "That Conway fellow isn't much of a cop. He wanted to suggest that Glory had turned them all on herself after the fire was over, just to back up her story. The fire marshal almost laughed in his face, and then asked him to try to turn one of the valves himself. Old Conway nearly busted a gut trying to break the knob loose."

"Did it happen?" Wyatt asked.

"Hell, no," Lane muttered, and scooped a piece of cherry pie on his fork. "The fire fused them in place. You couldn't budge one with a blowtorch."

"So, the official conclusion is in," Wyatt muttered. "Arson that resulted in two innocent deaths. The bottom line is, whoever did it is guilty of murder."

"Thank God," Glory said.

Both men turned at the sound of her voice. "At least now they *have* to believe me."

Lane grinned again. "Yes, ma'am, they do at that. Not that I didn't believe you myself…but hard proof is always good to have."

"So, where do I go from here?" she asked.

"Nowhere, unless I'm with you," Wyatt said. "Because if you're right about that, then you're right about why. Until they catch the man who's trying to hurt you, you will have twenty-four-hour protection."

Glory looked startled. *What do I do with two men the size of small horses in Granny's little cabin?*

Wyatt laughed aloud, startling Lane and making Glory flush. She'd forgotten his ability to read her thoughts.

"Well," she said, daring Wyatt to answer.

Lane wondered if he looked as lost as he felt. "I know when I've missed something, but the honest-to-God truth is I never saw it go by. What's going on?"

Glory frowned, and pointed at Wyatt. "Ask him. He's Mr. Know-it-All."

Wyatt grinned even wider. "Maybe you could bed one down in your daddy's barn and the other outside with the pup."

She raised an eyebrow, refusing to be baited by his words or his wit. "One of these days, you're going to eavesdrop on something you won't have an answer for," she said. Then she sat down beside Lane and began shuffling through the stack of pictures she'd left on the table.

The cryptic statement hit home as the smile slid off Wyatt's face. He knew she was right. Right in the middle of a new set of worries, Glory suddenly changed the subject.

"Lane, would you like to see my pictures?"

"Yes, ma'am, I would be honored."

Food and the future were forgotten as Glory led both men through her past, and as she talked, she absently caressed the pictures because it was all she had left to touch.

But while Glory was learning to heal, Carter Foster was festering into one big sore. His first choice for hit man was languishing in the state penitentiary. His second had moved to another state. He'd gone through the past seven years of his legal practice, trying without success to find a name to go with the game. It wasn't until he started on the files of his first year that he remembered Bo Marker.

It had been Carter's first big win in court. He'd successfully defended a man he knew was guilty as sin. Remembering the photographs he'd seen of Marker's victim, he was certain that this might be his man. Surely a man who was capable of killing a man with his fists was equal to pulling a trigger. He read through the file, making notes of the address and phone number he'd had at the time. He was certain that he'd have to do a little detective work on the side to find Marker, but it would all be worth it in the end.

He wrote quickly, returning the file as soon as he was through. Time was of the essence. The longer Glory Dixon remained alive, the shorter his own days of freedom. He'd lived in hell with Betty Jo long enough, and her death had, after all, been an accident. He deserved a break. Then he winced and ran his finger along his neck, loosening his collar and his tie. Just not the kind Betty Jo had gotten.

Chapter 6

Wyatt sat across the table from Glory, nursing a cup of coffee and watching the play of emotions upon her face as she went through the photographs she'd been given yesterday. At least they gave her pleasure, which was more than he could do. He'd lain in bed last night right across the hall from her door, listening for nearly an hour to her muffled sobs. It had been all he could do not to cross the hall and yank her out of that bed and into his arms. No one should have to cry like that alone.

Glory knew that Wyatt was watching her. Those dark eyes of his did things to her fantasies they had no business doing. They made her think things she shouldn't and want things she couldn't have. She should be thinking of him as nothing but a kind stranger, yet with each passing hour, he became more of a permanent fixture in her thoughts.

She sighed.

Thinking like that could get her hurt...very, very badly, and losing her family had been hurt enough. This man had already admitted to having doubts about himself. She didn't need to be falling for a man who would be here today and gone tomorrow. Glory was a forever kind of woman. She needed a forever kind of man.

The pictures slipped from her fingers and into her lap as she closed her eyes and leaned back against the couch, letting herself imagine what forever with Wyatt Hatfield might be like.

As her eyes closed and her head tilted backward, Wyatt froze. The delicate arch of her bare neck and the flutter of those gold-tinged eyelashes upon her cheeks were a taunting temptation to a man with deep need. He set his cup aside then got up, intent on walking out of the room before he got himself in trouble, wishing he'd gone to run the errands instead of Lane. But when he reached the doorway, he made a mistake. He looked back and got caught in a silver-blue spell.

There was a question in her eyes and a stillness in her body, as if she was waiting for something to happen. Wyatt ached for her…and for himself, well aware of just what it might be if he didn't readjust his thinking.

Suddenly, some of the pictures slid out of her lap onto the floor. He reacted before he remembered his intention to keep his distance, and was on his knees at her side, scooping them up and placing them on the table, before she could move.

Glory focused her attention on his hands, seeing strength in the broad palms, tenderness in the long, supple fingers and determination in the man himself as he persisted until every picture that she'd dropped was picked up. Forgetting the fact that he could tap into her thoughts at any given moment, she pictured those hands moving upon her body instead, and softly sighed.

"Here you go," he said, and started to drop the last of the pictures in her lap when an image drifted through his mind.

Skin...smooth to the touch, dampened by a faint sheen of perspiration. A pulse racing beneath it...a heartbeat gone wild beneath his fingertips. He rocked back on his feet and looked up at her.

Ah, God, Wyatt thought.

Glory saw the tension in his body, heard his swift intake of breath and remembered too late that, once again, she'd let him inside her mind. She held her breath, afraid to speak. How would he react, and what should she do? Ignore it...and him?

And then he lifted the pictures out of her lap and dropped them onto the cushion beside her, taking the decision out of her hands.

Mouths met. The introduction was short. It went from tentative to demanding in three short ticks of a clock.

Her lips were as soft as he'd imagined, yielding to a silent question he did not have the nerve to ask, then begging for more of the same. The sweetness of her compliance and the shock of their connection were more than he'd bargained for. Her breath was swift upon his cheek, her passion unexpected, and when he lifted his head from the kiss, as yet unfulfilled.

Oh, Wyatt!

"My sentiments exactly," he whispered, and ran his thumb across her lips where his mouth had just been. "Lord help us, Glory, but where do we go from here?"

Outside, the pup began to bark. Wyatt was on his feet in an instant, and out the door. The moment had passed.

Glory groaned, then buried her face in her hands. She'd been saved from having to respond. It was a small but much needed respite, because she had no answer for Wyatt. Not now, and maybe not ever.

Lane followed Wyatt back into the house, unaware of what he'd interrupted, and blurted out what had been on his mind all night.

"Glory, can you turn that psychic business of yours on at will?"

She seemed startled by the question, yet understanding dawned as to where he was leading.

"I've never tried. In fact, it's been quite the opposite. I've tried more than once to stop what I see, but I've never tried to start it."

"Don't you think now might be a good time to practice?" he asked.

Wyatt wanted to argue. Instinct told him this was too much too soon, but it was Glory's life that was on the line. It was her family who'd died. The least he could do was let her make the decision. Yet when she nodded, he frowned.

"Are you sure?" Wyatt asked.

She looked at him with a clear gaze. "About some things, no. About this, yes."

He didn't have to be a genius to read between the lines of her answer. She wasn't sure about what had just happened between them, but she was ready to try anything in order to find the person responsible for her father's and brother's deaths. All in all, he had to admit that her answer was more than fair.

"Then let's go," Lane said.

"Where to?" she asked.

"To where it all started."

Glory blanched, and in a panic, looked to Wyatt for support.

"I'm with you all the way," he said softly. "Want to walk or ride?"

"Ride, I think. The sooner we get there, the sooner it's over."

The drive was short, but the silence between the trio was long. When Glory got out of the car, she had to make herself look at the spot where her house had been standing. The blackened timbers and the rock foundation more resembled some prehistoric skeleton than the remnants of a home. It hurt to look at it and remember what had happened. But, she reminded herself, that was why she'd come.

Wyatt's hand cupped her shoulder. "How do you want to do this?" he asked.

"I don't know. Just let me walk around a little—maybe something will happen. I told you, I've never tried this before."

Lane had already found himself a seat in the shade. He watched Wyatt and Glory from a distance, thinking to himself that there seemed to be a lot more between them than the simple repayment of a debt. Wyatt hovered like a watchdog and Glory kept looking to him for more than support.

Lane's eyes narrowed thoughtfully as Wyatt caressed the crown of her head, his fingers lingering longer than necessary in the long silvery length. When he cupped her face with the palm of his hand, an observer might have supposed it were nothing more than a comforting touch. But Lane knew better. He saw the way Glory leaned into Wyatt's hand, and even from here, he could see a glow on her face that had nothing to do with the heat of the sun. If he wasn't mistaken, there was a slow fire burning beneath those two. Only time would tell whether it caught... or whether it burned out of its own accord.

Wyatt retreated, giving Glory space and time, but watched with a nervous eye as she paused on what was left of the back-porch steps.

As she stepped over the block foundation and then down onto the ground below, she stumbled. Instinctively, Wyatt started toward her, but then she caught herself, and so he paused and waited, watching as she started to move through the ash and the rubble.

Wyatt suddenly noticed that something seemed different about the site. It took a few moments for the reality to sink in. "That yellow crime scene tape is gone!"

Lane nodded. "They took it down after the fire marshal left. He said that it was impossible to preserve much of anything out in the open like this, and so he collected all of the evidence that he could. I think they took two or three of the small heating stoves in as evidence and took pictures of the rest."

"This is a hell of a deal, isn't it?" Wyatt muttered, taking consolation from Lane's comforting thump on his back.

Time passed slowly for the men, but Glory was reliving an entire lifetime as she walked through the rubble, and it was all too short a time considering what was now left.

She stood looking out across the broken foundation, trying to picture the man who'd invaded their home, and instead saw herself as a child, running to meet her father as he came in from milking. Seeing, through her mind, the way the solemnity of his expression always broke when he smiled. Almost feeling his hands as they circled her waist, lifting her high over his head and then spinning her around. Hearing his deep, booming laughter when he set her on his shoulders and she used his ears for an anchor by which to hold.

Oh, God, Glory thought, and swayed on her feet, overwhelmed by the emotion.

Angrily, she turned away, unwilling to savor the memory because of her loss. Black soot and ash coated the legs of her jeans and the tops of her boots as she trudged through what had once been rooms. Without walls to hold the love that had abounded within, the area looked pitifully small.

Again she stumbled, and something crunched beneath her boot. She bent over, sifting through the rubble to see what it had been. When she lifted it out, she choked back a sob. "Oh, no! I broke one of J.C.'s arrowheads."

She looked back down, and then gasped. There were dozens of them everywhere, shattered into remnants of their former beauty. What the explosion and fire hadn't ruined, the men who'd conducted the investigation had.

Tears flooded her eyes, then poured down her face, streaking the faint coat of ash on her skin as rage sifted through the pain.

Damn this all to hell!

She closed her fingers around the broken bits, squeezing until they cut into the palm of her hand. Anger boiled, then spilled, rocking her with its power. On the verge of a scream, she drew back her arm and threw. The broken pieces skipped through the air like rocks on water, and then disappeared in the grass a good distance away.

She was shaking when she turned, swiping angrily at the tears on her face. Crying would get her nowhere. She'd come to try to help find out who killed her family, not feel sorry for herself.

Wyatt could tell something monumental had just occurred. Her pain was as vivid to him as if it was his own. And when she turned toward them with tears running rampant down her face, he jumped to his feet.

"Damn it, that's enough," Wyatt said, and started to go after her.

Lane grabbed him by the arm. "Don't do it, brother. She'll stop when she's ready. Don't underestimate your woman. She survived real good on her own before you came. She's tough enough to do it when you're gone."

The look Wyatt gave him would have stopped a truck. It was somewhere between anger that Lane had dared to limit the time that was between them and fear that he might be right.

Wyatt turned, unaware that the look he was giving Glory was full of regret. "She's not *my* woman, she's… Oh, hell."

He bolted across the yard just as she staggered toward them. He caught her before her legs gave way.

"Glory…sweetheart…are you all right?"

His voice was anxious, his hands gentle as he steadied her on her feet. When she looked up, her face was grim and tinged with defeat, and for the first time since he'd come, he heard surrender in the tone of her voice.

"Damn, damn, damn. Nothing worked. Absolutely nothing. I couldn't think of *him* for remembering Daddy and J.C. I'm sorry. I just couldn't do it."

"To hell with this," he muttered. "I'm taking you home."

Her face was flushed and beaded with sweat, but her mouth twisted angrily as she looked over his shoulder. The dust of death was on her clothes, up her nostrils, coating her skin. At that moment, she hated. She hated her father and brother for leaving her, and herself for having survived. Pain came out cloaked in fury as she pointed to where she'd been.

"I am home, remember?" And she tried to push him away.

Wyatt ignored her anger, understanding it for what it was, and braced her with his hand. She trembled against him like a leaf in a storm.

Lane decided it was a good time to interrupt.

"Look, Glory, don't let it worry you. It was just an idea. I think I'm going to run into town and check on a few things. You just take it easy. We'll find him the good old-fashioned way." And then Lane gave Wyatt a long, considering stare. "I trust you'll take good care of her?"

Wyatt glared at the knowing look in Lane's eyes, then ignored him. When he thought about it, his brother-in-law could be a big fat nuisance.

"You're coming with me, Glory. You need a cool bath, a change of clothes and something to eat."

His proprietary manner was too new…and at this time, too much to absorb. She pushed his hand away. "Let me be, Wyatt. Don't you understand? I just want to be left alone."

Frustration was at the source of her anger, but the fact

that he'd been indirectly caught in its path hurt. He stepped back, holding up his hands as if he'd just been arrested, and gave her the space that she obviously needed.

"You don't want help? Fine. You don't want to talk to me? That's fine, too. But you don't get to be alone. You can have distance, but you don't get alone. Not until the son of a bitch is found who set fire to your world. So, do you want to maintain your solitary state in the front seat of my car while I drive, or shall I follow at a discreet distance while you walk?"

Lane hid a grin and headed for his car, thinking he'd be better off gone when the fireworks started. He'd heard that kind of mule-headed attitude before, only it had come out of Toni's mouth, not Wyatt's. Obviously that streak ran deep in the Hatfield clan. He wondered if Glory Dixon was up to the fight.

They were still staring, eye to eye, toe to toe, when the sound of Lane's car could no longer be heard.

Wyatt's eyes glittered darkly. He'd never wanted to swing a woman over his shoulder as badly as he did at this moment. For two cents, he'd…

I'm sorry.

"Well, hell," he grumbled, resisting the urge to kiss the droop of her lower lip. "If that's not just like a woman, expecting me to read her sweet mind for an apology."

Glory sighed, and then tried to smile. And when she held out her hand, he caught it, holding tighter than necessary as he pulled her up close.

"Apology accepted," he whispered. "I'm sorry, too."

"For what?" Glory asked. "You didn't do anything wrong.".

Wyatt grinned wryly. "I'd like to get that in writing," he said. "I know people who'd beg to differ."

But despair kept pulling her deeper and deeper back

into herself. "Dear God, Wyatt, there's nothing left to do but wait for him to try again."

He grabbed her by the arms and shook her, hating her for the fatalistic attitude. "Don't! Don't you even suggest that to me! You can't turn my world upside down, get into my mind and then give up on yourself without a damn fight! Do you hear me?"

After that, for a long, silent moment, neither spoke. And then Glory slowly lifted her finger and traced the path of the scar down the side of his face.

"Such a warrior."

Wyatt's confusion was obvious. "A what?"

Glory smiled, not much, but enough to let him know that he was off the hook. "You make me think of a warrior. For a while there, I forgot that you'd been a soldier. I'm sorry. I won't take you lightly ever again."

"Well, then," he muttered, at a loss for anything else to say.

Glory nodded, glad she was forgiven, and then turned back to stare at the rubble. Long minutes passed during which the expression on her face never changed, but when she abruptly straightened and put her hands on her hips, there was a glint in her eyes that hadn't been there before. Wyatt didn't know whether to be glad, or get worried.

"Wyatt."

"What?"

"I am going to rebuild."

His heart surged, and then he paled. *Dear God, if only I could be that certain about my life.*

"And, since you're bound and determined to dog my steps, you're about to get as dirty as I am." She headed for the barn with Wyatt right behind her.

"What are you going to do?" he asked as she began to push back the wide double doors hanging on tracks.

"I am going to clean house," she said. "Help me push this last door back. It always sticks."

Without giving himself time to argue, he did as he was told, and then watched her climb behind the steering wheel of an old one-ton truck that had been parked behind the doors.

"Better move," she shouted as the starter ground and the engine kicked to life. "The brakes aren't so good. I'll have to coast to a stop."

"The hell you say," he muttered, and then quickly moved aside, uncertain what to think of her newfound determination.

It was long past noon when Wyatt tossed the last board on the truck bed that it could possibly hold. Without thinking, he swiped at the sweat running down his face and then remembered the grime on his gloves and groaned. He yanked them off, but it was too late.

Glory turned to see what had happened, then started to smile. He frowned as she grinned.

"Well?" he grumbled, and she laughed aloud.

"What's so funny?" he said, knowing full well he'd probably smeared ashes all over his face.

Glory closed her eyes and grimaced, pretending to be lost in deep thought, and then started to speak in a high singsong voice.

"I see a man. I see dirt. I see a man with a dirty face. I see…"

Her playful attitude pleased and surprised him, despite the fact that he was the butt of her joke. He grinned, then without warning, scooped her off her feet, threw her over his shoulder and stalked toward the well house near the barn.

Glory was laughing too hard to continue her taunt. The world hung at a crazy angle as her head dangled halfway down his back. The ground kept going in and out of focus as she bobbed with his every step. And then her view shifted, and a corner of her mouth tilted. She knew just how to make him put her down.

Hey, Hatfield...nice buns!

"Lord have mercy, Glory, give a man a break," Wyatt muttered, suddenly thankful that his face was too dirty to reveal his blush. And while she was busy enjoying the point she had scored, he turned on the faucet, picked up the connected garden hose and aimed it directly at her face.

She choked on the water and a laugh, and then fought him for the nozzle. In the middle of the game, her participation suddenly ceased. Wyatt dropped the hose, letting it run into a puddle at their feet as he watched her withdrawal.

"What is it, honey?" he asked.

She started to speak and then covered her face, suddenly ashamed of what she'd been doing.

He grasped her hands and pulled them away. "Talk to me, Glory."

"I shouldn't have been... It isn't right that I..."

Understanding dawned. "You feel guilty for being happy, don't you?"

She nodded, and tried not to cry.

"Oh, honey, I'm sorry," Wyatt said, and wrapped his arms around her. "It's natural, you know. But you can't regret being alive, and I don't believe that your father would have wanted you to die with him...would he?"

She shook her head.

"So, okay, then." He picked up the hose, then handed it to her. "Come on, let's wash ourselves off before we go unload. And after I put some of that brake fluid you found in the truck, I'm driving. You, however, will have to navigate our way to the city dump. It wasn't on your town's tourist map."

She held the hose, watching intently as he washed his

hands, then lowered his head, letting the water from the hose run over the back of his hair and down his neck. He straightened quickly, shaking his head and wiping water from his eyes with both hands.

"Now you," he offered, and held the hose while she washed her hands, then cupped several handfuls of water and sluiced them on her face. "Feel better?" he asked, as he handed her his handkerchief.

"Wyatt?"

"What, darlin'?"

"Thank you," she said, and gave the used handkerchief back to him.

His gaze raked the contours of her body, now obviously revealed by the wet clothes clinging to her shape, and reminded himself of the task at hand.

"You're more than welcome."

The sign said Dump—$2.00 Per Load. But there was no one around to collect the fee, and so they drove right in and then backed up as near to the edge of the open pit as Wyatt dared. Taking into account the lack of decent brakes on the truck, he had no intention of going too close and then being unable to stop.

Glory got out of the truck with every intention of helping unload when Wyatt stopped her.

"Let me, okay?"

She relented. Her arms already ached from the strenuous job of loading the debris, and her legs were shaking with weariness.

"Okay, and thanks."

He smiled. "You're welcome. Now go find yourself some shade. This shouldn't take long."

Glory did as she was told, moving away from the side of the truck as Wyatt shed his shirt. She watched from a distance as he climbed up on top of the truck bed and began tossing the rubble, board by board, down into the pit, admiring the fluidity of his body and the grace with which he moved. After a while, she began to stroll around the area, stepping over bits of loose trash that had blown about and kicking at pieces of metal and stone lying haphazardly about the site.

Down in the pit, a huge, black crow began cawing loudly as it suddenly took flight, and two others followed. Glory turned, watching as they moved through the air on obsidian wings. She looked back to where Wyatt was working and saw that he had paused and was scanning the area with a careful eye. It gave her courage to know that he was ever on the lookout for her welfare.

He turned to her and waved. She started to wave back when his image began to waver like a fading mirage. Believing it to be caused by heat rising from the pit, Glory started to shade her eyes, and then felt the ground go out from under her. It was reflex that sent her to her knees to keep from falling face-first down in the dirt. And when her heart began to race and the mirage began to reshape itself, Glory grabbed on to the grass beneath her hands and held on, afraid to let go of the ride through her mind.

Bright sunlight was suddenly gone, as was her father's flatbed truck and Wyatt's image. Another had come to take its place. One stronger…darker…deadlier. She groaned, unaware that she was plunging her fingers deep into the dirt and grass in an effort to hold on.

Panic painted the man's movements, hastening his actions and coloring the short, uneven gasps of his breath. His rapid footsteps were muffled by the loose dirt and grass as he moved from the front of a car to the back.

A faint glow of a quarter moon glinted on the trunk lid of the car as it popped open. He bent down, then straightened, carrying something in his arms. Something heavy… something long…something white.

He staggered to the pit and then dropped it over the edge, watching as it fell, end over end, rolling, tumbling. Panic was beginning to subside. His relief was palpable.

Glory shuddered, trying to pull back from the scene in her mind, yet caught in a web not of her making. She watched as if through his eyes, unable to see his face. She rode with his thought, moved with his stride, paused with his hesitation. But when he stood on the edge of the pit and looked down, Glory's own horror pulled her out of the fugue. In spite of the realization that it was all in her mind, she began to scream.

The wind tunneled through Wyatt's thick dark hair, cooling the sweat upon his body and blowing away the ever-present stench of burned wood. Nearly through with the job, he paused and looked up, making certain that they were still alone, and ever careful to keep Glory within constant view.

Watching the wind play havoc with her hair made him smile. She'd already remarked while loading the truck that she should have done more than just tie it at the back of her neck, that it should have been braided to keep from whipping in her face and eyes.

And then he watched in horror as she suddenly dropped to her knees. Her name was on his lips as he jumped from the truck bed. And then he was running as fast as he could run, across the ground, past the edge of the pit, toward the sound of her screams. He yanked her out of the dirt and into his arms.

"Glory! Sweetheart! I'm here! I'm here. Let it go!"

She staggered, then swayed and, without thought, wrapped her arms around Wyatt's waist and held on, because he was her only stability in a world gone wrong.

"Dead. She's dead," Glory moaned. "All in white. And it came undone."

The plaintive wail of her voice sent shivers up his spine. She? Dead? What in God's name had Glory *seen* now?

He cupped her face with both of his hands, tilting it until she had nowhere to look but at him.

"Look at me!" he shouted. "Damn it, Glory, look at *me!*"

Her gaze shifted, and he could actually see cognizance returning. Breath slid from his lungs in a deep, heavy sigh as he wrapped his arms around her shoulders and rocked her within his embrace.

"Tell me, honey. Tell me what you saw."

And as quickly as her terror had come, it passed. There was intensity in her voice, in her manners, in the way she clutched at his bare arms.

"I saw a man take something white from a trunk of a car. I saw him drop it in the pit. It rolled and tumbled and..." She shuddered, then swallowed, trying to find ways to put into words what she saw in her mind. "He watched it fall. I felt him smile. The thing that he'd thrown came open. Like a candy that had come unwrapped. I could see her face. Her eyes were open wide, as if she'd been surprised. Oh, Wyatt, he threw a woman's body into the dump!"

"Good Lord! Are you sure?"

She nodded.

He stared down into the pit, noting the few bags of garbage that had been dumped earlier in the day, and then looking more intently at the huge layers of earth that had already been pushed over weeks of refuse.

"They probably cover this site every night. There's no way of telling how long ago this happened, is there?"

Her face contorted as she tried to remember everything that she'd seen and then she slumped in dejection. "No, it was so dark, I couldn't tell..." She gasped, and then cried, "A quarter moon! There was a quarter moon."

Wyatt tensed, then turned and stared at her face. "That was less than a week ago. I know because I sat on a porch in Tennessee, watching clouds blowing across a quarter moon and listening for the sound of your voice."

Glory shuddered. "What do we do?"

"We go tell Chief Conway."

She groaned. "He's going to laugh in our faces," she warned.

"Sticks and stones, honey. Sticks and stones. Now let's get the rest of that stuff on the truck unloaded and get back to the cabin. I think we need to look our best when we ask the chief to dig up a dump."

Chapter 7

Lane was waiting for Wyatt and Glory when they pulled up to the curb and parked in front of the police department.

"I got your message," he said. "What's up?"

"After you left, Glory wanted to haul some stuff to the dump. While we were there, she had a...uh, she saw..."

Glory sighed. Even Wyatt, who claimed to believe, had trouble putting into words what she so took for granted.

"Granny always called them *visions,*" she said.

Lane's attention piqued. "Look, Glory, you've already made a believer out of me, and that's no easy task. So what did you *see?*"

"A woman's body being tossed in the dump."

"Oh, hell," Lane muttered, thinking of the ramifications of convincing the law to act on a psychic's word. "This won't be easy."

After they went inside, he knew he'd been right. The police chief erupted as Glory started to explain, while the deputy slipped out of the room, hovering just out of sight on the other side of the door.

"You saw what?" Conway shouted, rising from his chair and circling his desk to where Glory was standing. "And I suppose you saw this incident *in your mind,* as well?"

Wyatt glared, inserting himself slightly between them. "There's no need to shout," he said.

A vein bulged near Conway's left eye as his face grew redder by the minute. "Let me get this right. You had this *vision,* during which time you saw a man throw a woman's body into the dump. Oh! And she was dressed all in white, right?"

Glory's stomach tightened. She wanted to turn and walk out and forget she'd ever seen what she'd seen. "Yes, I told you I saw her—"

Conway interrupted. "Can you explain why the man who works the bulldozer at the dump didn't see her...or why twelve men who work three different trash trucks on two different routes didn't see her while they were dumping loads?"

"No," Glory muttered.

Conway smirked. "I didn't think so." He glared at Wyatt, as if blaming him for this latest in a series of problems he felt unequipped to deal with. "Look, Hatfield. I deal in facts, and these...uh, impulses she claims to have are not facts. They're dreams. They're imagination. They're..."

The deputy slipped back in the room, unable to resist a comment. "But, Chief, she was right about them gas stoves."

"Shut up," he growled, and the deputy wisely retreated again, this time to the back room.

The chief's attitude did not surprise Lane. Law enforcement dealt with rules and givens. There were no rules for what Glory Dixon could do.

"I don't suppose you've had any missing person reports filed recently," Lane asked.

Conway made no attempt to hide his surprise. He apparently couldn't believe that a U.S. marshal would actually take any of this hogwash as fact.

"No, I don't suppose I have," he muttered.

"You're also real certain that none have come in over the wire from surrounding areas."

Conway flushed. He was pretty sure, but not positive. Obviously, however, he wasn't about to say it.

"Look, you two. You think because you're from the big city that the law in a little hill town like Larner's Mill can't cut the mustard, don't you? Well, you're wrong, and I don't like anyone buttin' into *my* business." His glare was directed as much at Lane as it was at Glory.

Before Wyatt or Lane could answer, Glory interrupted.

"I said what I came to say. What you do with the information is strictly up to you. However…if I'm right…and you're wrong, you've just let a man get away with murder. And that's your business, not mine, isn't it?" She walked out, leaving Wyatt and Lane to do as they chose.

They chose to follow her, and when they were gone, Anders Conway had no one to argue with but himself. It was a brief discussion that ended on a question. Just because Glory Dixon had been right about the fire that killed her folks didn't mean that she was always going to be right about that stuff floating around in her head…did it? He ran a hand through his thinning hair in frustration as he shouted at his deputy.

The deputy came running. "Yes, sir, what do you need?"

"I want to see everything we've got on missing persons in this county, as well as recent faxes along the same line." And when the deputy grinned, Conway glared. "Just because I asked to see the files doesn't mean I believe her," he grumbled. "I'm just doing my job. That's all."

Outside, Wyatt caught Glory by the arm as she walked toward the car.

"What?" she asked, still angry with the sheriff and the world in general.

"You did good," he said quietly.

Surprise colored her expression as Lane agreed.

"Wyatt's right. You said what had to be said. If the chief fails to follow up, then he's the one who's going to look like a fool. Now, if you two think you can make it on your own for a day or two, I'm going home to check on Toni and Joy, then swing by the office. I can access more information there than we're ever going to get out of Conway. Maybe something will turn up on the computer that fits what Glory saw."

"I'm really sorry all of this mess is taking you away from your family," Glory said.

Lane smiled. "My job always takes me away from my family, honey. We're used to it." And then his expression changed as he turned to Wyatt. "I've got some stuff I need to leave with you before I go. Why don't you pop the trunk of the car? I'll toss it in there."

"I'll do it," Glory said, and as she scooted across the seat, missed seeing the look on Wyatt's face as Lane set a handgun and several boxes of ammunition inside, then handed him his portable phone.

"Just so we can keep in touch," Lane said.

"And the other?" Wyatt asked.

"Just in case."

"Damn, I hate this," Wyatt said. "I thought I put all of this behind me when I left the military."

"Just take care of yourself," Lane said, and then gave Wyatt a quick brotherly hug. "I'll call you as soon as I know something."

Wyatt watched him drive away, then looked back at Glory, who sat patiently inside the car, waiting for him to get in. Her profile was solemn as she stared out a window, obviously lost in thought. Wyatt glanced at the trunk lid, picturing what Lane had put inside, and then looked up at Glory, struck by her repose and innocence.

Oh, Lord, I don't know what I'm afraid of most. Trying to keep you safe, or taking you to bed.

She turned. Their eyes met, and for a second, Wyatt was afraid that she'd read his mind. But when she did nothing but smile, he got in without hesitation, satisfied that his thoughts were still his own.

"Where do we go from here?" Glory asked.

He'd asked her that same question this morning right after the kiss, and like her, he had no answer.

"It's all up to you," he finally said.

"Wyatt?"

"What, honey?"

"Have you ever had so many problems that you just wanted to run away from everything?"

"Unlike you, sweetheart, I've been running all my life. We'll find a way to work this out. Just don't quit on yourself, and better yet, don't quit on me. I would hate to wake up one morning and find you gone."

An odd light glittered in her eyes, and then she turned away. "When it comes time to leave, I won't be the one with a suitcase in hand, and we both know it."

There was no way to argue with what she said and come out on the good side of the truth. Angrily, he started the car. Having done what they came to do, they headed back to Granny Dixon's cabin.

As they drove, Wyatt fought demons of his own that kept tearing at his concentration. Okay, he told himself, he didn't have to love her, and she didn't have to love him. All he had to do was keep her safe. He thought of the gun in the trunk and the look on Lane's face when he left. His stomach turned, imagining Glory in pain or danger, and he wanted to slam on the brakes and take her in his arms. He resisted the urge and kept driving. Yet the farther he drove, the more certain he became that it was too late. He didn't *have* to love her…but he did.

Thunder rumbled beyond the valley, and a streak of lightning crossed the sky. The rocking chair in which Glory was sitting gave an occasional comforting squeak as she kept up the motion by pushing herself off with the toe of her shoe. She looked up as Wyatt came in the door and dropped the magazine she'd been reading into her lap.

"Did you find the puppy?"

He shook his head. "Maybe he's afraid of the storm. He's probably under some bush or even gone back to the barn to a place that's familiar to him."

"Maybe."

But Glory couldn't shake the feeling that something was wrong. The puppy was all she had left of her life before the fire, and she couldn't bear to think of losing him, too. J.C. had adored him, and had sworn he would make a good hunting dog, but with her brother gone, the training sessions were over. If the pup came home at all, the only thing he would be hunting was biscuits. But her attention shifted from the missing pup to Wyatt as she noticed his behavior.

Rain began to pepper the glass behind the curtains, and although it wasn't really cold, she shivered, watching as Wyatt kept pacing from window to window, then to the other side of the house, ever on the lookout for something to come out of the dark. Something…or someone…that didn't belong. His every movement was that of a man on edge.

The more she watched him, the more fascinated she became. She thought back to the night of the blizzard and the first time she'd seen him, stretched out on a gurney and covered in blood. And then again, the day he'd been released from the hospital. Who would have guessed that one day, he'd be the single person who stood between her and death?

Looking back now, it hurt to remember how good and how simple life had been. Then she'd had a home and a family and a world that made sense. Now she had nothing but her life. And how Wyatt had come to her from across the miles was still a mystery; why he stayed an even bigger puzzle. As she rocked, he unexpectedly turned and got caught in her stare.

"Glory...what is it?"

"Why don't you doubt me? Everyone else does, except maybe Lane."

His answer was instantaneous, as if he'd thought about it himself, time and time again, and knew all of the words by heart.

"I don't know. All I know is, from the first there's been a connection between us. I don't understand it, but I know that it's there." He looked away, unwilling to say too much.

"Everyone thinks I'm crazy, so why are you different? Why do you stay with a crazy woman, Wyatt Hatfield? Why aren't you running as fast as you can from this mess?"

Now he hesitated. Telling the truth about his growing feelings for her could ruin everything, and yet lying to her was not an option. He had to find an answer somewhere in between. When he looked up, his eyes were full of secrets.

"Maybe I'm just waiting to hear you call my name."

The rocking chair came to an abrupt halt, ending in the middle of a squeak. *Oh, Wyatt. I'm afraid to. I'm afraid to love. I'm afraid that you won't understand me, and I can't change.*

Again, as he had in the past, he tapped into her thoughts and answered without realizing she hadn't spoken them aloud.

"I wouldn't change a thing about you, even if I could," he said. "I'm the one who's all messed up. I don't have it in me to make a good woman happy, because I've already tried and failed."

"No one is perfect, Wyatt. If you wanted to try, I believe that you could make anyone happy." And then her voice faltered, and she had to clear her throat before she could continue. "Even me," she whispered.

He froze. There was no mistaking the invitation, and ignoring it was beyond him. Because she sat waiting, he went to her, then held out his hands.

Glory took them without hesitation. The magazine in her lap fell to the floor when he pulled her to her feet, and when he began threading his fingers through her hair, her focus shifted, as it did when a vision was upon her. As he cupped the back of her head, tracing his thumbs across the arch of her cheekbones, she lost her center of gravity. Had it not been for Wyatt's arms, she would have fallen.

Even though she wanted this and much more from him, yielding to his greater strength was frightening. It was as if she'd suddenly lost her sense of self and was being consumed by his power. His voice rumbled too close to her ear, and instinctively she shivered. Wyatt read her actions as something other than desire and began feathering small kisses across her forehead, pleading his case as he drew her closer and closer against him.

"Don't be afraid of me…or of anyone else. Being afraid of love is like hiding from life. Sometimes you have to take a chance to be happy, and taking chances is what life is all about."

When his hands moved from the back of her head to the back of her neck, she sighed, giving way to a greater need within herself.

"Oh, Wyatt, I'm not afraid *of* you, only of *losing* you." *Lord help both of us.*

He lifted her off her feet. With her lips on his mouth and her body in perfect alignment with his, he began to turn, holding her fast within his arms as her feet dangled inches above the floor. Seductively, deliberately, with nothing but passion for music, they slow danced to a tune only they could hear.

Faintly aware of the ceiling spinning above and the lights blinking in and out of focus as they moved about the floor, she wanted to laugh, and she wanted to cry. She'd never known such joy…and such fear. She was hovering on the brink of discovery in Wyatt Hatfield's arms.

Wyatt ached, wanting more, so much more than the brief, stolen kisses that he was taking. *Time, I need to take my time.* But it was all he could do to heed his own words.

Unable to resist the temptation, he traced the curve of her cheek with his mouth and groaned when he felt her shudder. When he began nuzzling the spot below her ear with his nose, then his lips, savoring the satin texture of her skin, inhaling the essence of the woman that was Glory Dixon, she sighed, whispering something he couldn't understand. Her voice was soft against his cheek, and she yielded to him like a woman, giving back more than she got.

Clutching her fingers in his short, dark hair, she hid her face beneath the curve of his chin, ashamed of what she was about to ask but afraid this chance would never come again.

"Oh, Wyatt, I've learned the hard way that life is too uncertain. This time tomorrow you could be gone, or I could be dead. Please make love to me. I don't want to die without knowing what that's like."

He froze in the middle of a breath, with his mouth near her lips and his hands just below the curve of her hips. Except for the blood thundering through his veins and a pulse hammering against his ear, all movement ceased.

"What did you just say?"

Glory lifted her head. She wouldn't be ashamed of what she was. Truth was better said face-to-face.

"I asked you to make love to me," she whispered.

"Not that. The part about dying."

"I've never been with a man, Wyatt. I don't know what it feels like to have a man's hands on my body, or a man inside of me."

"Oh…my…God."

There was little else he could think to say. Nearly blind with need, it was all he could do to turn her loose, yet it had to be done. He'd started something in the wrong frame of mind, and had to stop it before it was too late.

"Well, damn," he said quietly, and walked out of the room.

She could hear the front door slam from where she stood. The fire that he'd started was scalding her from the inside out. She didn't know whether to cry or scream, to call out his name or go after him. She was still shaking from the hunger he'd started when she heard the door reopen abruptly and then slam shut, muting the sound of the wind accompanying the rain still pounding upon the roof. The click of a lock was loud in the sudden silence of the house. She held her breath, afraid to hope, afraid to care…and then the lights went out.

"Wyatt? Is that you?"

"Hell, yes, it's me," he growled. "Who else were you expecting? If anyone else touched you but me right now, I'd kill them with my bare hands."

Even in the dark, she started to smile. She wasn't going to question what had changed his mind, she would just be thankful that he had.

He found her right where he'd left her, and when his hands moved across her body in the darkness of the room, he felt her inhale, then sigh. He groaned with want as her breasts pushed against the palms of his hands.

"I didn't think you were coming back."

"I just went to my car…for these."

He caught her hands and flattened them against his rain-splattered shirt, guiding them to a shirt pocket to the right of his heartbeat.

Uncertain what was about to happen, she still followed his lead, feeling the pocket, then the flap, then at his instigation, dipping her hand inside. Thunder rattled the windowpanes as a gust of wind slapped tree limbs against the edge of the house. She gasped, spinning toward the sound behind them.

"It's all right, darlin'. It's just the wind."

And then he caught her hand and laid something into her palm.

Glory frowned as her fingers curled around the objects, unable to identify the sharp, clean edges of the flat, foil packets.

"I don't understand," she said. "What is it?"

"Your protection, sweetheart. I have never made love to a woman in my entire life without it in one form or another. I'm not about to put you at risk."

Oh!

"You guessed it," he said, and then laughed softly.

The sound of his laughter curled her toes and made her weak at the knees. Heat swept across her body, and she realized she was blushing.

"Where were we?" he muttered, and slipped his hands beneath her hips, cupping her body to his, and lowering his mouth in the darkness, searching for the sweetness of a kiss that he knew would be waiting.

The packets dropped to the bed behind them as she wrapped her arms around his neck. And then she moved against his groin, testing the bulge behind his zipper, and whispered against his mouth.

"Right about here…I think."

Moments later, Wyatt lifted her off her feet and laid her on the bed. The quilt shifted beneath her as his body pressed her deeper and deeper into the mattress.

Wyatt gritted his teeth, reminding himself that making love to Glory would be a whole new ball game, and took a long, slow breath to clear his senses. When he felt her shudder, his heart raced in sudden fear.

"Dear God, don't be afraid of me," he said. "I'll stop this right now if that's what you want."

Her hands moved up his thighs, pausing at the sides of his hips. "It's not fear that makes me tremble, Wyatt Hatfield, it's you."

"Have mercy," he said softly.

"Only if you hurry," she answered.

He did.

Clothes went flying in the darkness, landing where they'd been tossed with little care for the decorum. Now there was nothing between them but skin and need. Wyatt moved back across her body, settling the weight of himself upon her, testing the size of himself against her fragility. She was so damned tiny it scared him half to death.

Without wasted motion, he took her in his arms and rolled, taking her with him until he was flat on his back and she was lying upon him, mouth to mouth, breast to chest.

And when his hands cupped her breasts, rolling the hard aching peaks between his fingers with delicate skill, she instinctively arched, her mind blanking on everything but his touch.

Oh?

He smiled in the darkness, moving his hands upon her body, mapping the tiny bones and a waist he could circle with both hands, testing the gentle flare of her hips, then letting his thumbs slide down...down.

Oh, Wyatt!

Glory gasped, then moaned as her head fell back and her hips followed the pressure of his fingers. When her body swayed, and the long flow of her hair brushed across his thighs, teasing at the juncture of his turgid manhood, Wyatt shuddered with longing. Not yet, he warned himself.

His hands slid over the quilt top, finding then opening one of the packets he'd brought in from the car—doing what had to be done before it was too late to think.

The room spun and the bed tilted. Glory rode with the motion, afraid it would stop, afraid to let go of the man beneath her. He'd built too many fires with the touch of his hands and the sweep of his mouth. Something was building, tightening, spiraling inside her so deep that it had no name. There was no understanding of what would come next, only the mind-bending need for it to be.

"Oh…Wyatt."

Her cry was soft, almost unheard, but Wyatt felt it just the same. He was aware of what was happening to her and wished he could be inside of her when it happened. But he couldn't, not the first time, not until she knew that this act came with something besides pain.

"Wyyaatt?"

There was panic in her voice, riding along with a racing heart as he continued to stoke the fires he'd created.

"That's it, Glory. Don't fight it. Don't fight me. Just let it happen."

And then it did, breaking over her in swamping waves of heat, shattering in one spot and then spilling into every other part of her body.

"Ah, Wyatt," she groaned, and would have collapsed had he not caught her in midslump.

"Not yet, sweet lady. There's a thing I must do, and I ask your forgiveness now, before it's too late."

Glory's mind was still swimming in the midst of pure pleasure when he rolled with her once again. Vaguely aware of the bed beneath her bare back and the weight of the man above her, she was unprepared for the spear of manhood that gently shattered the dissipating pleasure. The pain was sharp, burning and, after such joy, unexpected. Unable to stifle a cry, her fingers dug into the sides of his arms as she instinctively arched against the thrust.

"Ah, Glory, I'm sorry, so sorry," he whispered, and gritted his teeth to maintain control.

A sob caught at the back of her throat. Afraid to breathe, she braced herself for the next wave of pain. It didn't come. Only an unexpected fullness she'd never known before. One slow breath after another, she waited for him to move, and only after she began to test the theory herself did he react.

Bracing himself above her, he shifted slightly, and then smiled in the dark when he heard a soft moan that had nothing to do with pain.

"Sweetheart, are you all right?" he whispered.

Her hands snaked around his shoulders. "I don't know yet. I'll tell you when it's over."

His laughter rocked the walls. When he lowered his head, feeling for her lips in the darkness, the smile was still upon his face. And then he started to move, slowly, tentatively, giving her time to adjust to his presence. Deeper and faster, he took her with him, driving like the rain that blew against the outer walls, losing himself in this woman who held his heart in her hands.

The end came almost without warning. One moment Wyatt was in total control, and then Glory moved unexpectedly, wrapping her legs around his hips and pulling him too far in to stop. Heat washed over him like a wave, sweeping everything from his mind but the feeling they'd created together. And then it was over, and he wanted her more.

Long silent minutes passed while he cradled her in his arms, whispering things in the dark that he could never have said in the light, stroking her body with the flat of his hand, unable to believe that this tiny, tiny woman was capable of such passion and love.

Finally he asked her again. "Glory?"

She sighed, and then slid one leg across his knees. "Hmm?"

"Now are you all right?"

He felt her smile against his chest, and dug his hands in the long tangle he'd made of her hair.

"Oh, Wyatt…I didn't know, I didn't know."

"Know what, honey?" he whispered, as he continued to cuddle her close.

"That love came in colors."

"That it did what?"

"It's true. When we…I mean, when I…"

He grinned. "It's okay, I know the moment you're trying to identify."

"I saw red…and then white."

Touched by her admission, he teased her, trying to alleviate his own emotions. "What…no blue?"

"Red was what I saw just before… When you… When we…"

His voice vibrated with laughter. "Darlin', we're going to have to find a way to get you past this mental roadblock. Just say it. When you lost your sweet mind, right?"

"I suppose it *was* right about then."

This time, he couldn't suppress a chuckle. And then her arms tightened around his chest and when he reached out to stroke her face, he felt tears on her cheeks.

"Tears? Don't tell me I was that bad," he whispered.

"No, Wyatt. I didn't cry because it was bad. I cried because it was so good."

He hugged her, too moved to respond to her praise.

A few seconds passed, and in that time, he felt her restlessness, and knew that there was something else she wanted to say. Then he remembered she hadn't explained the other color.

"So I made you see red. But what about the white?"

Excitement was in her voice as she lifted herself on one elbow and traced the lines of his face with her fingertips.

"Oh, Wyatt...just as everything within me gave way...I saw you...or at least the essence of you. There was no way to tell where I ended and you began. And the light with which you came to me was so bright...so pure...so white!" Her voice faltered, then broke. "That was when I cried."

Oh, my God!

More than once he tried to respond, but there were no words to express what he felt, only an overwhelming sense of inevitability, as if he'd been on the course all his life and the outcome was out of his hands.

And so they slept, wrapped in each other's arms while the storm front moved on and morning dawned to a damp, new day.

The sharp ringing of the telephone near his ear sent Carter Foster scrambling to shut off an alarm. By the time he realized that it was the phone and not the alarm, he had knocked a stack of papers onto the floor and cracked the plastic housing around his clock.

"Damn it," he muttered, and then picked up the phone. "Foster residence."

"It's Marker."

The skin on the back of Carter's neck crawled as his belly suddenly twisted into a knot. Hiring Bo Marker yesterday had been a last resort, but he hadn't expected to hear from him quite so soon.

"Is it over?" Carter asked.

Marker snorted loudly into the phone, his voice filled with derision. "Hell, no, it ain't over. You didn't tell me she had a bodyguard *and* a watchdog."

Carter groaned. He should have known Marker would screw up.

"For all I know, she could have three of everything,"

Carter snarled. "You're the one who claimed to be an expert. It's up to you to find a way to accomplish what you're being paid to do."

"I want more money," Marker argued. "I done been dog bit, and that man who hangs on the Dixon woman's arm is no slouch. I seen him take a handful of ammo and a piece out of his trunk that could blow a hole in an elephant."

"What did you think they would do, throw rocks at you?" Carter yelled. "And hell, no, you don't get more money. If you don't do what I paid you to do, you don't even get the last half of what I promised."

Then he pinched the bridge of his nose, took a slow, calming breath and stared out of the window at the rising sun. Screaming at Neanderthals was not something to which he was accustomed. Someone was going to have to do the thinking, and obviously, Bo Marker was not going to be it.

"Look, just get rid of the dog and…"

"Already done it."

Carter sighed. "Then why are you bothering me? You know what has to be done. Go the hell out and just do it. And don't call me again until it's over!"

Marker frowned. "Yeah, right," he muttered, and let the phone drop back onto the receiver, well aware that it would echo sharply in Carter Foster's ear.

Carter winced as he disconnected, and then fell backward onto his bed, staring up at the ceiling without seeing the fancy swirls of plaster that Betty Jo had insisted upon, contemplating how swiftly a man's life could change.

One day he'd had a wife and a business and a fairly normal life. That he no longer had a wife was not strictly his fault. He'd firmly convinced himself that Betty Jo had brought everything upon herself. And when he thought about it, he regretted the fact that he'd been forced to eliminate other lives in order to maintain his own…but not enough to sway himself from his chosen path. Yet think-ing about that Dixon woman and what she could do to his world made him sick with fear.

"Well, damn," he mumbled, and rolled off the bed and headed for the bath. It was time to start another day.

Chapter 8

With daylight came restraint. Glory wasn't versed in morning afters, and Wyatt looked even bigger and more imposing in the bright light of day as she lay in bed, watching him wake beside her.

The color of his hair was a stark contrast to the pillowcase upon which he lay. Dark to light. Black to white. His eyelashes fluttered as consciousness returned, brushing his cheeks like shadows moving in the night.

Glory shivered with longing as she gazed at his lips, remembering how he'd raked them across her body, and how she'd responded. He stretched, and she followed the path of muscles that contracted along his arms and chest, amazed at the size of him and of his obvious strength, yet remembering how gently he'd held her when they made love.

Nervously, she waited for those dark eyes to open, waited anxiously to see how he would respond, and reminded herself, *I'm the one who started this. I asked him to make love to me.*

Wyatt opened his eyes and turned to face her. An easy smile creased his lips as he scooped her up in his arms.

"And I will be forever grateful."

Glory blushed. "I thought you were asleep," she grumbled. "You could make a woman real nervous, sneaking in on her thoughts like that."

Wyatt grinned, then slid his hands down the length of her back, testing the softness of her skin. Stoking new fires, he began measuring the distance of his restraint between lust and passion. He wanted her to know pleasure before he knew his. But when her eyelids fluttered and her breath began to quicken, he knew it was time to ask.

"I don't want to insist, but I'd like to talk about, uh... losing our minds...just once more...before I get out of this bed."

"Talk's cheap," she said, and ran her hand down his chest, past his belly and beyond.

He grinned again as he caught her hand before she went too far in her exploration and ruined the extent of his plans, and then he paused, remembering last night had been her first time.

"But...I don't want you to do this if it's going to be uncomfortable for you," he whispered, tracing the shape of her mouth with a fingertip.

She raised up on one elbow and began digging through the tangle of bedclothes until she felt one of the flat packets beneath her hand. She handed it to Wyatt with only the faintest of blushes.

"Here. You're the one who feels uncomfortable, not me."

Again, in the midst of a most intimate moment, she had made him laugh by acknowledging that his manhood was hard and, most probably, aching. And in that moment, Wyatt knew a rare truth. Going from laughter to passion, without foreplay in between, was a rare and beautiful thing.

Like the bloom of the morning glory, a thing to be trea-
sured.

He took what she offered, and moments later he rolled
across the bed, taking her with him until she was firmly
in place beneath the weight of his body.

Glory looked up. The breadth of his shoulders swamped
her in size. The weight of his body was twice that of her
own, and yet she knew that she was in total control.

One word.

That was all it would take to change the drift of Wyatt
Hatfield's thoughts. But Glory wasn't a fool. If one word
need be uttered, it would be one of compliance, not rejection. The question was in his eyes, the thrust of his body
against the juncture of her thighs was all the proof that he
could show of his need. The muscles in his arms jerked as
he held himself above her, waiting for her decision.

"Glory...sweetheart?"

She lifted her arms and pulled him down. "Yes."

And when he slid between her legs and filled that in her
that was empty, she sighed with satisfaction. "Oh, yes."

Wyatt smiled, and then it was the last thought he could
manage as morning gave way to love.

Everything was wet. Last night's rain had soaked
ground, grass and trees, and the creek below Granny Dixon's old cabin was frothed with mini whitecaps from the
swiftly flowing stream. Wyatt stood lookout at the top of
the creek bank, watching as Glory searched the thickets
below, calling and calling for a missing pup that never
came.

"Give it up, honey," he called. "If the pup was anywhere
nearby, you know it would come to you."

She looked up, and the sorrow on her face was more than
he could bear. He started down the bank toward her when
she waved him away, and started up instead.

"We can go up to your house. Maybe the pup spent the night in the barn," he suggested.

She shook her head and all but fell into his arms as she reached the top. "Even if he had, he would have come back this morning begging for something to eat."

Weary in body and heart, she wrapped her arms around his waist and then suddenly gasped, jumping back in shock when her hands accidentally brushed across the pistol he had slipped in the waistband of his jeans. Her eyes widened with shock, turning more silver than blue as she looked up at Wyatt's face. It was all she could do to say his name.

"Why are you carrying a gun?"

His expression flattened. Once again, she saw the soldier that he had been.

"I want you alive. I want you safe. This is the only way I have of helping to keep you that way."

She paled, then spun away, and Wyatt watched as her hair fanned around her like a veil of pale lace. He wanted to touch her, but her posture did not invite intrusion. Instead, he waited for Glory to make the next move.

Glory stared blindly about her at the pristine beauty of the thick, piney woods that had always been her home, searching for the comfort that had always been there. Yet as she looked, the shadows that she'd once sought to play in no longer offered cool solace. Instead, they loomed, ominous by their mere presence. Trees so dense that it would be impossible to drive through no longer seemed a source of refuge. Now they seemed more like a prison. She doubled her fists and started to shake. Anger boiled up from her belly, burning and tearing as it spilled from her lips.

"I hate this," she muttered, and then turned back to Wyatt, her voice rising in increments with each word that she spoke. "I hate this! It isn't fair! My family was taken from me. I no longer have a home. And now J.C.'s puppy is gone." Her voice broke as tears began to fall. "It was the last thing I had from before."

Wyatt reached for her, but she was too fast. Before he knew it, she had started toward what was left of her home, splattering mud up the legs of her jeans and coating her boots as she stalked up the road.

He didn't argue, and he didn't blame her. Fighting mad was a hell of a lot healthier than a silent grief that never healed. He began to follow, never more than a few steps behind.

A slight mist was beginning to rise from the puddles as the midmorning sun beamed down through the trees, evaporating the water that had not soaked into the ground. The cry of a red-tailed hawk broke the silence between them as it circled high above, searching for food. Wyatt shaded his eyes and looked up, and as he did, missed seeing Glory as she suddenly veered from the road and dashed into the edge of the trees.

But when she screamed, he found himself running toward her with the gun in his hand before he realized that he'd even moved. Years of training and an instinct that had kept him alive in places like Somalia had kicked in without thought.

By the time he reached her, she was coming back to him on the run. He caught her in midstride, holding her close as he trained the gun toward the place she had been, expecting to see someone behind her. Someone who meant her great harm.

"Talk to me," he shouted, shaking her out of hysterics before it got them both killed. He needed to know what was out there before he could help.

She pointed behind her, and then covered her face with her hands and dropped to her knees in the grass.

"The puppy...back there...it's dead."

God! Wyatt ran his hand gently over the crown of her

head, then patted her shoulder, his voice was soft with regret and concern. "Wait here, sweetheart. I'll be right back."

It had been dead for some time. That much was obvious, due to the fact that while it had been shot, there was no blood at the scene. Last night's rain had taken care of that…and any other clues that might have led Wyatt to some sort of answer. And yet he knelt near the carcass, searching the ground around it for something, anything, that might lead to an answer.

He stared at the hole in the side of the pup's head, and another just behind one of its front legs. For Wyatt, it was total proof that it hadn't been some sort of hunting accident. One shot maybe, two, no. And then he noticed something beneath the pup's mouth and tested it with the tip of his finger. It was soft and wet and blue. Frowning, he pulled, then rocked back on his heels when a bit of cloth came away in his hands. It had been caught in the pup's teeth.

"Well, I'll be damned," he muttered, fingering the small bit of fabric. "Looks like you got a piece of him before he got to you, didn't you, fella?"

He stuffed the fabric in his pocket, then looked back at Glory. She was only a short distance away, and he could tell by the way she was standing that she'd been watching every move that he'd made.

Damn. He stood, then started toward her.

"Someone shot him, didn't they?"

He nodded.

"What was that you put in your pocket?"

He frowned, yet keeping the truth from her was dangerous. It could very well get her killed.

"I think maybe you had the makings of a good watchdog, honey. There was a piece of fabric caught in its teeth."

The anger that had carried her up the road simply withered and died as she absorbed the ramifications of what that could mean. Had the puppy died defending its territory from a trespasser? Maybe the same man who'd been in her house?

"So what do you think?" she finally asked.

What he was thinking didn't need to be said. He slipped an arm around her shoulder and hugged her gently. "Just that I need a shovel."

Her shoulders drooped. "There's one in the barn."

He held out his hand and then waited. This time, they traveled the rest of the distance hand in hand. But when they came out of the barn, Glory groaned in dismay. Edward Lee was walking toward them up the road, carrying the pup's limp body dangling across his outstretched arms.

"Oh, no," she said softly.

"What?" Wyatt asked.

"Edward Lee gave J.C. the puppy for a birthday present about six months ago. He's not going to take this well."

Sure enough, Glory was right. Edward Lee was sobbing long before he reached them.

"Look, Mornin' Glory, someone went and killed your dog."

"We know, Edward Lee. See, we have a shovel. We were about to bury him. Would you like to pick a place?"

Tears slowed as the idea centered within the confusion in his brain. He blinked, and then lifted his gaze from the pup to Glory.

He nodded. "I will pick a good place," he said. "A place that James Charles would like."

In spite of her pain, Glory smiled, thinking what a fit J.C. would have had if he'd heard that. Edward Lee was the only person who occasionally insisted upon calling her brother by his full given name. Everyone else had been forced to use the nickname, J.C., which he preferred.

And then Edward Lee looked at Wyatt, suddenly realizing he was there. "Wyatt is my friend," he said, assuring himself that the new relationship still held true.

Wyatt nodded. "Yes, I am, Edward Lee. Now, why don't you tell me where to dig, and we'll make a good place for the puppy to rest."

Glory watched from the shade of the barn while Edward Lee led Wyatt to a nearby lilac bush in full bloom. When he began to dig, she said a quick prayer and let go of her fear. A short time later, there was a new mound of dirt near the thick cover of lavender blossoms. It was a fitting monument for a short but valiant life.

They walked with Edward Lee to the end of the road, and then watched as he disappeared into the trees. A few moments later, as they were about to enter the cabin, the persistent ringing of an unanswered phone could be heard.

"Shoot." Wyatt suddenly remembered the phone that he'd tossed on the bed while getting dressed. He darted inside, and then toward the bedroom, answering it in the middle of a ring.

"Hello."

"Where have you been?" Lane growled. "And why didn't you take the damned phone with you? I left it so I could stay in touch. I was just about call out the National Guard."

"Sorry," Wyatt said, and dropped onto the side of his bed. "We were burying a dog."

"You were what?"

"The pup. Someone shot it while we were in town yesterday. We didn't find it until this morning."

"The hell you say. How's Glory taking it?"

"About like you'd imagine. It was her brother's dog."

Lane frowned. He didn't like what he was thinking, but it had to be said. "Look, Wyatt, remember when I was laid up at Toni's after the plane crash and your nephew's dog was killed?"

Wyatt grinned. "Yeah, was that before or after you got my sister pregnant?"

"Just shut up and listen," Lane muttered. "The point I'm

trying to make is that the inmate we all thought was dead was actually hiding in the woods. He killed the dog to keep it quiet during one of his trips to forage for food. I'm warning you to be careful. Bad guys have a habit of eliminating all obstacles in their paths, no matter what."

Wyatt dug in his pocket and pulled out the bit of fabric.

"Don't think it hasn't already crossed my mind. The pup got a bite of whoever it was that did him in, though. I found a piece of fabric caught between his teeth."

"Well, well! That's real good detective work. Maybe there's hope for you yet," Lane drawled.

Wyatt grinned. "Is there a real reason you called, or were you just checking up on me?"

"Oh, yeah, right! Look, I've been running a check on any or all missing person reports filed in the past two months in a five-hundred-mile radius of Larner's Mill. There are only two, and both of them are males. Glory is real sure the body she visualized was a female?"

"Absolutely," Wyatt said, and heard Lane sigh in his ear.

"Okay. I'll keep searching. Meanwhile, for God's sake, carry the phone with you. You never know when you'll need to reach out and touch someone...understand?"

"Understood," Wyatt said, and disconnected. When he looked up, Glory was standing in the doorway. She'd been listening to their conversation. There was a slight, embarrassed smile on her face, but stifling the question on her mind was impossible.

"Lane got your sister pregnant?"

Wyatt laughed. "It's a long story, honey. But don't feel sorry for my sister. She got exactly what she wanted. In fact, old Lane was the one who got caught in the Hatfield crossfire."

She smiled, trying to imagine anyone as big and forbidding as Lane Monday getting caught by anything.

"You're very lucky," she said.

Wyatt frowned as he tried to follow her line of thinking. "How so, honey?"

"You have a large family. I think it would be wonderful to be part of that."

"I'll share mine with you," Wyatt muttered. "Sometimes they can be a royal pain in the you-know-what."

If only I could share your family, Wyatt Hatfield. But she didn't say it, and walked away.

Wyatt sat on the side of the bed, calling himself a dozen kinds of a fool for not responding to her wish. But how could he say it when he wasn't sure what to say? All he knew was that he lived for the sound of her voice, rested easy only when she was within eyesight and came apart in her arms from their loving. It was definitely passion. But was it true love?

He followed her into the kitchen. "Don't cook. We need to get out of here for a while. Why don't you make a list? We'll do some shopping and then eat supper out before we come home?"

Glory turned. "I have to change. I'm muddy, and my hair's a mess."

Wyatt dug his hands through the long, silky length, then buried his face in the handful he lifted to his face.

"Your hair is never a mess," he said softly. "It feels like silk and smells like flowers." And then he leaned down and pressed a swift kiss on her mouth. "And...I love the way it feels on my skin."

And I love the way you feel on my skin, she thought.

Startled, Wyatt dropped her hair, and looked up. Glory arched an eyebrow, unashamed of having been caught.

"Did it again, didn't you?" she asked, and left him wearing a guilty expression as she went to change clothes.

Within the hour, they were in the car and on their way up the road. When they passed the old barn, Glory turned toward the new grave and impulsively pressed her hand against the glass.

"When this is all over, you could get another puppy," Wyatt said.

Glory shrugged. "If I'm still here to care for it, I might."

Wyatt was so angry he was speechless. That she kept referring to the fact that she might not live through all of this made him crazy. He couldn't shake the fear that she might be seeing something of her own future that she wasn't willing to share.

Sundown had come and gone while they were inside Milly's Restaurant on the outskirts of Larner's Mill. They exited the lively establishment into a crowded parking lot as the scent of hickory smoke from the inside grill coated the damp night air.

Glory walked silently beside Wyatt as they wove their way through the unevenly parked cars, absorbing the comfort of his presence even though she was unable to voice what she was feeling. And truth be known, she wasn't certain she could put into words the emotions swirling inside her head. All she knew was she wanted this man as she'd never wanted another.

A couple got out of a car just ahead of them, paused and stepped aside, giving Wyatt and Glory room to pass.

Pleasantries were traded, and then they walked on just as someone shouted Wyatt's name. He turned. It was the chief of police.

Anders Conway stepped off the curb and started toward them while Glory's good mood began dissipating.

"Oh, great," she muttered. "I'm not in the mood for any more of that man's sharp-edged doubt. Wyatt, could I please have the keys? I'd rather wait for you in the car."

He slipped his hand beneath the weight of her hair, caressing the back of her neck in a gentle, soothing touch, then handed her the keys without comment.

Beneath a tree a short distance away, Bo Marker sat in a stolen car, well concealed behind the dark tinted windows as the engine idled softly. When he'd seen the Dixon woman and her man come out of Milly's, he'd been satisfied that tonight he could quite literally kill two birds with one stone, get the rest of his money from Foster and be out of Kentucky before this night had passed. And then the chief of police had followed them outside.

"Son of a...!" he muttered, then shifted in the seat.

But berating himself for bad luck wasn't Bo Marker's style. All he needed was a change of plans, and when Glory Dixon suddenly walked away from her watchdog companion, Marker smiled. It creased his wide, homely face like cracks down the side of a jar. He leaned forward, hunching his great bulk behind the wheel of the car, and when Glory Dixon moved into the open, he quietly shifted from Park to Drive, and then stomped on the gas.

Bo Marker had stolen wisely. The souped-up hot rod could go from zero to sixty in seconds. The engine roared, coming to life like a sleeping lion. Tires squalled, gravel flew and the car fishtailed slightly as he shot out of a parked position, down the short driveway toward the highway beyond and right into Glory Dixon's path.

At the sound, Glory looked up and found herself staring straight into the blinding glare of headlights on high beam. Before she could think to react, a weight caught her from behind in a flying tackle, and before she had time to panic, Wyatt's arms surrounded her as they went rolling across the gravel.

Tiny shards of rock stung her leg as the car flew past, and she heard Wyatt grunt in pain as they came to a stop against the bumper of another vehicle. His hands were moving across her body before she could catch her breath to speak. She didn't have to hear the panic in his voice to know how close that had been.

"Glory! Sweetheart! Talk to me! Are you all right?" Before she could answer, she heard a man shouting orders and remembered. Chief Conway had witnessed it all.

"How bad is she hurt?" Conway asked Wyatt as he knelt beside them.

Wyatt's voice broke. "Oh, God, I don't…"

Glory caught Wyatt's hand as it swept up her neck in search of a pulse. In the second before she spoke, they stared straight into each other's eyes. There were no words for what they felt at that moment, nor were any necessary. He'd saved her life, as surely as she'd saved his all those months ago.

"Thanks to Wyatt, I think I'm all right."

"Damn crazy driver," the chief said. "I'm in my personal car, or I'd have given chase myself." And then by way of explanation, he added, "I couldn't catch a rabbit on a hot day in that thing, but at least I had my two-way. My men are already in pursuit."

Even as Wyatt helped Glory from the ground, the sounds of fading sirens could be heard in the distance.

"Oh, damn," Wyatt whispered, as he peered through the faint glow of the security lights to the dark stain coating his hand. "Glory…you're bleeding."

She followed the trail of a burning sensation on her left arm. "I just scraped my elbow." And then she shuddered and leaned forward, letting Wyatt enfold her within his embrace. "It wasn't an accident, Wyatt."

"I know, honey."

Conway frowned. "Now, it could have been a drunk driver, or a—"

Angry with Conway's persistent blind streak where Glory was concerned, Wyatt interrupted. His voice rose until by the time he was finished, he was shouting in the policeman's face.

"Last week, someone blew up her house, fully expecting her to be in it. Yesterday, someone shot her dog. We found this in his teeth when we went to bury it." Wyatt dug the bit of fabric from his shirt pocket and slapped it into the chief's hand. "Now, tonight, someone tried to run her down. And before you argue, consider the fact that the car wasn't already rolling when Glory stepped into the drive. I heard the motor idling. I heard him shift gears. He was waiting for her. When he had a clear shot, he took it."

Glory shuddered and Wyatt felt it.

"Now I'm going to take her to the hospital to be checked out. If you want to talk more, feel free to come along. Otherwise, I suppose you can file this information and the bit of fabric I just gave you where you've filed the rest of Glory's case."

"No hospital, Wyatt. Just take me home. There's nothing wrong with me that you and some iodine can't fix."

"Are you sure, honey?" he asked.

"I'm sure. Just get me out of here."

Conway felt restless, even guilty, although there was little else he could do right now other than what he'd just done. He followed them to the car as Wyatt helped Glory into her seat.

"Look, Miss Dixon. We're doing all we can to follow up on what you've told us. Maybe we'll have the man in custody before the night is out."

She didn't answer, and when they drove away, Conway was struck by the quiet acceptance he'd seen in her eyes. As if she knew that what he said was little more than whitewash for the fact that they had nothing to go on, so therefore, they were doing nothing.

"Damn it all to hell," Conway muttered. He looked down at the fabric that Wyatt had handed him, and then stuffed it in his pocket as he ran back to his car. The least he could do was get to the office and follow the pursuit from there.

As they drove through town on their way home, Wyatt couldn't quit watching the play of emotions on Glory's face.

"Honey…are you sure you don't want me to drive by the hospital?" His fingers kept tracing the knuckles of her left hand as he drove, as if he didn't trust himself to ever let her out of his grasp again. "When I took you down, I hit you hard…real hard. I just couldn't think of a quicker way to move you out of danger."

Glory turned sideways, staring at Wyatt's profile, wondering how she would bear it when he left her. Her voice was soft, just above a whisper as she reacted to his concern.

"It's all right, Wyatt. You saved my life tonight, and we both know it." She scooted across the seat and laid her head on his shoulder. "Thank you."

He exhaled slowly, finally able to shake off the panic he'd felt when he'd seen her in danger. With his left hand firmly on the steering wheel, he slipped his right arm around her shoulders and held her close. "Now you know how I feel about you."

She sighed, and her breath trembled, thick with tears she wouldn't let go. "Wyatt…oh, Wyatt, what are we going to do?"

God help us, I wish that I knew, Wyatt thought, but didn't voice his own fears. Instead, he pulled her that little bit closer and stared blindly down the road, aware that their fate was as dark and uncertain as what moved through the night beyond the headlights of their car.

Marker cursed loud and long. He knew the moment he sped past that he'd missed. And all because of that man who walked at her side. Instead of the solid thump he'd expected when bumper met body, he'd gotten nothing for his trouble but a high-speed pursuit that had taken him hours to escape.

Thanks to the fact that the car he'd stolen was faster than the police vehicles, he finally eluded the chase. He dumped the hot rod where he'd hidden his own vehicle hours earlier. When and if they found the car, they'd have nothing to pin it on him.

He'd made sure to leave no fingerprints behind, and he was an old hand at never leaving witnesses to his crimes. It was what had kept him out of prison this far, but cold-blooded murder was a different business and a little bit out of his class. Fed up with the hit-and-miss success of his strikes against Glory Dixon, as he drove, he made plans. New plans. Next time, he wouldn't miss.

Chapter 9

Moonlight lay across Glory's bare shoulders like a silver sheet, broken only by the presence of a long ivory braid down the middle of her back. Covers bunched around her waist as she struggled with nightmares she couldn't escape.

Wyatt heard her moan, and turned from the window where he stood watch, sickened by the darkening bruises on her shoulder and the bloody scrapes on her elbows. It was all he could do not to crawl in that bed with her and take her in his arms. But he didn't. He'd let down his guard once and it had nearly cost her her life. It wasn't going to happen again.

Even now, the playback of the engine as it accelerated and the tires as they spun out on the gravel was all too real in his mind. He didn't remember moving, only feeling the impact of hitting Glory's body and then rolling with her across the parking lot.

As he watched, a single tear slipped from the corner of her eye and then down her cheek like a translucent pearl.

Impulsively he reached out, catching it with the tip of his finger and then tracing its path with his lips, tasting the satin texture of her skin and the salt from the tear.

His breath fanned her cheek as he whispered, "Darlin', don't cry."

Her eyelids fluttered, and then she sighed. Reluctantly, he moved back to his post, took one last look out of the window by her bed, then picked up the phone and headed for the tiny living room.

The view from those windows wasn't much different from the view at the back, and yet he couldn't let go of the notion that something or someone watched them from the woods. Lightly, he ran his fingers across the gun in his waistband, waiting as his eyes adjusted to the dark, and then finally, he began to dial.

Lane Monday's voice was rough and thick with sleep, but he answered abruptly before the second ring.

"Hello?"

"It's Wyatt."

Lane rose on an elbow, leaning over Toni as she slept, to peer at the lit dial on the alarm. It was nearly one o'clock in the morning. That, plus the tone of Wyatt's voice, gave away the urgency of the call.

"What's wrong?"

"We went out to eat this evening. Someone tried to run Glory down in the parking lot. And before you ask, no, it wasn't an accident."

Lane rolled out of bed. Taking the portable phone with him so as not to wake Toni, he went down the hallway and into the living room where his voice could not easily be heard.

"I can be there in about six hours."

Wyatt cursed softly. "And do what?" he muttered. "I was right there beside her and I was almost too late."

"Is she all right?"

"Except for bruises and scrapes...and some more night-mares to add to the ones she already has...yes." Then Wyatt started to pace. "Look, I didn't call for backup. I just wanted to let you know what's happening. The only positive thing I can tell you is that Anders Conway witnessed the whole thing."

Lane sighed, torn between wanting to help and knowing that there was nothing he could do that Wyatt wasn't already doing.

"Okay, but keep me posted," he muttered, and then added, "Remember, all you have to do is call. If it's an emergency, I can hop a copter and be there in a couple of hours."

The nervousness in Wyatt's belly started to subside, if for no other reason than the fact that someone besides him knew what was going on.

"Thanks," Wyatt said, then added, "Oh...kiss Toni and Joy for me." Then he hung up and began pacing from window to window, afraid to sleep, afraid to turn his back on Glory...ever again.

Sometime before morning, Glory woke with a start, then groaned beneath her breath when aching muscles protested the sudden movement. Seconds later, she realized what was wrong.

Wyatt was gone!

Careful not to insult her injuries, she crawled out of bed, picked up the nightgown and slipped it over her head before leaving the room.

The floor was cool beneath her feet. The old hardwood planks were smooth and polished from years of use and cleaning, and as familiar to Glory as her own home had been. The half-light between night and dawn was just below the horizon as she made her way into the kitchen. He was standing at the window.

"Wyatt?"

Startled by the unexpected sound of her voice, he spun. When she saw the gun in his hand, she wanted to cry. He was holding fast to his promise to keep her safe, even at his own expense. She crossed the room and walked straight into his arms.

"Come to bed," she whispered. "Whatever is going to happen will happen. You can't change fate, Wyatt. No matter how much it hurts."

He cradled her face in the palm of his hand, tracing the curve of her cheek and the edges of her lips with his fingers as a blind man would.

"You don't understand, Glory. I don't quit. I don't give up. And one of these days, I'm going to get my hands on the bastard who's doing this to you. When it happens..."

Her fingers silenced the anger spilling out of his mouth, and in the quiet of Granny's kitchen, she took the gun from his hand and laid it on the table, then slipped her arms around his neck and whispered softly against his mouth.

"No, Wyatt, there's no room for hate in this house, only love. Now come to bed. It's my turn to take care of you."

Unable to resist her plea, he scooped her up into his arms and carried her back to her bed, making room for himself beside her. Just when Glory thought he was settling down, he suddenly rolled, then bolted from the room, returning only moments later. When she heard a distinctive thump on the bedside table, she knew he'd gone back for the gun.

"Don't say it," he growled, as he crawled in beside her. "Just let me have that much peace of mind."

Tears shimmered across her vision, but she didn't argue. Instead, she wrapped her arms around him and cradled his head on her breasts.

Just sleep, my love. It's my turn to keep watch over you.

For a moment, he forgot to breathe.

Like all the Hatfields, Wyatt had been full-grown in

size by the time he was sixteen years old. At three inches over six feet, he was a very big man and had been taking care of himself for a very long time. If anything, he was the caregiver, the fixer, the doer. That a little bit of female like Glory Dixon dared suggest she could take care of him might have made him smile…if he'd been able to smile through his tears.

Long after the quiet, even sounds of his breathing were proof of his sleep, Glory still held him close. Wide-eyed and alert, she watched morning dawn and then sunlight come, as it spilled through the slightly parted curtains and onto the man in her arms.

Sunbeams danced in the air above her head, bringing hope with the new day. Wyatt stirred, and Glory shifted, giving him ease and a new place to rest. When he smiled in his sleep, the scar on his cheek shifted slightly, reminding her of what he'd endured and survived. A deep and abiding ache resurfaced. She recognized it for what it was, and while he wasn't looking or listening, let herself feel what was there in her heart.

I love you, Wyatt Hatfield. And then a small, silent prayer to a much greater power. *Dear God, please keep him safe. Don't let me be the instrument of another man's death.*

Hours later, Wyatt rolled over in bed, reached out to pull Glory closer and then woke as suddenly as she had earlier. He was alone. But before he could panic, the scent of fresh coffee and the familiar sounds of a kitchen in use calmed his nerves.

He got out of bed and headed for the bathroom. A shower and a change of clothes later, he was entering the kitchen just as Glory set a pan of hot biscuits on the table. She looked up with a smile.

"Your timing is impeccable," she said.

Wyatt grinned. "So I've been told."

It took a second for the innuendo to sink in, and when it did, a sweet blush spread across Glory's face and neck.

"You are a menace," she muttered, and turned back to the stove just as his hands slid around her from behind and came to rest just below the fullness of her breasts.

"That, too." He chuckled, and kissed the spot just below her earlobe that he knew made her shiver.

She turned in his arms and let his next kiss center upon her mouth. It was hard and hungry, and just shy of demanding, and then he groaned, letting go as suddenly as he'd swooped.

"Glory...darlin', I almost forgot your bruises. How do you feel?"

"Like I was run over by a..."

"Don't!" His eyes darkened as he pressed a finger over her lips. "Don't joke. Not to me. I was there, remember?"

She smiled. Just a little, but just enough to let him know she was all right with the world.

"The biscuits are getting cold," she said, and aimed him toward the table. "Sit. I'm just finishing up the eggs."

"I should be cooking for you," he muttered.

"Lord help us both." When he smiled, she turned back to the eggs.

Later, Glory fidgeted as they ate, and Wyatt could tell there was something on her mind. But it wasn't until they were almost through with the dishes that she started to talk.

"Wyatt...last night at the restaurant...I nearly died, didn't I?"

"Don't remind me," he muttered, and set a clean glass in Granny's little cupboard.

"Oh...that's not what I was getting at," she explained. "What I meant was...if there had been anything left in this life I still wanted to do...it would have been too late."

"Hellfire, Glory! This is a real bad discussion right after a good meal."

She grinned. "Sorry. What I'm trying to say is…"

He tossed the dish towel on the cabinet and took her by the arm, careful not to touch the places that hurt.

"Look, girl! Just say what's on your mind."

She lifted her chin, pinning him with that silver-blue gaze that always made him feel as if he was floating.

"I need to go see my granny one more time…just in case. Chances are she might not even recognize me, but I don't want her to think that we forgot about her. Daddy always went at least once a month. It's past that time now. She's in a nursing home in Hazard. Will you take me?"

Wyatt felt the room beginning to spin. It scared the hell out of him just hearing her admit that she might not live another week as casually as she might have announced she wasn't going to plant a garden. Unable to keep his distance, he reached out for her, and when she relaxed against him, he shuddered.

"I'll take you anywhere you want to go. I'll stand on my damned head in the woods for a week if it will make you happy. But so help me God, if you don't stop forecasting so much doom and gloom, I'm going to pack you and your stuff and take you home with me to Tennessee. Then we'll see how far this killer wants to travel to die. I've got enough kin there to mount a small army."

She could tell by the tone of his voice that he was serious. But it was an impossible suggestion.

"No, Wyatt! It's bad enough that you've put your life on the line for me. I couldn't live with myself if any more people were put in danger because of this. I'll try not to be so negative, but truth is hard to ignore."

"The only truth is…your killer is a screwup. He tried to kill you and got your family instead, and then even later your dog. The fact that he was stupid enough to try a third time, and right in front of the chief of police, doesn't say much for his brains, only his desperation. Desperate men make mistakes, Glory. Remember that!"

In the face of all she'd lost, what he said shouldn't have helped, but for some reason, it did. She relaxed in his arms.

"Okay! I promise! Now let me change my clothes so we can go. And when we go through Larner's Mill, could we stop at the bakery? Granny loves their gingersnaps."

He nodded, and as she left, he retraced his path to the window, looking out into the bright sunlight of a brand-new day, wondering what it would bring.

As nursing homes went, it wasn't so bad. Like similar institutions across the country, it offered health care and comfort to people with aging bodies and minds. But the reason for its being was still the same. It was where the old went to die.

Wyatt caught himself holding his breath as they walked down the hallway. The scent of incontinence, cleaning solvents and medication was a blend impossible to ignore.

Somewhere ahead of them, an old man's cries for help echoed in the hall while other residents roamed at will, scooting along on walkers, thumping with their canes and wheeling the occasional wheelchair.

And then Glory touched his arm and paused at an open doorway before stepping inside. He followed. It was, after all, why they'd come.

She sat by a window, rocking back and forth in an uneven rhythm, as if sometimes forgetting to keep a motion going. Her body was withered and stooped, her snow-white hair as fluffy and sparse as wisps of cotton. The yellow robe she was wearing was old and faded to near white, but new, fuzzy blue slippers covered her feet. She had no memory of how she'd come by them, only that they kept her warm. Her eyes were fixed on something beyond the clear glass,

and her mouth was turned up in a soft, toothless smile…
quite lost in happier times and happier days.

"Granny?"

At the sound of her name, the rocker stopped and the
smile slid off her face. She turned, staring blankly at the
pair in the doorway and frowned.

"Comp'ny? I got comp'ny?"

Glory quickly crossed the distance between them to
kneel at her side, covering the gnarled, withered hands with
her own. The skirt of her only dress puddled around her
as she knelt and kissed her granny's cheek. "Yes, Granny,
it's me, Glory."

Wyatt watched while recognition came and went in
the old woman's pale, watery eyes, and then suddenly she
smiled and ran her hand across Glory's head, fingering the
long pale lengths of her hair. In that moment, he saw her
as the woman she once had been.

"Well, Glory, girl, it's been a while! I didn't think you
was ever comin' to see your granny again. Where's your pa?
I swear, that boy of mine is always late. I'm gonna give him
a piece of my mind when he shows up, and that's a fact."

There was a knot in Glory's throat that threatened to
choke her. Twice she faltered before she could speak, and
it was only after Wyatt touched her shoulder that she could
find the strength to continue.

"Daddy won't be coming today, Granny. It's just me."

A frown deepened the furrow of wrinkles across her
brow, and then she cackled and slapped her knee.

"That's good! That's good! Us women gotta stick together, don't we, little girl?"

Tears shimmered across Glory's eyes, but the smile on
her face was as bright as the sunshine warming Granny's
lap.

"Yes, ma'am, we sure do."

Granny's attention shifted, as if suddenly realizing that

Glory was not alone. She looked up at Wyatt, puckering her mouth as she considered his face, and then waved him toward a nearby chair.

"Sit down, boy!" she ordered. "You be way too tall to look at from down here." Then she cackled again, as if delighted with her own wit.

Wyatt grinned and did as he was told.

"Who's he?" Granny asked, as if Wyatt had suddenly gone deaf.

Glory smiled. "That's Wyatt Hatfield, Granny. He's my friend."

And then in the blunt, tactless manner of the very old, she looked up at Wyatt and asked, "Are you messin' with my girl?"

Glory rolled her eyes at Wyatt, begging him to understand, but it was a silent plea she need never have made.

"No, ma'am, I would never treat Glory lightly. I care for her very much."

Satisfied, Granny Dixon leaned back in her rocker and started to rock. Wyatt handed Glory the box of gingersnaps they'd brought from the bakery in Larner's Mill.

"Look, Granny, we brought you gingersnaps."

She set the box in Granny's lap, then patted her on the knee to remind her that she was still here.

The joy on the old woman's face was a delight to see, and when she opened the lid, the scent of molasses and spice filled the air.

"I do love my gingersnaps," Granny said. "But I reckon I'll save 'em till I get me some milk to sop 'em in. I don't eat so good without my teeth, anymore. Glory, girl, you set these by my bed, now, you hear?"

"Yes, ma'am," Glory said, and did as she was told.

When she returned, she knelt back at her Granny's knee. It was such an old, familiar place to be that before Glory realized what she was doing, she found herself leaning forward. When the rocking chair suddenly paused, she exhaled slowly on a shaky sob and laid her head in Granny's lap, waiting for those long, crippled fingers to stroke through her hair, just as they'd done so many years ago.

Suddenly, Wyatt found himself watching through tears and feeling the isolation that Glory must be feeling. Here she was, the last of her line, caught in a hell not of her making and seeking comfort from a woman who was fighting a losing battle with reality. He had the strongest urge to take both women in his arms and hold them, but reason told him to refrain. Here he was the onlooker. He didn't belong in their world.

Long silent minutes passed while Granny Dixon combed her fingers through the silken lengths of Glory's hair, soothing old fears, calming new pain. And then in the quiet, Granny paused and tilted Glory's face. She looked long and hard, then leaned closer, peering at the tearstained gaze in her granddaughter's eyes. Knuckles swollen and locked with age stroked the soft skin on Glory's cheek, brushing lightly against the halo the sun had made on Glory's hair.

"Such a pretty little thing...Granny's little Morning Glory. You been havin' them visions again, ain't you, girl?"

Glory nodded, unable to speak of the horrors she'd recently survived, unwilling to tell this woman that her only son was dead.

"It'll be all right," Granny said. "You jest got to remember that it's God's gift to you, girl. It ain't no burden that you got to bear...it's a gift. Use it as such."

"Yes, ma'am," Glory said, and when she heard Wyatt's feet shuffle behind her, she knew he was struggling with his own brand of pain.

Then the old woman's attention shifted, and once again, Wyatt found himself being grilled on the spot.

"You know 'bout Glory's gift, don't you, boy?"

"Yes, ma'am, that I do," Wyatt said. "It's because of her that I'm still alive. She saved my life."

Granny beamed, and the sunlight caught and danced in her eyes, giving them life where vacancy had just been. She clapped her hands and then patted Glory on the shoulder.

"That's my girl! You see what I'm a'tellin' you, Glory? You did good with your gift, and it brought you a man. That's good fortune!"

"But, Granny, he's not actually my—"

Wyatt interrupted, unwilling to hear Glory put the tenuous part of the relationship into words.

"I consider myself the fortunate one, Mrs. Dixon."

"That's good. That's good. You got yourself a man who has the good sense to know which side his bread is done buttered on."

When Glory blushed, Wyatt laughed, which only pleased her granny more.

"You understand your responsibilities of lovin' a woman as special as my Glory, don't you?"

Wyatt nodded. "Yes, ma'am, I believe that I do."

"Sometimes she'll ask things of you that you'll find hard to 'cept. Sometimes she'll know things you don't want to hear. But she'll be true to you all your life and that's a fact."

"Granny, he doesn't want to hear all about..."

Wyatt leaned forward. His brown eyes darkened; his expression grew solemn.

"Yes, I do, Morning Glory, yes, I do."

Glory held her breath as joy slowly filled her heart. She hoped he'd meant what he said, and then suddenly turned away, unwilling to look just in case he did not.

One hour turned into two as Granny Dixon regaled them with stories from Glory's childhood as well as old times before she'd ever been born. And while Wyatt listened, absorbing the love that had spanned all the years, bonding these women in a way no family name could have done, he knew that he'd finally found what had been missing in his own life.

Love.

The love that comes with knowing another as well as you know your own heart. The quiet, certain love that is there when all else has failed. The passionate, binding love that can lift a man up and keep him afloat all his life.

Before Glory, Wyatt had been running, always on the move, afraid of sinking before he had lived. Now the answer to his own brand of pain was sitting at his feet, and unless they caught the man who was trying to kill her, he could lose it…and her…before they were his. He believed that she loved him. He knew that he loved her. The uncertainty lay in keeping her alive.

And finally, when Granny's head began to nod, Glory motioned that it was time to go. As they stood, Granny reached out and caught Wyatt's hand.

"You'll bring my little Morning Glory back, won't you?"

"Yes, ma'am, I sure will."

Granny's mouth squinched in what might be called a flirtatious smile, although it was hard to tell with so much vacancy between her lips. "Since you're gonna be in the family, I reckon you could be callin' me by my given name."

Wyatt grinned. "I'd be honored. And what would that be?" he asked.

Granny thought, and then frowned. "Why, I should be knowin' my own name, now, shouldn't I?" And then a smile spread wide. "Faith! I'm called Faith." She shook her finger in Wyatt's face. "And you'll be needin' a whole lot of faith to love a woman as special as my Glory."

"Yes, ma'am, I suppose that I will."

"Maybe you'd be inclined to name your firstborn girl after me? I'd be pleased to know that my name lived on after I'm gone."

Moved by her innocence, Wyatt knelt, and took the old woman's hands in his own.

"I'm honored, Faith Dixon. And you have my word that it will be done."

Pleased that she'd covered all the bases with her granddaughter's new beau, Granny closed her eyes. Moments later, she began to rock, forgetting that they were even still there.

Wyatt slipped an arm around Glory's shoulder.

"Are you ready?"

Glory looked up, her eyes filled with tears, her lips trembling with the weight of unvoiced love for this man who held her.

"Yes, please."

She took Wyatt's hand and let him lead her out of this place. When they were in the parking lot, she knew there was one more place she needed to go.

"Since we're in Hazard, I suppose I should go by the lawyer's office. Daddy always said if anything ever happened to him that J.C. and I were to come here, that Mr. Honeywell would know what to do."

"Then we will," Wyatt promised. "You direct, I'll drive."

A short time later, they were sitting in the office of Elias Honeywell, the senior partner of Honeywell and Honeywell. He was still in shock at what he'd been told. His little round face was twisted with concern.

"Miss Dixon, I'm so sorry for your loss," he said. "But you needn't worry about your position. Your father was a farseeing man. Not only did he leave a will, but there is a sizable insurance policy, of which you are the sole beneficiary."

Glory had known of the will, but had had no idea her father had indulged in life insurance. Their life had been simple. Money had never been easy to come by. That he'd used it for a future he would not participate in surprised her.

"I had no idea," she said.

Elias Honeywell nodded solemnly. "Your father wanted it that way. He was concerned about your welfare after he passed on. I believe I recall him saying something to the effect that his daughter had more to bear than most, and he wanted to make sure you would not suffer unduly."

"Oh, my." It was all Glory could say without breaking into tears. Even in death, her father was still taking care of her.

Wyatt could see that Glory was not in any shape to question him. In spite of his reticence to interfere, he thought it best to ask now, rather than after they were gone.

"Mr. Honeywell, what will you need from Glory to proceed with the probate and claims?"

The little lawyer frowned, then shuffled through the file on his desk. "Why, I believe I have nearly everything I need," he said. "Except..." He hesitated, hating to bring it up. "We will need death certificates for her father as well as her brother before I can apply for the life insurance on her behalf. I have her address. If I need anything more, I will be in touch."

Glory rose with more composure than she felt. Had it not been for Wyatt Hatfield's presence, she would have run screaming to the car. The darkness within her mind kept spreading. She kept thinking this was all a bad dream, and that almost any time she would wake and it would all be over.

But reality was a rude reminder, and when they exited the office to resume the trip home, the only thing that kept her sane was remembering the promise Wyatt made to Granny. The fact that he'd made such a claim of the heart to a woman who would never remember he'd said it didn't matter to Glory. At least not now. He'd said she was his girl. He'd promised Granny that he would take care of her forever. Glory needed to believe that he meant every word that he'd said.

Long after they were back on Highway 421, driving south toward Pine Mountain and Larner's Mill, which nestled at its base, Glory still had no words for what Wyatt had given her this day. It wasn't until later when he stopped for gas that she managed to say what was in her heart.

"Wyatt?"

"What, darlin'?" he said absently, as he unbuckled his seat belt to get out.

"I will never forget what you said to Granny today. No matter what you really thought, you made an old woman happy."

He paused, halfway out of the car seat, and looked back at her. "What about you, Morning Glory? Did it make you happy, too?"

"What do you mean?" she asked.

"I didn't say anything that wasn't already in my heart."

"Oh, Wyatt! You don't have to pretend with…"

"If you need to go to the little girls' room, now's your time," he said quietly, aware that she looked as scared as he felt. But as Glory had said, who knew what tomorrow would bring? Denying his feelings for her seemed a careless thing to do.

She got out of the car with her head in a whirl, her heart pounding with a hope she thought had died. Was there a chance for her after all? Could she have a future with a man she'd just met? More to the point, would she even want to try it without him?

Chapter 10

Anders Conway entered his office with a beleaguered air. Having to explain to a U.S. marshal why two of his patrol cars had not been able to apprehend a hit-and-run suspect hadn't sat well with his lunch. His eardrums were still reverberating from the dressing-down he'd gotten over the phone from Lane Monday, and while he wanted to resent the constant interference of Glory Dixon's newfound friends, he couldn't bring himself to blame them. It was obvious they were truly worried about her welfare and afraid for her life.

What surprised him was that they believed her story without a single doubt. She'd lived in Larner's Mill all of her life and had been looked upon as something of an oddity. Why two strangers should suddenly appear in her life and take her every word as gospel was a puzzle.

But the fire marshal's report sitting on his desk was strong evidence that Glory Dixon had something going for her. After reading it, Conway been unable to deny the truth of the young woman's claim. Whether he believed her story of *how* she saw it happen was immaterial. Fact was, someone had meddled with gas stoves, causing the deaths of her father and brother.

Conway paced the room, mentally itemizing the series of events concerning her. Her claim that she'd been the target for the fire was too far-fetched for him to buy, and he chalked it up to a guilt complex for not having died along with her family. And then she wanted him to believe that she was still in danger, and had used the accidental shooting of her dog as more proof.

Conway snorted softly, muttering beneath his breath. "This isn't the kind of place where people go around killin' dogs for sport."

He started to pour himself a cup of coffee and then cursed when he realized it was cold. Someone had gone and turned the darn thing off, leaving the black brew to congeal along the sides of the pot.

"To hell with dogs…and coffee," he grumbled, and slammed his cup down with a thump.

But his mind wouldn't let go of his thoughts, and he kept dwelling on the oddity of the pup being killed so soon after all of the other trauma in Glory's life. He hadn't actually viewed the carcass, but he was inclined to believe that if it *had* been shot, it was most likely by accident, and someone hadn't been man enough to own up to the deed.

He fiddled with the papers in the file on his desk, staring long and hard at the evidence bag containing the bit of fabric that was supposed to have been caught in the dog's teeth, certain that it meant nothing, either.

Yet as hard as he tried to convince himself that there had to be a reasonable explanation for the things that had been happening to Glory, last night was an altogether different circumstance.

Watching that car take aim at her, and then seeing Wyatt

Hatfield suddenly turn and leap, had been like watching a scene out of a bad movie. Although it was an improbable thing to be happening in Larner's Mill, he *had* seen someone purposefully try to run her down.

"But, damn it, I can't take the word of a psychic to court. If only my men hadn't lost that damn hot rod on the logging road, I'd have me a bona fide suspect to question. Then maybe I could get to the bottom of this mess."

"You talkin' to me, Chief?" the dispatcher yelled from the other room.

"Hell, no, I am not!" Conway shouted, and then winced at the tone of his own voice. If he didn't get a grip, he was going to wind up a few bales short of a load and they'd be shipping him off in a straitjacket.

He cursed again, only this time beneath his breath, shoved the file back into the drawer and stomped over to his desk, slumping into his easy chair and feeling every day of his sixty-two years. If only his deputies had been able to keep up with that hit-and-run driver. Everything had hinged upon finding the suspect, and he'd gotten away.

His stomach began to hurt. The familiar burning sensation sent him digging into his desk for antacids and wishing he'd taken early retirement. But when he found the bottle, it was empty. With a muttered curse, he tossed it in the trash and then walked back to dispatch.

"I'm going to the drugstore. Be back in a few minutes," he said, and ambled out of the office without waiting for the dispatcher's reply.

As he walked down the street, a car honked. Out of habit, he turned and waved before he even looked to see who had hailed him. Across the street and directly in his line of vision, he saw Carter Foster locking his office and putting the out-to-lunch sign on the office door.

"Now there's another man with problems," Conway muttered, looking at the lawyer's rumpled suit and pale, drawn face. "Poor bastard. I wonder how much Betty Jo took him for when she left?"

Then he shrugged. He didn't have time to worry about cheating women. He had a belly on fire and an office full of trouble just waiting for him to return. Just as he was about to enter the drugstore, an odd thought hit him. He turned, staring back down the street where the lawyer had been, but Carter and his car were nowhere in sight.

Well, I'll be damned. We do have one missing person...of a sort...here in Larner's Mill after all. Old Carter is missing a wife, isn't he?

But as swiftly as the thought had come, he shoved it aside. "God Almighty, I *am* losing my grip. Everyone knows that Betty Jo would bed a snake if it held still long enough for her to get a grip. When her money runs out, or the old boy she took off with runs out of steam, she'll be back. And poor old Carter will probably be stupid enough to let her.

Satisfied with his conclusion, he entered the store, heading straight for the aisle where antacids were stocked.

Carter drove toward the café, unaware of the chief's discarded theory. Had he known, he might have kept on driving. As it was, he was going through the motions of normalcy while fighting a constant state of panic. He firmly believed that if Bo Marker didn't put Glory Dixon out of the picture, he was a ruined man.

But, Carter kept reminding himself, there was one thing about this entire mess that had worked to his benefit. No one questioned his drawn countenance or his lack of attention to details, like forgetting two court dates and missing an important appointment with a client. It *could* all be attributed to a man who'd been dumped by his wife, and not a man who'd tossed his wife in a dump.

He switched on the turn signal and began to pull into the parking lot of the café when a deputy stepped in front of his car and waved him to a different location. Surprised by the fact that nothing ever changed in Larner's Mill, he followed the officer's directions. But after he had parked, he couldn't contain his curiosity, and wandered over to the area to see what was going on.

"Hey, buddy, what's with the yellow tape?" Carter asked, and flipped it lightly with his finger as if he was strumming a guitar string.

"We had ourselves a crime here last night!"

Carter watched with some interest as another deputy was measuring some sort of distance between two points.

"What kind of crime? Someone steal hubcaps or something?"

"Nope. We had ourselves a near hit-and-run, and I got in on the chase afterward." And then he frowned and turned away, unwilling to admit how it galled him that the perpetrator had escaped.

Carter grinned. "How do you have a *near* hit-and-run, as opposed to an actual one?"

"Someone deliberately tried to run that Dixon girl over. You know, the one who just buried her daddy and brother?" He was so busy telling the story that he didn't see the shock that swept across Carter Foster's face. "Anyway…her and her friend was just comin' out of the café when some guy took aim and tried to run her down. If it hadn't been for that man who's stayin' with her, he would have done it, too."

Damn, damn, damn, Carter thought, and then worry had him prodding for more information.

"Have you considered that it might have been just a drunk driver?" he asked, hoping to steer their investigation in a different direction.

The deputy shook his head. "No way. It was deliberate! Chief Conway witnessed the whole thing. We was in fast pursuit within seconds of it happenin', and would have caught him, too, except the guy was driving a stolen car.

It was that Marley kid's hot rod. Ain't no one gonna catch that car, I don't care who's drivin' it."

The hunger that had driven Carter to the café was turning to nausea. He couldn't believe what he'd just heard.

"Anders Conway witnessed the incident? He *saw* someone try to run her over?"

"Yes, sir. Now, if you'll excuse me, Mr. Foster, I'd better get back to work. We got ourselves a felon to catch."

Carter stood without moving, watching as the officers picked through the scene. The longer he stared, the more panicked he became. The thought of food turned his stomach, and the thought of Bo Marker made him want to kill all over again. The stupidity of the man, to attempt a crime in front of the chief of police, was beyond belief.

Disgusted with the whole situation, he stomped to his car, then drove toward home while a slow, burning anger built steam. At least there he could eat in peace without watching his life go down the toilet.

He was already inside the kitchen, building a sandwich of mammoth proportions, when realization sank in. So Bo Marker was stupid. Carter had known that when he'd hired him. He'd counted on his dim wit to be the deciding factor when he'd offered him the job of murderer.

Carter dropped into a chair, staring at the triple-decker sandwich on the plate, as well as the knife he was holding, watching as mayonnaise dripped from it and onto his lap.

So, if I hired Bo Marker, knowing his IQ was that of a gnat, what, exactly, does that make me?

He dropped the knife and buried his face in his hands, wishing he could turn back time. A saying his mother once told him did a replay inside his head. It had something to do with how the telling of one lie could weave itself into a whole web of deceit. Carter knew he was proof of his mother's wisdom. He was caught and sinking fast.

Unless Bo Marker got his act together and did what he'd
been hired to do, he was done for.

Using the trees around Granny Dixon's cabin as cover
for the deed he had planned wasn't unique, but Bo Marker
didn't have an original thought in his head. He was still mad
about missing his mark last night, but had gotten some joy
out of the wild ten-mile chase afterward. Running from the
cops like that made him feel young again.

He glanced down at his watch, wondering when that
Dixon bitch and her lover would come back home, and
cursing his luck because he'd come too late this morning
to catch them as they'd left. It would have been so easy just
to pick them off as they'd walked out to the car.

He sighed, shifting upon the dirt where he was sitting,
searching for a softer spot on the tree against which he was
leaning. That knothole behind his back was beginning to
feel like a brick.

Bo was at the point of boredom with this whole procedure and kept reminding himself what he could do with the
money he would get from this job. As he sat, he rested his
deer rifle across his knees and then spit, aiming at a line
of ants that he'd been watching for some time. It wasn't the
first time he'd spit on them, and in fact, as he spit, he was
making bets with himself as to which way they'd run when
it splattered. But his mind quickly shifted from the game
at hand when something moved in the brush behind him.
He grabbed the rifle and then stilled, squinting through the
brush and searching for a sign of movement.

"Don't you think that rifle's a bit big for huntin' squirrels?"

Startled, Bo rolled to his feet, aiming his gun as he
moved. But the man who'd come out of the brush was ready
for the action. When Bo moved, the man swung his gun
downward, blocking the motion. It took Bo all of five sec-

onds to forget about tangling with the big, bearded mountain man.

The man stood a good four inches taller, and was more than fifty pounds heavier. And while Bo's gun was more powerful, that bead the man had drawn on his belly was all the incentive Bo needed to show some restraint. Being gut shot wasn't a good way to die.

"Who said anything about hunting squirrels?" Bo muttered, and tried taking a step back. The big man's gun followed his movement like a snake, waiting to strike.

Teeth shone white and even through the black, bushy beard. It might have passed for a smile if one could ignore the frosty glare in the mountain man's eyes.

Bo had no option but to stand and wait while the man took the rifle from his hands and emptied the shells in the dirt, then tossed back the empty gun.

Bo caught it in midair.

The man grinned again as he spoke. "Now, you're not about to tell me you're huntin' out of season…are you? We don't like strangers on our mountain…especially out of season."

Bo paled. The threat was all too real to ignore.

"Well, hell, if that's the way you wanna be, then I'm gone," he muttered, and tried a few steps of retreat.

"You know, that might be the smartest thing you did all day," the man said.

Bo nodded, then took a deep breath. Daring to turn his back on the man with the gun, he began to walk away. Just when he thought he was in the clear, a shot rang out, and he fell to the ground in mortal fear, fully expecting to be shattered by pain. Seconds later, something landed with a heavy thud in the middle of his back.

His face buried in his arms, sucking dirt and old leaves into his mouth, he began to shriek, "God have mercy! Don't kill me! Don't kill me!"

The man cradled his rifle in the bend of his arm and bent over Bo's body. "Now…whatever made you think you was in danger?" he asked.

Bo held his breath as the weight suddenly disappeared from his back. Shocked, he slowly lifted his head and then rolled on his back, staring up in disbelief at the big gray squirrel the man was holding by the tail. Blood dripped from a tiny hole in the side of its neck, and Bo had a vision of his own head in the same condition and shuddered.

The man waved the squirrel across Bo's line of vision, breaking the thick swirl of his beard with another white smile.

"Got myself a good one, don't you think?"

"Oh, God, I thought you was shootin' at me," Bo groaned. He started to crawl to his feet when the man stuck the barrel of the gun in the middle of Bo's fat belly.

"Should I have been?" the man asked quietly.

The tip of the barrel penetrated the fat just enough to hurt. Bo was so scared that had he been a cat, eight of his nine lives would have been gone on the spot.

"No, hell, no!" Bo groaned. "Now are you gonna let me up, or what?"

"Be my guest," the man said, and waved his arm magnanimously.

Five minutes later, Bo burst out of the woods on the run, sighing with relief to see his truck right where he'd left it.

Considering his bulk, he moved with great speed, his rifle in one hand, his truck keys in another. But his relief turned sour when he noticed the tires. All four were as flat as his old lady's chest, and just as useless. Fury overwhelmed him. He couldn't believe he'd let himself be bullied by some mountain man. And now this. He spun, staring back at the woods.

"For two cents," he muttered, "I'd go back in there and…"

And then the sound of breaking twigs and rustling

bushes made him pause. A picture of that squirrel's bloody
head and limp body made him want to retch. All of his bra-
vado disappeared as he pivoted. Dragging the empty rifle
behind him, he made a wild dash for the truck and moments
later, started down the mountain. The truck steered like a
man crawling on his belly, but Bo didn't care.

Putting distance between himself and this place was all
he wanted to do.

The sound of flapping rubber and bare rims grinding
against the gravel on the road could be heard long after
Bo had disappeared. And finally, the rustling in the underbrush ceased.

A short time later, the sounds of the forest began to re-
vive. Birds resumed flight, a blue jay scolded from an overhead branch and a bobcat slipped quickly across the road
and into the trees on the other side.

Pine Mountain was alive and well.

It was close to sundown when Wyatt turned off the main
highway and onto the one-lane road leading to the Dixon
farm. A soft breeze circled through the car from the half-
open windows, stirring through Glory's hair and teasing at
the skirt of her blue dress like a naughty child. She'd been
asleep for the better part of an hour with her head in his
lap, and without thinking, Wyatt braced her to keep her
from tumbling as the car took the turn.

He drove without thought, his mind completely upon
the revelation that he'd had this day. It didn't matter that a
week ago he hadn't even known she'd existed. In his heart,
it felt as if he'd known her for years, even from another
lifetime. The years stretched out before him in his mind,
and he couldn't see a future without Glory in it. But when
he drove past the burned-out remnants of her home and
headed down the old road toward Granny's cabin, his gut

twisted. Marriage was the last thing he should be worrying about. Right now all that mattered was keeping her alive.

His foot was on the brake when half a dozen men began coming out of the trees. They walked with the air of men who knew their place on this earth—with their heads held proud, their shoulders back. Some were bearded, some clean-shaven. Some wore jeans, others bib overalls. Some were short while others towered heads above the rest. It was what they had in common that made Wyatt afraid. To a man, they were armed, and from where he was sitting, they definitely looked dangerous.

"God," he said softly, and braked in reflex. He was at the point of wondering whether to fight or run when Glory awoke and stirred.

"Are we home?" She rubbed sleepily at her eyes, and it was only after Wyatt grabbed her by the arm that she realized something was wrong.

She looked up. "It's all right," she said. "They're neighbors." Before Wyatt could react, she got out of the car, beckoning for him to follow.

When Edward Lee came straggling out of the trees behind them, Wyatt began to relax.

Glory smiled and motioned Wyatt to her side.

"Hey, Mornin' Glory," Edward Lee said, and barged through the men as if they were not even there. He threw his arms around her neck, hugging her in a happy, childlike way. "Me and Daddy have been waitin' for you."

Glory nodded, and then watched as Edward Lee's father took him in hand. Although Liam Fowler was a very big man, his touch and words were slow and gentle.

"That's enough, Edward Lee. We came to talk business, remember?"

Edward Lee smiled, pleased to be part of anything his father did. And then he remembered Wyatt and pointed.

"This is Wyatt Hatfield. Wyatt is my friend," he announced.

"That's good, son." Liam Fowler's teeth were white through the thickness of his beard, as he acknowledged Wyatt with a nod. "But we need to do what we came to do, remember?"

Wyatt tensed. "And that is?"

"We came to warn you," Liam said. "There's a stranger in the woods."

Glory swayed. The shock on her face was too new to hide. She turned and fell into Wyatt's arms with a muffled moan. "Oh, God, will this never end?"

"Don't, honey," Wyatt said softly, and wrapped his arms firmly around her, willing her to feel his strength, because it was all that he had to give.

Because she was too weary and heartsick to stand on her own, she let Wyatt hold her, trusting him to face what she could not.

The men shuffled their feet, looking everywhere but at each other, uncomfortable with her fear because they had no way to stop it.

"How do you know about the stranger?" Wyatt asked. "Did you see him? Did you talk to him?"

Several of the men chuckled and then they all looked to Liam Fowler to answer. Obviously they knew more than they were telling.

Liam smiled. "You could say that," he said. "Now, back to the business of why we're here." He gave Wyatt a long, considering look. "My son says that you're a good man."

Edward Lee almost strutted with importance. It wasn't often that grown men took anything he said to heart.

Wyatt smiled at him, and then waited.

"He says that you came to take care of Glory," Liam persisted.

"Yes, sir, I did that," Wyatt said.

"We feel right ashamed that it took a stranger to do what we should have done on our own," Liam said. "Glory sort of belongs to us now, what with her family passin' and all."

Wyatt's arms tightened around Glory's shoulders. "No, sir. She doesn't belong to you. Not anymore."

When Glory suddenly stilled then shifted within his embrace, Wyatt tightened his hold and looked down, wondering if she would challenge him here in front of everyone. To his relief, he saw nothing but surprise and a little bit of shock, and knew that she hadn't been prepared for what he'd said.

The men came to attention, each gauging Wyatt with new interest as they heard and accepted the underlying message of his words. He'd laid claim to a woman most of them feared. More than one of them wondered if he knew what he was getting into, but as was their way, no one voiced a concern. Live and let live was a motto that had served them well for several centuries, and they had no reason to change their beliefs. Not even for a stranger.

Finally, it was Liam who broke the silence. "So, it's that way, then?"

Wyatt nodded.

Liam reached out, touching the crown of Glory's head in a gentle caress. "Glory, girl, are you of the same mind?"

Without looking at Wyatt, she turned, facing the men within the safety of Wyatt's arms. "Yes, sir, I suppose that I am."

So great was his joy that Wyatt wanted to grin. But this wasn't the time, and with these somber men judging his every move, it also wasn't the place. Like dark crows on a fence, they watched, unmoving, waiting for the big, bearded man to speak for them all. So he did.

"Then that's fine," Liam said, and offered Wyatt his hand. "Know that while you're on this land, within the boundaries of our hills, you will be safe. We guarantee that to you. But when you take her away from here, her safety is in your hands."

Aware of the solemnity of the moment, Glory stepped aside as Wyatt moved forward, taking the hand that was offered. And then each man passed, sealing their vow with a firm handshake and a long hard look. When it was over, they had new respect for the stranger who'd come into their midst, and Wyatt felt relief that he was no longer in this alone. And then he noticed that Edward Lee had stayed behind.

"Edward Lee, aren't you going to shake my hand, too?"

Wyatt's quiet voice broke the awkward silence, and his request made a friend of Liam Fowler for life. Wyatt had instinctively understood how the young man wanted so badly to belong.

He looked to his father, a poignant plea in his voice. "Daddy?"

Liam nodded, then took a long, deep breath as Edward Lee mimicked the seriousness of the occasion by offering Wyatt his hand without his usual smile. But the moment the handshake was over, he threw his arms around Wyatt's neck in a boisterous hug, and when he turned back around, the smile on his face was infectious. Everyone laughed. But not at him...with him. His joy was impossible to ignore.

"Then we'll be going," Liam said, and smiled gently at Glory. "Rest easy tonight, little girl. Your man just got himself some help."

"I don't know how to thank you," Wyatt said. "But be careful. Whoever is trying to harm Glory isn't giving up."

They nodded, then walked away. They were almost into the trees when Glory called out, then ran toward them. They paused and turned, waiting for whatever she had to say.

She stopped a few feet away, unaware that she'd stopped in a halo of late-evening sun. The blue of her dress matched the color of her eyes, and the hair drifting around her face and down her back lifted and fell with the demands of the breeze blowing through the clearing. More than one man had the notion that he was standing before an angel. Her eyes were brimming, her lips shaking with unshed emotion. But her voice was steady as she said what was in her heart.

"God bless you," she whispered. "My daddy was proud to call you his friends. Now I understand why."

Moved beyond words, they took her praise in stoic silence, and when they were certain she was through, turned and walked away without answering. Glory watched until they were gone, and then she turned.

Wyatt was waiting, and the look in his eyes made her shake. He was her man. He'd laid a claim before her people that they did not take lightly. And from the expression on his face, neither did he.

Chapter 11

Glory's eyes widened as Wyatt started toward her. Later, she would remember thinking that he moved like a big cat—powerful, but full of grace. But now there was nothing on her mind but the look on his face and the way that his eyes raked her body.

She held her breath, wondering if she was woman enough to hold this wild, footloose man. And when he was close enough to touch her, he combed his fingers through the hair on either side of her face and lowered his head. When his mouth moved across her face and centered upon her lips, the breath she'd been holding slipped out on a sigh. The impact of the joining was unexpected. She wasn't prepared for the reverence in his touch, or the desperation with which he held her.

Wyatt was absorbed by her love, drawn into a force that he couldn't control. It took everything he had to remember that they were standing in plain sight of whoever cared to look, and that she was still bruised and sore from yesterday's scrape with death. He groaned, then lifted his head, and when she would have protested, he silenced her plea by pressing his forefinger across her lips.

"Glory, I'm sorry. I almost forgot that you…"

"Take me to bed. Make me forget all this horror. Give me something to remember besides fear. I'm so tired of being afraid."

Ah, God.

She slipped beneath his arm, the top of her head way below his chin, and then looked up. Her silver-blue stare widened apprehensively as she waited for his response.

At that moment, Wyatt wasn't so sure that he couldn't have walked on water.

"I love you, Glory Dixon."

"I know," she said softly. "It's why I asked."

Hand in hand, they entered the cabin, for once safe in the knowledge that someone was watching their backs. The lock clicked loudly within the silence of the old rooms, and then there was nothing to be heard but the ticking of Granny's clock on the mantel and the heartbeats hammering in their ears.

Glory was the first to move. She slid her hands beneath her hair, tugging at a zipper that wouldn't give.

"Help me, Wyatt. I think my hair's caught."

And so am I, he thought, but never voiced his fear.

He thrust his hands beneath her gold strands, moving the heavy weight of her hair aside so he could see. His fingers shook as he unwound a strand from the metal tab. When it was free, he lifted the tab and pulled.

Slowly. Lower.

Revealing the delicate body that was so much a part of the woman he loved. Impulsively, he slid his hands beneath the fabric, circling her body and coming to rest upon the gentle thrust of her breasts. Glory sighed, then moaned, arching into his palms.

He shook, burning with the need to plunge deep within the sweetness of the woman in his hands, and yet he resisted. She wasn't ready. It wasn't time. She wanted to forget, and he hoped to hell he could remember what he was supposed to do, because every breath that he took was driving sanity further and further from his mind.

"Glory."

Her name was a whisper on his lips as she moved out of his grasp. When her dress fell at her feet in a pool of blue, leaving her with nothing on but a scrap of nylon that barely covered her hips, he started to shake.

Twice he tried to unbutton his shirt, and each time, his fingers kept slipping off the buttons.

"Oh, hell," he muttered, then yanked.

Buttons popped and rolled across the floor. Boots went one direction, his blue jeans another. Before Glory had time to think, he had her in his arms and was moving toward the bed with a distinct gleam in his eye.

They fell onto the quilt in a tangle of arms and legs as the last of their clothes hit the floor. At the last minute, Wyatt remembered protection and scrambled for the drawer in the bedside table.

There was no time for slow, easy loving, or soft, whispered promises. The passion between them was about to ignite. Glory's hands were on his shoulders, urging him down when he moved between her legs. When he slid inside, her eyelids fluttered, and then she wrapped her arms around his neck and followed where he wanted to go.

Rocking with the rhythm of their bodies, moments became endless as that sweet fire began to build. It was the time when the feeling was so good that it felt like it could go on forever. And then urgency slipped into the act, honing nerves already at the point of breaking.

One minute Wyatt was still in control, and the next thing he knew, she was arching up to meet him and crying out his name. He looked down, saw himself reflected in the pupils of her eyes and felt as if he was drowning. A faint look of surprise was etched across her face as shock wave after shock wave ebbed and flowed throughout her body. Caught in the undertow, Wyatt couldn't pull back, and then didn't want to. He spilled all he was in the sweet act of love.

For Glory, time ceased. The problems of the world outside were momentarily forgotten. There was nothing that mattered but the man in her arms and the love in his eyes. Seconds later he collapsed, lying with his head upon her breasts and his fists tangled tightly in her hair.

Replete from their loving, Glory reached out with a satisfied sigh, tracing the breadth of his shoulders and combing her fingers through his hair, letting the thick black strands fall where they might. Just as the sun sank below the horizon, she felt him relax and remembered last night, and how he'd stood watch while she slept.

Sleep, my love, she thought.

"Am I?" Wyatt asked.

Glory smiled. He'd done it again. "Are you what?" she asked, knowing full well what he was angling for.

"Your love."

"What do you think?" she whispered.

He lifted his head, his eyes still black from burned-out passion. "I think I'm in heaven."

She grinned. "No, you're in my arms and in Granny's bed."

He rolled, moving her from bottom to top. "Like I said… I'm in heaven."

Before Glory could settle into a comfortable spot, Wyatt's hands were doing things to her that, at the moment, she wouldn't have thought it possible to feel.

She gasped, then moved against his fingers in a tantalizing circle. "I don't know about heaven," she whispered, and then closed her eyes and bit her lower lip, savoring the tiny spikes of pleasure that he'd already started. "But if you stop what you're doing anytime soon, you'll be in trouble."

He laughed, then proved that he was man enough to finish what he had started.

Carter Foster stood at the window of his darkened house, peering through the curtains and cursing beneath his breath as the patrol car moved slowly past.

It wasn't the first time it had circled his neighborhood. In fact, it was a normal patrol for the officer on duty. But in Carter's mind, he saw the police searching for clues that would destroy his world. Guilt played strange tricks on a criminal's mind.

He let the curtain drop and began to pace, wondering if he should pack and run before they got on his trail. With every day that Glory Dixon lived, his chances of getting away with murder decreased. And as a man who'd made his living on the good side of the law, he knew exactly how deep his trouble was.

He moved room by room through his house, jumping at shadows that took on sinister forms. Sounds that he'd heard all his life suddenly had ominous qualities he'd never considered. And the bed that he and Betty Jo had shared was an impossible place to rest. He sneaked by the room every night on his way to the guest room, unable to look inside, afraid that Betty Jo's ghost would be sitting on the side of that bed with lipstick smeared across her face, and a torn dress riding up her white thighs.

"When this is over, I'll sell the house and move," he reminded himself. He had started down the hallway to get ready for bed when the phone rang.

Panicked by the unexpected sound, Carter flattened against the wall, and then cursed his stupidity when he realized it was nothing but the phone. He considered just letting it ring, and then knew that with the condition his life was in, he'd better take the call. Yet when he answered, he realized that, once again, he'd made the wrong decision. He should have let it ring.

"It's me," Bo growled.

"I can hear that," Carter sneered. "Now, unless you've called to tell me that you've finished something you so obviously botched last night, I don't think we have a damn thing to discuss!"

"I called to tell you that you owe me four new tires," Bo shouted.

Carter rolled his eyes. "Unless you get your butt in gear, I'm not going to owe you anything," he shouted back.

"Look, this job is more involved than you led me to believe. I ruined four tires today saving my own hide from some crazy hillbilly. You're gonna pay, or I know someone who'd be interested in my side of the incidents that have been happening to one Miss Glory Dixon."

Carter went rigid with disbelief. This was the last damned straw! The imbecile was trying to blackmail him. He took a deep breath and then grinned. Marker's gorilla brain was no match for his courtroom skills.

"Well, now, I'd be real careful before I went running to the law," Carter sneered. "They'd have nothing on me, and you have a rap sheet that dates back to your youth. You're the one who got bitten by a dog, and I'm a respectable lawyer. If some hillbilly took after you, why would they want to blame me? It wasn't my face that man saw, it was yours. And…to top that off, you're the one who stole a car and tried to run someone down, in front of the chief of police, no less. Now, you can talk all you want, but there is nothing…absolutely nothing…that links me to you. Not a dollar. Not a piece of paper. Nothing!"

Bo's response sounded nervous enough. "There's got to be a reason you want that Dixon woman dead, and I have no reason at all to care one way or another. If I tell them what I—"

Carter was so angry, he was shaking, but it didn't deter him from ending their argument with a resounding blow. One that got Bo's attention all too painfully.

"You do what you're told!" Carter screamed. "That crazy witch could ruin me. But, so help me God, if you talk, I'll make it my personal responsibility to see that you spend the rest of your life behind bars."

"Now, see here," Marker growled. "You can't—"

"Oh, yes, I can," Carter said. "Now. Either do what you were hired to do, or leave me the hell alone. Understand?"

Bo frowned, then slammed the phone back on the receiver. That had not gone exactly as planned.

"Now what?" he muttered.

He frowned, cursing both Carter and bad luck, and started up the street toward his house. Somewhere between now and morning, he had to find himself four new tires, or he'd never be able to finish the job. And if he had to steal them, which was his first choice of procedure, he could hardly be rolling the damned things down the street. He needed another pair of hands and a good pickup truck. As he walked, he wondered if his old friend Frankie Munroe was still around.

Anders Conway rolled over and then sat up in bed. He didn't know what hurt worse, his conscience or his belly. Grumbling beneath his breath, he crawled out from beneath the covers and started through his house in search of some more antacids. One of these days he was going to have to change his eating habits...or his job.

Today he'd faced the consequences of the law officer he'd become. With one year left to retirement, he'd let the office and himself slip. In spite of Glory Dixon's far-fetched claims about her psychic abilities, the fact still remained that someone was out to do her harm.

The stolen car that they'd recovered had been wiped clean of prints...all except for a partial that they'd found along the steering wheel column. They'd already eliminated the owner and any of his friends or family. It only stood to reason that it would belong to the thief. But it was going to take days, maybe weeks, to get back a report from the state office. During that time, Glory Dixon could be dead and buried.

He'd sent the bit of fabric along to a lab with the faint hope that something could be learned, although what they could possibly glean from a bit of denim cloth was impossible to guess.

He popped a couple of effervescent tablets into a glass of water, waiting while they fizzed, and consoled himself with the fact that at least he was doing his job.

Minutes later, he crawled back into bed, more comfortable with the situation, and with his belly. On the verge of dreams, the memory of Carter Foster's hangdog face drifted through his subconscious. But he was too far gone to wonder why, and when morning came, he wouldn't remember that it had.

Miles away, in a cabin nestled deep in the piney woods above Larner's Mill, Wyatt slept, with Glory held fast in his arms. The fear that had kept him virtually sleepless for the past two days was almost gone.

They'd gone to bed secure in the knowledge that somewhere beyond the walls of this cabin, there were six mountain men who'd sworn to a vow that he knew they would keep. He'd looked at their faces. He'd seen the men for what they were. The steadfast honesty of their expressions was all that he'd needed to see. With their help, maybe, just maybe, there would be a way out of this situation after all.

* * *

It was the quiet peace of early morning that woke Wyatt up from a deep, dreamless sleep. Or so he thought until he turned to look at Glory's face and saw it twisted into a grimace of concern.

He'd never seen horror on a face deep in sleep, but he was seeing it now. And as he watched, he knew what must be happening. Somewhere within the rest that she'd sought, another person's nightmare was taking place and taking Glory with it.

Except for the day at the city dump when she'd had the vision of the body being disposed of, he'd never witnessed this happening. His heart rate began to accelerate with fear. He wondered if this was how she'd been when she'd come to his rescue, then wondered whose life was about to take a crooked turn.

Uncertain of how to behave, or what to do, he realized the matter was out of his hands when she suddenly jerked and sat straight up in bed, her eyes wide-open and staring blindly at something other than the room in which she'd slept. Her eyes moved, as if along a page, watching a drama that only she could see. She moaned softly, wadding the sheet within her hands, rocking back and forth in a terrified manner.

Still. Everything was still. No wind. Not even a soft, easy breeze. Dark clouds hovered upon the early-morning horizon, hanging black and heavy, nearly dragging on the ground.

The outer walls of the white frame house were a stark contrast to the brewing weather. Fences ranged from barns to trees without an animal in sight.

And then everything exploded before her eyes, shattering the unearthly quiet by a loud, vicious roar. Trees bent low to the ground, and then came up by the roots, flying and twisting through the air like oversize arrows.

*Windows imploded. Glass shattered inward, filling the
air with deadly, glittering missiles of destruction. Everything that once was, was no more.*

*And then as quickly as it had come, it passed. Where
there had been darkness, now there was light. The house
was but a remnant of its former self. The limbs of a tree
protruded through a window. Beneath their deadweight,
a baby's bed lay crushed on the floor. And near the doorway, a clock lay on its side, the hands stopped at five minutes past seven.*

Glory shuddered, then fell forward, her head upon her
knees, her shoulders shaking as she pulled herself back
to reality.

"Honey…are you all right?"

Wyatt's voice was a calm where the storm had been. She
threw her arms around his neck, sobbing in near hysterics.

"The storm… I couldn't stop the storm."

Wyatt held her close, smoothing the tangled hair from
her face and rubbing her back in a slow, soothing motion.

"There's no storm here, honey. Maybe it was just a bad
dream."

Glory's eyes blazed as she lifted her head, pinning him
with the force of her glare.

"Don't!" she sobbed. "Don't you doubt me, Wyatt! Not
now! I don't *ever* dream. Either I sleep. Or these…things
come into my mind. I can't make them stop, and I can't
make them go away."

She rolled out of his grasp and out of the bed, desperate
to see for herself what it looked like outside. Wyatt followed
her frantic race for the door, grabbing for his gun as he ran.

Sunlight hit her head-on, kissing the frown on her face
with a warm burst of heat, while an easy spring breeze
lifted the tail of her nightgown and then flattened it against
her legs.

"Oh, Lord," she muttered, and buried her face in her

hands. "I don't understand. I saw the storm. I saw the…!" Her face lit up as she remembered. "What time is it?"

He looked back inside the house at Granny's mantel clock. "A little before eight. Why?"

Glory moaned, and began pacing the dewy grass in her bare feet. "This doesn't make sense. The clock had stopped at a little after seven. That time has already come and gone."

"Come here." He caught her by the arm, gently pulling her back inside the house. "Now sit down and tell me exactly what you saw. Maybe it was happening in another part of the country, and if it did, there's not a damn thing you can do to stop it, darlin'. You can't fix the world. I'm just sorry that you get pulled into its messes."

She went limp in his arms, and at his urging, curled up on the couch, tucking her bare feet beneath the tail of her gown to warm them. When she started talking, her voice was shaky and weak.

"It was so real. The house was white. And it's set on a hill right above a creek. There was an old two-story barn just below the house, and corrals and fences behind that stretched off into the woods."

Wyatt was in the act of making coffee when something she said made him pause. He turned, listening to her as she continued, the coffee forgotten.

"What else?" he urged.

She shrugged. "The sky. It was so black. And everything was still…you know what I mean…like the world was holding its breath?"

He nodded, although the description gave him a chill.

"And then it just exploded…right before my eyes. There was a roar, and then trees were being ripped out of the ground, and the windows…" She closed her eyes momentarily, trying to remember what had come next. Her lips were trembling when she looked up at him. "And then it was all over. There was a tree through a window, and a baby bed beneath it. And there was a clock on the floor that had stopped at five minutes after seven."

Wyatt shuddered. "Damn, honey. That's got to be hell seeing things like that and knowing you have no control of the outcome."

"Sometimes I do," she whispered. "Remember you?"

His eyes turned dark. "How could I forget?"

But the memory was too fresh to give up, and she thumped her knees with her fists in frustration.

"I just wish I'd recognized the place," she muttered. "It was so pretty. There was a rooster weather vane on the roof of the house, and it had a wide porch across the front, and a big porch swing. I love porch swings." And then she smiled sadly. "And there was the prettiest bunch of pansies growing in a tin tub beneath one of those old-fashioned water wells. The kind that you had to pump."

Wyatt paled. He listened to what she said as the air left his lungs in one hard gush. Panic sent him flying across the room. He pulled her to her feet, unaware that he was almost shaking her.

"Oh, God! Oh, God! What time did you say that clock stopped?"

Glory went still. The shock on Wyatt's face was impossible to miss. "Five minutes after seven," she said. "Why? What's wrong?"

He started to pace, looking at the mantel clock, then comparing the time that she'd stated.

"Oh, no!" He was at the point of despair when it dawned. "Wait! We're in a different time zone. It's not too late." Before Glory could ask what was wrong, he was running toward the bedroom, muttering beneath his breath. "The phone! The phone! I've got to find that phone."

Seconds later, she was right behind him.

His fingers were shaking as he punched in the numbers, and then he groaned as he counted the rings. Twice he looked down at his watch on the bedside table, and each time, the fear that had sent him running to call increased a thousandfold.

And then Lane's sleepy voice echoed in his ear, and Wyatt started shouting for them to get out of the house.

"Wyatt? What the hell's wrong with you?" Lane muttered, trying to come awake. He and Toni had spent sleepless hours last night with a sick baby, and when they'd finally gotten her earache under control and her back to sleep, they had dropped into bed like zombies.

"You've got to get out of the house!" Wyatt shouted. "There's a storm coming. You have less than five minutes to get everyone into the cellar. For God's sake, don't ask me why! Just do it!"

Without question, Lane rolled out of bed, grabbing at his jeans as he nudged Toni awake.

"Was it Glory?" was all that he asked.

"Yes," Wyatt shouted. "Now run!"

The line went dead in Wyatt's ear, and he dropped onto the side of the bed, shaking from head to toe as tears shimmered across his eyes. When Glory reached out, he caught her hand, holding it to his mouth, kissing her palm, then her wrist, then pulling her down onto his lap.

"It was my home that you saw," he whispered. "I'm glad you liked it. It was where I grew up."

Glory closed her eyes against the pain in his voice. "I'm sorry. I'm so, so sorry." She wrapped her arms around his neck and held him, giving him comfort in the only way she knew how.

Minutes passed, and then a half hour, and then an hour, during which time Glory tried to get him to eat, then gave up hoping he might talk. Wyatt sat, staring at the floor, with his hand no more than inches from a phone that wouldn't ring.

"Oh, God," he finally whispered. "What if I was too late?"

"Now you know how it feels to hold life and death in the palm of your hand," she said quietly. "I live with this every day of my life. Can you live with it, as well?"

He didn't answer, and she didn't expect one. He'd wanted to know all there was to know about her. And her heart was breaking as she realized that this might be too much to accept.

As Granny Dixon's mantel clock chimed, signaling the hour, Wyatt looked down at his watch. It was ten o'clock—nine o'clock for Toni and Lane. If they had survived, he would have heard by now...wouldn't he? He thought about calling his brother, Justin, and then couldn't remember the number. It was an excuse and he knew it. A simple call to Information would have solved that problem. But it also might have given him a truth he didn't want to face.

Seconds after he'd discarded the thought, the phone finally rang, startling them both to the point that neither wanted to answer the call. Glory held her breath and closed her eyes, saying a prayer as Wyatt picked up the phone.

"Hello?"

Lane's voice sounded weary and rough, but when it reverberated soundly in Wyatt's ear, he went weak with relief.

"It's me," Lane said.

"Thank God," Wyatt groaned. "I didn't think you would ever call. Are Toni and Joy all right? Did you—"

Lane interrupted. "I want to talk to Glory."

Wyatt handed her the phone.

"Hello?"

Lane swallowed a lump in his throat as he tried to put into words what he was feeling.

"How do I say thank-you for the only things that make my life worth living?" he asked quietly.

Glory started to smile. This must mean they were safe.

"I will never—and I mean, never—doubt a word you

say to me again. Five minutes later and we would have been dead. All of us. A tree fell on Joy's crib. It smashed the—"

"I know," Glory said softly.

Lane wiped a hand across his face and then smiled. "That's right, you do, don't you, girl?" He paused, then again wiped a shaky hand across his face. "There's someone else who wants to talk to you." He handed the phone to Toni.

"Is this Glory?"

Glory's eyes widened. She put her hand over the phone and whispered urgently to Wyatt. "I think it's your sister."

He smiled. "So tell her hello."

Glory dropped onto the bed beside Wyatt, anxiously twisting a lock of her hair around her finger. Except for Lane, this would be her first connection with any of his people.

"Yes, this is Glory."

Toni caught her breath on a sob. "I'm Wyatt's sister, Toni. You saved our lives, you know." And then she started to cry, softly but steadily. "Thank you is little to say for the gift that you gave me today, but I do thank you, more than you will ever know. If you knew what I went through to get this man and our child, you would understand what it means to me to know that they're safe."

A shy smile of delight spread across Glory's face as she caught Wyatt watching her. "You're very welcome," she said. "But it wasn't all me. Wyatt is the one who put two and two together. He's the one who made the call."

Toni sighed as exhaustion threatened to claim her. In another room, she could hear Joy as she started to fuss, and Justin's wife as she tried to console her. The call had to be short. With a trembling voice, she continued.

"When he comes back this way, I'd love for you to come with him. I've always wanted to hug an earthbound angel. Now put that brother of mine on, I need to tell him thank you, too."

Glory handed Wyatt the phone.

"Sis?"

At the sound of his voice, tears sprang again. "Thank you, big brother."

"You're welcome, honey," he said, and although he hated to ask, he needed to know. "Is the house gone?"

"No. It will take a lot of work, but it can be repaired."

"That's good," Wyatt said. "Are you at Justin's?"

She rolled her eyes as Joy's cries became louder. "Yes, but not for any longer than necessary. If you need Lane, call him here, at least for the remainder of the week. As soon as we get the glass out of the house and windows back in, we'll be able to do the bulk of the repairs in residence."

Wyatt grinned. He knew what a headache it would be for two separate families to be living under one roof, especially when two of the people were as hardheaded as Toni and Justin.

"Wyatt?"

"Yes, honey?"

"Don't you hurt that girl."

Glory saw the shock on his face and heard the pain in his voice, but she didn't know why.

"Why the hell would you say that to me?" he asked.

"Because I know you. You've got a kite for a compass. You go where the wind blows, and when her troubles are over, you'll be long gone again. Don't you leave her behind with a broken heart. If I find out that you have, I don't think I'll ever forgive you."

"That was never my intention," he muttered. "And I can't thank you enough for the vote of confidence."

"You're welcome, and I love you," Toni said. "Call if you need us."

The phone went dead in his ear.

"What's wrong?" Glory asked, aware that Wyatt was more than a little out of sorts.

He tossed the phone on the bed beside them, almost afraid to look at her for fear that she'd see the truth on his face.

"Nothing. She's just being her usual bossy self. She gave me a warning…and a little advice."

"And that was?"

He shrugged, then looked up as a reluctant grin spread across his face. He took her into his arms and dropped backward onto the bed.

"Something about hanging my sorry butt from the nearest tree if I didn't treat you right."

Glory laughed, and wrapped her arms around his neck. "I like the way that woman thinks."

Chapter 12

Just after noon, the sound of a car could be heard coming down the road to Granny's cabin. Wyatt watched from his seat on the steps as a black-and-white cruiser pulled to a stop only yards from the porch. When Anders Conway got out of the car, Wyatt couldn't resist a small dig.

"Are you lost?"

Conway had to grin. From the first time they'd met, he hadn't been as accommodating as he should have been, and yet this big, dark-eyed man didn't seem to hold a grudge.

"You might think so, wouldn't you?"

Wyatt motioned toward the single cane chair against the wall. "Have a seat."

Anders shook his head. "Maybe some other time. I just came out to update you on the investigation."

Wyatt made no effort to hide his surprise. "You mean there really is one?"

Conway frowned. He had that coming. "Yeah, there re-ally is. And I came out to tell you that, no matter what I believe about Glory Dixon's *powers,* I do believe that someone is out to do her harm." And then he scratched his head and took the chair that was offered, in spite of his earlier refusal. "The thing is, none of this makes sense. Why would anyone even *want* to hurt her? Hell, half the town is afraid of her, and the other half thinks she's a little bit…"

"Nuts?"

Both men looked startled as Glory came out of the cabin. Embarrassed at being overheard, Conway jumped up from his seat and yanked off his hat as a flush colored his skin.

"Now, Miss Dixon, I'm real sorry you heard that, and I don't mean anything personal by it," Conway said. "I was just stating a fact."

It wasn't anything she hadn't heard a hundred times before, and it wasn't what interested her. "What was that you were saying about an investigation?" she asked.

Conway relaxed, apparently thankful that the conversation had changed.

"We found a partial fingerprint on the car that tried to run you down. 'Course, it'll take a while for any results to come back, and you understand if the fellow that left it had no priors, then we have no way of identifying him, don't you?"

She nodded.

"And for what it's worth, I sent that scrap of fabric that you gave me off to the crime lab at the capital. Don't think we'll learn much, but we'll at least have tried, right?"

He hitched at his gun belt, and studied a knot on the plank beneath his feet. "What I came out to say is, I'm sorry. When you came to me for help, I let you down, and I can promise it won't happen again."

When the chief offered his hand, Glory didn't hesitate. And when he shook it firmly, in a small, but significant way, she felt vindicated.

"Thank you for coming," she said. "I appreciate it more than you know."

He nodded. "So, that's it, then," he said. "I suppose I'd better be getting back into town. It doesn't do to leave my two deputies alone for long. On occasion, they get ticket happy, and then I've got some angry townsfolk wondering why they could make a U-turn on Main Street one day, and then get fined for it the next. Besides that, we had ourselves a burglary last night. Someone kicked in the back door to Henley's Garage and Filling Station, waltzed in and helped themselves to a whole set of tires. From what we can tell, the thieves brought their own rims and mounted 'em right on the spot."

Conway shook his head as he started toward the cruiser. "I'll tell you, crooks these days either have more guts or less brains than they used to. And finding any fingerprints as evidence in that grease pit is impossible. Nearly everyone in town is in and out of there. Ain't no way to figure out who left what or when they left it, and old man Henley's fit to be tied. See you around," he said, and then left.

Glory turned to Wyatt, a smile hovering on her lips as Conway drove away.

"I didn't think this day would ever come," she said.

"What day?"

"The day when someone other than my family would bother to believe me."

He cradled her in his arms, hugging her to him. "After this morning, how can you forget the fifty-odd members of my immediate family who think you hung the moon?" He tilted her chin, then kissed the tip of her nose when she wrinkled it in dismay.

"Fifty?"

He grinned. "I underestimated on purpose so I wouldn't scare you off."

Glory shifted within his embrace. "As long as I have you, I'm not scared of a living thing," she whispered.

Joy filled him as he held her. "Lady, you take my breath away."

A light breeze teased at her hair, lifting then settling long, shiny strands across his hands. Unable to resist their offer, Wyatt combed his fingers through the lengths, entranced by the sunlight caught in the depths.

"Wyatt, there's something I want to talk to you about."

Play ceased immediately. The tone of her voice was serious, as was the look in her eyes.

"Then tell me."

She moved out of his arms, then took him by the hand and started walking toward the shade trees above the creek at the back of the cabin.

Wyatt went where she led, aware that when she was ready, she would start talking. As they reached the shade, Glory dropped down onto a cool, mossy rock, and then patted the ground beside it, indicating that Wyatt join her, which he did.

As she sorted out her thoughts, she fiddled with her hair. It was sticking to her neck and in spite of the shade, hot against her shoulders. Absently, she pulled it over her shoulders, then using her fingers for a comb, separated it into three parts, and began to braid.

"I have a theory," she said, as she fastened the end of the braid with a band from her pocket. "I don't know how to explain it, but I think that the body that was buried at the dump is somehow connected to what's happening to me."

A shiver of warning niggled at Wyatt's instinct for self-preservation as he gave Glory a startled look. "I don't like this," he said.

She shrugged, then stared pensively down the bank of the creek to the tiny stream of water that continually flowed. "I don't, either. But nothing else makes sense."

"What made you think like that?" he asked.

"It was something that Chief Conway said, about people being afraid of me." She turned toward Wyatt, pinning him with that clear blue stare. "What if someone thought my gift was like some, uh, I don't know…a witch's crystal ball, maybe? What if someone did something bad…really bad, and they thought that all I had to do was look at them and I'd know it?"

Wyatt's heart jumped, then settled. "You mean… something bad like committing a murder and dumping a body?"

She nodded.

His eyes narrowed thoughtfully as he considered what she'd just said. The more he thought about it, the more it made sense.

"It *would* explain why, wouldn't it?"

"It's about the only thing that does," she said. And then her chin quivered.

"Come here," he said softly, and she crawled off the rock and into his lap, settling between his outstretched legs and resting her back against the breadth of his chest. When he pulled her close, surrounding her with his arms and nuzzling his chin at the top of her head, she savored the security that came from being encompassed by the man who'd stolen her heart.

For a time, the outside world ceased to exist. For Glory and Wyatt, there was nothing but them, and the sound of the breeze rustling through the leaves, birdcalls coming from the green canopy over their heads, the ripple of the water in the creek below and the raucous complaint of a squirrel high up in a tree across the creek.

Bo Marker was back in business. He had shells for his rifle, wheels on his truck and a renewed interest in finishing the job he'd promised Carter Foster he would do. Now he didn't just *want* the money Carter had promised, he *needed* it to pay Frankie for helping him last night with the heist.

But Bo wasn't a complete fool. He had no intention of going anywhere near that Dixon farm again. He still had nightmares about that man who'd run him off, and hoped he never saw him again.

As he drove along the back roads, he kept his eye out for a good place to conceal himself and his truck. A location that would be close to the main road that led down from the mountain. That Dixon woman and her man couldn't stay up there forever. They'd have to come down sometime, if for no other reason than to get food. When they did, he'd be waiting. This time, he'd make sure that there would be no Kentucky bigfoot with a gun at his back when he took aim.

Pleased with his plan, Bo proceeded to search the roads, while Carter Foster lived each hour sinking deeper and deeper in a hell of his own making.

Carter was running. His belly bounced with each lurch of his stride, and his heart was hammering so hard against his rib cage that he feared he was going to die on the spot. With every step, the sound of his shoes slapping against the old tile floor of the courthouse echoed sharply within the high, domed ceilings.

He burst into the courtroom just as the judge was about to raise his gavel.

"I'm sorry I'm late, Your Honor. May it please the court, I have filed an injunction against the company that's suing my client."

The judge leaned over the desk, pinning Carter with a hard, frosty glare.

"Counselor…this is the third time you've been tardy in my court this week. Once more, and I'll hold you in contempt."

Carter paled. "Yes, sir. I'm sorry, sir."

And so the morning passed.

When they recessed for the day, it was nearly three o'clock. Carter's belly was growling with hunger. He'd missed breakfast, and because of his earlier dereliction, had been forced to skip lunch. Right now, he wouldn't care if his client got drawn and quartered—the only thing on his mind was food.

He came out of the courthouse, again on the run. He tossed his briefcase into his car and was about to get in when he heard someone calling his name. With a muffled curse, he turned, and then felt all the blood drain from his face. The chief of police was walking toward him from across the street.

"Hey there, Foster," Conway said, and thumped him lightly on the back in a manly greeting.

Carter managed a smile. "Chief, I haven't seen you in a while. I guess since the last time we were in court together, right?"

Conway nodded, while gauging Foster's condition. His supposition the other day had been right on target. Foster looked like he'd been pulled backward through a downspout. He needed a haircut. His clothes looked as if he'd slept in them, and there were bags beneath his eyes big enough to haul laundry.

"Say, I've been meaning to speak to you," Conway said.

"Oh? About what?" Carter's heart jerked so sharply that he feared he might die on the spot.

"Your wife and all," Conway said, a little uncertain how one went about commiserating with a fellow who'd just been dumped.

"What about my wife?" Carter asked, as his voice rose three octaves.

Conway shrugged and wished he'd never started this conversation. Old Foster wasn't taking this any better than he'd hoped.

"Well, you know, she's gone, and I heard that—"

"She ran off, you know," Carter interrupted. "She's been threatening to do it for years but I never believed her. I guess a man should believe his wife every so often. It might prevent problems later on, don't you think?"

The moment he said it, he gritted his teeth, wishing he had the good sense not to ramble, but when he got nervous, he always talked too much.

"I suppose you're right," Conway said. "Anyway, I just wanted to tell you I'm real sorry."

Carter sighed and even managed a smile. "Thanks. That's real nice of you, Chief."

Conway nodded, and then as Carter was about to get in his car, he asked, "Have you heard from her?"

From the look on Carter's face, the chief thought he was about to have a heart attack. Carter's mouth was working, but no words were coming out. Finally, he cleared his throat, and managed a small, shaky giggle.

"Actually, I have," he said. "I'm about to become the recipient of a Mexican divorce. Isn't that a laugh? Me a lawyer, and she felt the need to go to Mexico to have her legal work done."

Conway nodded, although he couldn't see much humor in the situation. And then he shrugged. He supposed it was every man's right to deal with hardship in his own way.

"Well, you take care now," Conway said. "I imagine I'll be seeing you real soon."

Carter paled. "Why?"

"Why…in court, buddy. In court."

Carter imagined all kinds of insinuations that were spelling out his doom, and in a fit of panic, fell into his car and drove off in a hurry, leaving behind a cloud of exhaust smoke and the sounds of tires shredding on pavement.

The chief shook his head, and ambled on into the court-house, thanking his lucky stars that he'd been the one who'd done the divorcing all those years ago. It must play hell with an ego when one was the dumpee.

It wasn't until later on in the afternoon that he received a phone call that set him to thinking along a completely different line.

"Chief, line two for you," the dispatcher shouted, and Conway rolled his eyes and picked up the phone. One of these days they were going to have to invest in some sort of intercom. Yelling at each other from room to room didn't seem professional.

"Chief Conway," he muttered, shifting files on his desk as he searched for clean paper and pen.

"Conway, this is Lane Monday. I thought I'd call and see how the Dixon investigation is going."

Conway was pleased to be able to count off the number of things that he'd done since last they'd talked. And when the marshal seemed satisfied, it pleased him even more.

"That's good," Lane said. "And it's one of the reasons I called. I had fully intended to come back that way within a day or two, but I've had a family emergency and a slight change of plans."

Conway frowned. "Nothing bad, I hope."

"No, and it's thanks to Glory Dixon," he muttered, thinking of the chaos back at their home, and then of Toni and Joy, and considered himself a fortunate man.

"How's that?" Conway said.

"All I can tell you is she knew about the tornado that hit our house this morning even before it hit. If Wyatt hadn't called us in a panic, screaming for us to get out of the house, we wouldn't have made it to the cellar in time. I don't know how Toni and I might have fared, but a tree came through the window and crushed our baby's bed. If she'd been in it…" He couldn't even finish the story.

"Well, I'll be damned," Conway said, and shuddered from the images the story provoked.

Unwilling to dwell on the horror still fresh in his mind, Lane quickly changed gears.

"That's not why I'm calling," he said. "It's with regards to the missing-person factor in Glory's story about the woman in the dump."

Conway fiddled with his pen, and wondered if he should admit to the marshal that he'd given that story little thought. Remembering Monday's earlier anger, he decided not.

"Yes, what do you have?" he asked.

"Well, you know how you said you had no reports of missing persons?"

"Yeah, go on," Conway said.

"I checked with the FBI. In my book, they're the experts when it comes to kidnappings and missing persons. The man I was talking to suggested that sometimes a person is actually missing for weeks, sometimes even months before it's discovered. Usually because a family member, or the community, believes them to be on a legitimate trip somewhere.

"He said they had a case once where a wife whose husband was in the oil business claimed that he'd made an unscheduled trip to South America and was then killed in a plane crash over there. Imagine their surprise when what was left of him surfaced months later in a fisherman's net off the coast of the Carolinas."

"Ooh, hell," Conway said. The image was startling, to say the least.

"Anyway, my point is, you might keep that in mind as you work the case."

"Yeah, right, and thanks," Conway muttered, and then disconnected.

He leaned back in his chair, propped his feet on the desk and locked his hands behind his neck, thinking as he did about what Monday just said. How did coincidence factor into a warning of impending danger? And how did...?

His feet hit the floor as his hands slapped the desk.

"Son of a..."

He jumped to his feet and stepped outside, staring across the street at the sign on Carter Foster's office.

Out To Lunch.

For a man who was supposed to be mourning the loss of a wife, he sure hadn't lost his appetite. "I wonder?" he muttered, then frowned, pivoted on his heel and stalked back into his office.

"Hey!" he shouted.

A deputy came running.

"I want you to check the bus station, the ticket counters in every airport within driving distance, and anyplace else you can think of that provides transportation."

"Yes, sir," the deputy said. "What am I checking for?"

Conway tapped the deputy on the shirt, lowering his voice in a confidential manner. "I want you to find me a paper trail. I want to know how and from where Betty Jo Foster left town, and if possible, who with. And I don't want to walk out of here this evening and find out that everyone in town knows what you're doing."

The deputy's eyes widened.

"What I'm saying is...do your job and keep your trap shut," Conway growled.

"Yes, sir," he said, and out the door he went.

Bo woke himself up when he snorted. The sound was so startling that he grabbed for his gun before he came to enough to realize that it was himself that he had heard. His legs were stiff, his butt was numb and his belly was pushing uncomfortably against the steering wheel of his pickup truck. He yawned, then stretched as he felt nature call.

Satisfied that from where he had parked, he was perfectly concealed from the road, he opened the pickup door and then scooted out of the seat, leaving the door open for privacy's sake as he did what he needed to do. Groaning beneath his breath as his legs protested his weight, he went about his business.

At that minute, a car came flying around a corner and then headed back up the hill. Confident that he was safe from being seen, he turned to look.

His heart jerked as he cursed. In a panic, he grabbed for his rifle, forgetting that he'd been using that hand for something else. To his dismay, he was too late to take aim, and found himself watching the taillights of Wyatt Hatfield's car as it disappeared over the hill.

Disgusted with his bad luck, he kicked at the dirt. Now there was no telling how long it would be before they'd come back.

Wyatt was carrying in groceries while Glory, at his insistence, had gone to her bed to lie down. Ever since she'd had the vision about the storm, she'd had a dull, niggling headache. It wasn't uncommon for such a thing to happen, but this time, she hadn't been able to shake the feeling of malaise.

Her head had barely hit the pillow when he came into the room with a glass of water and a couple of pills in his hand.

"Here, honey," he said. "See if these will help."

Gratefully, she accepted the water and the pills and swallowed them in one quick gulp. She set the glass on the table, and then lay back down on the bed.

"Thank you for taking care of me," she said.

Wyatt leaned over and softly kissed her cheek. "It's my pleasure," he whispered. "Now see if you can get some sleep."

She frowned. "I don't want to sleep. It's too late in the day. If I sleep now, then I'll never get to sleep tonight."

A cocky grin slid across his mouth. "Oh, that's okay," he said. "I can think of a few other things we might do instead."

In spite of her pain, she laughed. And at his insistence, rolled over and closed her eyes. *I do love the way his mind works,* she thought.

"To heck with my mind, how about the rest of me?" he asked, and left her grinning.

In spite of Glory's determination not to sleep, she quickly succumbed, and she was still dozing when Wyatt wandered outside to get some air. It was hard to keep his mind occupied with anything but Glory's safety, but he knew that he needed to take a break from the tension under which they'd been living.

For a few minutes, he wandered around the immediate vicinity of the cabin, but he was too cautious to go far. For lack of anything better to do, he picked up a stick, headed back to the porch steps, and then began to whittle. The activity had nothing to do with creativity. It was a thing to pass the time.

He had a good accumulation of wood chips going when he heard someone coming through the brush. For the first time since his arrival, he looked up with interest, not fear. When Edward Lee came ambling out of the trees, Wyatt stood up.

"Ma said I could bring you some cookies." He handed Wyatt the sack before adding, "They're my favorite kind."

Wyatt grinned, then opened the sack. "Would you like some?"

Edward Lee looked back over his shoulder. His father was right behind him, walking with the ease of a man who's at peace with himself and comfortable with the presence of the rifle he had slung on his shoulder.

"Daddy, Wyatt says I can have some of his cookies."

Liam Fowler grinned. "Then I suppose you'd better have some, son."

A wide smile spread across Edward Lee's face as he thrust his hand into the sack and came up with two cookies, one for each hand, then set about eating them.

"Had yourself any more trouble?" Liam asked.

Wyatt shook his head. "No, and I suspect that's thanks to you and your friends."

Liam nodded and absently stroked his beard, rearranging the thick black curls without care for appearance.

"What puzzles me is why Glory is suffering with this," he said.

"She has a theory," Wyatt said. "It came from something that Anders Conway said. He said that a lot of people are afraid of her."

Liam nodded. "That's true. It's a shame, but it's a fact. Lots of people fear what they don't understand."

"Are you afraid of her?" Wyatt asked.

Liam smiled, then looked down at his son. "No more than I'm afraid of Edward Lee. So, what's she getting at anyway?"

"Not too long after I arrived, she had a vision. She *saw* someone hiding evidence of a terrible crime. But she only saw it in her mind. She believes that whoever committed this crime is afraid that, because of her gift, she will be able to point the finger at him, so to speak. And that he's trying to get rid of her to keep his secret safe."

Liam frowned. "It sounds ugly, but it makes a lot of sense. I've known that girl since the day she was born. Rafe Dixon was one of my best friends. I've seen grown men say prayers when she crosses their paths, just because she has the sight."

Wyatt shook his head in disbelief.

With cookies gone, Edward Lee's attention wandered.

"Wyatt, where's my Mornin' Glory?" he asked, interrupting the seriousness of their conversation.

"She's taking a nap." As soon as he said it, he sympathized with the disappointment on the young man's face.

And then the door behind him suddenly opened, and Edward Lee bounded to his feet.

"Mornin' Glory! You woke up!" Delight was rich on his face as he threw his arms around her neck, hugging and grinning broadly as she greeted him with a kiss on the cheek.

"I thought I heard voices," she said, smiling easily at Liam and his son.

"Ma sent cookies," Edward Lee said.

Wyatt hid a grin. He could see where this was going and handed Glory the sack.

"They're my favorites," Edward Lee reminded her.

Glory laughed. "How many have you already had?"

"Only two," he said.

"Then maybe you could have two more?"

Liam laughed aloud at his boy's ingenious method of begging.

"Don't eat them all, boy!" he prodded. "Ma's got a whole cookie jar full saved for you at home."

Edward Lee nodded and chewed, unable to answer for the cookie in his mouth.

"Would you like to come inside?" Glory asked. "I could make a pot of coffee."

Liam smiled, and brushed his hand against the side of her cheek in a gentle, but testing gesture.

"No, thank you, girl. I just stopped by to say hello. We'd best be gettin' on home before my boy eats all of your food." And then he cast a long approving glance at Wyatt before tipping his hat to them both.

"You be careful now, you hear?"

Wyatt nodded. "Same to you, friend. Same to you."

When they were gone, Glory waited for Wyatt to say something, anything, to break the tension of the look he was giving her. But when he remained silent, she took the initiative.

"What?" she asked.

"I told Liam about your theory."

Her face lost all expression. She wouldn't allow herself to care if Edward Lee's father doubted her.

"So?" she asked.

"He said it made sense."

The tension in her body slowly disappeared as she dropped down to the porch steps and dug in the sack for a cookie.

"Want one?" she asked, and offered it to Wyatt.

He shook his head, then sat down beside her, slinging an arm across her shoulders.

"What I want is for you to be safe and happy. What I don't know is how to make it happen. This waiting is driving me insane."

She nodded in agreement, thoughtfully munching the cookie, savoring the spicy taste of cinnamon, oatmeal and raisin. When she was through, she brushed her hands on the sides of her jeans and then studied the toes of her shoes.

Wyatt could tell there was something on her mind, but he didn't know whether to ask or wait for her to say it in her own time. Finally, impatience got the better of him and he tugged at her braid to get her attention.

"So, are you going to say what's on your mind, or are you going to leave me hanging?" he asked.

"I think I should go back to the dump."

Wyatt flinched. He didn't like to think of what she'd endured before. Putting herself through torment again seemed more punishment than sense.

"But why, honey? You know what it did to you the first time."

She sighed, then leaned her head against his chest, relishing the comfort of his arms as he pulled her closer.

"Because if I'm right about why someone wants to harm me, then what happened there impacts my safety. When it happened before, I was so shocked by the horror that I pulled out of the vision before it had time to play out." Her voice deepened in dejection. "I don't even know, if we go back, that it *will* happen again, but if it does, maybe I will see something that will give us a face…or a name. As Chief Conway says, something solid to go on."

"I don't like it…but I'll take you."

She went limp in his arms. "Thank you, Wyatt. Thank you."

He frowned. "Don't thank me yet," he warned. "This mess isn't over."

Chapter 13

Wyatt was slipping the gun in the back of his jeans as Glory came out of the bedroom. He noticed her look of fear before she had time to hide it.

Watching him arm himself to protect her was a shock. She fiddled with the ends of her braid in embarrassment, unnecessarily tucked at the pink T-shirt already in place beneath the waistband of her jeans.

"It'll be all right," he promised, as he went to her side. "I won't take my eyes off you for a second."

"I know that." She let him hold her, relaxing against his chest and focusing on the constant and steady beat of his heart. "It's just that the sight of that gun reminds me that I'm no longer safe."

He tilted her chin until she was forced to meet his gaze. "You say the word, and this trip to the dump is off."

Dread of what lay ahead was overwhelming, but she was firmly convinced that if her life was ever to get back to normal, it hinged upon finding the identity of the man who'd dumped that woman's body in with the garbage from Larner's Mill.

"No. I want this to be over with."

He nodded. "Then let's get started. The sooner we get there…"

He left the rest of the phrase undone as they started outside.

Glory paused in the doorway, allowing herself one last look at the inside of Granny's cabin, absorbing the familiarity of its simple decor. The old wooden floors. The papered and painted walls, peeling and faded. The pictures and knickknacks that Faith Dixon had accumulated over her ninety-one years.

Wyatt put his hand on Glory's shoulder. When she turned, there were tears shimmering across the surface of her eyes. Her pain broke his heart.

"We'll be back, sweetheart. I swear."

Glory lifted her chin, then straightened her shoulders and nodded.

"I knew that," she said softly. "I just needed to remember my people."

There was nothing else to say as he locked the door behind her. Moments later, they were in the car and on their way down the road. When they passed the site where her home once stood, she frowned at the remaining rubble.

"This place is a mess," she muttered.

"It will get better," Wyatt said. "One of these days, everything will be better."

Glory sighed, then made herself relax. *This, too, shall pass.*

Wyatt heard her thought and had to restrain a shudder. He hoped to God that he wasn't destined to be part of her past. He couldn't imagine a future…his future…without Glory in it.

* * *

Bo Marker sat in the midst of the ruins of a late-night run for food that he'd made to a local convenience store. Potato chip crumbs were caught in the fabric of the truck seat, as well as hanging on the front of his shirt and jeans, leaving grease stains wherever they clung. An empty box that once held half a dozen chocolate cupcakes was on the floorboard, and the wadded wrappers from two deli sandwiches lay on the ground where he'd tossed them out the window. An empty liter of soda was on the ground beside them, and a half-empty bottle of the same was tucked safely between his backside and the butt of his gun.

His eyes were red-rimmed; his face itched from a three-day growth of whiskers. But he was determined that this time, he would not miss his chance. So when he heard the familiar sound of a car coming down the mountain, his pulse accelerated. If it was them, he was going to be ready.

He lifted the deer rifle from the seat beside him, angling it until it was pointing out the window. Adjusting the telescopic sight until the crosshairs were in perfect alignment with a tree on the opposite side of the road, he drew a deep breath and took aim at the peak of the hill down which they would come. And when the car topped the hill and started down, he squirmed with pleasure. It was them!

"All right!" he muttered. "Now it's my turn."

The speed at which they were traveling allowed him little time for error. He squinted, adjusting the scope as he followed the car's descent. Now the crosshairs were in alignment with the middle of the driver's face. The image he had was perfect, right down to the scar on the big man's face. And then he swung the barrel a few inches to the left, firmly fixing upon the woman in the seat beside the driver.

The nearer they came, the more certain he was that, in seconds, it would be over. His finger was firm upon the trigger, his breathing slow and even. He was counting his money as he squeezed.

When the car came even with his location, he was still scrambling to find the safety he'd forgotten to release. And when the car passed the trees behind which he'd hidden his truck, and then disappeared around the curve in the road beyond, he was cursing at the top of his voice and hammering his rifle against the door in unfettered fury.

"By God, you won't get away from me this time," he screamed.

He started his engine, gunning it until blue smoke boiled from the rear exhaust. When he launched himself from the trees and onto the road, he left a wake of overrun bushes and broken limbs behind him.

Potato chips flew, while discarded paper scooted from one side of the floorboard to the other as he followed Wyatt around the curve. The partial bottle of soda tipped over and began to leak upon the seat. Bo couldn't have cared less. He was on a mission, and this time, there would be no mistakes.

Their ride down the mountain had been silent. Wyatt was concentrating on what lay ahead, and Glory was locked in the past, trying to remember everything she could of what she'd seen before. But when she saw the sign indicating the way to the dump, she tensed.

Wyatt sensed her anxiety, and when he slowed to take the turn, he gave her a quick sidelong glance. Her face was pale, and her hands were clenched in fists.

"Honey, don't do this to yourself," he begged. "Either relax and let whatever comes come, or just stop it all now."

"It's too late to stop," she said. "It was too late the day Daddy and J.C. died." Her chin quivered as she tried to get past the pain. "Besides, I can't stop what I didn't start. This is someone else's game. My fear comes from the fact that I don't know all the rules."

"Then we'll just make some rules of our own," he said, and moments later, came sliding to a halt at the edge of the pit.

For a time, neither moved as they stared down into the morass. Scavengers had dug through part of the dirt covering the latest loads. Bits of garbage were blowing around the bottom, caught in a miniwhirlwind of dust and debris, and the usual assortment of birds were circling and landing with no particular rhythm. Even though the windows on the car were up, the odor of rotting garbage was invasive.

"Here goes nothing," Glory said, and got out on her side of the car as Wyatt exited on his. When he came around to get her, the gun was in his hand.

"How do you want to work this?" he asked.

She shrugged. "I don't know. I guess go back to the place where I was when it happened before." And when she started walking, Wyatt was right beside her.

She paused, then frowned as she remembered. "No, Wyatt. If this is going to work, then everyone has to be in the same position. You were on the other side of the pit with the truck."

"Damn it, Glory. I don't want you out of my sight."

Smiling, she lifted her hand, caressing the side of his face, and tracing a fingertip down the scar on his cheek.

"Then don't close your eyes," she teased.

He groaned, then pulled her into his arms and tasted her smile.

Like Glory, it was warm and light, and Wyatt held her close, demanding a response that was not long in coming.

She bent to him like a leaf to the wind. Absorbing his strength, taking courage from his presence, when he trembled beneath her touch, she knew that she was loved.

The rough squawk of an angry crow disturbed the moment, and brought them back to the task at hand.

Wyatt held her face in his hands, gazing down into those wide, all-seeing eyes, and knew a peace that he'd never known before. His voice was rough and shaky, but he was certain of his feelings. "God in heaven, but I love you, girl."

"Remember that tonight when we've nothing else to do," Glory said, and tried to laugh through an onset of tears.

And then before he could talk himself out of it, he jogged back to the place where he'd parked, then turned and waved, indicating that he was ready for her to proceed.

Glory took a deep breath, said a small prayer and started to walk, trying to remember her frame of mind that day, as well as where she'd been when she stopped and looked back at Wyatt, who'd been standing on the bed of her daddy's old truck.

The air was thick and muggy, and she wished for a breeze to stir the constant and often overpowering smell that went with this place. As she walked, she tried to let her mind go free, discarding her fears so that she would be receptive to whatever might come.

Long, anxious minutes passed, while Wyatt stood beside the car, watching her as she walked farther and farther away from him. Twice he almost called her back, but each time he resisted, remembering instead why they'd come.

And while he waited for something to happen, he constantly searched the line of trees around the dump. Now that they were off the mountain, he was solely responsible for Glory's well-being. Just when he feared this might be a wasted effort, she paused, and then her posture changed. He could tell, even from this distance, that she was lost in a world he could not see.

Glory was at the point of believing that this would be a repeat of the day she'd stood in the rubble from her home without seeing any more of the man who'd caused its destruction when everything shifted before her eyes.

The bright light of morning faded into night. Again, a quarter moon shed a faint ivory glow on the upraised trunk of a big gray sedan. A man stood hunched over the depths of the trunk, and then he straightened and turned. Again, Glory saw the long white bundle he held in his arms.

She shuddered, then moaned in fear—afraid it would stop and afraid that it wouldn't.

She watched through his eyes as the bundle toppled, end over end, then rolled down the deep embankment before coming to a stop against a mound of dirt. And as before, the wide-eyed but unseeing gaze of a dead woman's face stared back up at her.

She screamed, but it was inside her mind. No sound escaped her lips, and she remained motionless, waiting for a revelation.

A small cloud moved across the sliver of moon. Glory knew that it was so, because for a brief time, there was little to see but the darkness in the pit itself. And then as she watched, the cloud passed, and for a second, the copper glint of the woman's red hair was highlighted against the white spread in which she'd been wrapped.

Elizabeth.

The name slid into Glory's mind, and then suddenly, her vision switched from the pit to the man who was getting into the car. She fixed upon the stoop of his shoulders, the balding spot in the back of his head. He opened the door and began to turn....

Then, as instantly as she'd been drawn into the vision, she was yanked back out.

Glory gasped as the world about her returned to normal. The glare of sun against her eyes was suddenly too harsh to bear, and she shaded them with her hand. A dark and impending sense of doom was with her that had nothing to do with what she'd just seen. It came from here! It came from the now!

Glory spun.

"Wyatt!"

His name came out in a scream as she started toward him on the run.

Wyatt knew to the moment when she came out of the trance. But when she started toward him, shouting his name, he knew that something was wrong.

Years of military training kicked in, and he ran in a crouched position with his gun drawn, searching the thick boundary of trees that surrounded the dump as he tried to get to Glory before danger got to her.

And then out of the woods to his right, he saw the flash of sun against metal, and shouted her name. He heard the gunshot at the same time that he saw Glory fall.

"Nooo!" he raged, reaching her just seconds too late to shield her body with his own.

A heartbeat after he fell forward and then across her, the second bullet plowed up earth only inches from his head. Afraid to look down and see something he couldn't accept, he scooped her into his arms, then rolled, taking them both to a nearby stand of undergrowth. Once there, he quickly dragged her through the trees until he was positive that they were momentarily concealed from the shooter's eyes.

But when he started to search her body for a wound, she gasped, then choked, and grabbed at his hand instead.

"Glory! Where are you hit?"

"Oh, God. Oh, God." It was all she could say.

Another shot pierced the limbs over their heads, and Wyatt knew they had to move, or it would only be a matter of time before a stray bullet hit its mark.

"Where are you hit? Answer me, honey, where are you hit?"

Shock widened the pupils in her eyes until they appeared

almost black. "I fell. Dear God…the bullet missed me when I fell."

He went limp with relief, and had the strongest urge to lay his head down and cry. *Thank you, Lord.*

The sharp thump from a fourth shot hit its mark in a nearby tree. Wyatt grabbed her hand and started moving deeper into the woods, at an angle from where the last shot had come.

Yards away, Wyatt shoved Glory down between two large rocks.

"Stay here, and don't move. Whatever you hear or don't hear, don't come out until you hear me call." In fear for his life as well as her own, Glory started to argue when Wyatt grabbed her by the arm. "I said…don't move."

She stopped in the middle of a word. The look on his face was one that she'd never seen before, and she realized that this was the part of Wyatt that he'd tried to leave behind when he'd retired from the military. This was a man trained to kill.

She nodded as a single tear rolled down her cheek. And then he disappeared into the trees before her eyes. One minute he was there. The next, he was gone.

Periodic shots continued from the other side of the dump, and Glory could tell that the shooter was moving through the trees, circling the open pit. Overwhelmed by the horror of it all, Glory stretched flat in the dirt between the rocks, buried her face in her arms and prayed.

When Bo saw her fall, he was ecstatic. The fact that the man reached her seconds later was immaterial. He had a clear shot at a second hit, and took it without a qualm just as a gnat flew up his nose. One minute he was sucking air, the next, a bug. His finger twitched on the trigger, not much, but enough that it threw off his aim. And because it did, the bullet plowed into the dirt instead of Wyatt Hatfield's head. By the time he could react, the man had rolled, taking himself and the woman's body into a cover of trees.

"Son of a hairy bitch!"

Just to prove he was still in charge, he fired another shot into the location he'd seen them last, and then waited, listening for something that would indicate that they still lived.

Sweat rolled from his hair and down between his shoulder blades as he waited, holding his breath as he sifted through the sounds on the air. He heard nothing. Not a scream. Not a groan. And more important, not a return shot.

He knew that the man had a gun. He'd seen it in his hand as he ran. That he hadn't once fired back was to Bo proof that he'd crippled, if not killed him, outright.

But while Bo's elation was high, he'd had too many misses on this job already. He was going to see for himself.

As he circled the dump, angling toward the area where he hoped to find their bodies, he continued to threaten with intermittent fire, unaware that he was no longer the hunter. He'd become the prey.

Cold reasoning took Wyatt deeper into the woods, honing instincts he had perfected years ago. He moved with the stealth of a hunter, running without disturbing the ground upon which he moved, choosing his steps and his cover with caution.

As he ran, he realized that the rifle shots were also moving in a clockwise direction. A spurt of adrenaline sent him into a higher gear. He had to get to the man before the man got to Glory.

Once he had a momentary fix on the man's location as he glimpsed a second flash of sunlight on metal. But by the time he got there, the man was already gone.

And then luck changed for them both when Wyatt heard a loud and sudden thrashing in the underbrush ahead. Soft curses filled the air and Wyatt aimed for the sound with unerring instinct, hoping as he ran that the bastard had just broken his neck. It would save him the effort of doing it for him.

Bo was still trying to untangle himself from the rusting coil of barbed wire that he'd stumbled upon when he saw movement from the corner of his eye. Fear shafted, making his movements even more frantic and locking the barbs even deeper into his clothing as he staggered, trying to take aim without neutering himself in the process.

Wyatt came out of the trees at a lope. But when he saw Bo Marker struggling with the wire and the gun, he came to a stop and took aim.

"Drop the gun."

Bo gawked at the black bore of the automatic only yards from his nose, and could tell from the way the man was standing that he knew how to use it. But getting caught was not in his plan, and he feared jail almost as much as dying.

Wyatt could tell that the man was not in the mood to surrender. When he saw him shift the grip on his gun and tighten his finger on the trigger, Wyatt moved his aim a few inches to the right, then fired.

Pain exploded in Bo's arm, and his hand went numb as the rifle bounced butt first onto the ground.

"You shot me!" Bo screamed, and then fell to his knees, which, considering where he was standing, was not the smartest move he could make.

"If you move, I'll do it again," Wyatt said.

Bo wasn't smart, but he knew when a man meant business. And from the look on this one's face, he considered a broken arm a minor inconvenience. It was the barbs on which he was sitting that were causing him the misery.

The calm that had led Wyatt to this man suddenly disappeared. He was shaking with anger as he pulled him to his feet and started dragging him, wire and all, through the woods toward his car.

"You're killing me," Bo groaned, as Wyatt tightened his hold on his good arm and yanked him past a blackberry thicket.

Wyatt paused, then looked back. "Don't tempt me," he whispered. "You tried to kill my lady. It would be all too easy to return the favor."

Bo shrank from the venom in the big man's voice. Suddenly, the idea of getting to jail seemed a bit brighter than it had before.

"It wasn't personal," he whined. "I was just doing a job."

His words froze the anger in Wyatt's mind as a chill went up his spine.

"Someone hired you to do this?"

Bo nodded.

"Who?" Wyatt asked.

Bo shook his head. "Uh-uh. I ain't tellin' until I get to jail. If I tell you now, what's to keep you from shootin' me where I stand?"

Wyatt smiled, and Bo felt his potato chips curdle.

"Look," he cried. "I'll tell you who he is, I swear. But I need doctorin' first. Okay?"

"You are lucky that my father taught me to be kind to animals," Wyatt said softly. "Because I have the biggest urge to put you in the dump with the rest of the garbage."

"Oh, God," Bo said, and started to snivel. "Please, just get me to the doctor. I'll tell you everything I know."

At that moment, Wyatt hated as he'd never hated before. But he thought of Glory, who was still in hiding, and if this man was to be believed, still in danger. Without another word, he continued toward the car as if they'd not exchanged a word.

Minutes later, he dumped a bloody Bo, barbed wire and all, into the trunk of his car, and then started at a lope to the place where he'd left Glory in hiding.

* * *

She'd prayed until she'd run out of words, and cried until she'd run out of tears. The fear that held her captive between the two rocks was worse than what she'd felt when she'd witnessed her family die. Then it had been sudden and overwhelming in intensity. Now it was the waiting, the interminable waiting, that was driving her mad. But she had no choice. She'd trusted Wyatt with her life. She had to trust that he knew how to save it.

It seemed a long time before she heard the shot and the accompanying outcry. Terror for Wyatt sent her to her feet, and then fear that she'd endanger him further sent her back to her knees. She dropped between the rocks, rolling herself into a ball, and pressing her fingers against her mouth to keep from screaming.

Seconds turned to minutes, and far too many of them passed as she listened for proof that he still lived. Finally, she could bear it no more.

Wyatt...Wyatt...where are you? she thought.

"I'm here, Morning Glory. I'm here."

She caught her breath on a sob, and in spite of her fear, began crawling to her knees. When she lifted her head above the rocks where she'd been hiding, she saw him coming through the trees.

Seconds later, she was on her feet and running with outstretched arms. He caught her in midair, and then held her close, loving her with his touch as well as his words. When he could think without wanting to cry, he took her by the hand and began leading her out of the woods.

"Is it over?" Glory asked, and then took a deep breath, trying to steady the tremble in her voice.

Wyatt frowned, and slipped an arm around her shoulders as they came out of the woods. "Almost, sweetheart. Now, if I can get the bastard in my trunk to a doctor before he bleeds to death, we'll find out who hired him."

Glory stumbled, as a new wave of fear crossed her face. "Someone hired him? Oh, God! That means…"

"It means that whoever wants you dead doesn't have the guts to do it himself," he said harshly. "Don't worry. The loser in the trunk is going to talk, even if I have to beat it out of him."

Glory got in the car, a little leery of riding in the same vehicle with a man who'd been stalking her every move. But when Wyatt took off in a cloud of dust, bouncing over ruts and fishtailing in the loose Kentucky earth, the loud and constant shrieks of pain coming from the trunk convinced her that, at the moment, the man was in no shape to do her any more harm.

A short time later, Anders Conway was on his way out to lunch when he heard the sound of a car coming around the street corner on two wheels. He was fishing for the keys to his patrol car, expecting that he would have to give chase, when to his surprise, the car braked to an abrupt halt only feet from where he stood.

"You in a hurry to spend the night in my jail?" Anders grumbled, as he watched Wyatt Hatfield emerge from behind the wheel.

Wyatt grinned, but the smile never reached his eyes as he started toward his trunk. "No, but I brought someone who is."

Anders frowned as he circled the car. But when the trunk popped, shock replaced his earlier disgust.

"What in the world?" he muttered, missing nothing of the man's bulk, the shattered and bloody arm and the nest of barbed wire in which he was lying.

"That—" Wyatt pointed "—is the man who's been trying to kill Glory."

Conway gave Wyatt a long, considering stare. "Bo Marker…you sorry bugger…is this true?"

Bo groaned, considered lying, then looked at Wyatt's face and nodded.

Conway frowned, waving at a deputy who was just coming out of the office. "Bring me them bolt cutters from the closet," he shouted. "And then call an ambulance to this location."

The deputy pivoted, hurrying to do as he was told.

At this point, Bo began to bawl, aiming his complaints directly at Wyatt. "You nearly killed me with that crazy driving."

Wyatt leaned over the trunk. "I told you, don't tempt me, remember?"

Bo sucked up a squawk and then gave the chief a frantic look, as if begging for him to intervene.

And while no one was looking, Glory got out of the car. She was already at the trunk before Wyatt noticed her, and when he could have stopped her, realized that she needed to confront a ghost or two of her own.

Bo Marker felt the tension changing. As he tried to shift his head to see what they were looking at, she walked into his line of vision. Everything within him froze. It was the first time he'd gotten an up close and personal look at someone he'd spent days trying to kill.

He remembered what people said about her, and when he found himself staring straight into those pale, silver-blue eyes, he started to shake. There was no accusation, no demand. No shriek of dismay, no cry of fear. Only a long, steady look that seemed to see into his soul. Every black, rotten inch of it.

He shuddered as fear overwhelmed him. When she took a step forward, he shrank back into the trunk as far as he could go.

"Who?" she said.

His mouth dropped, and he stuttered out his own name.

"No," Glory whispered. "I want to know who wants me dead."

Bo stuttered again, then swallowed a knot of panic.

"I said that I'd tell when they fixed me up," he whined. "If I tell, what's to keep all of you from letting me die?"

"The same damn thing that's keeping you alive," Wyatt said. "I want to see you hang for what you did."

Bo shrieked. "They don't hang people no more! Chief, you got to help me! Tell this crazy sucker to leave me alone!"

Conway grinned to himself. Whatever Wyatt Hatfield had said and done to this man had made a believer out of him.

"Now, Bo, it was a figure of speech." Conway eyed the barbed wire snarling around Marker's body and shook his head. And when his deputy came dashing out of the office with the bolt cutters in hand, he grumbled, "Took you long enough," and began to cut.

An hour or so later, Glory and Wyatt, with the chief for added company, were waiting impatiently for Amos Steading to come out of surgery and tell them what they wanted to hear.

And when the doors at the end of the hall suddenly swung back, and he burst through with his usual gusto, Wyatt got to his feet.

"You could have aimed a little farther to the right and made my job easier," Amos growled, and then clapped Wyatt on the arm. "But he's fine, and will be in recovery for at least another hour. After that, you can have a quick go at him."

Conway nodded. "That's fine, then," he said, and then turned to Glory. "Miss Dixon, I'll be back at that time to interrogate the suspect. Rest assured that it will soon be over. Right now, I need to check in at the office. They're towing

Marker's truck from the dump as we speak, and I want to take a look inside before I talk to him. See you in a while."

They watched as he walked away, and then Amos Steading took a good long look at Glory, gauging the lingering shock in her eyes against the paleness of her skin and the way she clung to the man at her side.

"Are you all right?" he asked gently.

Glory slumped against Wyatt. "I don't know if I'll ever be all right again," she said softly. And then Wyatt's arms tightened around her shoulders, and she felt the strong steady beat of his heart against her cheek. "But I'm alive, and it's thanks to this man."

Amos shook his head in disbelief. "Well, little lady, a few months ago, I think he could have said the same thing about you."

Glory turned, her eyes wide as she gazed up at the doctor.

"Amazing, isn't it?"

The doctor's laugh boomed in the confines of the hall. "That's hardly the word, girl. Hardly the word."

Chapter 14

Carter Foster was on the phone when his secretary, Bernice, burst into his office waving her hand and mouthing for him to come look.

He covered the mouthpiece with his hand. "What? Can't you see I'm busy?"

"You've got to come see!" Her eyes were wide with excitement. "Some man just drove up in front of the police department and there's an ambulance on the way. I can hear it coming."

"So?" Carter growled. "It's the police department, for goodness' sake. Things like that happen over there."

"But that Dixon girl is there...and there's somebody screaming from inside the trunk of the car."

He blanched and hung up the phone without excusing himself from the conversation. As he rushed to the door, he tried to pretend it was curiosity, and not horror, that made him move.

He and his secretary stood in the doorway, curbside onlookers to the scene being enacted across the street. Even as Carter watched, he began to sweat. He couldn't hear exactly what was being said, but that voice coming from the trunk of the car was all too familiar. When he saw the chief take a rifle out of the backseat, he started to shake. It was the same kind of gun that Bo Marker had carried in the gun rack in the cab of his truck, right down to that telescopic sight.

Oh, no.

"Look, Mr. Foster. There's a man in the trunk, and he's all tangled up in some kind of wire. What on earth do you suppose happened?"

That stupid Bo Marker got himself caught is what happened, he thought, but it wasn't what he said.

"I have no idea," he said, and made himself smile. "You know what, Bernice? It's nearly noon. Since we've been interrupted, why don't we just go ahead and break for lunch? I'll be in court all afternoon, so why don't you take the rest of the day off?"

And then the ambulance pulled up and the show was all but over. His secretary was pleased with his offer, and anxious to share the gossip of what she'd seen with the dentist's receptionist down the street. She didn't give him time to reconsider, unaware that her work schedule was the last thing Carter Foster was worried about.

As she went to get her purse, he slipped out the door and into the alley, leaving Bernice to lock up. But he wasn't going to eat. Food was the last thing on his mind. It would only be a matter of time before that idiot, Marker, started blabbing. Carter knew that if he was to have a chance of escaping, he had to be miles away when it happened.

His hands shook as he slid behind the wheel of his car, and although he wanted to race through the streets at full speed, he made himself take the trip home with his usual poky ease.

Upon arrival, he began digging through closets, trying without success to find his big suitcase. It would hold all that he needed in the way of clothes. But the longer he looked, the more frantic he became. It was nowhere to be found.

He was at the point of hysterics when he remembered the last time he'd used it. It was the night Betty Jo had died. He'd packed a portion of her clothes into it to back up the story of her having left him, then tossed it in the dump when he'd tossed her body.

"Okay...okay. I'll improvise," he muttered, and headed for the kitchen.

Moments later, he was back in the bedroom, stuffing shirts and underwear into a garbage bag and yanking clothes, still on their hangers, from the closet. He had to get going.

Bo Marker came to in a frightening manner. One minute he'd been staring up at the bright lights of the operating room, and then everything went black. Now light was reappearing at the periphery of his vision. A woman's voice was calling his name and urging him to wake. It was the nurse who'd put a needle in his hand earlier.

Struggling against the desire to stay where he was, he finally opened his eyes, and then wished he'd followed his own instinct. People were hovering around his bed, staring intently at his face as he awoke. In a drug-induced state, he imagined them vultures, hovering over a carcass, readying to take a first bite.

"No. Go 'way," he muttered, and tried to wave them away when he realized that one of his arms was in bandages, and the other was connected to an IV line.

"Bo, this is Chief Conway. I understand you promised Mr. Hatfield here a name."

Bo groaned. "Can't you let a man rest in peace?"

Wyatt shifted his position, leaning over the bed so that Marker could see him clearly. "If I'd known that's what you wanted, I could have aimed a little to the left and saved the county the cost of cutting on you."

Bo looked up into eyes dark with anger and then closed his eyes, partly in pain, mostly in fear.

Amos Steading stood to one side, judging his patient's capability to communicate against the need these people had to find out the truth. After learning what Glory Dixon had endured at this man's hands, he had to remind himself of the oath he'd taken to preserve life, not end it.

Wyatt leaned closer until he was directly over Marker's face. "Give me the name now...or face murder charges on your own!"

It could have been the tone of Wyatt's voice, or the fact that Bo was in too much misery to put up a fight, but when the demand was uttered, words spilled.

"I didn't murder no one," he cried. "The only thing that I put away was a dog."

Wyatt's voice was almost at a shout. "Glory Dixon's father and brother are dead because of what you did. And you tried your damnedest to send her with them today. You might also like to know that they found a partial print on that stolen car that someone used in an attempted hit and run. What do you want to bet that it's yours?"

Bo groaned.

"Just don't give me any more of your crap, Marker. I'm already wishing I'd left you in that stinking dump."

The machine monitoring Marker's heart rate began to beep in a wild and erratic pattern.

Amos Steading frowned. "That's about enough for now. You'll have to come back later for further interrogation."

"I didn't kill no one!" Bo said. "Them people was already dead before Carter Foster hired me. I didn't have anything to do with their deaths...I swear!"

The chief frowned. "Now, damn it, Bo, I don't think you're telling me the truth. Why would Carter Foster want to kill the Dixon family?"

"Who's Carter Foster?" Wyatt asked.

"He's the town lawyer," Conway said. "And as far as I know, he doesn't have a vicious bone in his body."

But as soon as he said it, he remembered the investigation he'd asked his deputy to initiate, and wondered if anything valid had turned up on the whereabouts of Betty Jo.

Wyatt spun, staring back at the doorway where Glory waited.

"Honey, what do you know about Carter Foster?"

Surprise reshaped her expression. "Who?"

"The local lawyer."

"Oh! Why, not much. I don't think Daddy ever used him. When we had to commit Granny to the nursing home in Hazard, Daddy hired a lawyer there. That's the one who's handling the probate on Daddy's will, remember?"

Wyatt nodded, then turned. He could tell by the look on the doctor's face that they were about to be ejected.

"Please," he urged. "Just one more question."

Finally, Steading nodded.

"All right, Marker, let's say you're telling the truth. Did Foster say why he wanted Glory dead?"

Consciousness was beginning to fade. Bo's attention was drifting and his tongue felt twice its normal size. He licked his lips over and over, and it took everything he had just to get the words said.

"I don't know," he muttered. "All he ever said was that the crazy witch could ruin him."

"That's enough," Steading ordered, and finally ushered the trio from the room.

Once they were in the outer hallway, Conway paused, and scratched his head. "I don't get it. This doesn't really make sense."

Wyatt grabbed the lawman by the arm, desperate to make him believe.

"Look, Chief, there's something we haven't told you. Glory thinks that there's a connection between what happened to her family and the vision she had of that body being tossed in the dump."

The argument he expected didn't come. Instead, a strange expression crossed the chief's face as he turned and stared at Glory, as if seeing her for the very first time.

"Is this true, girl?"

She nodded. "That's why we went back there today. I wanted to see if the vision I had the first time would recur. I hoped that if it did, I might *see* something that I missed seeing before, like a face, or a tag number on the car."

"Well, did you?"

"Yes, sir."

"Then who did you see?" Conway asked, and then couldn't believe he was considering the word of a psychic as an actual fact.

"I didn't see a face, but I saw the man's back," Glory said. "He was stooped and starting to go bald on the crown of his head. He also drove a dark gray sedan. And,..I saw something else I hadn't seen the first time. The dead woman has red hair. And I think her name is Elizabeth."

Conway visibly staggered, then swiped a shaky hand across his face. "Good Lord, girl! Are you sure?"

"Yes, sir. Definitely sure about the red hair. Pretty sure about the name. It came to me out of nowhere, and I have no reason to believe that it is unconnected to what I was seeing."

Wyatt could tell by the look on his face that something Glory said had struck a chord. "Why? What is it you know that we don't?"

"It could be completely unrelated to what you saw. And it doesn't prove that what Bo Marker said is true. But..."

"Damn it, Glory has the right to know," Wyatt said. "Hasn't she endured enough?"

Conway looked at her where she stood, silhouetted against the bright backdrop of a wall of windows. Small in stature and fragile in appearance though she was, there was still something strangely enduring about her poise and the waiting expression on her face.

Finally, he nodded. "Yes, I suspect that she has." He made a quick decision and started talking. "A little more than a week ago, Carter Foster's wife ran off with some man. It wasn't her first indiscretion, and no one expected it to be her last. She's what you might call a loose woman."

Wyatt wasn't following this. If Foster's wife was gone, then why would he blame Glory?

"The deal is…to my knowledge, no one saw her leave. All we know of what happened is from Foster's version of the story. What gives me pause to wonder is what Glory just said. His wife was a redhead who went by the name of Betty Jo. But I've ticketed her myself on several occasions for speeding, and I distinctly remember that the name Elizabeth was on her driver's license."

Glory gasped, and then turned away. Wyatt came up behind her. His touch was comforting, but there was nothing he could do to ease the ugliness of what surrounded her.

"Why, Wyatt? Why did I get caught up in this?" she cried.

"Remember when you said the two incidents were connected?"

She nodded, then leaned against his chest, as always, using his strength when her own threatened to give. Wyatt's voice was low against her ear, but the truth of what he said was too vivid to deny.

"What if his wife didn't really leave him? What if he killed her, dumped the body and then feared you would *see* it and give him away? Bo Marker said that Carter claimed you could ruin him. Marker also claimed he had nothing to do with the explosion that killed your family. If he's to be believed, then that could mean Carter caused the explosion, and when he found out you escaped, he hired Bo Marker to finish what he couldn't."

She moaned and covered her face with her hands.

"Don't, honey," he said softly. "It's just about over."

"Look, I don't know quite know what to make of all this," Conway said. "But I need to get back to the office. I want to bring Foster in for questioning."

"I've got a cellular phone at the cabin," Wyatt said. "Here's the number. I'd appreciate it if you'd keep us abreast of what goes on, but right now I think Glory needs to go home. She's had just about all she can take."

The trio parted company in the parking lot of the hospital, and when Wyatt seated Glory in the car, she looked like a lost child. Heartsick at what she'd endured, he was about to get in when he glanced across the street and noticed the drugstore on the corner.

Just for a moment, he had a flashback of another time when he'd been in this lot, sitting in a wheelchair and waiting for Lane to pick him up. In his mind, he could almost see the peace that had been on Glory's face that day as she'd stood between her father and brother, safe in the knowledge that she was right where she belonged. But that was then and this was now. Now they were gone, and God willing, she would soon belong to him.

She leaned across the seat, then looked out at him through the open door.

"Wyatt? Is something wrong?"

Quickly, he slid behind the wheel, then cupped the back of her head and pulled her gently toward him until their mouths were a breath apart.

"Not anymore," he whispered. "Not anymore." He felt her sigh of relief as their lips connected.

* * *

Carter was at the end of the street and turning when he looked in his rearview mirror and saw a patrol car easing up his drive. There were no flashing lights or sirens squalling, but to him, the implications were all the same.

"Oh, my God," he gasped, and swerved, taking alleys instead of the streets to get out of town.

He cursed as he drove, damning everyone but himself as to blame. Once he barely missed a dog that darted across an alley, and then a few minutes later, slaughtered a pair of matching trash cans as he swerved to miss a pothole. On top of everything else, he now had a sizable dent in his left front fender.

"It's no big deal. I can handle this," he muttered, and then accelerated across a side street and into the next adjoining alley. When he realized he was on Ridge Street, he started to relax. He was almost out of town!

As if to celebrate his premature joy, a small dinging began to sound from the dash of the car. Carter looked down in dismay at the warning light near the fuel gauge. It was sitting on empty…and he had less than five dollars in cash to his name.

He slapped the steering wheel in frustration. He had credit cards he could use, but they left a paper trail. If he used them, it would be only a matter of time before they found him.

Frantic, he paused at a crossing and then saw salvation to his right. The First Federal Bank of Larner's Mill was less than a hundred yards ahead. Money was there for the taking. His money! And while he didn't dare enter, the automatic money machine in the drive-through beckoned.

Moments later, the decision made, he shot across the street and into the lane for the ATM, right behind a small brown coupe belonging to one Lizzie Dunsford, retired librarian. The moment he stopped, he realized he'd just made a mistake. Lizzie Dunsford was notorious for being unable to remember her own address. It was obvious by the way she kept punching numbers that she also could not remember her own personal identification number for her money card.

"No…oh, no," he groaned, and started to back out when a big red 4x4 pickup pulled in behind him. Although the windows were up, music could be heard as it reverberated loudly from the interior, marking time for the teenage driver and his young sweetie, who were making time of their own while they waited.

Carter waved at them to back up, but they were too busy locking lips to see him, and honking to get their attention was out of the question. Their music was so loud that they wouldn't have been able to hear, and honking his horn would only call attention to himself.

In a panic, he jumped out of his car, squeezing between it and the next car, until he was at Lizzie Dunsford's door.

"Miss Dunsford…it's me, Carter Foster. I see that you're having a little trouble. Maybe I could be of service?"

Hard of hearing, the old woman frowned. "I don't know any Arthur Fosser," she said, and started to roll up her window, certain that she was about to be the victim of a robbery.

By now, Carter was panicked. He stuck his hand in the gap between door and window, pleading his case with renewed vigor.

"I said, Foster! Carter Foster! You remember me. I'm a lawyer."

"Oh…why, yes, I believe that I do," she said.

Thank God, Carter groaned inwardly. "Now…how can I be of service?"

"I just can't get this thing to work," she said. "I keep punching numbers, but nothing comes out."

Carter peered at the screen, then frowned. "I don't know

what your identification number is, but this looks like a phone number to me. Are you sure you remember it right?"

She frowned, and then suddenly cackled in delight. "You know...I believe that you're right! Now, you run back to your car, boy. I'll try another. You're not supposed to watch me, you know."

"Yes, ma'am," he said, and jumped back into his car, praying that he hadn't been seen.

Afraid to kill the engine for fear there wouldn't be enough fuel to start it back up, he sat in horror as sweat rolled down his face and the gas gauge slid farther into the red. The only good thing about his location was that the patrol car cruising down the street didn't notice him sandwiched between the two cars.

In his mind, he was already preparing an argument to the court on his behalf when Lizzie's car suddenly sprang to life and bolted out of the lane and into the street, with Lizzie in less than firm control.

"It's about time," he muttered, and drove forward. Inserting his card, he began to withdraw all that he could from his account.

As Wyatt turned onto Main Street and headed out of town, he kept glancing back and forth at Glory. She was leaning against the seat with her eyes closed. More than once, he was certain that he'd seen her lips tremble. He kept watching for tears that never showed.

"Hey, little Morning Glory," he said, and slipped a hand across the seat toward her. "How about scooting a little closer to me?"

Glory opened her eyes and tried to smile, but there was too much misery inside of her to let it happen.

"What is it, baby?"

"Granny calls this...thing I can do a gift. But how can it be when it caused the deaths of my father and brother?"

"Your gift didn't cause them to die. Someone murdered them," he argued.

"Because of me," she whispered. "Because of me." Unable to accept his pity, she looked away.

There was nothing he could say to help. Only time and a better understanding of the frailties of the human race were going to make Glory's burden easier to bear.

"Just rest," he said. "We'll be home in no time. Maybe it will make you feel better."

As they passed, the buildings seemed to blur one into the other. Glory was lost in thought and on the point of dozing when the air inside the car suddenly seemed too close. And before she could react by rolling down a window, the skin on her body began to crawl. She went from a slump to sitting straight in the seat, searching the streets on which they drove for a reason that would explain her panic.

"Wyatt?"

Apprehension sent her scooting across the seat next to him, clutching at his arm.

"What is it?" he asked, and started to slow down, thinking she might be getting sick.

"No! No!" she shouted. "Don't stop. I think he's here!"

"You think who's h—" He swerved as understanding dawned. "Where?" he asked urgently, looking from one side of the street to another.

"I don't know," she said, and then pressed her fingers against her mouth and groaned softly. "I'm afraid."

"He can't hurt you, darlin'. I'm here."

Glory leaned even closer, her heart pounding, and let herself be pulled toward the fear. They had to find him. It was the only way she knew how to make it stop.

"Do I keep driving, or do you want me to stop?" he asked.

She closed her eyes, focusing on the fear, and then looked up with a jerk.

"Turn here!" she ordered, and Wyatt took the corner on three wheels.

Carter was stuffing money in his pockets when the sound of tires squalling on the street behind him made him look up in fright.

"Damn and blast," he groaned, and took off without retrieving his money card and receipt that were still hanging out of the machine.

"There!" Glory cried, pointing toward a dark gray car that was hurtling out of the drive-through at the bank.

Wyatt accelerated past the bank, and then swerved sharply to the right, blocking the car's only exit. Instinctively, he shoved Glory to the floor and then grabbed for his gun. He looked up just as the car came skidding to a halt. He jumped out with his gun aimed, unaware that Glory refused to stay put. The need to look into this man's face was, for her, overwhelming.

"Son of a...!" Carter's heart dropped.

But it wasn't the man with the gun who did him in. It was the sight of Glory Dixon, sitting up in the seat and staring back at him with those clear blue eyes.

"Nooo," he screamed, and shoved his car in Reverse. Rubber burned on the pavement as gears ground and tires began turning in reverse.

But no sooner had he begun to move than the big red 4x4 that was behind them turned the corner and hit his bumper with a thump. It didn't make a dent in the big truck or its occupants, but it jerked Carter's head, popping his neck like the crack of a whip.

Whiplash!

He groaned. A lawyer's favorite injury, and here he was without a prayer of collecting on the deed. He looked out his windshield and saw the man with the gun, waving and shouting at the kids in the truck. He was vaguely aware of them getting out and running toward the bank, and then of someone dragging him out of the car.

He was choking from the hold the man had on the back of his shirt. Every time he tried to move, the hold tightened and he would be all but yanked off his feet. The reality of his situation came swiftly when he finally heard Wyatt Hatfield's angry voice.

"Glory. Is this him?"

In a daze, she stared at his face, looking past the plain appearance of an overweight and aging man, to the evil in his eyes. And when she looked, it was there. The guilt. The shame. The fear.

She looked down at his hands and, in her mind, saw the same hands turning the jets on the cookstove in her house, then breaking a knob so that it would not turn off.

"Yes," she said. "That's him. That's the man."

Carter cursed and made a desperate effort to jerk free of Wyatt's hands, but the man and his grip were too strong. In the struggle, his jacket fell open, and money dropped from his pocket and onto the ground. A draft caught the bills, shifting and fluttering them along on the pavement, farther and farther out of Carter's grasp.

"My money!" he cried. "It's blowing away!"

"You're not going to need money where you're going," Wyatt said.

Carter's mind was whirling in desperation as the sound of sirens could be heard in the distance. Moments later, when the chief himself slid to a halt and exited his car on the run, Carter started babbling.

"Conway, thank God you're here. This stranger just tried to hold me up. Look! My money! It's blowing away! You've got to help me."

Conway motioned for a deputy. "Handcuff him," he said.

"No!" Carter screeched as the steel slid and locked

around his wrists. "You've got the wrong man! I didn't do anything wrong."

"That's not exactly what Bo Marker says," Conway drawled, and was satisfied with himself when all the blood seemed to drain from the lawyer's face. That was guilt showing, or his name wasn't Anders Barnett Conway.

"Who's Bo Marker?" Carter finally thought to ask, although he suspected his reaction might have come a little too late to be as believable as he'd hoped.

And then all eyes turned to Glory as she answered for them all. "He's the man you hired to kill me...isn't he, Mr. Foster?"

Carter looked away, unable to face her accusation.

But Glory wasn't through. "Why, Mr. Foster? Why would you want to harm me? I didn't even know your name."

He stared, unable to believe what she just said. She hadn't even known his name? Could that mean, if he'd let well enough alone, he would have gotten away with murder?

"Going on a trip, were you?" Conway asked, as he saw the bags and stacks of clothing in the backseat of the lawyer's car.

"Why, no," Carter muttered. "I was, uh...I was going to..." He brightened. "I was about to donate all this stuff to the Salvation Army."

Wyatt picked up a handful of money from the ground and stuck it beneath Carter's nose. "What was this for? Were you going to donate all of your money, too?"

Carter glared, then focused his anger on the chief of police. "Exactly what am I being arrested for?" he muttered.

"For the murder of Rafe Dixon and James Charles Dixon. For hiring a man named Bo Marker to kill Glory Dixon. And when we get through digging in the city dump to find the body, for the murder of Elizabeth Foster."

Carter tried to fake surprise. "Betty Jo! Murdered! You can't be serious?" And then he tried another tack. "You have no proof."

"When we get through digging, I will. I'm going to go back to the office and take this little lady's statement, just like I should have done days ago. And when we get through digging through the garbage, if I find myself a redheaded woman by the name of Elizabeth who's wrapped up in something white, then you're in serious trouble, my friend."

His eyes bugged. The description was so perfect that it made him sick. "That's impossible," he muttered, and then he thought to himself. *No one saw.*

Glory gasped, and answered before she thought. "Oh, but that's not true, Mr. Foster. I did."

Carter went weak at the knees. His mind was running on ragged, and afraid to stop for fear that hell would catch up with him while he was forced to face the truth of what she'd just said.

The witch, the witch. She'd read his damn mind.

Conway read him his rights as he dragged him away.

The ride home was quiet. Little was said until they pulled up in front of the cabin and parked. As they got out of the car, Liam Fowler and his friends walked out of the trees and into the yard.

"They've heard," Glory said.

"Already?" Wyatt asked.

She nodded. "It doesn't take long for word to get around up here."

Liam Fowler was grinning as he grabbed Wyatt's hand and gave it a fierce shake, then brushed the crown of her head with the flat of his palm.

"Glory, girl, you choose your friends well," he said. "We're all glad you're safe, and if you want to rebuild, just say the word. We'll be here."

Tears shimmered on the surface of her eyes as she nodded. But the emotions of the past few hours were too much for her to speak.

"Excuse me," she said, and ran into the cabin.

"It's been a bad day," Wyatt said.

"It's been a bad week, friend. Real bad. We lost two good friends. Thanks to you, we didn't lose another. If you happen to be a mind to stay in these parts, we'd be real proud to have you."

Then without giving Wyatt time to answer, they disappeared as quickly as they had come. As soon as they were gone, Wyatt went to look for Glory.

He could hear her sobs as he walked into the room. Without pause, he locked the door, set the gun on the mantel and followed the sound of her voice.

"It's all right, it's all right," he said gently as he crawled onto the bed with her. "Cry all you want. I've got you." When she rolled toward him and wrapped her arms around his neck, he groaned and held her close.

"Oh, Wyatt. His face... Did you see that man's face? He's not even sorry for what he did."

Wyatt felt as if his heart was breaking. If he could, he would have taken her pain twice over, just to make sure she never suffered again.

"I know, darlin', I know. Sometimes the world is an ugly place." He pulled her closer against him, comforting her in the only way he knew how. With love.

He held her until her tears dried, and only the occasional sound of a sob could be heard as she slept. And when she was fast asleep, he eased himself gently out from her bed, then went into the other room. There was something yet to be done.

Justin Hatfield leaned out the front door of his house and called to his brother-in-law, who was loading tools in the back of a truck.

"Lane! Telephone!"

Lane dropped a tool belt and a sack of nails into the bed of the truck and came running. He cleared the four steps up the porch in one leap and reached for the phone just as Toni walked into the room.

"Hello," he said, and gave Toni a wink.

"Lane, it's me, Wyatt. It's over."

Lane dropped into the chair by the phone. "What happened?"

"One of them started taking potshots at us at the dump. We caught the other one coming out of a bank. It's a long story. I'll fill you in on the details later."

Lane was surprised by what Wyatt just said. "There were two?"

"So it seems," Wyatt said. "At any rate, it's over. I just wanted to let you know that she's safe and everyone's in custody."

"What happens now?" Lane asked.

Wyatt rubbed his eyes wearily, then stared out the window over the kitchen sink into the nearby trees. The beauty of what was before his eyes was in direct contrast to what lay ahead.

"Tomorrow they start digging through the dump for a body."

Lane sighed with relief. He'd been living with guilt ever since the day he'd left, knowing that Wyatt was more or less on his own.

"You did a real good job, brother. Have you ever considered going into my line of work?"

Wyatt's answer was abrupt, but concise. "No. In fact, hell, no!"

Lane grinned. "Just thought I'd ask."

"Anyway, thanks for all you did."

"I didn't do anything," Lane said.

"Oh, yes, you did," Wyatt argued. "When I called, you came. A man couldn't ask for anything more."

"If there's one thing that living with the Hatfields has taught me," Lane said, "it's that…that's what families are all about."

Wyatt turned toward the bedroom where Glory lay sleeping. His eyes darkened. "I guess you're right," he said. "If you can't count on family…who can you count on?"

Long after their conversation was over, the heart of it was still with Wyatt. And as he lay beside Glory, watching her sleep, he felt the last of his uncertainties about himself slipping away.

Through a quirk of fate, he and Glory Dixon would be forever linked. He knew as surely as he knew his own name that he could not, and did not want to try to, exist without her. She was, quite literally, in his blood.

And with the acceptance of that fact came the acceptance of his own future.

Chapter 15

Wyatt stood at the edge of the pit, watching as men scoured the dump below. With more than a week's worth of dirt and garbage to move, he did not envy them their task.

Along with the local law, officers from the state police were on the scene, and at last report, Bo Marker was recovering by the hour. The better Bo felt, the more he talked. He was perfectly willing to admit to two counts of assault with a deadly weapon, but not murder. For once, he was innocent of something vile, and fully intended that everyone know.

Wyatt knew that while Marker's testimony backed up the truth of Glory's life having been in danger, there was still only her word—the word of a psychic—as to why Carter Foster wanted her dead. Carter was sticking to his story about his wife having left him for another man. Unless they found a body, he knew her story would stand on shaky ground.

Yesterday had been bad…both for Wyatt and for Glory. But that was yesterday. This was today. And the despair that he'd expected to see on her face when she woke had been absent. In fact, she'd greeted the day with eagerness, ready to put the past behind her. *If only I was that confident about losing my ghosts,* Wyatt thought.

Someone shouted from the line of cars behind him, and as he turned to look, he realized Glory was nowhere in sight. Only moments earlier she'd been at his side, squeezing his hand in intermittent bouts of anxiety as load after load of garbage was shifted down below. But now she was gone. A quick burst of nervousness came and then went as he reminded himself she was no longer in danger.

A hot gust of wind blew across the ground, stirring the air without cooling it as he moved away from the site. Just as he started toward the line of parked cars, he heard her calling his name.

"Wyatt!"

He spun, and when he saw her waving at him from the shade of the trees, he started toward her at an easy lope.

Glory watched him coming, looking at him as if seeing him for the first time, and marveled at the link they shared, as well as at the man himself.

In her eyes, he was as strong as the hills in which she'd been born. As brown as the earth upon which she stood. And he'd been as faithful to his promise as a man could possibly be. She wondered if after this was over, there would be anything left between them, or if he would consider this a promise made, a promise kept—and be on his way.

She said a prayer that it wouldn't be the latter. He was so deep in her blood that if he left her, he'd take part of her with him. How, she wondered, did one live with only half a heart?

Laughter was in his voice as he swung her into his arms and off her feet.

"I lost you," he said, nuzzling the spot below her ear that always made her shiver.

"No, you didn't, Wyatt Hatfield. You'll never lose me." She stroked her hand against the center of his chest. "I'm in here. All you have to do is look. I'll be waiting."

Whatever he'd been thinking died. All sense of their surroundings faded. The smile slipped off his face as he lost himself in a cool blue gaze.

"You would, wouldn't you?" he asked quietly.

But before she could answer, someone shouted his name. He turned, still holding Glory in his arms.

"Why, it's Lane!" Glory said, and then noticed the tall, pretty woman walking beside him. Neither the denim jeans and shirt nor the well-worn boots she was wearing could disguise her elegance.

"And my sister," Wyatt added.

Glory could see the resemblance in their faces, and the proud, almost regal way in which they held themselves as they walked. Both of them had hair the color of dark chocolate, and eyes that matched. Along with that, there was a similar stubborn thrust to their chins that made her smile.

Toni Hatfield Monday couldn't believe her eyes. Lane had said Glory Dixon was small. But she wasn't prepared for that fragile, fairy-looking waif who stood at her brother's side. And her hair! It was a fall of silver and gold that caught and held sunshine like a reflection on water.

But as she came closer, her opinion of helpless beauty disappeared. In spite of the fact that Toni was nearly as tall as Wyatt, she felt small and humbled by Glory's pure, unblinking stare. For several seconds, she was so locked into that gaze that she forgot why she'd come. And then Glory smiled, and the moment passed.

"So," Toni said. "We meet." A quick sheen of tears came and went as she spoke. "Do you remember what I said I wanted to do when that happened?"

"About wanting to hug angels?" Glory asked.

Toni nodded.

"Good. I could use a hug today," Glory said, and let herself heal in Toni Monday's welcoming arms.

Toni smiled at the nervous look on Wyatt's face, and then turned and kissed him on the cheek.

"Don't worry, big brother. I won't give away your secrets. I just came to see your lady, face-to-face."

Wyatt was playing it safe and accepted her kiss as his due.

"I have nothing to hide," he drawled.

Toni laughed aloud at her brother's audacity. "God save us from pretty men who lie as easily as they make love," she said, and winked at her husband as she took Glory by the arm. "Let's walk," she said. "I came a long way to say thank you."

Glory held the joy that was in her heart, savoring this moment to herself. It gave her a feeling of belonging to someone again.

"There was no need to say it again," Glory said. "I'm the one who's thankful that Wyatt could make sense of what I'd seen."

It was impossible for Toni to hide her amazement. "I won't pretend to understand," she said. "But I will never doubt your ability, of that you can be sure." And then her voice softened as she took Glory by the hand. "Lane told me what you've had to endure. I'm so sorry for your loss, but at the same time thankful that you and Wyatt have found each other."

Glory savored the words, hoping they were true. Had she and Wyatt truly found each other, or would he be saying goodbye now that she was safe?

"So, what are your plans now that the worst is behind you?" Toni asked.

Glory shrugged. "I have none, other than to rebuild my life."

A little surprised by the singular way in which she'd expressed her plans, Toni couldn't help but ask, "You sound as if you're planning to do this alone."

Glory paused, considering the best way to express her feelings, yet unashamed to admit what they were.

"I don't know," she finally said. "What happens between us now is not up to me. It's up to Wyatt. He knows how I feel." And then she smiled slightly. "In fact, most of the time he also knows what I think. I'm supposed to be the psychic and he reads *my* mind."

Toni's eyebrows arched, and she squeezed Glory's hand just a little, as if in jest. "You're kidding, of course."

"No, I'm not."

Toni gasped. "Really? He can do that?"

Glory shrugged. "For some reason, we now share more than a few pints of blood."

"Good Lord!"

Toni looked back at Lane as he stood talking to her brother, trying to imagine what it would be like to live with someone and have him know her every thought. And then something occurred to her, and she started to smile.

"So…my big brother knows what you think?"

"He sure does."

Toni put her hands on her hips and gave Glory a wicked smile. "Then give him something to think about. Let him in on some…uh, innermost thoughts, then see if he's man enough to take them."

The idea was audacious, just like Toni. She couldn't help but grin. "You're a lot like Wyatt, aren't you?"

"How so?" Toni asked.

"You don't waste time on details. You just jump in with both feet."

Toni grinned even wider. "Well, now, I didn't know I was so transparent, but if you need an answer, then I guess all you need to do is look at Lane Monday. I wanted that man from the time I pulled him out of a flood." And then she paused and grinned even broader. "I need to amend that slightly. I wanted *him,* but I was willing to settle for making a baby with him."

Glory couldn't hide her shock. "Good Lord, Wyatt was right."

"How so?" Toni asked.

"He said once Lane met you, he never had a chance… or words to that effect."

"Like I said," Toni reminded her. "If you want something but don't give it a try, you have only yourself to blame."

"Hey, you two, time's up," Wyatt shouted. "You've had time enough to plot the fall of man."

"Just about," Toni whispered, and winked at Glory.

Glory shivered with anticipation, and then started to smile.

"I'm glad you came," she said softly.

Toni hugged her. "So am I, Glory. So am I."

It was well toward evening on the second day of the dig when the revelation came. Birds, disturbed from their normal scavenging, were circling the air above the pit where the garbage was being moved. Yard by yard, earth was scooped then dumped as they continued their search.

Anders Conway stood on the precipice, wondering if he'd made a mistake by putting his cards on the table too soon by calling in the state police, and wondering how he was going to explain his mistake when someone shouted, and another man started running toward him, waving him down.

Wyatt stood alone, watching from a distance away as the men began to converge upon their latest location. Even though he was high above the spot and hundreds of yards away, Wyatt could tell they'd found what they'd been looking for.

He took a long, slow breath, and said a quiet prayer,

thankful that Glory wasn't here to witness it. Even from this distance, he could tell that what they found wasn't pretty. The once-white spread she'd been wrapped in was a stiff, dirty brown, and what was left of Betty Jo Foster was even worse. He turned away. He didn't need to see anymore.

"By God, Hatfield, they found her!" Conway said, as he came up and out of the pit a short time later.

Wyatt nodded. "I saw."

Conway looked around, expecting to see Glory Dixon somewhere nearby with a satisfied expression on her face.

"She didn't come with you today?"

"No," Wyatt said. "We were up late last night visiting with Lane and my sister. They left for home early this morning. Glory wanted to sleep in."

Conway nodded. "I guess it's just as well, but I thought she'd be here...wanting to know if the body was down there after all."

"You still don't get it, do you?" Wyatt said. "She didn't need to come for that. It was making you believe enough to look for the body that mattered. When your people started to dig, her worries were over. It was inevitable that you'd find what she already knew was there."

"You came," Conway said. "Does that mean you didn't believe her?"

Wyatt's smile never quite reached his eyes. "Oh, no. I came to make sure you didn't quit on her."

Conway flushed. "I suppose I had that coming."

"I think I'll be going now," Wyatt said. "Looks like you've got everything under control."

"Looks like," the chief said, but when Wyatt started walking away, Conway called him back.

"Hey, Wyatt!"

He paused, and then turned.

"I don't know how she does it," Conway muttered.

This time, Wyatt's smile was a little less angry. "Neither does she, Chief. Neither does she."

By the time they had Betty Jo Foster bagged and out of the pit, Wyatt was already gone.

Glory was down in the creek below the cabin, wading through the ankle-deep water with her jeans rolled up to her knees and her shoes in her hand. The soft, gentle breeze that had come with morning did not blow down here. Leaves drooped silently on heavily laden branches as an occasional dragonfly dipped and swooped only inches above the water. She moved without purpose, content only with the cool, constant flow between her toes and the ease that comes from knowing she belonged.

A squirrel scolded from somewhere in the canopy above her head, and she closed her eyes and took a slow, deep breath, realigning herself with the world in which she'd been born. Enclosed within the confines of the steep rocky banks, once again she felt safe and cleansed.

It would take longer for the anger to go away, and even longer before she learned how to live with the pain of her loss, but the guilt that had held her hostage was gone.

Something brushed against her ankle. She opened her eyes and looked down, smiling as tiny tadpoles wiggled past. And then something else, just below the surface of the water, caught her eye. As she stooped to look, her braid fell over her shoulder, baptizing the ends in the cool, Kentucky stream.

Her heart began to beat with excitement as she lifted a perfect arrowhead out of the creek.

"Oh, my gosh! J.C. is going to love…"

Realization struck. Staggered by the pain of loss, her lip trembled as she clutched it tightly in her fist. The time had come and gone for adding to her brother's beloved collection. Glory held it between her fingers, staring down at the cool gray piece and its perfect triangular shape.

Someday there'd be another boy who was as fascinated by the past as her brother had been. The arrowhead should be there, waiting for him to find. She held her breath and let it go, watching as it turned end over end, dropping into the water and then settling, once again, into the rocks.

And then she heard someone calling her name and looked up. Wyatt was standing at the top of the bank. She could tell by the look on his face that it was over. Without looking back, she stepped out of the water and started up the bank with her shoes in her hand. He met her halfway.

"I got your mail when I came by the box," he said. "There's a letter from your lawyer. It's on the table."

Refusing to cry anymore, she stifled a sob, and just held him.

"Are you all right?"

She nodded. "I am now," she said. "Help me up the bank."

But before they moved, he tilted her chin, forcing her to look him in the face.

"Would you like to go see your granny again?"

A smile of delight spread from her eyes to her face.

"Could I?"

"Honey, you name it, it's yours."

"Be careful what you say," she warned. "I may ask for more than you want to give." Then she laughed at the shock on his face.

It was as if the old woman hadn't moved since they'd been there last. She sat in the same chair, in the same clothes, with the same lost expression in her eyes. Staring out a window into a world from which she'd withdrawn, she rocked without thought, moving only when the urge struck her.

"Granny."

Faith Dixon blinked, and then turned her head toward the pair at the door.

"Comp'ny? I got comp'ny?"

"It's me, Granny. It's Glory."

Identity clicked as she smiled. "Well, come on in," she said. "I've been waiting for you all day."

As before, Glory knelt at her granny's feet as Wyatt took the only other chair.

"Did you bring my gingersnaps?" she asked, and then cackled with glee when Wyatt promptly handed over a small white sack bulging with a fresh spicy batch straight from the bakery in Larner's Mill.

"I'll save some of these for your daddy," she said. "My Rafe does love cookies."

It hurt Glory just to hear his name. But she knew that keeping silent about the truth was the best thing for all concerned.

"Yes, he does, doesn't he, Granny?"

The old woman nodded, and then patted Glory's head. "He's lookin' real good, don't you think?"

A frown marred Glory's forehead as she tried to stay with her granny's train of thought. She supposed she must be referring to Wyatt, although they'd been discussing her father only seconds before.

"Who, Granny? Who looks good?"

"Why, your daddy. Who else?" She smiled to herself, and then looked up at the sky outside. "He was here jest a day or so ago," she added, and then she began to frown. "At least I think it was then. I lose track of time, but I'm sure it warn't no longer than that."

Oh, Lord, Wyatt thought. *Maybe this wasn't such a good idea after all.*

"Honey?" He touched her shoulder, asking without saying the words.

Glory shook her head, and then whispered, "It's all right, Wyatt. It's not so bad."

Unaware of their aside, Faith was still lost in thought about her son's visit. Suddenly the frown slid off the old woman's face.

"No! I'm right. It was only a day or so ago cause I 'member askin' him why he didn't come with you before."

Glory froze. What kind of tricks was her granny's mind playing on her?

Granny started to rock, happy that she'd settled it all in her mind. "Said he was goin' on some trip." She slapped her leg and then laughed. "I swear, that boy of mine ain't been out of Kentucky three times in his life and now he's goin' on some trip."

"Oh, God," Glory said, and rocked back on her heels. When she felt Wyatt's hand on her shoulder, she all but staggered to her feet.

Faith frowned a little, continuing to talk to herself, even forgetting that they were still there.

"'I'll be seein' you soon,' he said." She nodded confidently as her tiny white topknot bobbed on her head. "Yep. That's what he said. 'I'll be seein' you soon.'"

Glory turned. Her eyes were wide, the expression on her face slightly stunned.

"Wyatt?"

There was little he could say. The implications of what Faith Dixon was saying were almost too impossible to consider. And then he thought of the connection that he and Glory shared. It was a bond stronger than love, which even death would not break.

"I heard."

"Do you suppose...?"

He pulled her to him. "It's not for us to wonder," he said. "Whatever happened is between that woman and her boy. If she believes she saw him, then who are we to question?"

Glory went limp in his arms.

"Are you all right?" he asked.

She nodded, and then looked back at her granny as she rocked. The scene was one that Glory had seen a thousand times before. But this time, she was struck by the peaceful, almost timeless quality of the sight. And as she looked, in a small way, she began to accept the inevitability of the circle of life. One was born. One died. And life still went on when yours was gone.

Suddenly, she reached out and took Wyatt by the hand.

He felt the urgency with which she held him. "What is it, sweetheart?"

"Take me home, Wyatt. I want to go home."

Moonlight slipped through the parted curtains, painting the bodies of the couple upon the bed in a white, unearthly glow. As they moved together in a dance of love, the sounds of their sighs mingled with those of the wind outside the door. Sometimes easy, just above a breath; often urgent, moving with the force that was sweeping them along.

With nothing but the night as a witness, Wyatt destroyed what was left of Glory Dixon's defenses. And when it was over, and they lay arm in arm, trembling from the power of it all, he knew that he would take the same road that he'd taken before. Risk losing his life all over again, for what he now held.

Wyatt smoothed the hair from her face, gentling her racing heart with his words and his touch. "I love you, Glory Dixon."

Weak from spent passion, Glory still clung to him, unwilling to let him go.

Ah, God, Wyatt thought. *Making love to you every night for the rest of our lives would be heaven.*

Glory gasped. She'd heard that! For the first time since their relationship really started, she'd read *his* mind. He'd said it couldn't happen. That he never let down his guard.

She turned her cheek, hiding her smile against his chest. He didn't know it yet, but he'd done more than let down his guard.

When he'd let her into his mind, he'd let her into his heart. Now she knew there were no more walls between them.

"Wyatt…"

The sound of his name on her lips was sweet music. "What, darlin'?"

"You're more than welcome to try…if you think you're able."

For a moment, he couldn't think past the shock. The little witch! She'd just read his mind!

"Oh, my God!" He sat straight up in bed. "What did you just do?"

She only smiled, then stretched enticingly, arching her body like a lazy cat.

"You heard what I thought…didn't you?"

"Why, yes…I believe that I did," she said.

"That does it," Wyatt said, and then pounced, pinning her with the weight of his body, and with the dark, hot fire in his eyes. "I'm done for." His words were rich with laughter; the kisses he stole from her smile were warm and sweet.

Glory shivered with longing. Even though they'd just made love, she wanted him all over again. And then she remembered his sister's advice about letting him know what was in her heart.

"Are you sure you're done?" she whispered.

"Lord, yes," he laughed.

I'm not done, Wyatt. I've only just begun.

The laughter stopped. And when he looked in her eyes, his heart almost followed suit. Although her lips didn't move, he heard her whispers as clearly as if she were leaning next to his ear. The surge of desire that came with the words made him shake with longing. What she said...what she asked...what she wanted to do!

"Have mercy," Wyatt muttered. "Not unless you marry me."

Glory blinked slowly as she began to refocus. "Is that a proposal?"

He raised himself up on his elbows and began to grin. "Why do I feel like I've just been had?"

Her eyes widened in feigned innocence. "Oh, no, Wyatt. You're the one on top. I believe it's me who was just had."

His eyes twinkled as he scooped her into his arms, rolling until the mattress was at his back and they were lying face-to-face.

"Now, then, where were we?" he whispered. "Oh, yes, I was waiting for an answer."

"I will marry you, Wyatt Hatfield. I will love you forever. I will make babies with you and share your life until I draw my last breath."

Tears came unexpectedly. The beauty of her vow stunned him.

"And I will be forever grateful," he whispered.

"So what are we waiting for?" Glory asked.

I guess I'm just waiting for the sound of your voice.

Glory paused, gazing down at the face of the man she'd come to love, and lightly traced the path of the scar across his cheek.

Quietly...in the dark...in the tiny cabin in the deep Kentucky woods, she called his name aloud.

A single tear rolled down his cheek, following the path of the scar. It was the sweetest sound that he'd heard on earth. Someone was calling him home.

Epilogue

Spring had been a long time coming. Kentucky had wintered through more snow than it had seen in years, delaying the finishing touches that Wyatt and Glory Hatfield kept trying to put on their new home. It hadn't been so bad, wintering in that tiny cabin nestled deep in the woods, but the ground had long since thawed, and Glory had already seen the first Johnny-jump-ups beneath the trees around Granny's cabin.

Their dark, shiny green spikes with a single white flower suspended at the end of a miniature stalk were among the first woodland flowers to part the mat of rotting leaves. They were nature's signal that it was time to work the ground and plant the crops.

And for Wyatt, spring was a homecoming in more ways than one. He'd started out a child of the land, and despite a lot of lost years between then and now, it had called him home, just as his wife had done. He couldn't wait to put plow into ground, and he'd been thinking of buying some Hereford heifers to start a herd of cattle.

And then finally, three days ago, the last nail had been driven in the house. Yesterday, two trucks from a furniture store in Hazard had delivered and then set up an entire houseful of brand-new furniture, which now resided in the rooms in shiny splendor, waiting to give comfort and ease.

A wide, spacious porch framed the entire front of the house, and along each side, brand-new lattice gleamed white in the noonday sun, waiting for the first tendrils of a vine...or a rose...to breach the heights. Hanging from the underside of the porch, and rocking gently in the breeze, was a white wooden swing just big enough for two.

Wyatt pulled into the yard with the last load of their clothes from the cabin and started carrying them through the back door. Inside, he could hear the frantic patter of Glory's feet as she scurried from room to room, making sure that everything was in its proper place. At any moment, the first attendees to their housewarming might arrive, and Wyatt knew that Glory would skin his hide if he wasn't dressed and waiting.

She gasped when she saw him coming through the kitchen. "Give those to me. I'll hang them up while you get dressed."

Wyatt's chin jutted as he lifted the hangers high above the reach of her hands. "No, darlin'. I've got them. I told you before, you're not carrying anything heavier for the next few months than my baby."

In spite of her anxiety, she savored the adoration in his eyes, as well as his tender care, absently rubbing the slight swell of belly barely noticeable beneath her white gauzy dress as he disappeared into the back of the house.

The dress, like the house, was new and bought especially for this day. The neckline scooped, almost revealing a gentle swell of breast. The bodice was semifitted, and hung loose and comfortable against her expanding waistline. The skirt hung midlength between knee and ankle, and moved with the sway of her body like a tiny white bell. The sides of her hair were pulled away from her face and fastened at the back of her neck with a length of white lace.

Minutes later, as Wyatt came out of the room buttoning a clean shirt and tucking it into his jeans, he looked up, saw Glory standing in the doorway, anxiously looking down the long, winding road, and had to take a breath before he could speak. She stood silhouetted against the bright light of day. For a moment, he thought an angel had come to bless this house. And then he smiled. What was wrong with him? One already had. Her name was Glory.

She spun, her eyes wide with excitement, a smile wide upon her lips. "Someone's coming!" she cried.

Wyatt swung her off her feet and stole a quick kiss, aware that it would have to last him awhile. "They're supposed to, darlin'," he teased. "We're having a party, remember?"

He clasped her hand, and together they went out to meet the first arrival.

An hour later, the party was in full swing and the air was full of laughter. A game of horseshoes was in progress over near the barn. A long picnic table had been set up underneath the shade tree at the edge of the yard and with every carful of well-wishers who arrived, more food was added to what it already held.

Children ran and climbed, shrieked and cried, and while Edward Lee was the only six-foot child in the midst of the play, he was having as much fun as the smallest.

Gifts for their new home were piled to overflowing on the porch, and Glory basked in the joy of knowing she was loved. Just when she thought there was no one left in Larner's Mill who could possibly come, more cars began to arrive.

But when the occupants started spilling from every opening, she started to smile. It was Wyatt's family.

"My goodness! Who are all of those people?" a woman asked.

Glory smiled. "My husband's family."

"Well, my word," the lady said. "I had no idea." She glanced down at Glory's belly, then back up at the brood moving like a groundswell toward the food and frivolity. "Fruitful lot, aren't they?"

Glory laughed aloud. "Yes, ma'am. I believe that they are."

Babies were napping on their mothers' shoulders and the older children were playing quietly in the shade. Typical of the mountains, men sat in one spot, gathered together by the bonds that made them head of the families, while women gathered in another, secure in the knowledge that they were sheltered by more than the breadth of their husbands' shoulders. And as one, they watched while Glory and Wyatt sat side by side on the front porch steps and began opening the gifts that had been brought to bless this house.

The thoughtfulness with which each gift had been chosen was obvious. Everyone knew that the newlyweds had literally "started with nothing." The fire that had destroyed Glory's family had also destroyed everything she owned.

Stacks of new linens grew with every package they opened. Often a gasp would go up from the crowd as Wyatt would hold up a particularly fine piece of glassware meant to be put on display. Mouth-watering jars of homemade jellies and jams lined the porch like fine jewels, their colors rich and dark, like the sweets themselves, waiting for a hot biscuit to top off. From the hand-embroidered tablecloths to the colorful, crocheted afghans, everything came from the heart.

And then Justin and David Hatfield, two of Wyatt's

brothers, came around the corner of the house, carrying their gift between them.

"It's been in the family for years," Justin said, setting it at Wyatt's and Glory's feet. "Nearly every one of us has used it for one baby or another, little brother. We thought it was time you had a turn."

Glory was overcome by the symbolic gesture. The rich, dark grain of the wood was smooth and warm to the touch. And when she pushed on the side, the old wooden rockers rocked without even a squeak. They hadn't just given her a cradle. They'd made room for her in their hearts.

"Oh, Wyatt, a cradle for the baby! It's fine! So fine!"

And so are you, darlin'. So are you.

Glory turned, and for just a moment, the rest of the crowd shifted out of her focus. There was nothing in the world except Wyatt's face and the love he felt for her shining out of his eyes.

"Thank you, Wyatt."

"There she goes. She's doin' it again," Justin grumbled. "All I can say is, thank God Mary can't read my mind or I'd be in trouble from sunup to sundown."

Everyone laughed, and the moment passed as they opened their next gift. The box was small, and the crystal angel figurine even smaller, but before she ever looked at the card, Glory knew that it had come from Lane and Toni. She'd been nicknamed the family angel, and took pride in their love and the name.

"It's from Lane and Toni," she said, holding it up for the people to see. "I'm going to save it for the baby's room. He'll need a guardian angel."

"He?" Wyatt leaned over and kissed the side of her cheek. "Do you know something I don't?"

"Figure of speech," she said, and everyone laughed.

But as she set the angel back in the box, Wyatt wondered

at her secretive smile. He'd already learned that the less he knew about what she was thinking, the better off he was.

The next gift was quite heavy and bulky. And when the wrapping came off and they realized it was a large sack of dog food from Liam Fowler and his wife, they tried to find a way to say thank-you for something they didn't need.

And then Liam grinned at the blank smiles on their faces and pointed toward his truck. Edward Lee was coming across the yard with a squirming black-and-white pup in his arms. He knelt at their feet, then set the pup down on the ground.

"He's a pretty one, ain't he, Mornin' Glory?" His long, slender fingers caressed the pup's ears with gentle strokes. "I'll bet he'll make a real good watchdog, too."

Glory held back tears, although it was hard to do. He was marked so like her brother's pup that she could almost hear J.C.'s shout of laughter. When Wyatt slid an arm around her shoulder, she leaned into his strength and found the courage to smile.

"Thank you, Edward Lee. It's just what we needed to make this house a home."

Pleased that his gift had been a success, he scooted back into the crowd, teasing the pup with a string of ribbon lying on the ground, while Glory and Wyatt continued to unwrap.

When all the gifts had been opened and thanks had been given for the fellowship that they'd shared, as well as for the presents, Wyatt held up his hand. He had a gift of his own for Glory, and he'd been saving it for last.

"Wait," he said, "there's one more left to open," and ran to their car.

Surprised, Glory could only sit and wonder what he'd done now. But when he came walking back to the house, carrying a box so big that he could barely get his arms around it, she started to smile. Just like Wyatt. He did nothing halfway.

He placed it before her like gold on a platter, then stepped back, becoming one of the onlookers as he watched her shredding the ribbon and paper.

Twice she laughed and had to call for his help when the knots in the ribbon wouldn't come undone. And then finally, there was nothing left but to open the top and look in.

At first, she could see nothing for the folds of tissue paper. And then the paper finally parted and she peered inside. The smile of expectation slid sideways on her face.

"Oh, Wyatt."

It was all she could say. As hard as she tried to stop them, the tears still came, filling her eyes and running down her cheeks in silent profusion.

Stunned by her reaction, the guests shifted uneasily on their feet, uncertain whether to watch or turn away, yet wanting desperately to know what had sparked such a reaction.

And then as they watched, they saw. Handful by handful, she began to pull the contents out of the box, piling them in wild abandon into her lap. By fours and sixes, by ones and by threes. And with each handful she took, her movements became more eager, laughing through tears while they spilled out of her lap and onto the steps beside her. As nothing else could have ever done, they filled her hands and her heart.

And when there was nothing more to take out, she wrapped her arms around the lot as Wyatt knelt at her feet and began wiping the tears from her cheeks.

"I couldn't give you back what you lost," he said softly. "But it's something to remember it by."

"Will you help me plant them?"

Wyatt grinned, and then stood. "We all will. Why do you think I got so many?"

And then he grabbed the packets of seeds by the handfuls and started tossing them to the crowd.

"Plant them anywhere. Plant them everywhere," he shouted. "By the barns, along the fences, down by the well. Run them up the mailbox and the old windmill. But not here." He pointed toward the two, shiny new trellises on either side of the porch. "Glory and I will plant here."

Caught up in the fantasy of the moment, people began claiming their spot, and before long, the place was crawling with gardeners on their hands and knees, planting the tiny seeds with makeshift tools in the rich, spring earth.

Wyatt took Glory by the hand and led her to the side of the porch.

"I'll dig, you drop," he said.

Careful of her dress, she went to her knees, and through a veil of tears, planted the seeds that, weeks later, would grow into vines. And from the vines would come flowers that gave bloom in the mornings. Blue as a summer sky, she could almost see the fragile little trumpets that would hang from these walls like small bells.

They were the morning glory, her daddy's favorite flower, and her namesake.

Like nothing else they'd been given this day, these would make their house her home.

Glory's hands were shaking as she dropped the last of her seeds into the ground. When she looked up at the man at her side, she knew that she was loved.

"I wish Granny had lived to see this day," she said softly.

Tenderness colored his words and his touch as he cupped her face with his hand.

"What makes you think she didn't?" Wyatt asked. "Remember, darlin', time doesn't break the bonds of love."

* * * * *

We hope you enjoyed reading

RIDER ON FIRE

and

WHEN YOU CALL MY NAME

by *New York Times* bestselling author

SHARON SALA

If you liked these stories by SHARON SALA, then you will love **Harlequin® Romantic Suspense.**

You want sparks to fly!
Harlequin® Romantic Suspense stories deliver with strong and adventurous women, brave and powerful men and the life-and-death situations that bring them together.

Heart-racing romance, high-stakes suspense.

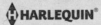

ROMANTIC suspense

Enjoy four *new* stories from
Harlequin® Romantic Suspense every month!

Available wherever books and ebooks are sold.

SPECIAL EXCERPT FROM

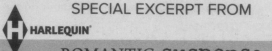

ROMANTIC suspense

Sheri Marcoli is searching for two things: her missing aunt and her fairy-tale prince. The damaged and fierce detective Jimmy Carmani is nothing like the man she envisions, but when the kidnapper sets his sights on her, it's Jimmy who rides to Sheri's rescue.

Read on for a sneak peek of

LONE WOLF STANDING

by *New York Times* bestselling author
Carla Cassidy,
available July 2014 from
Harlequin® Romantic Suspense.

"That's better than being poisoned, right?"

He was aware of the weight of her intense gaze on him as he pulled out of the animal clinic parking lot. "I'm no veterinarian, but I would think that definitely it's better to be tranquilized than poisoned." He shot a glance in her direction.

She frowned. "That man in the woods broke Highway's leg. I don't know how he managed to do it, but I know in my gut he probably broke the leg and then somehow injected him with something. Highway would never take anything to eat from anyone but me, no matter how tasty the food might look or smell. Jed and I trained him too well."

They drove for a few minutes in silence. "Sorry about the pizza plans," she finally said.

He flashed her a quick smile. "Nothing to apologize for.

I'm guessing you didn't plan for a man to attack your dog and then chase you in the woods tonight. I think I can forgive you for not meeting up with me for a slice of pizza."

"Thank God you came to find me." She wrapped her slender arms around her shoulders, as if chilled despite the warmth of the night. "If you hadn't shown up when you did, I think he would have caught me. I will tell you this, he seemed to know the woods as well as I did, so it has to be somebody local."

"We'll figure it out." He seemed to be saying that a lot lately. "Maybe in the daylight tomorrow we'll find a piece of his clothing snagged on a tree branch, or something he dropped while he was chasing you."

"I hope you all find something." Her voice was slightly husky with undisguised fear. "I felt his malevolence, Jimmy. I smelled his sweat."

"You're safe now, Sheri, and we're going to keep it that way. Highway is going to be fine and we're going to get to the bottom of this."

"So...so, what happens now?" she asked.

"Since we didn't get our friendly meeting for pizza, we're going to do something else I've heard that other friends do," he replied.

"And what's that?" she asked.

He flashed her a bright smile as he pulled in front of her cottage. "We're going to have a slumber party."

Don't miss
LONE WOLF STANDING
by Carla Cassidy, available July 2014 from
Harlequin® Romantic Suspense.

ROMANTIC suspense

SECRET SERVICE RESCUE
by Elle James

The Adair Legacy

Heartstopping danger, breathtaking passion, conspiracy and intrigue. The Adair legacy grows...

Secret Service agent Daniel Henderson saves the rebellious secret heiress Shelby O'Hara from a cartel looking to pressure her grandmother to drop out of the race. But when they're forced into hiding, sparks fly and Daniel realizes the biggest threat is to his heart.

Look for the final installment of *The Adair Legacy*— *SECRET SERVICE RESCUE* by Elle James in July 2014.

Don't miss other titles from
The Adair Legacy miniseries:

SPECIAL OPS RENDEZVOUS by Karen Anders
HIS SECRET, HER DUTY by Carla Cassidy
EXECUTIVE PROTECTION by Jennifer Morey

Available wherever books and ebooks are sold.

Heart-racing romance, high-stakes suspense!